BRADFORD
Bastard

Sheridan Anne
Bradford Bastard: Bradford Bastard #1

Copyright © 2022 Sheridan Anne
All rights reserved
First Published in 2022
Anne, Sheridan
Bradford Bastard: Bradford Bastard #1

This book is a work of fiction. Names, characters, places, and incidents are products of the author's imagination. Any resemblance to actual events or persons, living or dead, is entirely coincidental.

No part of this book may be reproduced, stored in a retrieval system or transmitted in any form or by any means, without prior permission in writing of the publisher, nor be otherwise circulated in any form of the binding or cover other than in which it is published, and without a similar condition, including this condition, being imposed on the subsequent purchaser.

Cover Design: Sheridan Anne
Photographer: FXQuadro
Editing: Heather Fox
Formatting: Sheridan Anne

BASTARD!

To all the readers who have fallen down the dark RH rabbit hole and have been missing your past love of high school, enemies to lovers drama. I know you crave all that meat, you nasty little minx, but I promise, Tanner Morgan is going to hit that spot just right!

CHAPTER 1
Brielle

Confession.

When I was fourteen, in the prime of my pre-teeny-bopper years, my lip was almost torn right off my body, and unfortunately ... I don't mean the lip on my face.

Let me explain ...

I was a snoopy kid. Every conversation that wasn't meant for my ears was listened to. No matter what. I couldn't help myself. It was a sickness, but how else was I supposed to learn anything? I was the annoying little sister of the family, and no one told me shit, so I learned to adapt. Sue me. I don't regret it, except once...

I'd overheard a bunch of senior boys talking about some chick they'd seen online. At the time, I'd assumed they had seen something in a movie, but now at eighteen, I see it for what it was—those fuckers were watching porn like some kind of bonding experience in the back of the school bus. Perverts.

They ogled her tits and snickered like bitches when she started moaning, pretending they weren't rock hard with pre-cum smearing through the inside of their basketball shorts. For the most part, I tried to ignore them, but when another girl joined and one of the guys scoffed at her body hair in disgust, I was all but running to the drug store.

I was fourteen. I didn't know what boys liked, but the idea of being disgusting to a senior boy inflicted a fear in my young chest that I'd never felt before. My feet had barely hit the pavement before I was already halfway to the store.

I wanted a boyfriend. I wanted the older guys at school to not only notice me, but desire me, and I wanted all the girls to know that I had it all. In hindsight, my priorities were a little fucked up, but that didn't stop me from grabbing the first tub of hot wax off the shelf and handing it over to the cashier while my cheeks flamed with embarrassment.

The memory of that day sends a shiver sailing down my spine. Maybe things would have gone differently if I had an older sister or a mother who wasn't too busy working long hours. But lucky me, I was stuck with an older brother who was too cool to let his little sister in on the most important things in life. Besides, I wasn't about to have this conversation with him. No way in hell.

I was on my own, and I was determined. I was going to be as bare as the day I was born.

It seemed easy enough, so I shoved the hot wax into the microwave and followed every instruction until it was time to finally spread my legs. I swallowed my fear and held my head high. I knew other girls in my class who'd tried it and they didn't have too many complaints. It couldn't have been that bad, right?

Fucking wrong. So fucking wrong.

With the small handheld mirror propped up against the bathroom wall, I lost my pants and dropped to the ground. One leg went to the left, braced against the shower glass and the other to the right, propped up over the edge of the bathtub. It was the most dazzling sight, you know, minus the bush between my legs.

The freezing bite from the tiled floor assaulted my asshole as I crouched over and got into a good position.

After scooping out a large dollop of wax, I smothered it over my most intimate parts. The hot wax burned my lips and I cried out, trying to blow on it to cool it down as it ran and made a mess. The wax slowly hardened in delicate places it wasn't supposed to find itself, and I told myself that the first time is never supposed to go well. I'd know better next time. In hindsight, I now know the importance of trimming first, not that I've ever attempted this shit again.

Next came the mental pep talk good enough for an Olympic-level coach prepping his star athletes for the biggest game of their lives, and with that, I clenched my eyes and tore that wax off my coochie as hard as humanly possible.

My hand slipped off the edge of the wax and I gave myself a black eye, but that didn't matter because half of my left lip was HANGING

OFF MY FUCKING COOCH! Blood was spurting as agony tore through me. I screamed until my throat was raw, terrified I was going to bleed out and my mom was going to come home to find me dead, spread-eagled on the bathroom floor.

It was a bloodbath. A massacre of the highest degree.

Only moments had passed, and I was contemplating my death, when my older brother came storming through the bathroom door, all but breaking the damn thing down. His eyes were wide and frantic after hearing me scream, but nothing was worse than watching as his gaze dropped and saw the wax, the bush, the blood, and the hanging lip.

The big bastard had to carry me out to his car, still spread eagle and screaming while the neighbors watched in horror. Then to make matters worse, he made me wait while he laid a towel down because I couldn't possibly risk bleeding all over his stupid wipeable leather seats. Asshole.

Not going to lie, that was the most humiliating moment of my life.

Or so I thought, until half an hour later when I was lying on a hard bed in the emergency room with an ice pack on my face and a team of doctors and nurses studying my vag. Not to mention the hundred-year-old nurse at my side telling me all about the dilemmas she has with her own bush.

My brother was off in the corner on the phone with Mom, unable to look me in the eye while a male nurse on his first day of prac stood between my legs with a hair dryer, trying to heat the wax enough to start removing it. After all, they couldn't possibly stitch me up with the mess surrounding the disaster that shall not be named, and I quickly learned that scissors and shaving weren't going to do the trick.

Thirteen stitches later, a night in the hospital, and a vow to never speak of it to another soul, and I was home free. To this day, my secret has remained my own—apart from the millions of medical staff who insisted on coming to have a peek. That was the worst day of my life. Not even the day my father walked out on us can top that shit. Though to be fair, he was a spineless sack of shit who was only holding us back.

Nothing has come close to the humiliation I felt that day, until right this very minute.

Music blasts through the McMansion. At least, it's a McMansion to me. To these rich kids around me, this place is probably sub-standard with its three levels, private bar, and a pool that is somehow both inside and outside at the same time. Either way, it doesn't matter to me because I have absolutely no plans to return here ever again.

My shoulder presses up against the doorframe of one of the many spare bedrooms, watching as my boyfriend, Colby, goes to town on some cheerleader-looking princess, giving her the whole experience, grunts and sweat included.

I shake my head as the party rages around me, the rest of the world completely oblivious to the humiliation washing over me. It's the last party of the summer, and despite knowing I don't belong here, I let him drag me along. I'm such a fucking idiot. I knew he asked me to come just so he could get blind drunk and have some sorry loser waiting for him to decide when he's ready for her to drive his bitch ass home.

Fuck me, I'm such an idiot. I knew I should never have come here with him.

Usually, there are more public parties than I can count on the last weekend of the summer, but after the incident a few weeks ago and the cops shutting down every last hint of fun in town, no one bothered. Which is exactly how we ended up at a private school party.

This shit isn't my scene. No, wait. Back that up. This is definitely my scene. I love a good party, and if it gets out of hand, even better. It's just that I'm not feeling it tonight, especially now that Colby's dick is currently impaling a cheerleader.

Letting out a sigh, I pull my phone from the back pocket of my jeans and waltz into the room. I've not been feeling our relationship for the past few months and just haven't had the balls to break up with him. Though, I guess there's nothing stopping me now. Bonus points for getting to leave him while also being able to make him the bad guy. Nothing better than being able to claim you're the innocent one in a breakup.

The music is so loud that neither of them hear me until I'm standing right beside them, my camera up and a wide grin across my face. "Hey Colby," I say, snapping a quick shot of the two of them. "Smile."

Colby's head whips around as cheerleader bimbo screeches and reaches for the blanket, tearing it up to cover her tits. Not gonna lie, she's got a nice rack on her. If I weren't so humiliated by being the oblivious woman who allowed a piece of shit like Colby Jacobs to cheat on her, then I might even send her a compliment or two. Hell, my friends even tried to warn me, but I told them they were wrong about him.

"Bri," Colby rushes out, his face paling as his jaw drops, more than just caught in the act. Fuck, it was almost worth it to see the sheer panic taking over him. "Fuck, babe. What are you doing?"

I flip my phone around and show him the picture of him fucking the girl. "Oh this?" I question. "Just giving myself something to look at every time you blow up my phone asking for me back. This will make sure that I never fall back into that trap again."

He shakes his head, scrambling for something to say. "I … I didn't mean to, Bri. You have to believe me. It just happened. She … she came onto me."

I laugh, grinning at the asshole. "Really? You're going to try and feed me your bullshit excuses while your three-inch cock is still buried inside the cheerleader? Shit, Colby. I almost feel sorry for the girl."

"I, uhhmmmm," the cheerleader says awkwardly, brushing her messy brunette hair off her face and drawing my attention down to her, sprawled across the bed. She looks awkward and more than uncomfortable, and for just a second, I wish that I could do something to put her at ease, but then I remember that I don't give a shit. "I'm not a cheerleader by the way. I'm a dancer."

A beaming smile cuts across my face, and I almost wish she knew me better to be able to read the sarcasm in my tone. "That's fabulous."

She pushes Colby off her and I scoff at the way he flies back on the bed, his hands dropping to cup his deflating junk. The girl pulls herself up on the bed and holds her hand out to me, and for some ridiculous reason unknown to me, I take it. "I'm Ilaria," she says before adjusting the blankets over her body. "For what it's worth, I didn't know he had a girlfriend. I'd never have even looked twice if I knew."

Realizing far too late that I just touched her dirty sex hands, I start to back away. "Appreciate it," I tell her, having to remind myself that this isn't on her. She's just a clueless victim in all of this. The bastard here is Colby. "As for you," I say, turning to my now ex-boyfriend who's scrambling to get himself dressed. "You can go and fuck a cactus. We're over. Done. And for the record, I'm not above telling the whole fucking school that you wear women's underwear and cry when you come."

"Babe," he gasps, his eyes wide. He starts to scramble after me, but I'm already gone, slamming the door behind me, the sound drowned by the thumping music.

Knowing Colby all too well, I make a break for it while trying not to think about the agonizing sting in my chest. I'm not about to have this argument out in the middle of a private party surrounded by a bunch of rich kids who are only going to laugh at my humiliation. All I want is to get out of here, get my ass home, and lock the door. The second I take off, Colby won't be able to come after me. He'll be stuck here, figuring out how to get himself home, and by the time his remaining two brain cells figure it out, it'll be far too late.

Bodies cram the stairs, and I squeeze through them, shouldering my way past jocks of all shapes and sizes. Unfamiliar faces ripple with cocky grins as I pass them, their hands groping at my ass, seeing me as nothing but fresh meat.

Making my way to the bottom, I hear Colby calling my name from the top and risk glancing back. His shirt is unbuttoned and to anybody looking, it's clear that he just got sprung doing something that he shouldn't have been. But lucky for me, he's had far too much to drink to concentrate on the crowd below. He scans over the bodies and I'm not going to lie, for once, I'm glad I'm vertically challenged.

I easily get lost in the crowd and beeline for the absurdly grand entrance of the home, trying to remember my way there. This place is like a maze, the dancing bodies and dark, flashing lights not making it any easier.

Taking a left, I try to peer around the bodies and crash straight into a hard wall of muscle, a red solo cup flying out of the guy's hand and drenching his tight black shirt. "Oh fuck," I screech, my stare snapping up to find a set of dark eyes glaring back at me.

Beer soaks through the guy's shirt, sticking the material to his wide, toned chest, and if he weren't so fucking terrifying, I might even take a moment to gape at how gorgeous he is. He's tall and muscular with dark brown hair that probably shimmers in the sun and a jaw sharp enough to slice a woman's underwear right off her body. Sleeves of tattoos wind up each of his arms, the tops of them peeking out around the neckline of his shirt and making something clench deep inside of me.

But those eyes. Fuck, they're scary. These are the kind of eyes that are capable of destroying a woman.

He glares at me, and even though barely a moment has passed, he holds my stare hostage, every passing second making me feel as though I'm getting smaller and smaller. I struggle to catch my breath, absolutely certain that I'd rather deal with Colby than be stuck in this awkward stare-off with this dude. "I, ummm ... I'm sorry. I was just trying to find my way out of here," I tell him. "I didn't mean to ruin your shirt."

The guy clenches his jaw, and I shrink further under his monopolizing stare, even more so when his hand crushes the empty solo cup in anger. My knees weaken and my heart starts to race, certain that he's about to curse me out and destroy me in one simple go.

Feet, meet the floor. NOW FUCKING WALK ACROSS IT. NO. RUN. Run as fast as you can.

Realizing that he's more than content with staring at me until I wet my pants, I go to sidestep around him when another guy pushes in beside him, throwing his muscular arm over his shoulders, a drink in hand. He's gorgeous with his flirty smile and sandy blonde hair. His gaze sails over me, his eyes lighting with the challenge. "Oh, fresh me—" he says before cutting himself off and scrunching his face in disgust, pulling back from his friend. "Bro, what the fuck? You're drenched."

Scary dude grunts, still not taking his eyes off me. "I know, and I have this little bitch to thank for it."

His attitude rubs me the wrong way and my brow shoots up. "Excuse you?" I demand, my fiery, public-school attitude rearing its ugly head. "I'm just trying to get out of here. You're the idiot not watching where he's going. This isn't all on me."

His flirty friend laughs and my gaze darts to the way his button-down shirt gapes in the front, showing off his strong, tanned pecs. He watches me, his intrigue growing by the second, and I'm not going to lie, his attention is fun, but I'm in no mood for eighteen-year-old dudes and their need to get their dicks wet. "Shit, bro. This one's got a bite as well as a bark. I wonder what else she can do."

"Don't even think about it, asshole," I say, knowing I should reel it in before this gets any worse, or hell, before Colby finds me and insists on defending my honor by trying to beat the shit out of these guys, though he would lose. These guys look as though they eat bitches like Colby for breakfast. "If you need someone to suck your dick, why don't you ask your friend here? He seems to have a big mouth. Clearly he needs something to shut him up."

A strange hush falls over the room, the music still thumping but the bodies all seem to have stopped. Unease settles over me, and as I glance to the side, I realize that everyone is watching me. Now, I don't know shit about private school politics, but I know drunk high school kids, and when something gains the attention of the whole room, it's not good. These guys are obviously a big deal, and I just got myself into a world of trouble—exactly where I don't want to be.

Flirty guy looks nervously toward the scary dude, and I conclude that I just insulted the king of the jocks. He doesn't respond, and I don't know if his silence should intimidate me, but as it is, I just have to dig myself a deeper hole. "Let me guess," I say, trailing my gaze over him, taking in his big shoulders and strong chest, right down to the way his wet shirt sticks to his holy grail of bodies. "Quarterback? Whole school thinks you're a bigger deal than what you are? Bad attitude and gets whatever he wants by acting like a twat, but gets away with it because the school sees you as royalty? 'Bout right?"

Flirty guy laughs, throws his heavy arm back over his friend's shoulder and slaps his hand across his chest. "Holy fuck, bro. She got you down in one go." He turns his attention back to me, the corner of his lip pulling into a cocky grin. "It's been fun, but you're climbing up the wrong tree, baby. I suggest you back the fuck down. I wouldn't want to see a pretty little thing like you find herself in trouble."

Reading into his words, I take it for what it is. He's letting me off the hook, giving me a chance to run before shit goes any further south, and not needing to be told twice, I give him a tight smile and nod. "You and I know it's already too late for that, but good idea nonetheless," I tell him, averting my gaze, hating the way I can still feel his heavy stare on the side of my face.

I go to step away, but his hand shoots out and captures my chin. Scary dude steps into me, forcing my chin up until my eyes lock on his, holding me captive. "Where the fuck do you think you're going?" His tone is deep and murmured, and despite the music, I hear every last word as though he spoke straight to my soul.

I try to keep myself calm despite the way my heart thunders erratically in my chest, so wild and terrified that it hurts. "Don't make me knee you in the balls," I warn him. "It's a cheap shot, but trust me when I tell you, I am not above taking it."

His gaze narrows and I try to keep myself breathing.

A moment of silence passes before his fingers begin to loosen on my chin. "Watch yourself," he tells me as I tear my chin free from his warm grip. "I never forget a face."

His threat is loud and clear. I've insulted him here tonight. I've spilled beer all over him, suggested he suck his friend's dick, and called him out for being a typical douche jock. He won't forget it, and at some point, I'll have to pay. I refuse to release his stare, showing that I'm not scared of him despite the terror causing havoc over my body. "You sound like a treat," I tell him. "Listen, great meeting you and all, but I've had a shit night and I'm not about to stick around and wait for one of your friends to start groping me, but it's nice to know that you'll be spending your days unable to forget my face when I can guarantee that the moment I walk away from here tonight, I won't even think twice about yours."

He continues watching me as his friend just stares, looking between the two of us as though he's never witnessed someone having the balls to fight back. He's almost mesmerized by me, and if I were on my own turf, I might even feel good about it, but the rich boys of a private school are unpredictable, and I want nothing to do with them.

I hear my name hollered through the room and my heart stops for only a moment.

Colby.

Fuck, I'd almost forgotten that asshole was looking for me. So, without wasting another moment, I shoulder past the Adonis and barrel toward the grand entrance, determined to get out of here. I don't dare look back at Mr. StickUpAss or his friend Mr. TannedGoldenAndCocky and take off like Cinderella, bolting down the front steps as though her life depended on it. Though unlike her, I leave absolutely nothing to come back for.

CHAPTER 2
Brielle

Slamming the door of my old Honda Civic, I grip the steering wheel and let out a shaky breath.

Okay, so tonight could have gone a bit smoother. Sure, Colby was asking for a verbal smackdown and a shitload more, and I probably should have handled the whole beer on jock situation a little better, but what's a girl to do? I'd just found out that my boyfriend had been screwing other girls, not to mention literally walking in on him with his dick buried in another girl's pussy, and I hadn't even had a chance to scream about it. To be fair, I think the scary jock dude got off easy. Plus, he's an asshole, so I'm sure my bitchy attitude is nothing that he doesn't handle on a daily basis. A guy like him is probably getting panties in a twist left, right, and center.

Wanting to get home, I shove the key in the ignition and feel the soft rumble of the engine vibrate through the car. Hitting the gas and easing out of my parking space, I spy Colby racing toward me, and I laugh as his hands fly up, trying to flag me down.

Asshole. He's kidding himself if he thinks I'm about to give him a ride home so he can rattle off bullshit excuses, throw up in my backseat, and then insist that I'm to blame for his cheating.

No thanks, not today, Satan.

I flip off Colby and fly past him, loving the look of astonishment that crosses his stupid face, like he's actually surprised I'd leave his ass behind.

My phone immediately begins blowing up and I silence it until a new call comes through.

"Girl, what the hell is going on?" Erica demands, not bothering with a hello, though what's new? When you've been best friends since kindergarten, the formalities quickly fade away. "Colby's blowing up my phone, demanding you call him back. What happened?"

I groan and hit the speakerphone button on the cracked screen before tossing my phone back onto the passenger seat. "Are you kidding me?" I mutter. "The dude—"

"There he goes again," she says, cutting me off as I hear the familiar beep of her incoming call. "The asshole won't quit calling. Does he think you're with me or something? I thought you guys were going to that private party."

"We were," I tell her, rolling my eyes as her phone beeps again. "I mean, we did. I just left. He was fucking some dancer chick with great tits in one of the upstairs bedrooms. I walked in to find them and then broke up with him while his limp dick was still inside her. But on the plus side, the girl seemed nice."

"WHAT?" Erica screeches. "HOLY FUCK."

"Yeah," I mutter to myself. "That's what I thought."

"Shit, Bri. Are you alright?" she questions, her tone breaking, reflecting my own pain. "I mean, I know you haven't been feeling it much lately, but nothing is going to take the sting away from something like that. Do you want me to come over? It's still kinda early. We can watch shitty reruns and curse him out all night."

A soft smile pulls at my lips, and while I appreciate her wanting to be there for me tonight, I just want to go to bed. "Nah, that's alright," I tell her. "I'm just going to head straight to bed and try to forget that I just wasted six months of my life on a jackass like that."

"Tough shit," she cuts in, groaning when her phone starts beeping again. Rustling sounds through the phone, and when she speaks, she sounds as though she's running around her room. "I'm packing my stuff now. I'll be there in ten."

Fuck.

Erica ends the call before I get a chance to tell her not to bother, and I let out a heavy sigh. I could call her back and insist she doesn't come. She'll eventually give in, but there's no doubt that she'll bring cookie dough and ice cream, and I simply can't pass that up.

Erica is a great friend, and though I feel like shit, she'll somehow have me laughing so hard that I forget who Colby even is and fall into a peaceful sleep. And damn, that sounds so good right now. She's been there for me through thick and thin, even nursed me back to health after the great lip incident of ninth grade. Though to be fair, she thinks I was stuck in bed after having my appendix out. She would have cared for me either way, but she also would have never let me live it down.

My Civic rolls to a stop in front of the small garage, and I push my door open while silencing another call from Colby. Not trusting this shitty, run-down area, I quickly lock my car before racing toward my front door. The dark and I don't exactly get along, and while I know the likelihood of someone actually jumping out at me is low, my brain can't help but take me there.

Mom's car wasn't in the driveway, so I have to assume that she's still out on her hot date with the fancy lawyer, and I roll my eyes as I shove the key into the front door. I met this new guy last weekend, and I can only assume that she's going to fall madly in love with him. She's always been that way. Either all in, or nothing at all, and after eighteen years of life, I still can't figure out if it's a good thing or not.

Our home isn't exactly falling down, but it's certainly no McMansion either. We live out in the dodgy part of Hope Falls, though to be fair, when we first moved here, the crime rate wasn't so bad, and the area had a good name. That shit went downhill fast. Now, we're all just trying to get by each day without getting jumped on the street.

Stepping through the door, I go to close it just as Erica's familiar yellow Beetle pulls to a stop. I hover in the doorway, watching as she quickly locks her car and races toward me.

She runs at me, only slowing a few feet away before coming to a full stop in front of me, her face falling as she takes me in. "You okay?"

she questions, her voice low while trying to hide the heartbreak she holds for me.

My bottom lip pouts out, and without warning, she crashes into me, throwing her arms around me and squeezing the life out of me. The momentum has us falling back into my home, and she kicks the door shut behind her. "You're going to be just fine," she promises me as we move into my cramped living room. "Now, I don't really know what I'm doing, but I googled voodoo dolls on my way over here and I think I can pull something together."

I laugh and she finally releases me. "Uh-huh," she beams, grabbing my shoulders and looking at my face. "I knew I could make you smile."

And with that, I flick the lock on the back of the door, and she loops her arm through mine before dragging me to my bedroom. My room is an absolute mess, but Erica is more than used to it by now. I'm not proud of it, but it is what it is.

Four different outfits lay scattered across my bed after not being able to decide what to wear to the private party, and I groan at my hair straightener on my dresser. I didn't use it tonight, but clearly Mom did, and that one piece of knowledge has me sailing across the room to double check that she remembered to turn it off.

Mom is my world. She's amazing and I love her. She works crazy hours and puts up with the worst kind of shit at her job just to keep a roof over our heads, and I respect that. She's a smart woman and would do anything for me, but put an attractive, rich man in front of her, and the woman turns to Jell-O.

Pushing the clothes off my bed, I drop down at the end of it and fall back against my pillow while Erica does the same, only flipping around so her feet are up near my face. "Tell me all about it," she says as I grab the other pillow and throw it down to her.

"Which part?" I question with a breathy scoff, leaning across my bed to reach the old blinds above the small window, knowing that my neighbor likes to look in, especially when I have friends over. "The party or the awkward, sweaty fucking?"

"Definitely the awkward, sweaty fucking," she laughs. "We can get to the party later."

Pushing up onto my elbow, I look down at her at the opposite end of my bed, a grin pulling at my lips. "Did I ever tell you how Colby does this weird grunting thing? Like he matches his grunts to his thrusts. It's very off-putting. A girl doesn't stand a chance with him. It's impossible to get in the zone with that going on in your ear."

Erica snorts a laugh, which only makes us both crack into uncontrollable fits of laughter, and just as I expected, all thoughts of Colby fade away, leaving me with nothing but talk of Mr. StickUpAss and his spilled beer.

Just as I finish telling Erica all about our intense stare-off and my bold attitude, my bedroom door flies open and Mom stands in my doorway, her lips pressed into a hard line. I didn't even hear her come in, but I rarely do. She's more than considerate when she's coming in late and always takes her heels off at the door so she doesn't wake me.

She looks amazing, and I don't even comment on the fact that she's wearing one of my dresses. "What's wrong?" I ask, sitting up on my bed and taking in the odd expression on her face. When Mom comes home from a date and she's not beaming from ear to ear, it only ever means one thing—her date was an ass. "Did he call you a cougar like the last guy?"

Mom sighs and gives Erica a quick smile before welcoming herself into my room and dropping down beside me on my bed. There's no doubt about it, my mother is stunning. I can only hope that I look this put together when I'm her age. With that long, blonde hair, dazzling blue eyes, and toned waist, any man would be lucky to have her. It's all too common for her to come home after a date to tell me that some douchebag guy just saw her as a piece of ass to screw over for the night. She's not down for that. She's looking for a real connection, someone to build a life with and make her feel like the luckiest woman on earth.

Mom bites the inside of her lip, and I can't help but notice the flicker of nervousness that settles deep in her bright eyes. Erica must notice it too as she excuses herself with some bullshit excuse about getting ready for bed, and I can honestly say that in the thirteen or so years that I've known her, she's never once bothered with a bedtime routine.

"How was your night?" Mom asks, giving me a fake smile that doesn't reach her eyes. "Did you have a good time? I wasn't expecting to see you home so soon."

I shake my head, my eyes narrowing in suspicion. "Don't even think about it," I warn her. "What's going on?"

She presses her lips into a hard line again, and if there's one thing I know about Cara Ashford, she never hesitates, not unless it's really fucking bad. The last time she hesitated to tell me something, she told me my brother had enlisted in the marines and was taking off for God knows how long.

"Honey, I …" she pauses, draping her delicate hand over my knee as if to somehow soften the blow for whatever's about to come flying out of her mouth. "You know I've been concerned about the growing violence in our area. Gangs are starting to move in, and the kids are getting out of control."

"Okaaaay," I say slowly. This isn't anything new. It's been the same old crap for years.

"The attack on that poor girl a few weeks ago has really rattled me," she continues, the memory of that night coming back to haunt me. "I know you may not understand this, but as a mother, I'm terrified. Do you know how easily that could have been you?"

I go to cut her off, but she beats me to it. "Don't even try to tell me you weren't at the party that night. I know you were, and I know you are careful, but it only takes one asshole to slip something into your drink. I just …" She pauses again, her lips pressing into a hard line as she slowly raises her gaze to mine, preparing to hit me with whatever it is she needs to say. "I was speaking with Orlando about it on our date. You know he's a lawyer and had quite a bit of insight on the issue, and he agrees, this area is too dangerous for us now. What would we do if someone broke into our home? We have nothing to defend ourselves with, no way to protect ourselves. I'm always working, Brielle. You're here alone far too often, and the idea of something happening to you has been eating at me."

My brows furrow as I take her in, wishing she would just say whatever it is she's trying to say. "Just tell me," I insist, spying Erica at my bedroom door, unable to keep from listening in.

"Orlando has offered to move us into his home in Bradford, with him and his son, and I have accepted."

I stare at her, my eyes going wide as I replay every word of what she just said inside my head. "Excuse me?" I breathe, hearing her but unable to comprehend what she's actually saying. "You want us to move into his place?" I ask. "With his pervert son?"

"Oh, stop," Mom says, immediately jumping to the dude's defense. "Jensen is not a pervert. He's perfectly acceptable."

"Listen to you," I scoff. "You even sound like a country club wife already. Where has my real mother gone? You and I both know that Jensen is a weirdo. It was no coincidence that he walked in on me in the bathroom at brunch last week."

Mom flies to her feet, her brows pinched with irritation. "Don't you speak like that about another human being. Orlando is doing us a huge favor by allowing us to move out of this dangerous area. We should be thankful rather than attacking his son like that. Jensen is … strange, yes, but to make awful assumptions like that is a despicable trait, and I will not tolerate it from my daughter. You know how dangerous words can be, and you will not destroy somebody's life by being careless with how you speak. Is that understood?"

I let out a heavy sigh and drop my gaze. I can't stand Jensen. He's creepy and weird, but she's right. "I know, I'm sorry," I murmur, the words tasting like lead on my tongue while also hating how much of a stranger my mother sounds to me right now. "I just … I don't want to move away, and I sure as hell don't want to move into a home with a bunch of rich guys that we don't really know."

"Honey, I know this is a big change for you, but Orlando and I have been dating for a little while now. I trust him, and I'd like it if you could trust him too, or at the very least, trust my judgment on this." She takes a breath and moves back toward me, reaching for my hands. "This is the best move for us. With Damien joining the military, he could be gone for any length of time, and I would never forgive myself if I left you in a position where you were unprotected. This area just isn't safe for us now."

"But …" I let out a heavy sigh, understanding her point but not liking it one bit. "It already takes me fifteen minutes to get to school. This is going to add …" I pause, trying to do the math. "Another forty minutes minimum, considering there's no traffic. That's … THAT'S ALMOST AN HOUR! EVERY MORNING. WHAT? NO. Absolutely not. I'd have to leave at like seven in the morning just to get to my classes on time. It's my senior year, Mom. That's not fair. There's gotta be something else we can do. Moving in with this guy isn't it."

"I'm sorry, Brielle," she tells me, her stare hardening with authority. "That's the other thing I wanted to discuss with you."

I shake my head before she has a chance to utter the words I fear the most, and a sense of dread washes over me.

"I've enrolled you in Bradford Private. You'll no longer be attending Hope Falls Public."

Erica's shocked gasp sounds from my door as I stare back at my mother, tears threatening to fill my eyes. I stand, shaking my head. "No," I tell her, gripping her hand tighter. "No. You're not pulling me out of Hope Falls. All my friends are there, my teachers, my … my …"

"I'm sorry, Brielle. It's a done deal. Orlando has paid your tuition fees and we'll be making the move to Bradford first thing in the morning. This isn't up for discussion."

Mom gives me one last tight smile before squeezing my hand and turning on her heel. She hightails it out of my bedroom as though she can't get out of here soon enough, and before she even crosses the threshold, Erica is already barging straight back in, her arms flying around me and holding me tight. "It's going to be okay," she tells me. "We're going to be okay."

CHAPTER 3
Brielle

Bradford can suck my big-ass metaphorical dick.

I've been here for all of thirty seconds. I haven't even stepped inside the stupid house and I already hate it. Mom and I had brunch here last week, and I didn't give two shits about the home because there was no way in my wildest imagination that I would ever have to be here again, let alone moving all my worldly possessions into it.

This can't be happening. It's just after midday, and it's as though I've been living inside a nightmare all morning, unable to wake myself and make it all go away.

The movers arrived at the crack of dawn, and I had to scramble out of bed to pack my things before they came barging into my room and insisted on doing it for me. Now, I'm not one to care about random people seeing my underwear but having strangers in my space and touching all my things just feels wrong.

Mom gives me an encouraging smile as we look up at the big house we're about to call home. It's not massive like the mansion I'd been in last night, but it's definitely a huge upgrade from the modest three-bedroom shack I've called home for the past six years.

The house is situated toward the end of a private road with others, nearly identical, lining the street around us. It's not exactly a gated community, but it's well on its way. Expensive BMWs, Mercedes, and Audis line the road, and I find my gaze settling back onto my old Honda Civic. She definitely doesn't fit in here.

The houses up and down the road are huge, taking up as much of the property as possible and making it look as though they practically live on top of their neighbors. All the yards are perfectly landscaped, and I'd bet that every single property has a pool and an extravagant entertaining area out back.

This is rich man's territory here, though it could be worse. Another five minutes down the road and we get into billionaire territory where the properties are simply insane. These McMansions lining the private road are the modest version of those; the homes that the billionaires turn their noses up to. Shit, I can only imagine what they'd think of the small, falling apart, three bedder that I just vacated.

Grabbing the box of my most important possessions from the passenger seat of my Civic, I walk toward Mom and meet her by the side of her car so that we can walk up to the front door together.

The truck is just pulling up to the curb and we barely get another step before the door opens wide and the famous Orlando Channing, number one criminal lawyer in the state, appears before us.

He doesn't look the tiniest bit pleased to see us as he stands fully decked out in a suit that cost more than my car. His graying hair is swept back, and there's no doubt that he's a bit of a silver fox, just my mother's type.

Orlando's gaze rakes over me before settling on my mother, who beams back at him, turning to mush at the sight of the man who's made her all kinds of promises that I know he won't be willing to keep. I just can't figure out his angle here. He's a smart man, a lawyer at the top of his game. Why would he be so reckless in inviting his new girlfriend and her daughter to live with him? Does he like it when women are dependent on him? Does alienating them from their independence get him hot? All I know is that I don't like him, and I sure as hell don't trust him.

"Ahh, Cara, truly a radiant sight as always," he says, working her just right, though the words don't quite match the lack of interest in his eyes. "I was starting to wonder if you'd changed your mind."

"Not at all," Mom says, leading us up the path to the front door, her cheeks glowing with a soft blush at his compliment. "Packing all of our things took a little longer than anticipated, but we're here now."

We step up to the door and Orlando's gaze falls on me once again. "You remember my daughter, Brielle?" Mom continues. "She was thrilled to learn that we were going to be spending our time together."

Orlando narrows his gaze on me, knowing damn well that's not how the conversation went down. After all, he has a teenage son of his own, one who I'm sure has his own issues with authoritative figures making demands of him.

I give the guy a forced smile and he gives me an even faker one in return. "It's a pleasure to have you stay with us," he says. "I'm sure you and Jensen will get along just fine. I know he is looking forward to your arrival."

I'm sure he is.

Orlando points to the box in my hands. "Here, let me take that for you and I'll show you up to your room."

I pull away from his grabby fingers. "No, it's fine. I can—"

He takes the box right out of my hands, no questions asked, and turns his back before stalking into the house. Having no choice, I follow Mom and Orlando inside as the movers remain behind, opening the back of the truck and starting to pull out boxes of junk that Mom, Damien, and I have spent a lifetime collecting.

"This way," Orlando says with Mom hurrying to keep up with his long strides, doing everything she can to appear like the perfect guest. I wonder if Orlando is the type of man who thinks women should be seen and not heard.

The house is immaculate and boring as fuck. White walls, white floors, white decor. I mean, there's a slight gray to some of it, but for the most part, it's all white. It's the kind of place I'd be too scared to sneeze in on the off chance I accidentally shit myself in the process. When I say this isn't the kind of place you want to be in when you get brought down by a gastro bug, I truly mean it. There will be no racing in and traipsing mud through the house, no grabbing pizza and taking it up to my room, no drinks other than water allowed anywhere within this house.

It's boring. Fucking boring.

Reaching the top of the stairs, I glance around at the open living space. It's way too formal for someone like me to be comfortable, though judging by how perfectly it was put together, I doubt anyone actually uses this area. It leads directly off from the stairs with large windows sending waves of sunlight dancing across the floors. It has a fully stocked library, probably filled with books that I've never even considered glancing at, and an off-white concrete-style coffee table with big couches on either side. There's a rug across the living room, almost the same off-putting white as the marble beneath it, and while I'm sure it would feel heavenly beneath my feet, I don't dare test it out. We'll be out of here in only a matter of weeks, and I refuse to be the reason this place wasn't left in pristine condition. A guy like Orlando would probably send us off with a bill for a cleaner.

We follow Orlando deeper into the upstairs living areas, and I commit each turn to memory as he leads us down a wide hallway. It doesn't escape me that there's shitty emo-screamo music coming from the end of the hallway, and I sigh realizing just how close my bedroom is going to be to his pervert son's. I'm going to have to lock my door each night just to keep myself from being groped while I sleep.

Jensen's bedroom door remains closed, and I take that as a bonus as Orlando turns into a room and waits just inside the open door, inviting us in.

Mom steps inside just a fraction before I do, and her pleased gasps sail through the big room. I quickly move in around her and take it all in.

It's fucking huge. No, fucking huge is an understatement. This room is bigger than all three bedrooms at our old place combined.

A queen-sized bed sits directly to my left, with a private bathroom just beyond that. Everything is white, which is no surprise, and the closet is big enough to be considered a separate bedroom. Instead of a simple desk, there's an entire space carved out to be an office. I guess Orlando is serious about education and good grades.

The whole room has been decorated perfectly for a teenage girl, and I can't help but wonder if it was created specifically for me, or if it's just always been like this.

"This will be your room," Orlando tells me, shuffling in toward the bed and placing my box of precious items on the bedside table. "I hope everything is as you imagined. You should be very comfortable here. I'm not sure how much your mother has discussed your schooling with you, however you start at Bradford Private first thing in the morning. Your uniform is hanging in your closet and your textbooks are on your desk. Now, I know you will be busy unpacking today, but please set aside some time to go over your class schedule and the student handbook. School commences at 8:40 and not a moment after. You will need to arrive with plenty of time to visit the student office and meet your advisors. However, since you have your own transportation, there should be no issues there. Do you have any questions?"

My jaw goes slack, and I scramble to remember everything he just said as I shake my head. "Um, no. Thank you. I'm sure I will be fine."

"Good." Orlando gives me a tight smile and, with that, bows his head and walks out of the room.

The tension in my shoulders evaporates the moment he's out of sight and I move deeper into my new bedroom, brushing my fingers over the soft blankets of my bed and taking it all in, my gaze shifting over the walk-in closet and spying the private school uniform that's staring back at me. I've never worn a uniform in my life, so this is bound to be interesting.

Two big windows don the walls—one directly in front, looking over the front of the property, and one to the right of the room that showcases the pristine landscaping around the side of the house ... and gives my new neighbors the perfect view right into my room. I'm going to have to remember to close the blinds each night, but what's new? I already spend my days avoiding the leering stares from my creepy neighbor.

Glancing back at Mom, I find her all but bouncing on her toes, desperately trying to reel in her wide grin. "Well?" she rushes out, her eyes darting around the impressive room. "What do you think? It's nice, huh?"

"Nice?" I scoff. "More like a pay-off to ensure Orlando doesn't get any trouble from me. Don't you think it's a bit much? My old room wasn't even a third of this. Plus, there's a private bathroom and a walk-in. I mean, what am I going to do with all of that? My clothes wouldn't even begin to fill that."

"Oh, come on," she says. "Can't you just allow yourself to enjoy this? It's not every day we find ourselves able to live in such luxury. I know Orlando runs a tight ship. He's strict and will have rules which I'm sure are bound to ruffle your feathers, but in the long run, I know you're going to be happy here."

"And his pervert son?"

Mom's eyes go wide as she whips her head around, making sure we haven't been overheard. "What did I tell you about that? There is nothing wrong with Jensen. He is a perfectly acceptable young man, and you will do well to make friends with him. Just because he is different to you, does not mean that he is an awful person. I know he graduated last year, but I'm sure he wouldn't mind showing you the ropes around here, help steer you in the right direction."

My lips twist with unease. "Maybe you're forgetting about the whole bathroom situation at brunch last week."

"A simple misunderstanding, I'm sure." Mom huffs and rolls her eyes as she moves back toward the door, already frustrated with me, but what did she expect? That I would take the word of a stranger without question? She's completely uprooted my life, taken me away from the friends I've grown up with, and shoved me in this robotic world full of white walls and strict rules, a world that I never once imagined myself having to become accustomed to.

Mom stops by my door, glancing back at me with a firmness I rarely experience from her. "I will have your boxes sent up to you. Unpack quickly and ensure you have enough time to go over your class schedule."

And with that, she's gone.

Frustration burns through me like lava in my veins, and I narrowly avoid sprinting after her just to slam the door in her face. She's completely screwing me over here, only thinking about herself and what she wants. Does my life not matter to her? She claims this whole move was about finding us somewhere safe to live, but she's already made it clear that this is all about becoming Orlando's newest show pony and getting to live out some ridiculous fantasy of being a trophy wife.

The shrill ring of my phone brings me out of my rage-induced panic, and I dart across my new room before scrambling through the box on my bedside table. My fingers close around my phone and I bring it up to find a facetime call from Erica and I quickly accept.

"Oh my God, show me," she says, as usual, not bothering with a hello.

"Ugh," I grumble, crossing the room to close the door only to stumble back a step, finding Jensen peering in. "Can I help you?"

A grin settles across his face and unease drops into my gut like a lead weight falling from the sky. "Not at all," he says, leaning against the doorframe, his hands shoved deep into his pockets, probably cupping his cock as we speak. "Just thought I'd do the hospitable thing and check in on our new guest. After all, we're practically siblings now."

Gross.

"Let's get a few things straight," I snap, stepping closer to grip the handle of the door, more than ready to slam it in his face. "We are not siblings. We are not friends. We are nothing, just two people who have to live down the hall from one another. You don't come into my space, and I won't come into yours. Touch me and I will make your life a living hell. I will make sure you rot and burn. Your life will not be worth living. Got it? I'm not here to fulfill your gross stepsister fantasy."

Jensen winks and it has a chill sailing down my spine. "Got it, little sis. I'll make sure you feel perfectly welcome here. You don't need to worry about me."

He backs away, grinning to himself, and I don't hesitate in making the door fly. It slams shut with a loud bang and I don't doubt Mom is going to berate my ass for being so disrespectful, but fuck it. I'm sure if she wasn't so blinded by Orlando's silver fox status, she'd see that his son is an asshole.

"Was that your new roomie?" Erica asks.

I bring the phone up and see her face staring back at me. "Yes," I grumble. "That was Jensen. He's such an ass. I'll have to search the room for peepholes and spyware."

"Don't forget to search for gloryholes," she mutters. "The last thing you want is to reach for the light switch only to get a handful of cock poking through the wall."

An unladylike snort pulls from the back of my throat. "Where the hell do you come up with this shit?"

"Hey," she snaps back at me. "I don't ask you about your childhood trauma, so don't bring up mine. Now, show me your new room. Is it fit for a princess?"

"It's certainly fit for something," I mutter darkly as I switch cameras on my phone and begin scanning the room, showing off the monstrosity around me. Though, in all fairness, this room is incredible. It's certainly more than I ever expected for myself and definitely something I never thought I'd ever get to experience. Mom was right about that. I should be grateful. I'm probably just acting like a brat because I'm hurt about the sudden move. Perhaps I owe her an apology.

Regret settles into my chest as I show Erica around the room, listening to her impressed oohs and ahhs, especially when I get to the private bathroom. Not going to lie, I'm just as impressed as she is, while also kinda put off at the bidet sitting beside the toilet, staring back at me like some kind of challenge. The shower is huge and the detachable showerhead …

"Holy shit," she breathes. "You've literally hit the sugar daddy lottery. Do you think he'll let me move in too? Imagine the parties we could throw in that place."

"Call him my sugar daddy one more time and see what happens," I warn her. "It's bad enough that—"

A loud, obnoxious rumble tears through the property, practically shaking the foundations of the house and my brows furrow, cutting off whatever point I was trying to make. "What the hell is that?" I murmur, striding across my room to the window overlooking the front of the property.

A sleek black motorbike slows before the neighbor's house, pulling into the driveway, and I hold up the phone. "You seeing this?" I ask Erica, my gaze feasting over the helmeted rider in his black shirt that sticks to his strong, muscled body, his sleeves tightening around his shoulders and biceps.

Thick thighs straddle the bike and my mouth waters as Erica gushes. "Fuck me. Is that your new neighbor?"

"I fucking hope so," I tell her, watching as the guy brings the bike to a stop and climbs off, his heavy boots hitting the ground. He looks dangerous and sexy and holy hell, if he is my new neighbor then staying here might not be so bad after all. I wouldn't mind waking up every morning and peering out my window to see that.

Erica groans, taking him in. "I pray for your little dried up, underused pussy that he's a fuck boy."

A laugh vibrates through my chest, and I roll my eyes, unable to pull my gaze away from the intriguing sight. The devilish man kicks the stand out and balances the bike before gripping his helmet and making my heart race, the anticipation of finding out if his face matches his body growing wild within me.

"That's right, baby," Erica murmurs. "Take it off. Let me see what's hiding under there."

I hold my breath as the helmet comes up over his head, my eyes feasting on every inch of newly exposed skin, and as the black helmet finally lifts off his head, my whole world crumbles, burning to ashes around me.

My eyes bug out of my head, panic tearing at my chest. "OH FUCK."

"Oh, fuck is right," Erica laughs. "Girl, you're in so much trouble. New neighbor dude is so damn hot. He's going to have you up against a wall and destroying you in minutes. Shit. Who needs Colby's awkward grunts with that hanging around? Fuck, I'm so jealous."

"No. I don't mean *oh fuck,* he's going to rail me until I scream. I mean *oh fuck,* I'm in actual trouble. That's the dude from the party last night. The one I spilled beer all over and then suggested his friend shove his dick down his throat."

"Oh, babe," she laughs. "You really are fucked."

CHAPTER 4
TANNER

You've got to be fucking kidding me.

I kick the stand out under my bike and make sure she's balanced when I find the little bitch from last night peering out at me through one of the many spare bedrooms of the Channing property next door. There's a moving truck blocking half of my driveway, a piece of shit Honda Civic parked on the street, and another car I haven't seen around here parked in the driveway. All signs that the asshole next door has asked his gold-digger girlfriend to move in.

Just fucking perfect.

Anyone but her.

I'm not surprised. This is Channing's third girlfriend in two years. It's his fucked-up routine. He takes them in, makes them think they can't live without him, and then the bullshit starts. He's an asshole, but who isn't around here? Everyone has their dirty little secrets.

My gaze raises to the feisty blonde in the window. I clocked her the second I pulled into my driveway. I don't know if she's dumb or desperate, but just because I'm wearing a helmet doesn't mean I can't see straight through the crystal-clear window. She's been blatantly staring like a little puppy starved for attention, and if she weren't so fucking hot, I would have flipped her off by now. There's no doubt about it, she's fresh meat, and I don't plan to burn that bridge quite so soon. At least, after her performance at Riley's party last night, I'll have her on her knees begging for it first.

I don't know who this girl is, but she's got a feisty attitude. I've never seen her hanging around here, and now I see her twice in as little as twelve hours. Riley was right, she's got a nasty bite, but it was her bark that intrigued me. I can't say that any chick who's drenched me in beer and called me out has ever gotten me hard like that, but she did. Maybe it was the fire in her eyes, or maybe I'm just into petite blondes now.

Riley's end of year party was a drag. At least, for me it was— he had a fucking great time. It was supposed to be my last shot at relaxing, forgetting all the bullshit, and chilling out with the boys before school starts, but nothing has been the same this summer. The party was flooded with losers from the public school just outside of town, bringing their problems to our turf as though we give a shit about them.

Riley's party though, Riley's rules.

If it were me, I would have locked their asses out and watched them beg for attention. Not Riley though. He's a flirt. To him, any hole is a goal as long as she's eager, willing, and wet, and when carloads of chicks he's never played with turned up, the fucker couldn't say no.

Not gonna lie, he's a dick, but he's my best friend, and I wouldn't have it any other way.

Stepping back from my bike, I reach for my helmet and pull it over my head. My eyes immediately snap up to the girl in the window as a shit-eating grin stretches across my face. Her eyes bug out of her fucking head and it's damn near the funniest shit I've ever seen.

Panic surges through her wide stare, and I can almost hear her fear pounding through the glass, desperate to get out. She scrambles like a terrified mouse, darting behind the curtains, and it forces my grin wider.

I wasn't wrong, living next to little miss no name is going to be fun. A lot of fun.

What I wouldn't give to be a fly on the wall inside her bedroom, to brush my fingers over her pulse and feel the rapid thrum as her heart races with fear, to watch her hands begin to shake and hear her soft gasping breaths as she tries to calm herself.

She fucked up last night. She might not have known who I am or just how fucking stupid it was to mess with me, but she'll learn quickly. No one throws down a challenge that I don't rise to, and if a rivalry is what she wants, then who am I to deny her?

Not gonna lie, the fact that she's absolutely stunning is just the cherry on top, and I'm going to enjoy watching her purse those full lips around my cock, but not as much as I'll enjoy fucking her. It's only a matter of time.

Knowing damn well that she's not about to risk looking down here again, I make my way inside, following the sound of my mother's heels clicking against the Italian marble she imported last year.

"Tanner? Is that you, honey?" she calls out from the living room.

I roll my eyes and shake my head. I love my mother, but sometimes she needs to think before she lets the words fall from her lips. "Who else would it be?" I throw back, making my way across the foyer and past the kitchen. "Expecting anyone else with a motorcycle?"

"Ha. Ha. You know sometimes I forget how funny you are," she says as I finally reach her, only to find her scrambling for her things, most likely on her way out. "You get that from your father."

"Wow. Woke up and chose violence," I tease. "Fuck, Mom. I wish you'd given me the heads up. Maybe I would have waited until you left before coming home."

Her soft eyes narrow into a hard glare. "Watch your language, Tanner Morgan. I brought you into this world, and I sure as hell can take you out of it."

A wide smile stretches across my face, one I know she can't resist. "You wouldn't dream of it."

Mom holds my stare as if to say, *try me* and I let out a heavy sigh, knowing damn well that she would win this round. She's no idiot. She's the woman who raised me and the one I could never hurt. I don't know what kind of motherly black magic she's got going on, but she has this way of putting me in my place without even saying a damn word. What can I say? I love my mom.

"Heading out?" I ask, moving across the living room to the fruit bowl Mom keeps on one of the many decorative tables. I grab an apple and grin at her as I take a bite. She fucking hates it when I do this. Apparently, this particular fruit bowl is for decoration only. Its contents are not to be consumed and the bowl is not to be fucked with.

Mom lets out a heavy sigh. "You know I hate it when you do that. There's a perfectly good bowl of fruit in the kitchen."

"You know, normal people eat their fruit," I tell her, just in case she hadn't quite figured it out, but just to get my point across, I take another bite. "What's wrong with vases or flowers or shit like that? Do you know how uncomfortable it is when the guys are here and I have to explain why they're not allowed to eat the fruit in the fruit bowl that's right in front of their faces? It's like dangling a hooker in front of Riley and telling him he's not allowed to lick it."

Mom's eyes go wide. "TANNER MORGAN!" she gasps, horrified by my loose tongue, though I don't know why, she's heard a lot worse slip from my mouth. But hell, Mom thinks I'm her precious little star. In her eyes, I can do no wrong and that's the way it's going to stay. She doesn't need to know about the list of women I've worked my way through, the amount of hearts that have broken under my boots, or the number of jaws I've dislocated and broken.

Not going to lie, I've been in more shit than anyone at my school. I all but live in the principal's office. Me and Principal Dormer have a solid understanding. He leaves my mother out of it and allows my father to deal with me, and in return, I ensure that he has the number one high school football team in the country. Who knows what he's going to do when I graduate next year, but I suppose that's not my problem. I'll be onto bigger and better things with a long list of college teams begging me to join them.

"If you must know," my mother continues, realizing that she's not about to get an apology out of me, "I'm heading out. I've got a bunch of chores to do and then I thought I'd go visit your sister."

I nod, having figured as much. "Tell her hi for me."

Mom rolls her eyes and gives me a hard stare. "You could always come with me and say it yourself."

My face scrunches. Mom knows how visiting my sister fucks with my mood. Every time I've seen her over the past few weeks, it sends me into a blind rage. Don't get me wrong, I love my sister. She's the reason I push myself so hard. I want to show her that anything is possible, but right now, I'm not sure I can be the kind of brother she needs.

Mom doesn't bother waiting for a response, knowing where I stand on the topic. She loops her handbag over her arm and makes her way to the door, digging through her bag for her keys. Being the gentleman she thinks I am, I pull the door open and hold it for her.

Mom steps out and raises her head only to let out a heavy sigh. "Oh damn. The neighbor's truck is blocking our driveway," she mutters to herself, irritation lacing her features. "How am I supposed to get out around that?"

"Do you want me to ask them to move?"

She presses her lips into a hard line, her eyes flicking between the truck and her car. "No, it's alright. I think I'll be able to squeeze past."

"Sure?" I question, looking up at the narrow space, not feeling good about the safety of her new Merc. Mom isn't the greatest driver. There's a reason we have a brand-new mailbox, and it has nothing to do with dumbasses driving past and knocking it down with baseball bats. "I can back out for you. It's no problem."

Mom scoffs. "Oh please, you ride around on that silly motorcycle all day. Besides, I have been driving for much longer than you have. I'll be perfectly fi—" she trails off, watching as Channing's new girlfriend steps out of the house and strides up to the movers, collecting boxes and taking them inside.

I can't help but watch the show. She doesn't strike me as the typical gold-digging girlfriend I'm used to seeing come and go from the house, but she holds all the typical qualities of a woman Channing likes—bleach-blonde hair, big eyes, and false lashes. Plus, she's got a killer body to go with it. Clearly this is where her daughter gets it from.

Mom's lips pull up in irritation and I smirk at her response. "What? Not keen on the new neighbor? Usually, you'd already be over there with a fresh tray of brownies, welcoming her to the street. I'm appalled, Mrs. Morgan. Where are your neighborly manners?"

Mom shrugs. "I don't have time for that today. Besides, I wasted good brownies on the last two women who came through here and neither of them even bothered with a thank you, but I suppose that's what you get when you date women lower than your class. They lasted only a few months each. If this new floozy makes it past the four-month mark, then I'll introduce myself."

"Shit, Mom. You really did wake up and choose violence," I laugh, loving this side of her. "Is something bothering you? Do I need to beat someone's ass?"

Mom walks down the front steps and moves in beside her car before looking back at me, a smirk stretching across her face. "Oh honey, it's nothing your daddy can't fix with a good beating."

Oh my fucking God. Tell me she did not just say that.

Bile rises in my throat as I listen to the sheer laughter booming out of my mother. Fuck, she thinks she's so funny. One more joke like that and I'll be buying a lifetime of sessions with the best therapist in Bradford.

I shake my head, the images already intruding in my mind and making me feel sick. "Low blow, Mom," I mutter, watching as she opens her car door and lowers herself into it. "Low fucking blow."

"Listen," she calls out her window, her engine mostly drowning her out. "The girl next door; Orlando mentioned she'll be starting new at Bradford Private first thing in the morning. She's a senior like you, so I expect you to be welcoming. Show her around, introduce her to some friends."

"You're joking right?"

"I am absolutely not joking, Tanner Morgan. Just because I'm not doing the neighborly thing, doesn't mean that you won't be."

Mom fixes me with another hard stare, not relenting until I give in and dazzle her with a tight smile and a nod, but she's fucking kidding herself if she thinks I'm about to be Killjoy's new BFF.

Despite wanting to shove a hot poker through my ear just to singe the visual of my parents fucking out of my head, I wait and watch her leave. A part of me would like to say that it's because I worry about her safety while backing out around the truck, but in all honesty, I just want to be here when she inevitably realizes that I was right and has to get out and ask for help.

What can I say? I'm such a selfless son. Always there for her when she needs me the most.

It takes Mom ten minutes just to back out, inching out of the driveway and refusing to meet my eye. She's stubborn, just like me, but I don't blame her. Were the situation reversed, I wouldn't ask for help either. But on the other hand, I wouldn't have had the issue in the first place. Those movers would have known to move out of my fucking way, and if they refused, they would have learned really fucking fast what it means to cross me.

I'd wave goodbye, but my arms ache after spending most of my morning working out. The twins fucking killed me. Their dad just completed their new home gym, so naturally they pestered me until I showed up on their doorstep, Riley in tow. Their father, who is also my uncle, is a bigshot movie producer and will flood Jax and Logan with expensive presents and shit just to ease the guilt of being away all the time, but they don't seem to care. Not anymore. They've gotten used to it after so many years.

The twins, Logan and Jax Morgan, are my cousins, best friends, and fucking killers on the football field. All of us are. Logan, Jax, me, and Hudson Bellamy. We've been tight for years. Riley's on the team too, but he's too busy chasing pussy to care about being at the top of his game—not that it makes him any less of a fucking superstar on the field. Even without putting in the effort, he's still one of our best players. Not above me though, and that's not my ego talking. It's just a fact.

School starts tomorrow, my senior fucking year. I've got everything going for me. Colleges are already interested, I'm at the top of the food chain, plus I have a brand-new hobby to fill my spare time. What more could I possibly need?

Letting the door fall closed behind me, I skip up the stairs two at a time while reaching over the back of my head and gripping the fabric of my black shirt. I shrug out of it and toss it aside as I enter my bedroom, my hands falling to the button on my pants. It's been a long morning and after sweating it out in the twins' new home gym, I could use a shower.

Stepping out of my jeans, I go to make my way into my bathroom when movement through my bedroom window catches my eye, and I find Killjoy directly across from me, reaching up to hang clothes in her closet, her shirt riding up and exposing the toned skin of her waist.

My cock flinches with hunger, fire burning through my veins.

"Down boy," I mutter, gripping onto my hardening cock and giving him a firm squeeze. What is it about this chick that keeps setting me off? After she'd bailed out of the party last night, I couldn't stop thinking about the rage in her eyes. Something had pissed her off and she wasn't above beating a bitch down to let it be known. Lucky me, I just happened to be the asshole standing in her way.

I watch her for a moment, hanging her clothes and bending down to grab some more out of a large box, her ass high in the air and making the hunger soar deeper through my body. Can't lie, the girl is fine. Her blonde hair falls over her shoulder, exposing the curve of her neck, while her slim, toned waist looks as though it could fit perfectly between my hands, but her ass … fuck. I could bury myself in that ass.

Without even realizing, my hand begins moving up and down the length of my cock, imagining her plump lips circled around it, her tongue rolling over my tip. A groan rumbles through my chest as my lips begin twisting into a wicked smirk, knowing just how much fun it's going to be living next door to this little vixen. I just hope her bite really is as bad as her bark.

Killjoy hangs the last of her clothes, and as she steps out of her closet, her head snaps up, her soft blue eyes landing directly on mine. I can almost hear her gasp.

Her gaze drops, her jaw going slack as those blue eyes widen and snap back up to mine. A laugh booms out of my chest. I'm in no way ashamed of my body, in fact, I'm pretty fucking proud of it, and just to let her know, I move my fist up and down and wink before watching as she dies of embarrassment.

She immediately looks away, her cheeks flaming bright red as my grip tightens on my cock. She spins around and all but runs back inside her closet before grabbing the door and slamming it behind her.

Another laugh rumbles through my chest and I move across my room into my private bathroom as I thank whoever exists above that she hadn't considered closing her blinds. Though something tells me that won't be the case from here on out.

Leaving the door wide open, I step into my shower and go to fucking town, knowing damn well that the second she steps out of her closet, she's going to be watching the whole damn show.

Whoever said fucking with your neighbors shouldn't be fun?

CHAPTER 5
Brielle

*B*eep. Beep.

Beeeeeeeeeep. Beep. Beep.

"Ugggggh," I groan, rolling over and slamming my hand down over my phone. It hasn't shut up for the past half an hour, and I'm one *beep* away from throwing it across the room and shattering it against the wall. I'm not proud of my violent ways, but I'll do anything to make it stop.

Beep.

"FUUUUUCK!"

I curl the cool metal around my hand and lift it over my face to see what the hell is going on, only to feel rage boiling through my veins as I find a slew of missed calls and texts from Colby. Does this guy not get the hint? We're over. So fucking over. I don't want anything to do with him. I mean, I know he clearly has no self-respect, but I sure as hell do.

Not having the restraint to control myself, I open his messages and realize they start right from the night of the party.

Colby - Babe, please. I swear, it's not what it looked like. Come back. We can talk about this.

A booming laugh tears from my chest. He's kidding, right? I literally walked in and saw his three-incher buried inside Dancer Girl. The need to respond with the photo I'd taken blasts through me, but I don't dare give in to him. The moment I reply is the moment he gets me right where he wants me, and that's not about to happen.

I scroll down.

Colby - Missed Call.
Colby - Missed Call.
Colby - Missed Call.
Colby - Where are you? Why aren't you answering my calls? Don't be like this, babe. Please, we can work through it. I was just drunk and stupid, but what we have means so much more.
Colby - Why are you throwing this away?
Colby - Missed Call.
Colby - Come on. Stop being so dramatic. That slut came onto me. What was I supposed to do?
Colby - Answer your fucking phone.

Colby - Real fucking mature, Brielle. Do you know who I am? I'm the fucking captain of the football team, I'm the fucking king of the school. Without me, you're nothing. I will destroy you. You're just some dumb bitch with a nice rack. One word from me and you'll be the school outcast. Is that really how you want to start senior year?

Colby - Missed Call.

Colby - Missed Call.

Fucking hell. My heart races with anger and I clench my jaw, the struggle not to respond testing me like never before. All of those messages are from the night of the party, and clearly he was a little sore after having to find his own way home, but what did he expect? Maybe he's forgotten that I have actual proof of him fucking that girl.

What does it matter now anyway? I've moved homes, I live far away, and won't even be going to school with him. His threats mean nothing, and despite how much I don't want to be living here with creepy perv dude down the hall and naked, tattooed, horny guy next door, it's somehow a fresh start.

Call me a sucker for punishment because I keep scrolling, finding the messages from yesterday and this morning.

Colby - I'm sorry, babe. Can we just start over? I was drunk and didn't know what I was doing. Surely you can forgive me, right? I didn't mean to hurt you. It was just a mistake. I'm human. What more do you want from me?

Colby - Missed Call.

Colby - Missed Call.

Colby - Missed Call.

Colby - Why aren't you answering your phone? Erica's not taking my calls either. Please, babe. Just tell me we're cool. I'll pick you up for school in the morning. We can ride in together and talk.

Colby - Bri, can you just reply? Tell me you're okay.

Colby - I'm out front. Come out.

Colby - Missed Call.

Colby - Missed Call.

Colby - Where the fuck are you? Your house is empty!

Colby - Brielle. Where are you?

Colby - Missed Call.

Colby - Missed Call.

Colby - ANSWER THE FUCKING PHONE.

Colby - Missed Call.

Colby - I'm so fucking done with your shit. Good luck being the school reject, bitch. I'll have Kate on her fucking knees, sucking my cock by lunch. I don't fucking need you. I'm out.

Letting out a breath, I drop my phone into the sheets and stare up at the ceiling. I suppose this is what I get when I don't answer my phone all weekend. Though, it's not my problem anymore. Good luck to him. I'm sure it'll be fun trying to make me the reject of a school I no longer attend. It's Erica I worry about. It won't take long before he's cornering her in the hallway, demanding answers. She can handle assholes like that though. She's been waiting six long months to put him in his place, and I can guarantee that she won't hold back.

My gaze lingers on the ceiling, desperately wishing I could sleep another few hours. I spent most of the night unpacking my things. You know, after I found the nerve to escape my closet, but damn, that scary dude was butt naked with every single tattoo on full display, staring right at me with his monster dick in hand and his eyes sparkling, daring me to come over and play. I don't think my heart has ever raced so fast.

When I realized the guy from the party was my new neighbor, dread filled me. I knew I wasn't going to get away with the bullshit I pulled at that party. I was angry and hurt and my attitude flew free. I don't usually speak so bluntly to strangers, and I sure as hell don't pick fights with them, especially when they're twice my size.

I'm not going to lie, I laid awake for most of the night, unable to stop picturing the way his hand moved up and down his thick shaft, unable to stop imagining just how good it would have felt had it been my hand, wondering what was rushing through his head.

Shit, I know I shouldn't go there. I know that I should take the image of his thick, veiny cock and that devilish grin and burn them to ashes. It's dangerous territory, but when a girl is all alone with a beast of a man just one window away, it's almost impossible not to go there.

Without thinking, my gaze falls to the window, my breath catching in my throat as my bottom lip catches between my teeth. With my blinds pulled, I can't see anything but the inside of my new bedroom, but just the knowledge of Jock Dude being so close, asleep in his bed, probably looking like some kind of wet dream, makes it hard to focus.

Ha. Maybe if Colby had ever satisfied me, I wouldn't be so caught up on this. I'm so hungry for it that it scares me. I'm going to get myself in trouble, trouble I can't afford.

Beeeeep.

"Fucking hell."

My hand slams back down on my phone and I clench it between my hands, raising it above my head to spy the screen. I immediately swipe the new message away and my gaze settles on the time across the screen.

7:48 am.

"Oh, fuck."

I scramble out of bed and race across the room, bolting into my massive walk-in closet. I didn't get a chance to go over my class schedule or the student handbook like Orlando had so kindly suggested. I'm sure he's going to be so proud. School starts promptly at 8:40, and I'm going to have to find time to get dressed, make myself presentable, eat, and get my ass to school while leaving time to figure out the whole parking situation and get to the student office.

Great. This is exactly what I *didn't* want for my first day.

Orlando is far from a father figure in my life, but something tells me that he won't hesitate to give me the usual *you're such a disappointment* speech that most money hungry fathers give their children when they embarrass them in front of their other money hungry friends. Now I'm not one to judge, but I assume scary Jock Dude next door is probably very familiar with that speech.

After quickly getting dressed and feeling like an absolute idiot in my new uniform, I hurry into the bathroom and race through my morning routine. After putting on a flick of mascara and tying my hair into a loose braid, I sling my bag over my shoulder, moving toward the full-length mirror across the room. I have no idea how strict this school is, but I'm not taking any risks, not when I already have Jock Dude to manage.

My gaze raises to the mirror, preparing to give myself the best pep talk of my life, only I stop. My eyes widen, and a gasp rests on my lips as I scan the words scrawled across the mirror in bright red lipstick.

SO PRETTY WHEN YOU SLEEP.

My heart kicks into gear, my hands immediately growing clammy.

What the ever-loving fuck?

Falling back a step, my knees hit the edge of my bed and I collapse, my gaze locked on the lipstick on the mirror. I've known fear in my life, plenty of it. You don't grow up in Hope Falls without learning the true meaning of fear at a young age, but I have never felt anything like this.

Jensen Fucking Channing.

My heart pounds. The guy is a creep, but to sneak into my bedroom while I sleep? To invade my personal space like that? No, absolutely not. I won't stand for that shit. I warned him yesterday what would happen if he were to fuck with me. He kept referring to me as a sibling, calling me lil sis and trying to get into my head. He's the worst kind of predator, and I don't want to end up as one of his victims. That isn't the life I want for myself. I have to shut this shit down.

I told Mom what he was, I told her what I thought of him, and she still brought us here, still pushed me into this life I didn't want. What am I supposed to do with that?

Swallowing hard, I throw myself to my feet, the anger pulsing heavily through my veins. Do I tell Mom? Orlando? And if I do, are they just going to shrug it off or are they going to put a stop to this? I know what Mom would have done had Orlando been some random guy that she wasn't screwing, but now? I'm not so sure.

Stepping out of my room, I scoff to myself, my gaze sailing toward the end of the hallway at Jensen's bedroom door. It's shut and there's not a sound coming from within, but I'm not surprised. I'd still be sound asleep if I spent my night creeping around random girls' bedrooms and watching them sleep.

Fucking creeper. I'm so angry. I need to vent, but right now, I need to get to school.

I make a point of pulling my door closed firmly behind me before racing down the stairs. I make my way through the big house, stopping by the kitchen to find a small container filled with fruit salad and a side of yogurt with muesli sprinkled on top.

My stomach growls and I scoop it up while glancing around. I'm assuming this is for me, and I suspect that there was some kind of personal chef here early this morning to make it happen. My mom hasn't made breakfast a day in her life and Orlando … no. It definitely wasn't him.

Hurrying out the door, I fix my backpack over my shoulder and scurry toward my Honda, ignoring the house directly to my right. I'm just unlocking my car when I hear the front door of my new monstrosity open and glance up to find Mom in a white pantsuit, her hair curled and sprayed, and her makeup flawless.

"Where the hell are you going?" I grunt, my hand pausing on my car door as I stare at her in confusion. She works a million dead-end jobs, each one as shit as the next, but she's never once missed work and she's never once come strutting out the door looking like that … except when she's got a date.

Mom's head snaps up and she takes me in with wide eyes. "Bri," she gasps. "What on earth are you still doing here? You should have left ages ago. You're going to be late for your first day."

"Yeah, I'm well aware," I grumble, deciding now probably isn't the time to bring up the creepy message from my new roommate. "Why are you dressed like that? Don't you have work?"

Mom glances away, shame flaring in her eyes. "I, ahhh … no. Orlando and I decided now that we're living here, there wasn't a point in me working so many jobs. I was overworked and exhausted. I needed a break, so he offered me the legal secretary position in his firm. Better pay and less hours. I'll have more time to be here with you."

I give her a blank stare. "But you don't know anything about being a legal secretary. You don't even know the correct terminology."

"I'll be just fine," she says, her tone short and sharp, clearly irritated with being questioned on her abilities. "Now hurry along and don't get yourself in any trouble. The kids at this school … they're not like the ones you are used to back home. These people solve their issues with money, not words, so keep your head down. Everything we do reflects on the Channing name, so keep that in mind. Now, hurry along. You cannot be late on your first day."

My gaze narrows as I slip inside my car and kick over the engine, unable to look away from her. Less than twenty-four hours living under Orlando Channing's roof and she's already a complete stranger.

I don't like it. I don't like it one bit.

CHAPTER 6
Brielle

Holy fuck, Toto. We're not in Kansas anymore.

My Honda inches through the gates of Bradford Private and into the student parking lot as I gape at the world around me. I feel like I've just entered an alternate universe as rich teens with Lamborghinis, McLarens, and Ferraris loiter around the parking lot.

The girls wear their short uniform skirts with their nails in perfect talons while their bleach-blonde hair falls in long curls down their backs. The jocks walk around in their stupid letterman jackets despite the sun already scorching, looking as though they spent the summer shooting up on roids.

I've never felt so out of place.

This school is filled with the kind of girls and guys that I make a point of keeping away from—trouble.

Letting out a shaky breath, I scan through the parking lot and find an empty space. Gently hitting the gas, I ease toward it, not wanting to be responsible for running over this year's prom queen on my very first day. I can practically feel the sneers and disgust coming from the students around me, taking in my Honda as though it's so far below them that they either assume I'm lost, or I'm the new janitor.

Turning my steering wheel, I start guiding my car into the parking space when a loud, roaring engine echoes through the lot. A shiver sails down my spine and my whole body tenses, knowing exactly who it is. I don't even have to look. The guy has been causing havoc over my every thought since he decided to drop his pants and play with his junk without closing his blinds.

I wish I knew his name just so I know what to yell when I'm cursing him out …. or maybe I just want to know what it feels like to have his name whispered on my lips when I test out that new showerhead.

Shit no. Don't go there, Brielle Ashford. Playing with fire is going to get you burned.

Focusing on the task at hand, I keep moving into my parking space when the black motorbike cuts in front of me and comes to a skidding halt in my spot. I slam on the brakes, desperately trying to avoid hitting his stupid bike as I gape at the asshole, all thoughts of his long, thick cock gone from my mind.

Fury boils through me. Can this morning seriously get any worse?

Lord of the douches climbs off his bike, his jet-black helmet barely gone before he's completely surrounded by his loyal fans. He hangs his helmet off the handlebar and strides toward the front gates of the elitist private school, completely swallowed by the crowd. He doesn't even glance back or acknowledge that he just stole my parking space, and the way he pretends to not see me only pisses me off more.

Reversing back and repositioning my car, I avoid every eye of the judgmental students around me before putting my Honda back in drive and searching for a new space. I'm all too aware of the minutes quickly counting down, warning me that if I don't hurry up, I'll be more than just a little bit late for my first day.

I find a space in the back of the lot, and honestly, while it's frustrating as hell to have to walk so far, it's a relief to know that I can't accidentally ding the door of a car that's worth more than my home back in Hope Falls.

After locking my car and slinging my bag over one shoulder, I hurry up to the front gates and frantically search for the student office. They would have been expecting me at least thirty minutes ago and probably wanted to spare a minute to introduce me to the student guidance counselor and senior advisor, but that'll have to wait.

My phone buzzes in my pocket and assuming Colby just arrived at school and realized I'm not there, I promptly ignore it and ask the first person who doesn't snub me where the hell I need to go.

It takes way too long to find the student office, but after meeting Principal Dormer and trying not to roll my eyes at the huffy office assistant, I'm free to find my locker and get sorted out for the morning.

Students linger in the hallway and the smell of coffee assaults my senses. My stomach growls. I haven't had a chance to eat my fruit salad or yogurt, and I could really use a coffee, but I have no idea where all these students are getting it from. There seems to be one in every set of hands.

Bodies pack the hallway, and it's almost impossible to figure out where the hell I'm going. Groups of guys laugh and whistle at the girls that pass by in their short uniform skirts, and their giggles only fuel the shameless flirting. Conversations and gossip drift down the hall, all about summer flings and who had the most extravagant vacation.

Some people keep their heads down, keeping to themselves, while others draw attention as though holding a sign reading, *I give good head*. The pecking order of this school is crystal clear. If you're a jock, a cheerleader, the richest of the rich, or simply just blessed with undeniable beauty, then your opinion matters and people want to be around you. Anyone else is just a punching bag for the elite assholes.

Finding my locker, all too close to Mr. WankInFrontOfMyBedroomWindow who's surrounded by a bunch of guys that look just as intimidating as he does, I figure out the lock and get busy jamming my things inside. I don't have time to do all that girly decorating shit to my locker, and honestly, I don't think I'll be here long enough to even bother.

I don't waste any more time grabbing my class schedule and flipping through the student handbook to find the map of the school, having only just enough time to figure out how to get to my first few classes before the bell for homeroom sounds. I grab what I need and make a move for it, knowing that today is going to be nothing but fresh hell topped with a splash of complete and utter bullshit.

Closing my locker, I take off down the hallway, following the map held tightly between my fingers. I only get a few steps before a large body steps in front of me, blocking my path. My head snaps up and I have only a second to stop myself before slamming headfirst into his wide chest.

Just when I thought I could get away with a peaceful morning. I should have known better.

King Jock stands before me, his lingering gaze locked on my face as his friends move in beside him, looking over me like a new toy they're figuring out who gets to play with first. "Well, if it isn't the little Killjoy from Saturday night."

Unease settles heavily into the pit of my stomach, and I clench my jaw, doing what little I can to appear as though I'm not about to shit myself. "Is there something you need?"

Big guy smirks back at me, his dark eyes dancing with amusement. "Just wanted to give you the big Bradford welcome," he says, moving in closer, his gaze getting darker and hotter all at the same time. He stands over me, the smell of his cologne wrapping around me and holding me hostage. His words are kind, but there's a clear threat in his tone, reminding me that I'm nothing but the girl who threw down a challenge that I'm in no way, shape, or form prepared for. He takes a step closer, forcing me to back up, and I don't miss how a crowd has begun to form around us, phones out recording every minute of my humiliation.

Not wanting to be an easy target, or someone he'll freely be able to walk over, I stop backing up and hold my ground. "That's so kind of you, but if you don't stop intruding on my personal space, I'll have no choice but to shove my foot so far up your ass that you feel it in your throat."

He just stares at me, his gaze getting harder by the second. "You wanna talk personal space, Killjoy?" he questions, his eyes lighting once again. "Why don't we talk about your little Peeping Tom routine. Looking into my room like that, you should be ashamed."

My face flames as embarrassment takes over, but there's no way he's about to drop a bomb like that without a little bit of context for the masses of students swarming around us. "Ashamed? Not at all. I think embarrassed is the right word, embarrassed for you, that is. Though it's okay, I'm sure you were only half-hard, right?" I reach up and give a pitying pat against his wide chest, hating how the touch of his warmth beneath my palm sends a bolt of electricity pulsing through my body. "It's fine, not everyone can have a monster cock. The small guys have to get love too. But hey, if you want to fuck your own palm in the privacy of your bedroom, then that's your business. Self-love and all that, it's healthy, right? But I just ask that next time you get hard staring at me like a dirty perv, perhaps close your blinds before you start rubbing one out, okay? I mean, I appreciate your attempt to entertain me, but I wasn't all that impressed."

I give him the most condescending smile I can possibly manage and step around his bitch ass as his friends gawk. Every nerve in my body demands that I turn back just to get the smallest glimpse of the rage burning through his eyes, but I won't dare give him the satisfaction of having my attention. So instead, I keep walking, hoping that was enough of a warning to get him to back off.

By the time I reach my homeroom, the students are already buzzing with gossip, whispers about Tanner Morgan shutting down the new girl, and I can only assume that Tanner is the one and only King Jock. But honestly, if they think that's what shutting me down is, they've got another thing coming. Back home, something like that wouldn't even be worthy of morning gossip, not unless a few fists got thrown in the process.

"Holy shit!" A chirpy, feminine voice calls across the classroom.

I follow the sound, my head snapping up to find a petite brunette who sends a cold rush swarming through my veins like a million little needles pricking at my skin. She stares straight back at me, and all I can think about is the way Colby's cock looked buried deep inside her lady taco.

The need to bail sails through me, but she quickly stands and waves me over, a bright, genuine smile stretching across her face. I hesitantly make my way across the room, the other students watching me like a disease spreading throughout the school.

"You must be the new girl everyone's talking about," the girl says, propping her ass back onto the edge of the table as she waves me toward the empty space beside her. "How funny. Out of all the people who could have walked through that door, it just happened to be the girl who saw her boyfriend railin—"

"No! I don't need the visual," I say, holding my hands up as I reluctantly take the seat beside her, though unlike her, I actually drop my ass into the chair rather than propping myself against the table.

"Oh, right," she laughs. "I'm Ilaria, by the way. I can't remember if I introduced myself or not the other night. I was in a bit of an awkward position, and when that happens, I tend to ramble useless things that don't matter."

"Yep, I figured that much out," I confirm, remembering the moment all too clearly while desperately wishing I couldn't. "I'm Brielle."

"I … yeah," she says, biting her bottom lip and averting her eyes as shame flashes in her pretty features. "Listen, I tried to find you afterward, but judging by the way your boyfriend was running up the street, I kinda figured you bailed. I just … I want you to know that I'm not *that* girl. I don't go out with the intention of finding some other girl's man and stealing him from her. That's not me. I know we don't know each other and a promise from me is probably worth absolutely nothing, but I swear to you, I wasn't aware he had a girlfriend. He told me he was at the party alone and that he was single. I never would have touched him otherwise."

I give her a tight smile. Despite the honesty in her words and the shame in her tone, it still stings. I know she's not to blame, this is all on Colby. She's just as much a victim of his lies as I am, but I still want to hate her, and I'm sure that makes me an awful person, but every time her eyes meet mine over the desk, I picture them together and it sucks.

It makes me feel weak, used, and pathetic, and I'm so much better than that. This girl is better than that. Hell, I don't even know her, but I know enough. She is kind and honest and probably the type of girl

I should be trying to make friends with. Colby used her for her body, he played her just as he played me, but luckily for her, she didn't spend six months trying to feel something for the guy.

Fuck, I'm such an idiot. Colby really wasn't the kind of guy I thought he was.

"Do you ..." she glances away, looking nervous. "Do you think you could forgive me and we could be friends? You're going to need someone to show you the ropes around here, and I have a group of friends who are amazing and will welcome you with open arms. Besides, us girls have to stick together, right? This isn't exactly a nice school to be the new girl at, and from what I hear, you've already pissed off Tanner Morgan, which means you're going to need all the help you can get."

My eyes widen just a fraction. "Is he really that bad?"

Ilaria laughs and I can't help but wonder if she's pitying me. "Yeah, girl. He's about as bad as they come."

"Shit. He's my new neighbor. His bedroom looks directly into mine, and last night he got naked, stared at me through the window, and rubbed one out while watching me. Then when I actually looked up and noticed, the asshole winked at me."

Ilaria laughs again. "Oh, girl. You're in deep trouble."

"He won't ... he won't actually hurt me, will he?"

"Physically, no," she says. "He'd never touch a woman, but he'd sure as hell use all the tricks in the book. Intimidation, threats, toying with your heart. Nothing is off-limits to Tanner Morgan, and if he's chosen you to be his little toy, then it's guaranteed you'll be crushed. He's the type of guy who lets you think you're winning and right when you become vulnerable, he'll pull the rug out from under you and watch you burn. You need to be careful."

"You sound like you're speaking from experience."

Ilaria shakes her head. "Not me," she says. "My friend, Chanel. She was close to him last year … until she wasn't. But honestly, I don't think she's ever really gotten over it. He's not the type to do things halfway. If there's a target on your back, he's going for the kill."

Well, fuck. That's just what I need.

"So, I suppose that means I'd be stupid to push away someone offering to be a friend, huh?"

"Yeah," she says, her lips pulling into a delighted smile. "It would make you a real fucking idiot."

"Good thing I'm only an idiot when it comes to choosing boyfriends."

"Yeah, I'm not going to lie, you picked that one really well. Where were your friends when you made that mistake? Surely someone was whispering in your ear to run for the hills."

I laugh, shaking my head. "They weren't just whispering, they were practically screaming it, but I just had to see it though. My best friend, Erica, she couldn't have been happier when I told her we were finally over."

"I bet," Ilaria says, reaching over and gripping the class schedule out of my hand before scanning over it. "Ah, you have first period history with me. I'll take you there, but second period you're on your own. I'll introduce you to the girls during break and then we can work out how we're going to destroy Tanner Morgan and his band of douchebag friends."

CHAPTER 7
Brielle

Mrs. Porter welcomes me into her history class, and I'm only just saved from standing and introducing myself to the class when none other than Tanner Morgan strides through the door.

Juuuust great. I was hoping to avoid sharing any classes with the guy, but let's face it, I haven't exactly been the poster child for luck over the past few days.

Tanner barely spares a glance toward Mrs. Porter before he slinks through the classroom, turning down the first row and heading to the seat right in the very back corner. I'm not surprised he's late to class. He's the type of guy who'd probably be late to his own funeral.

"Make it quick, Mr. Morgan. You're late," Mrs. Porter scolds, though her tone is far too lenient compared to the scolding tones I've become accustomed to at Hope Falls Public. "I don't need to remind you how bad that looks for your first class of your senior year. Let's not make this a habit."

My stare flickers up to Tanner, watching as he saunters down the narrow walkway toward his seat, his hands deep in his pockets. A soft grin lingers on his lips, probably pleased to have irritated Mrs. Porter so early in the day, but it quickly fades as his sharp gaze snaps to mine.

The tension in the room builds and my breath catches in my throat, waiting for him to pass, but it feels as though it takes a lifetime. How is it possible to have this many encounters in such a short amount of time? Fuck, I've seen this guy naked and fondling his manhood, and damn it, it was one hell of an impressive manhood. He's a girthy motherfucker, but also long, and while I wasn't even a little close enough to tell if it has thick, protruding veins, I just know it does.

And just like that, my cheeks flame the brightest shade of red and he smirks, knowing exactly what's circling my head.

Crap.

I turn away, unable to handle his intensity, and just when I think he's about to pass, Tanner moves in behind me, one hand braced against the corner of my desk as his other comes down by my opposite elbow, caging me in like some kind of wild animal. My stare remains locked straight ahead, and I stop breathing completely when he begins to lower himself down, his breath gently brushing over the sensitive skin of my neck.

Tanner doesn't say a word, but I'm pretty sure the teacher does. I don't hear it though. I don't hear a damn thing except the ferocious, heavy beat of my pulse in my ears. My hands curl into fists on my desk, and I consider the consequences of slamming one of them back, right into his junk, but figure violence on my first day isn't going to go down well.

So I wait, watching him from the corner of my eye as I sense Ilaria beside me, openly gawking at the scene before her. I can only imagine what she is going to say ... actually, I can't. I don't know her well enough, but I'm sure it's not going to be good.

Tanner's hand slips off the edge of the desk, but he doesn't move, slowly breathing me in until his hand is right back again, a familiar tube of dark red lipstick clutched between his fingers. He places it dead center of my desk, standing it up for the world to see, knowing damn well that my world is caving in on me.

My eyes widen in horror, realization dawning on me. I suck in a breath, my head whipping around to meet his intense stare, but he's already gone, his back turned to me as he makes his way to the back of the classroom.

That fucker.

It wasn't Jensen in my room last night, it was Tanner.

He watched me sleep, snuck in through ... I don't know, the window? Maybe he broke in through the back door and found his way up to my room. Hell, maybe he has some twisted friendship with Jensen and he let him in. All that matters is that he was there, violating my privacy and space, and that's not okay.

That asshole. I bet he's so fucking smug sitting in the back of the room, his stare boring into the back of my head, just waiting for me to scoop up the offending lipstick and hide it away like it's some kind of big secret.

No, he won't get away with this. It's one thing to throw taunts at me, block my way in the hallway, and make out like he's some kind of king on campus, but I draw the line at sneaking into my bedroom. If that's how he wants to play this, then I'll rise to the occasion. He may look scary as hell with his bike and all those tatts winding up his strong arms, but he'd be wrong to assume he intimidates me.

I'm not going to lie to myself, it's comforting knowing that it wasn't Jensen watching me sleep, but I can't explain why. Both of them could easily overpower me, however I don't think Tanner would hurt me … at least, not physically. Jensen on the other hand, he lacks morals, and I don't doubt that given the chance, he'll try to take things further. Either way, I'm locking all windows and doors from here on out.

"Alright," Mrs. Porter says, her narrowed, pissed-off stare sailing across the room and lingering on Tanner, clearly not pleased with his little show. "Get your books out, we'll be starting the term with a deep dive into the Civil War."

Keeping my stare locked on the front of the classroom, I grab my notebook and open to a new page before scrawling today's date in the top corner. I don't dare look back, and I don't dare allow him to take another moment of my time. At least, for now. Something tells me that the asshole at the back of the room is going to demand all too much of my attention.

"What the hell was that?" Ilaria screeches under her breath, leaning across from her desk directly beside me as the room fills with noise of rustling papers.

"That," I murmur back, trying to keep our conversation somewhat private. "Is the bullshit Tanner has been hitting me with. This lipstick," I say, taking the offending item and sliding it to the top of my desk to allow space for my books. "Is the lipstick he used to write a message on my mirror in the middle of the night."

"Your mirror?" she questions. "Wait … what do you mean?"

I quickly glance around, making sure no one is listening. "He broke into my room in the middle of the night while I was sleeping and wrote on my mirror like a fucking creeper. I thought it was Jensen at first, but clearly Tanner wanted me to know it was him."

Ilaria's jaw goes slack, her eyes widening like saucers as she grips the edge of her desk and leans in closer. "Hold up. There is so much to unpack right now," she says. "We'll circle back to the lipstick. But Jensen? Do you mean Jensen Channing? Like, you're living with Jensen Channing now?"

"Unfortunately, yes."

"Shit, girl. That's messed up. I don't want to freak you out but that guy … he's a bit of a creep. You need to be careful. Last year, a freshman accused him of trying to force himself on her. Luckily, someone walked in and she ran off, but nothing came of it. It was he said, she said, and his father—"

"Best criminal lawyer in the state," I finish for her. "Trust me, I know. His dad is just as much of an asshole as he is, only in a cocky, untouchable way. But you don't need to warn me about Jensen, I'm already watching him closely. After I moved in, he referred to us as siblings and promised to make me feel extra welcome."

"Fuck, you know what? My parents don't let me have friends stay late on weeknights, but on the weekends, if you wanna crash at my place, you can."

Relief floods through my chest and I let out a breath, not realizing just how much fear I've been holding over Jensen's games. "You know, I might just take you up on that."

"Eyes to the front," Mrs. Porter says. "Let's get started."

Fifty minutes later, the bell has hardly sounded and Tanner is already out the door, whipping past me, his manly scent practically hitting me in the face. I can't help but breathe him in. He's intoxicating, and the smell sends a rush of heat through my veins. I find myself silently begging him to look down at me, just one small glance in my direction, but I get nothing.

I can't explain it. I don't know why I want his eyes on me, but I do, and that one little desire is going to get me in a world of trouble.

Why do I find him so thrilling? He makes me want to get in his face again, want to throw insults just so I can be close to him, just so I can see the way his eyes flare when he's around me. There's no mistaking it, I make him feel some kind of way. I just don't know what kind of way that is.

The door slams shut behind him, and I hastily pack up my things before slipping the tube of lipstick into my skirt pocket. Ilaria gives me directions to my next class and tells me where I can meet her during our first break, and just like that, I'm moving out of the classroom and bumping shoulders with the other students trying to go about their day.

An hour later, I step through the open doors of the biggest cafeteria I've ever seen. "Holy crap," I murmur to myself, needing to pause just inside the door to take it all in. The cafeteria at Hope Falls was practically nonexistent. There were a few tables and an overworked lunch lady. For the most part, students would just pack their own lunch and sit outside to eat, but this right here, this is the heart of the whole damn school.

Large circular tables fill the room and noise bounces off the walls. A few teachers casually stroll around, keeping the peace while students relax and catch up with friends they haven't seen since before the summer. A soft smile pulls at the corners of my lips, one I can't explain. Maybe it's the sense of community here or just the way that the whole student body can sit in one room without tearing shreds off each other. It's chaotic, but it's also calming.

I find Tanner almost immediately, his dark eyes watching me like a hawk as he sits in the furthest corner of the cafeteria with his friends all around him, hyping him up like he's some kind of god. Cheerleaders loiter around the guys table, and I have to stop myself from scoffing. It's the same hierarchy at every school. I don't doubt that there's one cheerleader in particular who thinks that she has some kind of claim over Tanner and his friends, though I'd bet everything I have that Tanner doesn't feel the same way.

All I know is that there are two groups of people I need to steer very clear of.

His stare is electrifying and sends a tingle sailing down my spine, making me feel uneasy and nervous. I look away, not wanting my first cafeteria experience to revolve around him, while also not wanting to draw any more attention to myself. It's bad enough being the new girl, but to have the eyes of the most popular guy in school on me is bound to raise a few eyebrows.

A hand shoots up out of the crowd, and I find Ilaria waving me down. "Bri, over here," she calls through the masses.

I give her a tight smile and make my way toward her, noticing that she sits with two other girls. One looks as though she just came from a photo shoot with her long golden hair falling in perfect waves down her back and a sharp stare narrowing at the sight of me, as though I'm some kind of threat. The other girl doesn't seem to even notice me coming—or just doesn't care. She's petite, unlike her supermodel, golden friend beside her who has legs for days. There's something warm about this petite girl, she seems kind and almost fragile with her soft features and light eyes.

"I take it that you made it through Bio without incident?" Ilaria asks as I reach the edge of the big table.

She grins up at me, and I can't help but grin right back. "Only just!"

Her friends watch me with furrowed brows, but Ilaria is quick to do the introductions. "This is Chanel and Arizona," she tells me, pointing out the golden model as Chanel and the fragile petite girl as Arizona before turning to them. "This is Brielle. She just started today and has already become Tanner's new project."

"Oh shit," Chanel laughs, her brows flying up as she shuffles over and makes space for me. "You're going to need all the friends you can get."

Ilaria smiles as I take the space beside her, clearly pleased that her friends are being so welcoming, and honestly, so am I. Chanel was right, I'm going to need as many friends as I can possibly find. "Tell me about it," I say. "That guy is intense."

"Chanel knows all about how intense Tanner Morgan can be," Arizona laughs. "She had the misfortune of having his interest last year, and trust me when I tell you, it didn't end well."

My brows shoot up and I gape at Chanel beside me. "No way, really?" I ask, way too intrigued by the topic. "What did he do?"

Chanel scoffs and takes a bite out of an apple. "What didn't he do?" she says, a heaviness falling over her shoulders. "I used to be the head cheerleader and most popular girl in school until he came along. He has a kink for ruining people's lives."

"Really?" I breathe, nerves swelling in my chest. "He has *that* much influence over this school?"

Ilaria nods. "What did I tell you?" she says with a smug, knowing grin. "You're in a world of trouble."

Well, crap. This is almost worse than waxing off half my meat curtain. My heart races. Colby threatened to make me the outcast of

Hope Falls, and now there's a chance that Tanner could do the very same thing, after crushing me first.

"How did you even get on his radar?" Arizona asks. "It's only your first day. Either you work fast or something else is going on here."

Both Arizona and Chanel furrow their brows as Ilaria cringes, recalling the many events that have brought me to this very moment. I turn to Chanel, my brow arching. "You don't still have a thing for the guy, do you?"

She gapes at me as though I just grew an alien lifeform out of my ass and shakes her head. "Hell no."

"Good, because I don't think any of what I'm about to say is going to be very nice, but it all started at that party on the weekend, right after my boyfriend cheated on me." Both Chanel and Arizona gasp and I glance at Ilaria, wondering how much of this she's comfortable with me sharing, but just that glance alone has the girls putting the pieces together.

"NOOOOOO," Chanel laughs, slamming her hand onto the table and meeting Ilaria's gaze. "The Hope Falls dude you hooked up with was her boyfriend?"

Ilaria rolls her eyes, looking more than ashamed of herself. "Yup," she says, popping the 'p' sound. "I had no idea he was with her, so I want that on record. I'm not a boyfriend-stealing whore … at least, not knowingly."

Arizona smirks. "Noted."

"Go on," Chanel tells me, her gaze slowly narrowing with curiosity. "I don't see how any of this has anything to do with Tanner."

"Right, so I'd just sprung my boyfriend going to town on your girl here and naturally, I was a little upset, so I stormed out and accidentally ran into him. I was trying to get out of the house and turned a corner just as he stepped around it, and I knocked the beer right out of his hands. He must have just gotten it or something because the guy was drenched."

Chanel laughs. "That was you? I heard something going on with Tanner but couldn't see past all the bodies."

"Yeah, unfortunately. Anyway, I was a little upset, understandably, and Tanner was all glaring and angry and then his friend came over acting like I was some kind of fresh meat who he could persuade onto her knees, who—"

"That would have been Riley," Arizona cuts in. "The guy who looks like Thor's younger, flirtier brother?"

"Yeah."

"He's Tanner's best friend. You don't need to worry about him. All he'll try to do is get between your legs, but now that Tanner's got you in his sights, Riley will back off … at least, he should. He'll still flirt. I don't think he's capable of not chatting up a girl."

"Great, just what I need," I laugh. "Anyway, he was being all *I wonder if she bites,* so I let him know that I wasn't about to suck his dick, but that if he needed to stick it somewhere, Tanner's throat seemed like a good place, which apparently made things worse, so then I called him out on his bullshit, which again … worse."

Ilaria shakes her head. "Literally the worst way you could have possibly handled any type of situation with Tanner Morgan."

"Yeah, I'm figuring that out," I tell her, before glancing back at Chanel. "Anyway, I got out of there, went home, and my mom hit me with the whole *we're moving in with my fancy new boyfriend* bombshell, and now, I'm somehow Tanner's new next-door neighbor."

Her eyes bug out of her head. "WHAT?"

"Yeah, his bedroom looks directly into mine," I say, pulling the lipstick out of my pocket and slamming it down on the table. "So, he took it upon himself to break into my room in the middle of the night and leave me a message on my mirror in lipstick."

"The fuck?" Arizona grunts. "That's messed up."

"Could have been worse," Ilaria tells me. "It could have been Jensen."

"Jensen Channing?" Arizona gasps. "Holy fuck. Don't tell me you're involved with that asshole too?"

"Unfortunately. He's my new roommate. My mom is dating his father."

Chanel shakes her head. "You're fucked, so fucking fucked," she says, glancing toward Ilaria and Arizona across the table. "What the hell are we supposed to do about this? There's no way she's going to survive the year living right next door to the guy. Plus, who knows what Jensen is capable of." She turns back to me. "Does your mom know about him, what he's like?"

I nod. "Yeah, when I first told her about the vibe I got from him, she seemed horrified, but now that we're living there, she's turning a blind eye to it. I don't know, it's been one day and she's already slipping into the role of country club housewife. He already got her to quit her job and start working as his legal secretary, wearing ridiculous pantsuits with hooker heels."

"Shit."

I nod and my gaze drops to the lipstick in the middle of the table, my heart heavily thumping in my chest. I thought I could handle all of this but seeing just how concerned they are is alarming. Maybe this whole situation is worse than I'd assumed.

A moment passes as I stew on everything that's gone down, before finally raising my head. "I don't know what I'm going to do about Jensen, but as for Tanner Morgan, I'm not about to sit back and let him railroad my senior year. I'm more than happy to face this alone, but if you guys are down, I'd love some back up."

Arizona grins, a wicked spark hitting her soft eyes. "Just tell me where you want me."

I grin right back at her. "Ever broken into someone's house before?"

CHAPTER 8
TANNER

"Fuck bro, if you don't rail that chick soon, I will," Jax says, slinging his arm over my shoulder and slapping his hand against my chest, all but howling his appreciation for Killjoy as we watch her making her way back down to the student parking lot.

Shrugging his arm off my shoulder, I keep walking down to the football field for our after-school training session. It's the first of the season, and I don't doubt it's going to be killer, especially after spending the last three months drinking and partying. "I'm sure you'll get your chance," I tell my cousin, unable to resist rolling my eyes as I smirk back at him. "But I can't guarantee that after being with me, she'll have any interest in your pin dick."

Jax stops walking and gapes at me as though he's never been so offended. "Pin dick?" he questions, a hard edge in his tone. "Nah, you've got me confused for Hudson. You know damn well that I've got a king cobra between my legs. It's a motherfucking python, baby! This beast needs his own zip code." I scoff and he gapes some more. "Are you fucking kidding, bro? I'll drop my pants right now if I have to."

"Go ahead," I tell him, a smirk resting on my lips. "Whip your dick out. Maybe do a dance, shake that thing around, but I can guarantee that no matter how big you think you are, she won't even look twice." I spin around to face him while still moving away, walking backward as I tap my fingers to my temple. "I'm already in her head, bro. Every waking second, she's already thinking about me."

Spinning around, I walk forward as Logan falls into my other side, glancing back at his twin brother, his helmet pinned between his hip and arm. I have to do a double take, making sure it actually is Logan. I don't know what's going on with these guys, but the older they get, the more similar they appear, but I suppose that's just what you get with identical twins. Same dark hair, same chiseled jaw, same fucking laugh that throws me off.

"Jax talking about his dick again?" Logan asks.

"You fucking know it," I sigh. Jax is just one of those guys who will mention his dick, even when the conversation doesn't call for it, but I can't blame the guy. He's proud, and he sure as fuck has a right to be. I might tease the guy about having a pin dick, but that's certainly not the case. I've shared enough girls with each of my friends to know exactly what they're packing. They're all doing just fine.

Logan sighs and shakes his head. Out of all of us, he's the one who has to put up with Jax's shit the most, but they're both as bad as each other.

Jax catches up just as we meet Hudson and Riley down on the field with the rest of the team, and I roll out my shoulders, preparing for what I assume is going to be a killer session. Noise stirs up from across the school and I glance back at the student parking lot, finding Brielle Ashford huddled around her new group of friends. Ilaria, Chanel, and Arizona. And honestly, I don't know how I feel about it. There's nothing wrong with them, in fact, they're probably good friends to have when stepping into a new school. They'll show her the ropes, teach her how things are done around here, and keep her on track, but they're not fucking pushovers, and that's what bugs me. They'll keep her away from me, warn her off. They're not going to make it easy for me to destroy her, but that's alright, I like a challenge, and Brielle Ashford is one hell of a challenge to have.

"What's the deal with this chick?" Hudson asks, stretching out his calves and catching me staring at the feisty blonde I've studied all day. "It's been one day and she's already getting to you."

"She's just some random girl," I grunt, turning away and focusing on the boys, hating the way Riley watches me in return, his eyes narrowed as if he knows my darkest secrets … Well, he does know them, every last one of them, and they have never made him watch me the way he's looking at me now. "I'm just toying with her, letting her know how things go around here. She'll break and then I'll fuck her out of my system."

Logan scoffs. "Right, you know she's been hanging out with Chanel all day. That bitch ain't going to let you get close enough to fuck the new chick over."

I arch a brow, surprised by his bluntness toward Chanel. *"That bitch?"*

Logan glances away. "Lay off, man. She means nothing to me."

Jax scoffs and shoves his twin brother against his shoulder. "Right. So, you haven't had a hard-on for her since Tanner was through with her last year?"

Logan grunts something none of us can make out and stalks away as Jax grins proudly after him. There's nothing the twins like more than getting under each other's skin, and lately, throwing Logan's fucked-up crush on Chanel in his face is all it takes for Logan to get his panties in a twist. I swear, that motherfucker must have a serious case of blue balls. He hasn't been able to fuck her out of his system because the girl won't go anywhere near him, and sure, that's partly my fault, but it's not like any of us knew that Logan was going to fall for the broken, sad girl when she cried on his shoulder.

Hudson glances back at me. "Logan was right though, you're not getting anywhere near that girl. This is different. Forget about it before she starts to fuck with your head. This is your senior year, and we have a championship to win," he says, the afternoon sun smacking him right in the face and making his eyes sparkle a blinding emerald green. "I know you've already got colleges lining up for you, but the rest of us need this win."

"Chill out, man," I say, my gaze flicking toward Riley to see his stare still locked on mine. "She's not fucking with my head. It's just a little bit of fun to pass the time. Don't stress, I'm all in for this season. We're taking the championship no matter what."

Riley stares back as he stretches his quads, knowing damn well the coach will have us running all session. "So, if she's just some random chick," he says, glancing up toward the parking lot, taking her in. "Then you wouldn't mind if I take a shot, yeah? She's fucking hot, and we all know those new friends of hers are warning her away from you."

I clench my jaw, unsure why the idea of my best friend going after Killjoy doesn't sit right with me. I know he has no real interest in her, but if she offers to get on her knees or spread her pretty thighs for him, he's not going to say no. He's simply asking to see my reaction, so I play the game, not ready to admit out loud that after only a short weekend, she's already intrigued me more than any woman has before. Hell, I won't even admit it to myself. "Like I told Jax, you can try all you like, but we both know that she's not interested in anything you've got."

"Oh, yeah?" he questions, his eyes sparkling with excitement. "Care to make it interesting?" I watch him carefully, my nerves on fucking fire as I wait for him to go on. "If I can get her in bed by the end of the week, you have to ditch this revenge plot and focus on football."

I narrow my gaze on him, my hands balling into fists at my side. "And if you can't?"

"Then she's all yours, man," he says. "I'll back off and you can have her, make her your fucking girl for all I care."

I fall back a step, my brows furrowed. "My fucking girl?" I grunt, the horror of what he just said messing with my head. "The fuck are you talking about? I don't want her like that. I just want to show her who's boss around here, and once I have her right where I want her, I'll fuck her and send her on her way."

"Right," Riley laughs, backing further away from our group and toward the rest of our teammates. He spares one more glance toward the student parking lot to where Brielle is ducking into her piece of shit Civic. Riley looks back at me, a cocky grin resting on his lips. "I bet she's going to taste so fucking sweet."

Something cracks inside my chest and a protectiveness comes over me, but I don't dare speak on it. I hold my position as Riley laughs and takes off at a light jog, deeper onto the field. "What's it going to be, Morgan? Do we have a deal?" he calls loud enough that every one of my team members looks back at me.

Fucker. He knew exactly what he was doing.

Glaring back at him, I nod, knowing damn well that I could regret this. "One week, man. If you can get her, she's yours," I tell him, but that doesn't mean that I won't stop trying in the meantime. No matter what, I will see this through. Brielle Ashford is going to succumb to my hold. She's going to fall at my knees, and she's going to beg for forgiveness, and only then will I give her exactly what she's been craving.

It doesn't change the fact that picturing Riley beating me to her makes me feel sick, makes something tighten in my chest and I don't fucking like it. To Riley, this is just a game, but for some reason, it feels like so much more to me.

Seeing the frustration in my eyes, Hudson knocks my shoulder, encouraging me to run along with him. "Come on," he murmurs, Jax stepping into my other side. "If coach catches us down here fucking around instead of warming up, he'll fucking destroy us."

He's right. Coach Wyld is tough. He's strict and has high expectations for his team, expectations that we always strive to meet, and I'm not about to fuck with that on day one.

Taking off at a jog with the boys by my side, I call out to the team, knowing they need their captain more than ever this season. "Alright boys, let's do this," I demand, knowing an order from their captain will be respected without questions. I glance back at the parking lot one more time, watching as the sky-blue Civic pulls out onto the road, probably heading right home, and with that, I put the feisty blonde to the back of my mind. Riley was just messing with me when he said that I could make her mine. That's not what I want. All that matters to me is this season, leading my team to victory, and getting one step closer to my future.

The team grunts their approval, and just like that, we take off around the field, Riley taking the lead while I follow up the rear, pushing the stragglers along, more than ready to dominate this season.

CHAPTER 9
Brielle

Nerves pound through my body as I pull my Civic right into the driveway of my new home. The girls said that Tanner will be in football practice for another few hours, but that still doesn't keep me from glancing toward his house.

I must be insane for wanting to do this. I'll be starting a war, and while all three of the girls warned me off doing this, the thrill is too intoxicating. The idea of making a stand and capturing Tanner's attention, if only for a moment, makes adrenaline thrum through my veins like a potent drug.

Arizona's Audi pulls to a stop on the curb, and she bails out of her car, racing to meet up with me by the front door. "You sure about this?" she questions, still having my back despite knowing it's a bad idea. She's really going to make a great friend. "It's not too late to bail. Or we could wait till tomorrow when we have both Chanel and Ilaria to play lookout."

Unlocking the front door, I glance back over my shoulder with a sadistic grin. "But doesn't the idea that we could get caught thrill you?"

"I don't know what terrifies me more, the way Tanner is going to try and destroy you, or the way you're going to fight back. You both play dirty."

My grin widens. "Exciting, isn't it?"

She shakes her head but can't stop the shit-eating grin that tears across her face. "Fuck, yeah. Let's do this."

I laugh as I finally unlock the door and push through to the polished foyer, thankful to find that we're home alone. Perhaps now might be the time to do a little recon on Jensen as well. I give Arizona the grand tour and she nods with each passing room, not exactly impressed by the place, but I suppose she wouldn't be when she's lived in McMansions her whole life.

At lunch, Arizona had explained that her father was some big businessman, important in the fuel industry, while Chanel's mom is a socialite living the rich and famous lifestyle, but to be honest, I haven't got a damn clue who her mom is. I've never heard of her before, but I still smiled and nodded as if it were a big deal. Ilaria though, she comes from old money. Her great, great grandfather was a big-time land developer with billions of dollars under his belt. Though when I asked what he was responsible for developing, she had no freaking idea, and honestly, I don't blame her.

Both Ilaria and Chanel wanted to be here this afternoon, the idea of breaking into Tanner's home was too thrilling to pass up, but Ilaria has dance class and Chanel was grounded over the weekend for apparently getting a little too drunk at Riley's party and passing out on her front doorstep. So, it's just me and Arizona.

We make it up to my bedroom and stand at the window, peering straight through to Tanner's room. "We're idiots, right?" I question her, my nerves starting to creep up once again. "This is insane."

"It is," she agrees. "But I'd feel like a loser if we bitched out now. I bet Tanner didn't think about bitching out. He would have just done it and laughed about it afterward."

"You're right," I tell her, both of us swallowing hard. We talk a big game, but when it comes down to the crunch and the panic starts to take over, we're like two little field mice running from the big bad wolf. "We can do this. What's a little breaking and entering between friends?"

She lets out a few quick breaths, her shoulders bouncing as she pumps herself up. "We've got this. It's only Tanner Morgan and his whole crew that will come for our blood."

"So, ummm …" I say, my gaze sweeping over the massive house before us. "I know we've got this and all, but how exactly do you think we're going to get inside?"

Arizona looks over the house just as I am, her brows furrowed as she considers my question. "Do you think the back door would be open?"

I shake my head. "Nah, there's no way, plus everyone has home security around here, right?"

"Right," she says, her gaze fixing on Tanner's bedroom window, making my stomach drop. "Do you think we could get in if we climb that tree and scale the side of the house?"

My gaze falls to the tree in question, and my heart gives out. I'm a little sporty, but definitely no athlete, and tree climbing certainly isn't a strong point. "You want to climb the tree and scale his house?"

"Great story for the grandkids," she tells me. "Besides, look at his window. It's not closed properly, it's open just a sliver, practically daring us to open it. If we could get our fingers through that, we can pry it open. In and out in two seconds. Plus, I get the opportunity to snoop through his room. Win-win."

Well, shit.

"You know, when I first walked into the cafeteria and Ilaria waved me over, I thought you were the innocent one, but I think I was wrong."

Arizona laughs, her wicked tone filling my room. "So very wrong, girl. Now let's go and teach Tanner Morgan a lesson."

Within two seconds, Arizona and I are standing out on the manicured lawn, staring up at the overgrown tree between the two big houses. "Okay," Arizona says, swallowing the lump in her throat. "I exaggerated. Maybe I'm not as wild as I think I am."

I shake my head, trying to figure out the best path up the tree. "I think we can do it," I tell her, pointing out my trail. "If we find a step or something to boost us up, we can get to that low branch, step up to the next, then go to the right, and assuming that's not actually as high as it looks from down here, we should be able to swing up to that top branch and reach the second story roof."

"That's all we gotta do, huh?"

"Yeah," I say, my mouth going dry. "You wanna go first?"

"Fuck, no, girl. This is all you."

A nervous laugh rumbles through my chest as I step toward the tree, looking directly up, wondering how the hell I'm going to make this work.

"Here," Arizona says, dashing across the yard to grab a large rock. She bends down to try and hoist it up and groans, her cheeks blowing out. "Fuck, that's heavy," she says, giving up and rolling it instead. She pushes it right to the base of the trunk and I test its stability, knowing damn well that the slightest wobble could send me crashing and burning in a big way.

"You good?" she asks as I step up, holding her hand up toward my back in case I fall.

Hoisting myself up, I grip the lowest branch and pull, feeling like a damn queen for even attempting this. There's still a long way before I reach Tanner's bedroom window, and I'm not entirely sure I'll make it. "I'm good," I call down to her, pretty damn pleased with myself. "You sure Tanner's got football practice? Like, he's not just going to show up, is he?"

"Certain," she laughs.

I crouch down on the thick branch and catch her hand as she steps up onto the rock below me and help pull her up until she's safely beside me. We straighten up, looking up at our next step and when her eyes meet mine, we each grin like fucking idiots. "Oh, we so got this," she says.

I muffle my laugh, all too aware that while Tanner and his family aren't home, that doesn't mean that we don't have other neighbors who are probably just as snoopy as the rest of us.

Arizona and I fly up the tree, the dash to the top a lot easier than we anticipated, and before we know it, we're clutching onto the side of his second story roof and shuffling across the tiles to his bedroom window.

Dropping to my knees, I slip my fingers through the small crack and jimmy it open, both of us laughing like hyenas as it slides open with ease.

The nerves have completely faded away, and I'm left with nothing but the thrill of being one step closer to revenge. We slip inside his bedroom, and I'm immediately hit with that same manly scent that captivated me at the end of history class. It's intoxicating and makes my heart thrum a little faster.

"Well, well," Arizona says, her feet dropping to the plush carpet beside mine. "I never thought I'd step foot in the devil's lair."

She doesn't waste time breaking free and exploring just as I do. "Tell me more about him," I say. "What's there to know about the star of the school?"

"Uhhhh, not much," she says, distracted by his bedside table, which surprise, surprise, is filled with condoms. "He has a younger sister, Addison, but she goes by Addie. She was supposed to be a junior at Bradford this year, but she wasn't there today. No one has really seen her for a few weeks and the rumor going around school was that she got a late acceptance into some big-time performing arts school."

"No way," I say, moving through the room, scanning over the framed pictures, and taking in the books on his desk, each of them focusing on football.

"Yeah, she's talented, just like her brother."

"What else?"

"Umm, I don't know. He's pretty much been the popular football star since the start of high school. He's got his crew—the Bradford Bastards—him, his best friend, Riley, the twins Logan and Jax, who are also his cousins, and then Hudson Bellamy. He's kinda the black sheep of the group, but he just kinda fits in. I don't doubt that all five of them will have colleges fighting for them come the end of the season."

"Oh, really? I ask. "They're *that* good?"

"Hell yeah, just you wait until the first game. It's insane."

"Don't tell me you're going to make me go to that shit."

"School spirit, baby!" she sings. "Besides, you kinda have to go. It's practically social suicide to not attend."

Dread sinks heavily into my gut. The last thing I want to spend my time doing is sitting in a packed grandstand watching the school assholes strut around the field, pretending to be gods while allowing the rest of the school to treat them as such. I wouldn't be surprised if Tanner literally had girls falling at his feet.

His room is big, much bigger than it appears looking in from across the yard. He's got the typical rich kid bedroom, almost mirroring the room that I just moved into, only instead of whites and soft pink hues on the bedsheets, they're gray. His room is tidy and put together and I just know this is the kind of man who puts his laundry away as soon as it's done.

But unlike my room, there isn't a full-length pedestal mirror waiting for me to destroy.

While Arizona busily makes herself at home, getting a feel for Tanner Morgan, I move toward his bed. Hoisting myself up, I stand by the headboard, gripping onto it to keep myself steady as I dip my hand into my skirt pocket and pull out the lipstick that has haunted me all day.

My stare lingers on the wall over his bed. It's practically screaming blank canvas, and it would only be the neighborly thing to do to help him with a little bit of art. What can I say? I'm a neighborly kind of girl, so I uncap the lipstick and get to work.

Arizona gapes as she watches me, and I try not to grin like an idiot. This is more thrilling than it has the right to be. I just hope the lipstick doesn't stain the wall, though it shouldn't. It's not like I can afford the good shit.

When I'm done, I cap the lipstick and leave it balanced right in the center of his headboard just as he had done when putting it on my desk. Arizona offers me her hand and I jump down before the two of us stand at the end of his bed, admiring the priceless artwork scrawled across the wall.

KEEP IT. IT'LL LOOK BETTER ON A BITCH LIKE YOU.

"You're dead," Arizona laughs. "You know that, right?"

Moving toward his window, I glance back over my shoulder and grin at her. "I know. I can't wait." And with that, we climb out, leaving his room just how we found it, minus one exquisite new artwork.

Arizona hands me a mimosa and we make our way out the backdoor into the warm sun. The pool glistens, almost daring me to dive in, and I have to take a moment to appreciate just how fortunate I am. I mean, sure, I don't exactly want to be here, and I don't exactly like the company I have to keep, but there's no denying that this new home comes with certain advantages that I simply would never have been able to obtain in Hope Falls.

This lifestyle is beyond anything I could have dreamt for myself. I feel like Ryan from *The OC* being thrust into this luxurious life that I did absolutely nothing to earn, but hell, that doesn't mean I won't soak up every last second of it while I can. Who knows when Channing will decide that he's had enough of us. I can't get too comfortable here or make friendships that are only going to be stripped away.

"Tell me about this ex-boyfriend," Arizona says, slipping her glasses over her eyes and dropping down onto the sunchair.

"Uggggh, the guy is an asshole," I tell her. "I don't know what I was thinking."

Beep. Beep.

My gaze drops to my phone as I make myself comfortable on the sunchair beside hers and groan when I see Colby's name flash across the screen. I don't even bother looking at it before handing her my phone and showing her the slew of texts I've received from him since Saturday night.

"Holy shit," she gasps, her eyes widening in horror. "This dude is intense."

"Yeah," I laugh. "Apparently, it's unreasonable to dump a guy for cheating on you, but it's even worse not to be present for him to unleash his revenge tactics. Who would have known?"

My phone rings in her hand and she quickly holds it out to me. "Sorry, didn't mean to look. It's Erica," she says as I take the phone back and scan the name flashing on the screen.

Warmth surges through my chest as I answer Erica's call and hold the phone to my ear. "Well, well, look who couldn't go a whole day without me."

I can almost hear Erica rolling her eyes. "I'm more than happy to end the call and leave you to discover all of Colby's bullshit on your own."

"No, no, no," I rush out, laughing. "I'm sorry. Don't hang up. I want to hear all about it."

"There's a lot to unpack," she says. "Are you sure you want to know? Colby was in fine form. He was so freaking pissed when he got there this morning. I almost got my head bitten off. He wanted to know where you were, but don't worry, I didn't tell him shit."

"Damn. I'm sorry you have to play this in-between thing."

Erica scoffs. "In between would imply there are two sides here. It's literally just him spewing insults and rage at me as though I'm the one to blame for his limp dick ending up in some whore's cooch."

"Actually," I say with a cringe, almost guilty for having judged her so fast. "She's not a whore. She's actually really nice."

"What? We're friends with the dancer girl now?"

"Yeah," I laugh. "Her name is Ilaria, and she introduced me to some of her friends. One of them is here now actually. We're having mimosas by the pool."

"You're having mimosas and are only just telling me now? Shit, Bri, you're losing your edge. Make space. I'll be there in twenty and then I can tell you everything in person, and you can introduce me to these new friends so I can decide if they're worthy replacements."

I roll my eyes, a grin spreading from ear to ear. "No one is replacing you."

"Damn straight and don't you forget it."

And with that, the line goes dead, and I drop my phone back into my lap and bring the champagne flute to my lips. This is going to be interesting, my two worlds colliding … Well, maybe not so much of a collision. More like a soft love tap, though there's no doubt in my mind that Erica will love Arizona, especially when she finds out she helped me break into Tanner's room.

Just the thought of the red lipstick smudged across his wall makes me laugh. Arizona was right, I'm so dead, but I'm looking forward to it. He'll retaliate, but the question is, how?

Arizona and I fly through our mimosas, and by the time we're back in the kitchen, Jensen is just getting home and letting Erica in with him. He gives me an awkward leer before disappearing deeper into the house, and as Erica waltzes into the kitchen, her lips twist with unease, sensing that same discomfort from Jensen as the rest of us.

"What's that dude's problem?" she whispers, walking into me. I go to give her a quick hug at the same moment her fingers curl around the glass flute, leaving us in an awkward half hug. "I mean, I was just going for your drink, but if you want to make this a whole hugging event, I suppose I could go back and try it again."

"Shut up and hug me and then make your own damn drink."

Erica laughs and wraps her arms around me, and as she squeezes me tight, she looks over my shoulder at Arizona. "You must be one of these new friends," she says. "What's your stance on revenge sex?"

Arizona pours another drink and holds it up for Erica to take. "As long as it's hard and fast and you call him by his best friend's name, then I'm all in."

Erica laughs and clicks her glass against Arizona's. "You and I are going to get along just fine."

Erica finally releases me from her hug, and as we make our way back out to the pool, she tells me all about the bullshit Colby played today, dragging my name through the mud over and over again, but Erica and my other friends were right there to put him back in his place. By the end of first period, the whole school knew what Colby had done. Though, that didn't stop the other girls trying to console him with a nice, tight hug … you know, the kind of hug that's not given with your arms, but more like your mouth wrapping around a cock, but it's fine. Colby's the very definition of a minute man, in and out in under sixty seconds, so I'm sure he had plenty of time for all the hugs on offer.

I can't lie, I thought the rumors he would spread would sting. I thought his dismissal and the whole school's rejection would kill something inside of me, that my pride would be shot down, but I don't even feel it, don't even care that the people I used to know have been fed bullshit lies about me. It simply doesn't matter anymore, though it should. When Orlando inevitably decides that my mom and I aren't good enough for this life, we'll be right back there.

The afternoon sun beams down on my skin, and I soak up every second of it as I tell Erica all about my first day of school with Arizona cutting in to tell the parts she thought were important. We're only halfway through explaining our journey up the tree between the two big houses when the familiar rumble of a motorcycle cuts through the peaceful afternoon.

My eyes snap to Arizona's and her wide grin confirms what I already know.

Tanner Morgan is on his way home.

Erica's gaze darkens, her devilish need to cause havoc stirring deep within her, part of the reason I was drawn to her in the first place. She holds up her glass, her eyes sparkling with mischief. "Let the games begin."

And with that, she throws back what's left in her glass, and we prepare for the most thrilling games of our lives.

Tanner Morgan, welcome to your first day of hell.

CHAPTER 10

TANNER

My bike rumbles between my legs and I cut the engine, letting the deafening sound fade away as Riley pulls up in his Escalade behind me, blocking the rest of my driveway. My helmet comes off with just enough time to catch what Riley is saying, and I glance back over my shoulder to see him indicating toward the sky-blue Honda Civic parked in the neighboring driveway.

"Hot mess express is home," he says, his bet brimming in the forefront of my mind. "I wonder if she's down to chill. You know, a good girl like her is probably untouched territory. I could break her in for you."

Anger bubbles in my chest. It was a shitty practice and I'm fucking exhausted, so I don't trust myself not to clip my fist across his fucking jaw. He knows this chick is in my head, which was clear enough during practice, and damn it, it pissed me off. She's no one to me, just some random chick living next door, but watching her eyes widen when she's near me, watching her cheeks redden when she saw me through my window, and watching the way she gets all worked up makes something stir deep in my gut, and I fucking hate it.

The only thing stopping me from flying across my driveway and beating Riley's confidence out of him is the fact that he's dead wrong. Brielle Ashford is not a good girl, despite how she presents herself to the world. Just one look into her eyes and it was clear to me. She thrives on the adrenaline, the thrill of getting caught makes her heart race, makes excitement pulse through her veins. It's only been one day at Bradford, one night as my new neighbor, and she's already addicted.

Riley can read me like a fucking book, always has, but that's a two-way street. I know him just as well as he knows me, which is usually a good thing, except for right fucking now. He sees what I'm refusing to admit out loud, and the fucker will do whatever it takes to force it out of me.

"Lay off it," I tell him, turning my back so that he can't see the fire burning through my eyes. Heading for the front door, I glance back over my shoulder. "Get some drinks and I'll meet ya out back."

Just as I slip in through the front door, Hudson and the twins show up, more than ready to waste away the rest of the afternoon. We're all fucking wrecked after that training session. Coach Wyld went hard. He wants the championship again this year, and we're going to give it to him, which means endless training sessions and nights pushing ourselves at the gym.

No one will come close to us this season. No one will beat us.

Knowing Mom would flip her shit if I were to dump my bag at the door, I race up the stairs two at a time, my muscles burning from practice, before I push through my bedroom door and dump my bag and helmet just inside.

Pulling the door closed, I go to turn back down the hallway when a flash of red pulls me up short and I do a double take toward the back wall of my bedroom.

"What in the ever-loving fuck?"

Pushing the door wide open again, I step through to my bedroom and stare at the wall above my bed, a shit-eating grin stretching across my face.

I knew Killjoy had balls; I just didn't realize they were this big. She's a little spitfire and I fucking love it. Fucking with her is going to be better than I imagined. She just made this the most intriguing game I've ever played, and she has no fucking idea.

My gaze scans over the bold capital letters on my wall, and if I didn't know better, I'd say that it almost looks like it was written in blood. Though, the small tube of lip shit on my headboard suggests otherwise.

KEEP IT. IT'LL LOOK BETTER ON A BITCH LIKE YOU.

Only one person has ever gotten away with calling me a bitch, and that was my younger sister. She was wasted and didn't like that I was dragging her home, but it's not like I was about to leave her stupid ass at that rager. Who knows what could have happened to her. All I know is Brielle Ashford is going to regret breaking into my room, but she'll regret her choice of words more.

A feminine laugh cuts through the silence of my room and my brows furrow. Who the fuck was that?

Trudging through my home, I walk to the back of the house and through my sister's bedroom to the closest window which overlooks the yard and my jaw snaps together finding Riley and my boys over in Channing's yard chilling with Killjoy, Arizona, and some other chick I don't know.

Jax is getting handsy with her and I shake my head, watching as this new chick eats up his attention, just as every girl does, but it's Riley's lingering stare on Killjoy that grinds on my nerves. The asshole works fast. He saw his opportunity and he took it, didn't even wait two minutes before jumping the fence and intruding on the girls' afternoon. I just wish I could understand why it makes me so damn cocky to see that she doesn't seem to give two shits about Riley's attention.

Letting out a sigh, I filter through my options. Stay locked up in my room like a fucking loser or go over there and end up looking like a jealous asshole who can't handle one little fucking bet.

Shit.

On the other hand, if I don't go over there, I don't get the rush from watching the fear flash in her eyes or the hunger from when she watches my every move, remembering what she saw through my bedroom window yesterday.

Fuck it. Call me a sucker for punishment. I want to be over there, and I want to see the fear in her eyes. Screw the boys and their opinions. If they want to give me a hard time about it, then so be it. I'll just have to kick their asses harder on the field. A few stray tackles won't hurt.

Taking off down the stairs, I all but blast my way through the front door, the anticipation of fucking with her afternoon too good to pass up. The boys would have slipped through the side gate of Channing's property, but if I'm doing this, I'm making it count.

Striding over the boundary line, I make my way right to the front door and grip the handle before welcoming myself in. I strut through the house I know all too well and a rush of memories of growing up alongside Jensen Channing assault me. Rumor has it that he assaulted some chick at school last year. I never got that vibe from him, and while he never got arrested or charged, there's no way of knowing if he actually did it. It was her word against his. All I know is that the guy is a fucking loser. Killjoy really hit the jackpot by becoming his new roomie. She's going to have to watch her back.

Making my way through the kitchen, I scrunch my face at the chick drinks covering the counter. Jax and Riley would be all over that fruity shit, but the rest of us have respect for ourselves. Logan and I prefer bourbon, whereas Hudson gets hard for whiskey.

The bifold doors are wide open and their mindless conversation flows into the house, slowly killing my brain cells one by one. Jax is shamelessly flirting with the chick I don't know, leaning into her and whispering in her ear while she goes all doe eyed. Logan and Hudson have made themselves comfortable on the end of Arizona's sun lounger, to her dismay, of course, while Riley sits on the edge of Brielle's lounger. His positioning forces her to cross her legs to leave enough space for him, but he still takes up all the space he can, making sure that her skin is pressing against his thigh.

I try to ignore it as I reach up and grip the frame around the bifold doors and watch the performance before me. "The fuck are you assholes doing here?"

The boys all look my way, but I keep my eyes on Brielle, watching as her back stiffens and her head whips around, her hair flowing over her shoulder in the process. Her eyes widen just a fraction, and she pauses a moment, almost as if trying to decide how she is going to handle this. Not going to lie, my heart is beating just that little bit faster. Getting this reaction from her is like a drug I'm already becoming addicted to. She fucking hates me and I love it.

Riley watches me with a smug expression, one I plan to knock right off his face. He knew exactly what he was doing and once again, I've just played right into his fucked-up games.

"Holy hell," the new chick breathes, her eyes flashing toward Arizona. "Who the fuck is that?"

I don't wait to hear the response as my attention is solely on Brielle and the way she flies up off the sun lounger, anger burning in her narrowed stare. "Who let you in here?" she spits, striding up to me and putting herself right in my way, her chin tilting to meet my gaze.

I don't dare look away, capturing her stare with my own and holding her captive. Most chicks break, unable to handle the intimidation. They have no choice but to look away, but she doesn't back down, just dares me to continue. Can't lie, I'm impressed. "What's the matter, Killjoy? I figured you'd be the last person to bitch about breaking and entering."

Amusement flares through her bright blue eyes, and without a doubt, she knows that I've seen what she did to my room. All eyes fall on us, their heavy, concerned stares lingering and waiting to see how this is going to go down, waiting to see who will break first.

"Not at all," she tells me, stepping in even closer and lowering her tone. "I just have issues with assholes like you making yourself welcome somewhere that you're clearly not wanted."

I move in closer, just as she had done, leaving barely a breath between us, and I don't hesitate, reaching out and curling my fingers around her throat, trailing my thumb up and down her soft skin. I feel the rapid beat of her pulse beneath my thumb and a wicked satisfaction tears through me. She's coming alive for me, her eyes are wide, all of her attention on me as her breath catches in her throat, unlike when talking to Riley. Just as I told Jax, I'm already in her head. They can try all they like, but she's already mine.

To fuck, to torture, to play. I will get whatever I want from this girl. She will fall at my feet, and I won't even need to try.

"Not wanted?" I question, leaning in even closer, feeling the sharp inhale of her chest as it presses up against mine. I lower my voice to a soft whisper, letting my breath brush across her skin. "Quit lying to yourself, Killjoy. You might not want this, but your body sure as fuck does. I bet you're soaking wet for me, aren't you?" she leans in, her head tilting to the side, inviting me in. "You want to feel my tongue brushing over your clit, my thick cock pushing up into that tight little cunt. You're desperate for it. Tell me, baby, did you fall asleep thinking about what you saw? Did you fuck yourself while thinking about the way I stroked my cock and watched you through your window?"

I pull back just a fraction to see the way her eyes become hooded and her tongue rolls over her bottom lip, and I almost falter, my knees threatening to fall out beneath me. She's so fucking gorgeous. Hating her is going to kill me, but it'll be so worth it.

Brielle's gaze drops and her fingers slip up under my shirt, pressing against my abs. Her fingers flare against me and then slowly move up to my chest. "Tanner," she breathes, and just like that, she has my complete, undivided attention. I wait for her, wait to hear whatever the fuck she has to say, hanging on her every word. "Quit kidding yourself. I would never lower my standards and fuck someone like you, but please keep trying. Your desperation is the best entertainment I've ever had."

She pulls back from me, her eyes as hard as glass as her hand falls from my chest, and I realize that the panting breath and hooded eyes were all part of her game. She fucking played me just as I was trying to do to her, but unlike never before, she bested me, and I don't know whether to fall to my knees and worship her or make her pay. Instead, I just meet her smug grin with one of my own, undoubtedly impressed.

Before I get a chance to remind her where her place is in all of this, Riley approaches, moving in just behind her, his hand falling to her waist and slowly curving around until the tips of his fingers are slipping inside the top of her waistband. My stare falls to his touch and I barely resist curling my hands into fists and giving myself away. "Yo,

Tanner. Everything chill over here?"

She pulls her hand from my chest and swings it back, nailing Riley right in the junk and dropping him to his knees. "Ahhh, fuck," he groans, holding on to his balls for dear life.

Brielle whips around to face him, bending over to grip his chin and force his stare to hers. "Riley, is it?" The fucker nods, trying to breathe through his pain, and she gives him a dazzling, sugar-sweet smile that nearly knocks me off my fucking feet. "Let's set some ground rules, shall we? I don't give a shit about whatever fucked up game you two have going about who can fuck the new girl first. It's perverted and quite frankly, ain't ever going to happen. So hear me, and hear me loud and clear, if you ever put your hands on me without my consent again, I will pull your testicles out through your throat, pulverize them into dust, mix it with whatever steroid powder shit you inject yourself with, and feed them to you. Is that understood?"

Riley's eyes go wide as he gapes at her, his balls almost forgotten. "Holy fuck," he breathes, unable to tear his gaze off her, watching her with wonder. "I think I just fell in love with you."

Brielle scoffs, her gaze flickering to mine as a smugness pulls at the corner of her lips. "Join the club."

I can't tear my eyes off her as she barges past me back into the house and goes about fixing herself a drink, and it sure as fuck doesn't go unnoticed that not once in the past few days when I've touched her has she had any objections. She all but welcomes it, she breathes me in, she leans closer, and there's no feigning the feel of her rapid pulse beneath my fingers.

Riley gets to his feet, peering inside at Brielle as he shakes his head in disbelief. "Holy fuck, bro. No chick has ever dropped me like that." He can't look away from her, watching her with a strange mix of awe and confusion as an uncalled-for panic spears through my chest. I've seen that look before. It's the look he had when he saw the twins' mom in a bikini for the first time after she had her tits done, the same look he gave her before spending the next six months obsessing over her and convincing himself that he was in love, and I don't fucking like it.

"Get the fuck out of here, man," I tell him, giving him a shove into the house and watching as he goes. "Go get cleaned up. You have your father's dinner tonight."

Riley groans, the mention of his father like a bucket of ice water tipped over his head. "Fuck, I'd almost forgotten about that," he says, turning back and glancing at Brielle in the kitchen as she pours herself another drink. "It was a pleasure, but I must see myself out."

Riley tips his imaginary hat to her and she narrows her eyes as she watches him leave, not bothering with a goodbye. Riley takes off and I turn back to my boys outside. "I'm out," I tell them, not giving two shits if they stay and fuck Bri's friends. As long as they keep their filthy hands off her, I'm good.

Turning around to head back in the house, I find Killjoy trailing toward me, sipping on her fruity shit. "Leaving so soon?" she smiles. "What a shame. I was really looking forward to whatever riveting conversation I'm sure you're capable of."

"Aww, Ashford's got jokes," I say, hating how much I'm enjoying this, but loving how much she hates it. "Shouldn't be surprised, chicks like you have to rely on your personality. Don't get by on much else—unless you like getting on your knees."

"Ohhh, ouch," she says, looking bored. "Was that one supposed to burn? Maybe I'll ask your friends. I'm sure they might see things a little differently. Or who knows, maybe I might just get on my knees … *for them.*"

She's fucking bluffing and we both know it, but it doesn't lessen the sting of thinking of her on her knees for anyone but me. Fuck, I'm getting too caught up. If I'm not careful, this girl will become my obsession.

My hands slip into my pockets, and I give her the most condescending scoff I can possibly come up with. "I'll be seeing you, Killjoy."

And with that, I stride out of the house before I can convince myself to turn around, slam her up against the wall, and fuck her until we're both panting on the ground.

CHAPTER 11
TANNER

It's well after dark when I emerge from my bedroom and scavenge through the fridge for something to eat. Mom got back late, so she grabbed dinner on her way home and left me to fend for myself. Usually, it'd bug me, especially after a big training day, but I couldn't even bring myself to think about food. Not after those few minutes standing in Brielle's presence.

I'm starting to wonder if Killjoy is an appropriate name for her. That first night it sure as fuck was, but now? I'm not so sure. Every last encounter I've had with her has left me more than excited for our next meeting. It's addicting to watch her scramble with fear only to remember that she has a backbone and fight back.

Grabbing some leftover spaghetti Bolognese from last night, I shove it into the microwave and hit start just as Mom strides into the kitchen, looking frazzled, her eyes darting around the room, unable to focus. "Oh, honey, you didn't have to do that," she tells me, noticing my dinner heating in the microwave. "I could have made you something fresh."

"It's fine. I got it covered," I say, noticing her phone locked in her tight grip. I cross the kitchen and pry it from her hand before taking her shoulders and forcing her stare to mine. "What's wrong?" I ask, my brows furrowed, hating seeing her like this. "Is Addie alright? Did something happen?"

Mom looks directly at me, yet she still seems so far away. "Ummm, yeah. Yes, of course Addie is okay. Same as yesterday, no change. It's just …." she pauses as she indicates toward her phone I carelessly tossed on the counter. "I just had a call from the police station. They have a suspect. Someone came forward and gave a name."

"What?" My eyes widen and I step away from my mother, my chest heaving as I stare back at her, fury rippling through me as I picture my little sister lying in her hospital bed, imagining the sounds of her heart monitor beeping steadily. It's been nearly five long weeks since the fucker who drugged and raped her left her in a coma, and I've wanted nothing more than to get my hands on the bastard. "Who, Mom? Who was it?"

She shakes her head. "I … I didn't recognize his name, but they've taken him in for questioning."

"Mom," I demand, unable to control the anger poisoning my veins. It's more than likely that I wouldn't recognize his name either.

Addison was at a Hope Falls party during the summer because she was trying to avoid me, trying to avoid my watchful eye as she hung out with her friends. If I hadn't been so overprotective, always fucking with her nights, maybe she wouldn't have felt the need to slip away from us, wouldn't have gone all the way out to a public party. I'll never forget her call, listening as she screamed for help while the bastard laughed and raped her. It makes me fucking sick.

I got there just in time to save her life, but not fast enough to see who the fuck had hurt her, and I will never forgive myself for it.

"Colby Jacobs," she finally says.

"Jacobs?" I question, my back stiffening as I clench my jaw so hard that I fear I'll crack each of my fucking teeth. "Colby Fucking Jacobs? Are you shitting me?"

Uncontrollable rage pounds through my veins. That fucking prick. This was never about my sister. This was about me. The asshole has been waiting nearly two years to screw me over and the second he saw his opportunity, he fucking took it.

Two years ago, I fucked his older sister right before her senior prom. It was a drunk, sloppy, encounter, but I got what I needed from it. She didn't mention she was damn near engaged to some NFL tight end that was traded to an out-of-state team. Some drunk bitch barged in and told everyone what went down. For me, it was just another drunken conquest that I barely remember, but I imagine her boyfriend didn't take the news so well. Her whole school was talking about it. She was labeled the slut of Hope Falls, a jersey chaser, and her dream of being an NFL trophy wife was over before graduation. Her reputation was destroyed. I heard a rumor when she disappeared that her mom sent her to some small town to live with a distant uncle. I felt bad for the girl, but she made her own decisions. Who the hell knows what she's doing now. It's not my problem.

Despite how eager Rachael was to slide into bed with the star player of Bradford Private's football team, Colby blames me for destroying his sister's future. Every time I face him in the field, he takes it personally. The fucker hates me, but I never gave him a second thought until now.

Mom grips my hands, trying to calm me while also desperate for answers. "Tanner, do you know this boy?"

I scoff. "*Know* is a loose term for it. He's fucking scum. He's the captain of the Hope Falls football team and plays dirty. If he fucking did this …" I curl my hands into fists around my mother's fingers and she has no choice but to pull away from me. "If he did this, it was to send a message to me, and the fucker used Addie to do it."

A loud roar tears out of me, and I slam my hands against the counter, imagining what fresh hell my little sister went through all because of my decision to let some loose bitch fuck me two years ago and this asshole's need for vengeance. "I'm going to fucking kill him."

Mom grips my arm and tears me back to face her. "The hell you are," she spits, her tone full of venom. "You're not going to do a damn thing except eat your dinner and go straight to bed. The police haven't even confirmed that this boy is the culprit. They're simply questioning him. No arrest has been made and no charges filed. He could have an alibi or might have been mistaken for someone else, so until we know for sure, there's not a damn thing you will do, do you understand me, Tanner Morgan?"

"Mom, no. If he did—"

She grips my chin and forces her stare to mine, that same venom pouring out of her again, demanding obedience. "I said, do you understand me?"

"Yes, alright. I won't do anything."

"Good. He made the worst mistake of his life when he touched my little girl, so don't be fooled, Tanner, he will go down for this, but it will be with the law on our side. You will not get your hands dirty, and you sure as hell will not throw your future away. Addison would not want you to jeopardize yourself no matter how angry you are. The moment the police can prove this young man raped our girl, we will hit him with the full force of the law, and he will spend the rest of his life behind bars, but until then, you keep yourself out of it. You will not jeopardize this case by becoming involved."

I step away, trying to find some self-control. I know what she's saying, and I get it, but the need to get out there and make this fucker pay for what he did controls my every instinct, my every thought, my every need. The only thing keeping me grounded is the fact that the bastard is probably being held in police custody for questioning.

Mom crosses the kitchen and takes my dinner out of the microwave, but I've completely lost my appetite. That doesn't stop her from almost shoveling it down my throat though. "Now, tell me how school was? Did anybody ask about her?"

I shake my head as I grab a fork and start spinning the spaghetti.

"It's fine," I tell her, hating that I have to keep this secret about where Addie has been all this time. The boys only know because they were with me when she called. They were right there by my side as we tore through Hope Falls to find her, but apart from that, the rest of the school believes she's at some performing arts school. I get it though. It's Addison's choice if she wants the world to know her story, and until she gets the chance to make that decision, my mouth will stay shut. "No one questioned it, but her friends were wondering why she hasn't been texting back."

"Oh?" Mom questions, panic flaring in her dark eyes. "What did you say?"

I shrug my shoulders. "Just told them she's not allowed her phone on campus. It's no big deal, Mom. It's a simple fib. When you make it complicated is when people start to ask too many questions. Besides, Addie has applied to that school every year and has cried to her friends every time she didn't make it in. It's no leap for them to believe she received a late acceptance. Addie can clear it up when she gets better if that's what she wants to do."

Mom nods and takes a shaky breath. "And football training? How did that go?"

"Mom," I say, reaching across the counter and taking her hand in mine before giving it a gentle squeeze, somehow finding the ability to calm myself despite the rage burning a hole through my chest. "You don't need to do that. School was fine. Why don't you go call Dad, let him know what's going on and then spend the night with Addie? I'll be fine by myself."

"I … no, I couldn't."

"Mom, it's okay. You need to be with her tonight. I'll keep my phone on and you can call me if you need me."

Relief surges through her stare and I watch as her shoulders sag. "Are you sure?"

"Sure. It's late anyway. I was just going to eat and then crash. Go."

Mom moves around the counter and steps straight into my arms, holding onto me tightly. "You're a good boy, Tanner Morgan. We're going to catch this guy and then everything can go back to normal."

I rest my chin on her head and let out a sigh. "Nothing will ever go back to normal," I tell her, hating to break her heart like that. "You need to be prepared for that. From the moment Addie wakes up, her whole life is going to change. She's not going to be the same girl we knew before that night, and it's going to take a while before we see that sparkle in her eye, but she'll get there because she has you and Dad at her side. She's going to be alright."

Mom pulls out of my arms and hastily looks away to wipe the tears in her eyes. She hates crying in front of me or Addie. She likes to be strong for us, especially because Dad is gone so often, but over the past few weeks, the tables have turned, and it's been me trying to keep her together.

"Okay," she finally says. "I'll call your father in the car and check in with you in the morning."

"No problem, Mom."

And with that, she's all but racing out the door in her desperation to get to Addie—a feeling I know all too well, a feeling that haunts me every night in my sleep.

The house is quiet, and I force myself to eat the rest of my dinner while trying to keep calm but having a face to put to the monster who hurt my sister doesn't help. Pulling my phone from my pocket, I bring up anything and everything I can find on the guy online but get nothing but his football stats. The fucker isn't even that good, definitely not deserving of being team captain. He has no social media pages and is all but a ghost online, and it does nothing but piss me off more.

Knowing all I'm going to do is work myself into a blind fury, I put my phone away and ditch my plate in the dishwasher before heading upstairs. I push into my bedroom and just like every time I walk in here over the past two days, my gaze sweeps across to my bedroom window, and knowing she's in there settles me. Her blinds are drawn and the lights are out, but there's the smallest opening I can see straight through, and despite what she might think of me, I'm not about to spend my night creeping on her.

Letting out a breath, I drop onto my bed and prop my hand behind my head, not bothering to wipe the lipstick off the wall behind my head. Instead, I grab the small tube and flick the lid on and off with my thumb just to give me something to do. I lay in complete darkness, not in the mood to bother with the TV.

Moments pass before light outside my window catches my eye and I turn my head, finding Brielle's bedroom filled with the dim light shining from her open bathroom door. Her silhouette moves across the room, and she darts into her closet before quickly dressing. The lights go out and her room is flooded with darkness … until it isn't.

A soft lamp shines through the room, and I watch through the small opening as she walks to the window and double checks that it's locked before doing the same to her bedroom door. A smug grin ripples across my face knowing she's doing that solely for my benefit. She has no fucking idea how I got into her room last night, and I don't plan to share that information with her. Though I'm all too aware that she could be locking that door just to keep Jensen at bay, and that worries me more than it has the right to.

Killjoy settles herself in bed and I turn over in mine, being the creeper I promised myself I wouldn't be, but I can't stop looking at her, far too intrigued by this girl who's not afraid to stand up to me. No girl has ever done that before, and they certainly haven't captured my attention the way she has. She's living next door, yet a part of me feels like that's still so far.

I go to look away just as her hand lifts and my eyes focus on the movement, watching as it skirts down her body, brushing over her tits and down past her ribs, her back arching up off the bed as her head tilts back. Her other hand cups her breast as her knees come up and fall open.

No fucking way.

I sit up straight on my bed, my eyes as wide as saucers as my heart races.

Holy fucking hell, she's not …

Her hand lowers further down her body and my heart jolts in my chest, my cock stiffening, already in my hand.

Fuck me. I should look away. This isn't my business, but my eyes are glued through the window, watching as her hand slips under the blanket and she shudders, her fingers clearly brushing over her clit.

"Oh, fuck," I groan, my dick rock fucking hard.

Brielle squirms from her own touch, and I'd do anything to be under that blanket with her hand, tasting her on my tongue and making her scream my name. She's so fucking gorgeous, and now I sound like a goddamn stalker.

Great. Fucking great. Before I know it, I'll be stealing her panties out of her dresser and sniffing them during the night. What the fuck is wrong with me? I need to get a grip—*Yeah, a fucking tighter grip of my dick, that is.*

FUCK!

Look away, bro. Look. Away.

Bri throws her head back as she reaches lower, and I can only imagine the way she pushes her fingers inside her sweet pussy, the way her walls would contract around them, *the way they'd contract around me.*

My hand moves slowly as I watch her, stroking up and down my thick length, feeling like a fucking perv, but she's doing the impossible—making me think of something other than Colby Jacobs and what he did to my sister—and for that, I can never thank her enough.

She picks up her speed and I match her pace, more than ready to explode the second she does, and knowing her body and exactly what she needs, she tips herself right over the edge not a moment later, coming hard and muffling her cries so Jensen down the hall doesn't come looking.

Unbelievable pleasure rocks through me, and I come with her, spurting hot cum into my hand like a fucking tween coming for the first time. I'm hot and heady, panting and desperate, and without even knowing it, she's got me right where she wants me.

I'm fucked, but one thing is for sure—I will be visiting her room again tonight, and this time, I'm taking things to a whole new level.

CHAPTER 12
Brielle

That fucking asshole. I'm going to kill him. I'm really going to kill him, and damn it, I'm going to enjoy it. I've never hated anybody like the way I hate Tanner Morgan.

Humiliation sweeps through me as I stare at the mirror across my bedroom, taking in the words written in black eyeliner as my cheeks flame. Waking up yesterday to realize he'd been in my room is one thing, but now this … fuck.

NEXT TIME, YOU CUM ON MY FINGERS.

I might as well dig a hole and fall into it. How the hell am I supposed to face the day knowing he watched me getting myself off last night? Hell, how the fuck did he even get in here? I made sure the window was locked, plus the door too. I was careful. The blinds were drawn and all my bases were covered. He shouldn't have been able to come in.

But those fucking blinds. I'll be replacing those fuckers the first chance I get.

How could I be so stupid? I suppose I'm lucky, I was mostly hidden beneath the blanket. He couldn't have seen anything, though how can I ever be sure? Does the asshole have cameras in here? I wouldn't put it past him. He's got a sick mind.

Fuck, fuck, fuck. Why couldn't I have just gone to town on myself while I was locked away safely in the shower? I had to do it in bed, had to do it right by the window that I know Tanner Morgan likes to look through. I'm an idiot, no doubt about it.

Trying to put it to the back of my head, I throw my blankets back and get ready for school before grabbing some wet wipes and trying to get the eyeliner off the mirror. It's one thing for someone to walk in and see his other message in lipstick, but this one … no. I'd die if anyone saw this, especially my mom.

Making my way downstairs, I find Mom and Orlando in the kitchen while Jensen sits at the breakfast bar, helping himself. "Morning, honey," Mom sings as she busily goes about her morning, today wearing a pristine cream pantsuit that probably costs more than my car. "Are you hungry? I made pancakes."

My stomach rumbles but seeing the pancakes over by Jensen, I'd rather starve. "I'm okay. I wanted to get to school early," I say, secretly happy that Jensen seems to be giving me space. "My English teacher wants me to write an essay to get a feel for where I am academically, and I wanted to get a start on that before I get lumbered with more homework."

"Don't be ridiculous," Orlando says, turning to face me with a heavy scowl. "Your mother has slaved in the kitchen to prepare you a nice meal. Now take your seat and eat your breakfast. You can work on your essay this afternoon."

I gape at him before flicking my gaze toward Mom, who watches me with a cringe, and without a doubt, I know she's not going to have my back on this. I barely resist scoffing at her. There was once a time where nothing was more important than my schoolwork. Mom wanted me to succeed, push myself and get the hell out of Hope Falls to create a better life for myself, but now, what her filthy rich sugar daddy wants, her filthy rich sugar daddy gets.

"With all due respect, sir. You may have offered up your home, but don't be mistaken. You are not my father, and you certainly don't get a say in how and when I tackle my schoolwork. I appreciate that you have paid my tuition to a fancy private school, really, I do. However, I didn't ask for this. I was taken from the home that I loved, from the school where I grew up, from my friends, and thrown headfirst into this life that more than likely comes with an expiry date. My education comes before … whatever this is."

"Brielle," my mother gasps, feigning surprise despite having seen it coming a mile away. "Apologize right this instant."

"No, don't *Brielle* me, Mom. Do you know you're his third or fourth girlfriend to have moved in here over the past two years? TWO

YEARS, MOM! Do you not see how messed up that is? This is all an act. You have literally never cooked me breakfast on a school day, like ever. This is all a show for your new boyfriend and his pervert son, and it's all for nothing because in a few months, he's going to be done with you, and we'll be right back where we started, only you'll be broken and hating yourself for falling for his charm."

"You are out of line," Orlando demands, rage burning through his features as Mom presses her hand to her chest, gasping in horror for my terrible behavior. "My son is not a pervert. He is a respectable young man with a promising career at his fingertips. How dare you make such an allegation."

"I said what I said," I tell him, holding my ground, almost feeling guilty about it. "Though I'm curious, have you disclosed the fact that your son attacked a girl on school grounds last year before you asked my mother to move herself and her eighteen-year-old daughter into your home, or did that just slip your mind?"

Orlando's face turns bright red as his son sits back and watches the show with an amused smirk playing on his lips, as though he's never been so entertained in his life. My mother looks absolutely horrified and sick. "Jensen was not charged with any wrongdoing. That girl was out to get him. She confessed to lying out of sheer embarrassment for getting caught, and I ensured that she was charged appropriately."

"Orlando," Mom gapes, her gaze shifting to the sick bastard in question as a wave of confusing emotions crash through me. "Is this true? Did he attack a minor?"

"No, certainly not," Orlando says. "This is all just exaggerated school yard gossip."

"Right," I laugh, wondering if maybe I've judged the guy too soon. Maybe he is just weird and that's all there is to it. Maybe the rest is only schoolyard gossip, but how will we ever really know? Orlando is the best at what he does, and I wouldn't put it past him to intimidate the girl into a confession. "You keep telling yourself that while blatantly ignoring the fact that he constantly leers at me like I'm a fucking meal. Real nice, Orlando. You must be so proud." I fix my bag over my back and check the time, making sure I have enough time to grab something to eat on the way to school. I go to leave when I turn back to find my mother staring at Orlando as though he's some kind of stranger. "I don't know what's going on with you, Mom, but we've only been here for a few days and you're already a stranger to me. I miss my real mother, and I hope to God that she comes back to me."

And with that, I grab my keys off the edge of the counter and make my way out to the car, listening to the utter silence behind me. Guilt fires through me and the need to text Mom with an apology itches at my fingers, but I hold off. I don't know why I'm particularly crabby today. Perhaps it was the embarrassment of knowing Tanner saw me last night, or maybe it was Mom's refusal to have my back and allowing her boyfriend to speak to me like that. Hell, maybe it's just the fact that she's so desperate for this bullshit lifestyle that she refuses to see what's clearly in front of her, refuses to listen, and refuses to put me first.

Or … I just had one too many mimosas yesterday.

In the space of three days, I feel like my mother has flipped a switch and is a complete stranger. She's so desperate to impress this asshole, that she doesn't remember what's important in life. I mean, who just moves out of their home on a whim, uproots her daughter's life, and becomes a cheerleader for a guy just because he can offer her a life full of luxury?

Dropping into my car, I pull my door shut and just sit, needing a moment. Only when I see my mother racing out the front door with a takeout container filled with breakfast, I wish I had just driven off.

She opens the door and thrusts the pancakes at me, and I reluctantly take the container. "Please just eat something, honey," she says, looking at me with sad eyes.

"Are you serious?" I laugh. "That's all you have to say?"

Mom presses her lips into a tight line. "I'm sorry, but Orlando has promised me that Jensen is perfectly safe. It was just a silly teenage girl who was embarrassed that she'd been caught with him, so she accused him of an ugly, heinous crime rather than own up to the fact that she had consented. She didn't want her parents to know that she was sexually active."

I stare at my mother, not knowing this stranger before me. "Are you kidding me?" I question. "Tell me that you're not blaming the victim here. Let me guess, her skirt was too short, so she was asking for it? She bent over in front of Jensen and he accepted that as her consent? What if that were me? What if he forced himself onto me and raped me? What would you say then? Would you tell me it was my fault, or would you just insist that I was lying?"

"Brielle, what on earth has gotten into you?"

I shake my head and thrust the pancakes back at her before slamming the door between us. What the hell has gotten into me? More like, what the hell has gotten into her? She gets dicked down every night now, so apparently, she doesn't need to have respect for herself, her morals, or her family. Give me a fucking break.

Slamming my Honda in reverse, I floor it, peeling out of the driveway before I get the chance to really let my mother know what I think of her right now.

I pull up at school ten minutes later, the early hour allowing me to bypass the usual morning traffic, and instead of going in and working on my essay, I just sit and stare up at the big school, unable to stop replaying my morning. That wasn't right, that wasn't my mom. Had I said that to her this time last week, she would have fought tooth and nail to protect all innocence, but now, she's taking on Orlando's corrupted views and bullshit morals. This isn't right. Is he forcing this on her? Is he making her say these things? Is there more at play here?

Heaviness weighs down on my shoulders and minutes begin to pass where I just stare out the window, feeling more lost than ever before. A loud rumble of a familiar motorcycle cuts through my thoughts, and I jump, my gaze falling to the small digital clock. I've been sitting here for over an hour.

Students fill the parking lot, lingering around Tanner, trying to get his attention, and I use it as my chance to escape through the crowd. My stomach grumbles as I dart toward the school, and having a few spare minutes, I detour past the cafeteria and grab myself a slice of toasted banana bread with a caramel latte.

The hot beverage sails down my throat and somehow manages to warm the chill left behind from my morning. It's exactly what I need to be able to face the day. Making my way through the crowded senior hall, I find my locker and throw everything inside before quickly glancing at my class schedule again.

As I'm finding what I need, Ilaria appears at my side, a grin on her face while Chanel and Arizona talk shit behind her. "Did you do it?" she asks, her eyes sparkling with excitement.

"Do what?"

Ilaria rolls her eyes and laughs as I close my locker and start sipping my latte once again. "Break into the lion's den," she murmurs, looking around to make sure no one is overhearing.

I laugh, unable to believe I didn't catch onto that one, but it feels like so much has happened since then. "Oh, yeah," I tell her. "We scaled a tree outside his bedroom and slipped in through his window."

"What did you end up doing?"

"I returned the lipstick and casually let him know that particular shade would look better on a bitch like him."

Her eyes bug out of her head, and I watch as Chanel catches onto what we're discussing and moves in closer to hear the rest of the story, Arizona grinning proudly. "Bullshit," Ilaria laughs. "Did he retaliate?"

Panic slams through my chest, not ready to share the fact that he sure as hell did. I'm trying to choose my words carefully when Arizona cuts in first. "Fuck yeah, he did," she says. "He came over."

Chanel's eyes go wide. "What?"

"Yeah," Arizona continues. "All his friends were there anyway because we were having mimosas and they made themselves welcome when they heard us, but then Tanner let himself in through the front door a few minutes after. It was clear that he'd just seen her message, and he was pissed."

"What did he say?"

Arizona shakes her head. "I … I don't know. Bri went over to kick his ass out and then he grabbed her and said something, but we couldn't hear it. Looked kinda hot though, but knowing Tanner, it was probably some kind of threat."

All eyes turn to me, gaping and demanding answers, and I roll my eyes, trying not to remember just how hot he'd made me in that moment. I was so close to caving, so close to giving him exactly what he wanted. "Nothing, he was just talking a big game, acting like he could get me on my knees anytime he wanted. Usual ego bullshit from a football god."

Ilaria laughs. "Not gonna lie, if a guy like Tanner Morgan was asking me, I would have just done it."

An unladylike snort pulls from the back of my throat, and before I can even respond, a heavy arm drops over my shoulder. "Morning, babe," Riley says, leaning into me, a cocky grin spreading across his face. "What's going on?"

"Ugh," Chanel groans. "You hung out one time. Don't tell me that this is going to become a thing?"

"Damn right," Riley says. "What can I say? She's got a nasty backhand and I fucking love it. No one has ever dropped me to my knees like she did, and for that, I claim her as my own."

I scoff, slipping out from under his arm. "No chance in hell," I tell him. "Besides, it's bad enough that I already have to deal with Tanner on the regular, I don't have time to brush you off too."

"Then don't brush me off," he says simply, his lips pulling into a cocky, shit-eating grin. "Let me take you out. Just you and me. I'll show you a good time, then you can return the favor. It's a win-win all around."

I look up at him, staring deeply into his eyes and watching how his body stiffens. My hand falls to his strong chest as I push up onto my tippy toes, getting so close that I feel his breath brushing over my cheek. "Over my dead body," I whisper.

His face falls and he slams a hand to his chest before falling back against my locker. "Oh fuck," he says, clutching his chest. "That one hurt."

I laugh and he pulls away from the locker, reaching for my hand. "Seriously, though," he says with an odd rawness in his eyes that I'm not prepared for. "I like you. I don't know if it's the feisty attitude, the way you sucker punched me in the balls, or just because you're fucking gorgeous, but I wanna take you out."

As if on cue, a hand shoots out and smacks Riley on the back of his head and my eyes snap across to meet Tanner's as he walks by. He doesn't say a damn word, but the way he holds my stare, his eyes sparkling with our latest secret, keeps me completely captivated. Just the knowledge of knowing he saw me last night scares the crap out of me, but it's also the most thrilling thing that has ever happened to me.

We share this dark, sexy secret, and I want more, but not before he suffers the consequences of breaking into my bedroom ... twice. Though, does that make me a hypocrite for doing the same to him? At least I wasn't watching him get off ... but then, I kinda did. Unintentionally.

Tanner keeps on walking, pulling his gaze from mine and leaving me breathless. And that right there is why I won't even give Riley the time of day. His best friend, without even trying, has got me hook, line, and sinker, and I hate him for it.

The bell sounds through the hallway, and I quickly drink what's left of my caramel latte while my friends openly gape at me, having watched that brief moment between us, but Riley steals my attention once again. "You and me, babe," he says, walking backward as he follows after Tanner. "It's going to happen. We were meant to be."

Rolling my eyes, I dive back into my locker and grab my things, only to turn back to find the girls still gaping at me. "Ummm ... what just happened?" Chanel demands, a strange hard edge to her tone.

I shake my head and step around them, avoiding each of their stares. "Nothing," I say, holding my books close to my chest. "Gotta run. Don't wanna be late for homeroom."

And just like that, I take off down the hall, all too aware that I share homeroom with Ilaria and that I haven't avoided this conversation yet, not even a little bit.

CHAPTER 13
TANNER

NEXT TIME? YOU COULDN'T HANDLE A NEXT TIME

Why is getting home after football training and seeing her bullshit responses to my messages the best part of my day? I've barely spoken two words to the girl and those words have all been insults or threats. She shouldn't be holding my attention like she is, and I sure as fuck shouldn't be holding hers.

I'm going to break her, she … fuck, she might even break me first.

The boys took off half an hour ago, and just like last night, Mom has taken off to sit by Addie's side. Each passing minute that she's stuck in this coma kills me. The doctors believe that her body has had a reaction to the cocktail of drugs she was fed and that's why she hasn't woken up yet. I hate it. I need to see her eyes, need to see her smile, and hear her tell me that she's okay.

The doorbell rings and I walk out of my room, taking off down the stairs to the front door. I'm fucking starving and this Uber Eats driver can't get here soon enough. It's been a long day, and I've spent most of it staring at Brielle from across the room, picturing the way she came on her fingers. I'd give my left nut to see that up close in person, and be the one who made her feel that way.

Riley spent most the day doing the same damn thing and it's fucked with my head. This new obsession of his is in full force, and I fucking hate it. I hate how he watches her, hate how he's so comfortable to walk up and shamelessly flirt, hate how she smiles up at him. Brielle knocks him back every time he tries, and a part of me should be happy about that, but at some point, she's going to cave. They always do.

Pulling the door open, I find the Uber Eats guy and he hands me my food just as my phone rings. "Thanks, man," I say, taking my meal while digging in my pocket.

Mom's name flashes on the screen and I take her call immediately. She rarely calls me while spending time with Addison, so it's got to be some kind of news—good or bad, who fucking knows. "Mom?" I rush out, hovering in the open doorway.

Her sobs cut through the silence and my heart shatters.

"What happened? What's wrong?"

She sniffles and sobs and I put my food down by the door and step out into the warm night, listening as she tries to calm herself enough to tell me what the fuck is going on. "She stopped breathing," she tells me, every word breaking her even more. "The doctors intubated her and she's on a ventilator to help her breathe."

I drop into the grass, my head falling to my knees. "Is she ... is she dying?"

"No," Mom says. "The doctors are still hopeful that she will come through this. Her heart is strong and there's still positive brain activity. They say ... they say it's a common occurrence and that we shouldn't worry."

"Shouldn't worry?" I demand, my voice rising with fear. "She has fucking tubes keeping her alive. Mom—"

"No," she cuts in, trying to keep from breaking. "I know what you're thinking, and the answer is no. Your sister needs you here with her, she doesn't need you locked up in a cell. She is going to pull through this, Tanner. You have to have faith. She's strong enough to pull through."

I drop my phone into the grass and hit the speaker button before rubbing my hands over my face. "I know, Mom. I know she's strong enough. She's going to get through this, but I just can't let him get away with it. Have you heard anything from the police?"

Mom goes silent and I laugh, the agony of the situation weighing me down. "You're fucking kidding me," I murmur. "They let him go, didn't they?"

Mom sighs. "They didn't have enough evidence to hold him. He claimed he wasn't even there that night and now we're back to square one. He hired that asshole from next door and the next thing I know, he was walking free. But don't worry, Tanner. We will catch this guy, whoever it is, he will pay for what he's done to my little girl."

I shake my head, not believing it for one second. The moment the name Colby Jacobs was thrown into the mix, I knew it was him. I knew it deep in my gut. There have been other names tossed around, but none of them felt right, but this ... this one is personal. I know it was him and the fucker is about to walk free, especially with Orlando Channing working the case. That bastard has never lost a case, and not because he's just that good. He's fucking shady and wins on intimidation tactics and false evidence.

Not on my fucking watch.

"The doctors are here to take her for more scans. I'll call you if there are any updates."

"Alright. The second you know anything—"

"I know, love. You'll be my first call."

With that, the call goes dead, and I remain sitting in the grass, my elbows braced against my knees as I stare at my hands, devastation washing through me.

"Hey," a voice calls from behind. Glancing back over my shoulder, I find Brielle sitting out on the roof, looking sorry for herself, a bottle of tequila hanging between her fingers. She holds it up. "Wanna drink?"

My brow arches and I stare at her for a moment. "How long have you been out here?"

"Long enough," she tells me, letting me know that she'd overheard my whole conversation. "Your sister isn't at a performing arts school, is she?"

I get to my feet and stare up at her, not ready to answer that question out loud, it's not my place. "What are you doing out here?"

She shrugs her shoulders before taking another swig of tequila. "Had a fight with my mom," she mutters, rolling her eyes. "Apparently the fact that Jensen Channing may or may not be a rapist isn't my business despite living with the guy, and now somehow I'm the bad guy because I pointed out that she's turning into Orlando's groupie and throwing all her morals out the window."

"Shit. Tough break."

"I'm not looking for your pity."

"And I'm not looking for yours."

"Good."

She takes another swig and I let out a heavy sigh. That bottle is nearly full and if she drinks that whole thing on her own, she'll be finding a bed right beside Addie's. "You hungry?"

Bri nods and without another word, I walk back into my house, grabbing my dinner by the door and searching for two forks. A moment later, I emerge back on the lawn and walk around the side of Channing's home, effortlessly pulling myself up on top of the fence before hoisting myself onto the roof.

Walking across, I meet Brielle by her open bedroom window and hold out my hand for the tequila. She offers it up and I pass her my takeout before making myself comfortable beside her. She digs straight into the food as I take a long swig, hating the burn as it sails down my throat. I'm not a massive fan of tequila, but I'm not going to say no if it'll help ease the ache of what's going on with my sister.

"You wanna talk about it?" she asks around a mouthful of noodles.

I shake my head and glance across at her. "Nope. You?"

"Nope."

Perfect.

We eat in silence and the calm that settles through my chest puts me at ease for the first time in five long weeks. I've been nothing but angry but sitting in her presence soothes me, and I'm already addicted to it.

Once the takeout container filled with noodles is completely demolished, Bri leans back onto her hands as I sip at the bottle of tequila, welcoming the way it dulls my emotions. "You know," she says after being silent for nearly forty-five minutes. "Watching me through my window is next level fucked up."

Don't I fucking know it!

A grin lingers on my lips as I turn back to meet her heavy stare. "I don't know what you're talking about."

Bri rolls her eyes, unable to hide the smirk that plays on her lips. She reaches forward and snatches the tequila from my hands before taking another swig. "Sure you don't."

Taking the bottle back from her, I place it down on the roof between us before catching her wrist and pulling her to me. She doesn't flinch away or even hesitate, so I take her waist and lift her right onto my lap until she's straddled over me, her hands clutching my shoulders to keep steady.

My fingers curl around the back of her neck, my thumb brushing over her jaw and watching as she tilts to the side, her eyes fluttering at my touch. I draw her into me, and she comes willingly, curling her arm further around my neck until her body presses against mine, the heat of her pussy rocking against my hardening cock.

My lips press to her shoulder and slowly work their way up her neck, moving gently and watching how she reacts. Her breath grows heavy, and her fingers dig into my skin, probably leaving perfect little half-moons from her nails.

A soft moan slips between her lips, and I crave to capture them in mine, but she's been drinking, and I'm not about to kiss her when any other day, she would have pushed me away. My lips work her neck with hunger, trailing up to the sensitive spot below her ear. She groans, grinding down against me as my arms wrap around her petite body.

Her hand shifts around me and I hesitantly pull back, knowing damn well if I don't stop, I'll pick her up and take her straight back to her room where neither one of us will be able to stop. Heat shines through her eyes as she looks back at me, her need evident all over her body. "Why aren't you pulling away from me, Killjoy?"

"Probably for the same reason you came up here."

"I highly doubt that."

She arches a brow and presses her hands against my shoulders, pulling back and giving herself just a fraction of space. "You watch me all day at school. I feel your eyes on me every time I walk into a room. You search me out just as I do to you, only every fiber of my body is screaming at me to hate you, and don't even try to deny that you're trying to hate me too. But you can't. I'm your distraction from the real world. Tormenting me is the best fun you've ever had, and you know what? For some fucked-up reason, I can't get enough of it."

I shake my head and reach up, brushing her golden blonde hair off the side of her face. "I think you're thinking too hard into this," I tell her, cupping the side of her face and becoming addicted to the feel of her body against mine. "I do hate you. You don't mean shit to me."

"Uh-huh," she says. "Sure I don't."

I lean back against the roof and hold her stare. "You know Riley is into you," I tell her, not wanting to tell her how much this bothers me.

"He's not," she tells me, making my brows arch. "He only thinks he is. Don't get me wrong, messing around with him would be fun. He's a flirt but that's all it is. He'd keep it lighthearted, and I bet he fucks like a pornstar, but he wants what he can't have. He sees whatever … this hot mess is and knows that I'm not interested in him, so he's turning his attention on me because he knows that as long as you hold my attention, it will never be anything real."

Before I can even formulate a response, she pushes against my shoulder and stands, using her hold on me to keep balanced as she steps back toward her window. She sits her ass on the frame and glances down at me. "I think you should go before we both end up doing or saying something stupid."

A laugh rumbles through my chest, but I stand, knowing damn well that she's right. "I think we flew past stupid days ago," I tell her, bending down to grab the takeout container and empty bottle of tequila. Straightening up and backing away from her, I find myself pausing, watching her as she sits in her window. "You know, if Jensen gives you trouble …"

Brielle nods, reading the rest of my comment loud and clear, and a part of me relaxes, knowing that she would feel comfortable enough to ask for my help if she were in trouble. "For the record," she says, hooking one leg inside her room. "This didn't happen. The second you step off this roof, we go right back to hating each other."

I wink and her cheeks flush, sending me into fucking heart failure. "Going back to hating you would imply that I ever stopped."

I turn to leave and start making my way toward the fence to jump back down when her soft tone calls through the silence of the warm night. "Tanner?" she questions, hesitation in her tone.

Glancing back over my shoulder with furrowed brows, I pause, watching her struggle with the emotion written across her face and not understanding this need to console her. "What's up?"

"I'm sorry about your sister," she tells me. "I don't know the details, and I'm not going to ask for them, but if you need to talk it out or just want to scream … I'll keep quiet about it. You don't need to worry about me spreading shit."

My stare lingers on hers for a moment and I can't bring myself to respond. The idea of breaking down in front of her scares the shit out of me. I don't want her to see me as vulnerable or weak. I can't … no. Tonight was already pushing the limits. I've already crossed a line that I shouldn't have.

Seeing that a response isn't coming, Brielle slips back into her bedroom and watches me through the window as she pulls it closed and reaches up to lock it. I can't look away. My body craves her, needs her like an addict desperate for his next hit.

Before I do anything I'll regret, I jump down from the second story roof and land in the grass, my hand already slipping into my pocket. I pull my phone out, press a few buttons as I dump the empty bottle and takeout container in the trash can and hold the phone to my ear.

It rings twice before Riley's voice sounds through the phone. "What's up, man? Your sister alright?"

"Nah, the fucker walked and now she's on a ventilator."

"What do you need?"

I step into my darkened home and move up the stairs until I'm standing in my bedroom, a clear view of Brielle Ashford directly across from me. I lean against the window frame, watching as she sits on her bed with her laptop, busily typing away. "I want to know every last thing there's to know about Colby Fucking Jacobs, and then we're going to fucking end him."

CHAPTER 14
Brielle

The noise of the busy cafeteria drowns out the plaguing thoughts circling my head about my stupid decision to ask Tanner up on the roof. I can't believe how bold I was. I labeled it … whatever it is. I was happier pretending that there was nothing between us, but I was too obvious. I called us both out and now, I can't stop remembering his hands on my body, his cock grinding between my legs, and his warm lips tormenting me like the sweetest caress against my neck.

Stupid. Stupid. Stupid.

When I woke this morning, there was no message scrawled on my mirror, and a part of me hated it. I've started to look forward to his creepy little lipstick messages and knowing he was in my room while

I slept. How fucked up is that? Maybe I'm wrong and just missed it after oversleeping and waking up with a killer hangover. I had to grab the essay that I spent the rest of my night typing and then rush out of there in the hopes of making it to school on time.

I didn't. I barely scraped by and barged into homeroom just as the teacher was marking off students' names. He gave me a free pass because I'm new, but the warning in his tone was clear—I won't be so lucky next time.

English was up first, and I handed in my essay, which took a weight off my shoulders. Following that, my day went back to normal ... well, as normal as it'll ever be at this school.

My phone buzzes on the table and I drop my gaze to find a text from Miranda, one of my friends from Hope Falls, and I welcome it greedily, scooping up my phone, more than grateful for the distraction. Only it doesn't stop buzzing, message after message pops up, and I scan over them, my brows furrowing deeper the further I read along.

Miranda - Dude, WTF???? Where have you been? Erica is saying your mom moved you to Bradford. BRADFORD!!!!

Miranda - Fuck me! Tell me you're not one of those hoity-toity uniform wearing rich bitches now, coz if you are, you know I'll have to come and kick your ass.

Miranda - Alsooooo....... Colby? Why's he telling everyone that you sucked every dick you could find over the summer and that he dumped you? He's calling you a cunt to anyone who'll listen.

Miranda - He's lying right? You guys were tight and I know you're not a cheater. He's saying you're being a stuck up bitch and not responding to any calls. Like he dumped you and then you just ghosted big time.

I let out a breath and get busy responding.

Brielle - The fuck! As if anyone is going to believe that shit. First up, yes. Mom moved us in with her rich boyfriend and kinda sprung it on me last minute, so I'm stuck in Bradford until he decides to break up with her. And second, you know I'm not some dick sucking whore! Colby was screwing around behind my back. I literally walked in on him mid-fuck and he's pissed that he got caught! I cut all communication with him and he can't handle it.
Miranda - No freaking way!
Brielle - How do you not know this? Didn't Erica tell you guys?
Miranda - No, that bitch hasn't told us shit!

What the hell? That doesn't make sense. Erica told me that she was doing damage control all that first day. How can people not know this? But then, does it even really matter what they all think of me? As long as my friends know the truth and have my back, that's all that matters.

Before I get to respond, another text comes in and my gaze drops down the screen.

Miranda - Is this why Colby was arrested? Did he do something?

My brows shoot right up into my hairline, my eyes widening like saucers. Colby got arrested? What the fuck? No, that couldn't be right.

Colby was an ass, but he's not a criminal.

Brielle - What do you mean he got arrested? What happened? Have charges been pressed?

Miranda - I've got no idea. We've all been trying to figure it out, but since you've been MIA all week, I just assumed it had something to do with you. He's at school today so I guess that means whatever he did couldn't be that bad, right?

Brielle - Suppose so. Let me know if you find out anything.

Miranda - Sure, girl. Gotta run. Principal Fanning just sprung me on my phone and he's coming this way!

I laugh, able to imagine the scene so clearly because the exact thing has happened to me so many times. Phones are prohibited to use at Hope Falls, but here, they seem chill about it, as long as phones are on silent and aren't visible or distracting during class time.

Even knowing the strict phone rules of Hope Falls, I can't resist scrolling through my recent contacts list and pressing on Erica's name. Bringing the phone up to my ear, it rings twice before she accepts the call. "Colby got arrested?" I screech down the line. "How could you not tell me that? What happened?"

"Chill out," she laughs. "Apparently the cops raided his house and arrested him on Monday night, but he was let go after twenty-four hours. I wasn't at school yesterday. I was feeling sorry for myself at home after allowing you to get me wasted on mimosas, so I only just found out this morning. I've been trying to get a message off to you all morning, but it's been a busy day."

"Oh, shit sorry. I didn't mean to accuse you of not telling me. I just figured you'd already have known about it," I say with a cringe. Ilaria, Chanel, and Arizona are watching me through narrowed gazes after catching my earlier question. "Do you know what's going on? What did he do?"

"I've got no idea. Everyone thinks it has something to do with you because you're not here anymore. You know, the timing is coincidental, and despite how much I tell them that you have nothing to do with it, they don't want to hear me."

I groan, rolling my eyes as I slump down in my chair. "It's bad enough that he's talking shit about me to anyone who'll listen, but now they think I tried to have him arrested? That's bullshit."

"I know, Bri, but this will pass. Colby is an asshole, and you don't deserve to be dragged down for this. Besides, this is Colby. If anything, he probably got busted for drugs or letting off illegal fireworks. He's a little bitch who thinks he's tough. I doubt he would have done anything worthy of jail time."

"Drugs?" I question, laughter bubbling in my chest. "Nah, there's no way. It would have been something stupid. Can you imagine that bastard locked up? He wouldn't be able to cut it."

"Hell no. He'd be calling some big dude Daddy by the end of his first night."

My laugh dies the moment I see Riley cutting across the cafeteria, his gaze locked on mine with hunger deep in his stare. One of the twins comes with him, both of them looking as though they're up to no good. I let out a heavy groan. "Shit, girl. I have to go. I'll talk to you later."

"Alright, babe. Call me later. I've been dying for an update on your new neighbor."

She cuts the call and I bring my phone down just as Riley drops into the empty space beside me, his arm slinging over my shoulder. "Sup, babe?" he asks, as whichever twin it is drops down directly opposite him. A flash of guilt settles through me at not knowing which one he is, but who can blame me? I barely know these people and they're freaking identical. It's impossible to tell them apart.

"Chanel," the twin spits, narrowing his eyes at my new friend who looks just as displeased to see him.

"Logan," she fires back, the two of them caught in each other's heavy stare, almost becoming entranced and then as if they never said a thing at all, they look away.

"Ummmmm, what the hell just happened?" I question, looking between the two and hating Riley's arm still slung over my shoulder but kinda loving it because I can feel Tanner's heavy stare from across the room like laser beams trying to get right inside my head.

Riley laughs and leans in. "They're in love but refuse to acknowledge it."

Chanel gapes at Riley, looking absolutely disgusted. "Over my dead body. Have you met the guy?" she demands. "He's a certified asshole, and if you ever try to insult me like that again, I will reach between your legs and stretch your balls right up over your shoulders before tying them around your neck like a bowtie."

Riley laughs as Logan scoffs. "Keep lying to yourself all you want, babe, but you can't resist me."

Chanel scoffs right back at him before leaning across the table, giving him the perfect view right down her cleavage and plastering a sultry smile across her face. She reaches across and brushes her fingers across his toned forearm like a gentle caress, and I watch the way he falters, completely struck by her beauty. "You're right," she whispers. "What was I thinking? It's always been you, Logan."

Logan's jaw drops and he stares for a moment, trying to find some composure, and I lean back, watching the two of them. Chanel is so clearly screwing with him, but Logan's response is genuine. He's in love with her, but I don't think Chanel feels the same. Either way, this is an interesting turn of events. I don't consider myself a meddler, but if it helps get my mind off the asshole across the cafeteria who is still staring at the back of my head, then I'm down.

"Chanel, angel, if you don't take your hand off me right fucking now," Logan warns, his tone deepening with a fierce hunger that's also mixed with fury, clearly pissed that she's playing with his emotions. "I'm going to throw you down and fuck you right here in front of the whole fucking school. Mark my words."

Chanel withdraws from him, a cocky smirk across her face, and it's clear that not only does she not feel the same, but she despises the guy. "Just fucking try me, Logan Morgan. It's never going to happen."

"Ouch," I murmur a little too loudly, getting his sharp glare thrown across the table at me.

Logan stands, slamming his hands on the table. "I'm done with this shit," he snaps, his irritated stare falling back to Chanel. "You're not worth waiting for." Logan stares back at Riley. "You coming or are you going to waste your time trying to fuck a chick who doesn't want you?"

"Fuck off, bro," Riley says, laughing at his performance. "Go rub one out in the locker room and calm down, then you can come back here and apologize to Chanel before I deck you."

Logan's stare burns with fury and he storms away just as his twin brother approaches, his wary gaze flicking toward Chanel before glancing back in the direction Logan just went, concern in his eyes. "What the fuck just happened?"

"Logan's just being Logan," Riley tells him. "He's pissed, man. Just give him space. He'll be good by practice this afternoon."

Jax sighs and drops down into Logan's vacated space before reaching across and stealing the french fry right out of Arizona's fingers. He glances toward me. "So, what's up with you?"

"Huh?"

His gaze flickers toward Riley's before turning back to mine. "Before when you were texting, you looked like you wanted to murder someone. That's why this asshole came over here in the first place."

"Oh," I say, glancing up at Riley. "That true?"

"Yeah," he says. "And seeing as though Tanner didn't seem to be brooding any more than usual, I figured it was someone else. I was curious what could have possibly gotten you all worked up like that."

I smile up at him, feeling guilty because at some point, I'm going to have to shut down this strange little crush of his. "It was nothing," I assure him, the girls still listening to my conversation. "Just bullshit drama with some people from my old school."

"Which school was that?" Riley asks, his brows furrowed as though not knowing these tiny details of my life is bugging him to no end.

Glancing over his shoulder, I find Tanner still watching me, and I remember our conversation up on the roof, and I stand by everything that I said—Riley doesn't really like me, he likes the idea of me, likes the idea of a girl he has no chance of getting close to. Because if he did, he'd have to open up and become vulnerable, and guys like Riley simply aren't capable of that ... at least, not yet. One day he'll find that one girl who makes him want to share every aspect of his life, the good, the bad, and the ugly. But until then, I'm not going to be the one to lead him on, not when something between us could cause all sorts of fresh hell between him and Tanner.

"I was at Hope Falls," I tell him. "Nothing fancy like this place."

His brows shoot up. "Hope Falls?" he questions, glancing toward Jax through a curious stare. "No shit. So, you would know the guys on the football team?"

I roll my eyes and let out a heavy sigh. "Unfortunately," I murmur. "Just like the school, they're nothing special either. They're all assholes and will most likely spend the rest of their days washing cars or serving hamburgers."

"You're not a fan of the team, I take it."

"Nope. Not a fan of football. Period."

His eyes bug out of his head, his hand pressing against his chest. "That was like taking a bullet right to the heart," he tells me as Jax grins at his performance. "I'm highly offended, and now you have no choice but to make it up to me."

"I've told you a million times before, Riley, I'm not getting on my knees for you."

Riley laughs and shakes his head, a grin resting on my lips. "As much as I'd like to see that happen, I mean a date. Let me take you out."

I stare at him in horror. "You're kidding, right?"

"Absolutely not."

"But ... why?"

The dude looks gobsmacked and Jax laughs. Watching his friend get shut down is clearly the highlight of his day. "What do you mean, why?" Riley asks me. "I'm hot, you're hot. We'll both look hot together. I can take you to an Italian restaurant and we can do that Beauty and the Beast spaghetti noodle thing and then afterward, we can fuck, and that'll also be hot. I'll even ask before I start recording."

I laugh. "First off," I say, grabbing his arm and shoving it hard off my shoulder. "It's Lady and the Tramp, not Beauty and the Beast, and second, how many times do I need to tell you no before you'll get the hint? You've been going hard for the last two days when it's clear that you and I are not going to be a thing. I think you're a cool guy and all, you're probably a great football player too, but why bother with me when you can stand on this very table and tell the whole school that you're available and have nearly every last girl around here spreading their legs without question?"

Guilt flashes in his eyes and he glances toward Jax before looking back at me. "I, ummm—"

"Holy shit," I gasp, realization dawning on me. "It's a bet, isn't it? You have some sick bet about who can fuck me first, right? Tanner put you up to this to humiliate me, didn't he? He wants to call me out for giving myself up and label me the new school slut. Get fucked."

Ilaria scoffs, shaking her head. "What did I tell ya?" she says, a disgusted bite in her tone. "These guys are nothing but assholes."

"No, no," Riley rushes out. "That's not how it went down, I swear, that wasn't my inten—"

Disbelief pounds through my chest, and before I get a chance to even think about what I'm doing, I'm stepping up onto the table with every eye in the cafeteria staring back at me while my gaze remains locked on Tanner Morgan's. "This is a public service announcement," I say proudly, cutting off whatever bullshit explanation Riley was about to throw in my face. "To all the gorgeous women in this room, this is your official warning that Riley … wait—"

Leaning down, I meet Riley's nervous stare. "What's your last name?"

"Sullivan."

"Right, thanks, cupcake."

I straighten up and address my audience again. "That Riley Sullivan is a man whore. It's only my third day at Bradford Private, and already this asshole sitting beside me is trying to convince me to spread my legs so he can win some bullshit bet. Real gentleman. Third freaking day, ladies. Watch your backs around guys like this. They're only after one thing."

A round of applause sounds through the room, quickly followed by an echoing boo aimed at Riley, and as I climb back down to my seat, he simply stares at me, his eyes filling with wonder. "Yeah, if I wasn't in love before, I sure as fuck am now."

Well, shit.

CHAPTER 15
TANNER

The ball lands in my hands, and without skipping a beat, I clock Logan already taking off, sprinting down the field with Jax and Hudson taking off after him. My arm rears back as I launch the ball through the air, watching Jax and Hudson do what they can to intercept.

They get close, but nobody on this team is as fast as Logan, especially after the bullshit with Chanel at lunch. Logan has a skill for channeling his rage and putting it into his training, and right now, he's un-fucking-stoppable, desperately trying to work it out of his system. He jumps, springing high into the air, and plucks the ball out of the sky before effortlessly hitting the ground and continuing a few steps.

"Nice," Coach Wyld says. "Again."

The twins and Hudson jog back, exhaustion heavy on all their faces. We've been running drills for the past hour, but I can tell from the lack of commentary from Coach Wyld that this will be the last one.

It's been a long day and an even longer week, but no one expected this season to be easy. Coach has been riding our asses hard. He wants that championship just as badly as we do, and he's making sure we put in the work to make it happen. We all fucked around during the summer, and it's an adjustment getting back into the routine, but I know the boys can handle it. They'll pull through. They'll push themselves to the breaking point and then push themselves some more.

Everybody gets into position, and on Wyld's whistle, we run the drill again flawlessly. The ball sails perfectly into Logan's waiting hands, and out of habit, I glance toward Coach Wyld, waiting for his approval despite knowing we won't get it. The only time the asshole has ever cracked a smile was after we won that big-ass trophy at the end of last season, and even then, it only lasted all of three seconds.

"Right, pack up this shit and hit the showers," he calls to the team. "We've got a big session planned for tomorrow, so don't fuck around. Get a good night's rest and come prepared to work hard."

With that, he's gone, and the boys and I quickly go about cleaning up the field, knowing the sooner we get it done, the sooner we can get out of here.

Walking into the locker room fifteen minutes later, Riley's booming laugh bouncing off the walls gives me an instant headache. All I want is to get home and put today to rest, but apparently, I can't do that without dealing with Riley's bullshit first. Don't get me wrong, I love the guy, but sometimes he doesn't know when the hell to shut up. "You fucking know it, man," he says as I round the corner into the lockers to find his back to me, tearing off his sweaty uniform. "Two days left to bone the bitch, but you know me, all I need is fifteen minutes."

Anger pounds through my system, knowing he's talking about Brielle. He's been bragging about it all week, and the closer he gets to her, the more it fucks with my head. She has no interest in fucking him, but I don't know her all that well. Riley is an easy fuck, he'll screw any woman who'll offer him a good time, and if Bri gives him even a hint that she's down, he'll see her as nothing more than a target to add to a long list of women.

And if he does, if he touches her, I'll fucking kill him.

Jax watches me over Riley's shoulder as I make my way to my locker, and as I see his eyes sparkle, I know he's about to stir the pot. "Don't know about that," he says to Riley. "Seems your girl already has her pussy wet for someone else."

A grunt tears from the back of my throat as I open my locker and glance back at Jax, his eyes already on me. "Call her his girl one more time and see what happens."

Jax laughs, rubbing his hand over his bare chest. "Ooooh, getting attached, cousin?" he says, delight brimming in his eyes. "Tell me, whose fucking girl is she? Yours? You claiming that fine ass officially?"

My teeth grind together as I clench my jaw, venom pooling in my stare. Fucking asshole, he knows damn well I'm not about to claim her as my own, but the very thought of her belonging to someone else … fuck. I need to shake this.

Last night, up on that roof, touching her, feeling her body against mine ... that was dangerous. Too fucking dangerous. The lines are blurring, and I can't handle it. I'm spiraling out of control.

I turn back to my locker and reach for my things. Fuck this. I'll shower at home. I barely get a chance to close my locker before Riley is there, his heavy arm draping over my shoulders. "Come on, man. We're only fucking around. I know you're into her, which is exactly why, after the races on Friday night when I fuck her into oblivion, I'll share. We could tag team her like old times. Do you think she'll be down for that?"

Rage shatters the little control I have left, and I grip my best friend and slam him up against my locker. "The fuck did you just say?" I roar.

"Chill, bro," he laughs, his eyes darkening, knowing exactly where this is leading but doing absolutely nothing to defuse the situation. "Why does she have you so worked up? She can be our little secret. Suck you off while I fuck her from behind."

My fist slams against his jaw and he shoves me back, anger bursting through me like never before, anger for not understanding what the fuck is happening with Brielle, anger for what happened to my sister, anger that she's not fucking waking up, anger that my father is always away when my mother needs him by her side.

Riley hits me right back as our teammates crowd around, half of them urging us on while the other half try to pull us apart. He gets a clean shot to my gut, but I fire back with another, splitting his lip. "That all you got, asshole?" he spits. "Fucking hit me harder."

I push him hard, my knuckles bleeding as we beat the shit out of each other, but with every punch, I feel that anger burning out of me until I'm able to relax enough for Hudson and Logan to tear me off him, both of us panting and covered in blood.

I get to my feet, keeping my stare on Riley and without saying a damn word, each of the boys finally get just how messed up I am over this girl, despite preaching that she means nothing to me. Riley nods and just like that, I storm back to my locker, grab my shit, and get the fuck out of here.

I'm home within five minutes, pushing through the front door and storming up to my room. I see her through my window, but I don't stop to linger as I move through to the bathroom, the ride home doing nothing to ease the rage boiling through my system. Beating the shit out of Riley helped, and on some level, I think he pushed me on purpose. He's been watching me all too closely this week, he knew I needed that outlet, and I don't doubt that sooner or later, he'll be wanting to talk it through. I hate that I used his face as a punching bag, hate that I split his lip, but that's just how it's always been between us. I can't count the number of black eyes I've come home with over the past few years after Riley's been fucked over by his parents once again.

Bracing myself against the counter, I hang my head, taking a few deep breaths before slowly looking up to find my reflection staring back at me. My eyes are wild, my hair a fucking mess, and there's blood splattered across my face and uniform. I need to check myself. I need to find control before I break.

What I fucking need is to get this chick out of my head.

Yanking my bloodied uniform off, I toss it into the hamper,

turning the hot water on full. It takes only a moment to heat, and I step into the harsh spray before bracing my hands against the cold tiles. Tipping my head forward, I let the hot water rush over me as I try to focus on calming myself.

She's just the new girl, and sooner or later, Channing will be done with them and send them back to wherever the hell they came from, and I'll be done. Addie is going to be okay. She's going to wake up, and she's going to breathe on her own, and then she's going to come to me and demand I put Colby Jacobs in the ground, and I'll do whatever the fuck I have to do to make it happen. I might lose everything, but at least I'll feel like myself again.

Just when I think I've got myself under control, I step out of the shower and I wrap my towel around my waist, catching a glimpse of bright blue eyes staring back at me through the mirror.

The fuck?

Moving to the open doorway, I find Brielle perched on the end of my bed, concern flooding her heated stare, watching me as though she knows I'm straddling the line of insanity. Reaching up, I grip the frame of the bathroom door and stare back at her, letting her see the full rage that's been plaguing me and hating how she doesn't back down from it. "What the fuck are you doing in here?"

Brielle stands and moves across my room, getting closer with every step until she's standing right before me, her eyes scanning over the light bruises decorating my skin. "You look like shit," she tells me, her fingers flinching at her sides, trying to convince herself not to reach out and touch me.

The need for her to brush her fingers across my skin storms through me, knowing that just one touch from her will send a wave of relief settling through my chest. I crave it like never before, but I won't dare beg for it. If anything, she needs to fuck off out of here because every moment alone with her only screws with me more.

I need to push her away. I need this girl out of my head. I can't afford to throw everything I've worked for out the window, and that's exactly what's going to happen if I allow myself to let her in. I have a team to think about, a championship to win, colleges to impress, and none of that is going to happen if I'm obsessing over some girl, a girl who shouldn't matter to me.

It's only been a few days since I first saw her at that party, and already, I'm too fucking deep.

"What are you doing?" I question, my tone filled with venom. "We have one conversation on the roof and you suddenly think we're friends?"

She flinches at my tone, her stare hardening. "*What am I doing?* What the fuck do you think you're doing?" she throws back at me. "I came to make sure you were alright because you stormed in here like a fucking bull, bleeding and out of control, and you want to give me this bullshit attitude? Absolutely not, Tanner Morgan. You don't get to be so hot and cold with me, acting like we're besties one minute then being a complete ass the next."

My glare hardens and I lean into her, that familiar scent of her perfume or shampoo lingering in the air and making me high. I capture her stare and watch as she shrinks under it. "Get the fuck out."

She swallows hard, her stare taking on a rage of its own. "Cut the attitude and just put it aside for like, three seconds," she demands. "You're acting like a fucking idiot all because ... what? Because someone got in your face at training? Maybe said something they shouldn't have? Who fucking cares? It's over, and judging by your cracked knuckles, you let them know they were out of place. So, calm down and get over it for just a minute so I can stop the bleeding."

"What do you think this is?" I question. "I'm not your fucking charity case, Brielle. Get the fuck out and don't come back here. And while you're at it, do me a favor and fuck Riley already."

Brielle scoffs and looks at me as though I'm the most pathetic creature on earth, but the understanding that dawns in her eyes puts me on edge. "That's what this is about, isn't it?" she questions. "Riley has the balls to do something about the way he feels about me and you don't. Well guess what, asshole?" she murmurs, stepping in even closer, her fingers coming up to brush over my chest as she lowers her voice to a breathy whisper. "I think I might give him exactly what he wants. Let him strip me naked and fuck me until I scream his name. Is that what you want? Is that what you need to finally get me out of your head?"

She's fucking lying. She wouldn't spread those pretty thighs for Riley, she wouldn't dare because despite how much she denies it, she's already mine. Doesn't make her words sting any less, and fuck, it only pisses me off all the same.

"You don't know what the fuck you're talking about."

Brielle laughs and steps away from me, moving toward my

bedroom door. "Right," she says, stopping and turning back to me with her fingers curling around the door handle. "You might be able to lie to yourself, but if you want to lie to the rest of the world, try not being so damn obvious about it."

FUCK. Fuck. Fuck. Fuck!

She doesn't wait for a response as she flies out through the door, slamming it behind her. "Bleed out for all I care, Tanner," she calls through the closed door, already halfway down the stairs. I listen as she makes her way out of my house, and before I know it, I hear another door slam from within the house next door.

Anger burns through me, making my chest ache and I walk into my closet, my hands balling into fists. I hate being a fucking ass to her, hate seeing that flicker of hurt shining through her eyes, but I have to. A part of her hates me, and I'm fine with that, but that small sliver of hate mixed with that strange pull between us doesn't keep her away.

No matter how much she hates me, she's going to keep coming back, she's going to keep showing up for me, and keep being drawn toward me just as I am to her.

No, hating me isn't enough. I need Brielle Ashford to despise me.

CHAPTER 16
TANNER

Bile rises in my chest as Jules Macey from my third period math class presses her body against mine, her hands roaming over my chest and arms as her lips press against my neck. The feel of her tongue moving over my skin makes me want to hurl, but I don't stop her. She's been begging for this for three years, so the moment I shot her a text, she was already knocking on my door.

I make it a rule not to have random chicks over at my house, and there's a damn good reason for that, but this is different. I need Killjoy to see. I need her to watch, but most of all, I need her to hurt.

If Brielle Ashford doesn't despise me yet, she will after this.

Jules' fingers grip the hem of my shirt, raising it up over my head and tossing it aside before she greedily roams her hands over my bare chest, trailing them down my abs and rubbing them over the front of my pants, feeling just how hard I am. She groans, her lips still moving against my neck, thinking this hard-on is for her. I figure it'd be a dick move telling her that she's not doing it for me, but that the blonde goddess glaring at me through her bedroom window is what's got me on edge.

Jules pulls her lips free and tries to kiss me, but I shake my head, taking her shoulder and pushing her away a step. Meeting her cautious stare, I lower my voice, letting her know just how serious I am. "You want this, then you play by my rules." I pause, watching as she takes it in. "Is that clear?"

She nods and I raise my gaze back to my window to find Killjoy moving toward it, her stare not daring to lift from mine. She was fucking pissed when she stormed out of here, but this …

I know how this looks, and I've never hated myself more than in this very minute, but I need it to sting. I need Brielle to remember this every time she looks at me, remember why she needs to back away every time she's pulled toward me, and I don't care how many girls I have to work my way through to make it happen.

Jules stands before me in nothing but a lacy white bra and matching thong. She's gone all out with the makeup and thigh-high stockings, and I'm not going to lie, she's sexy as fuck, but I'd prefer to be doing this with the vixen staring at me through her window.

She steps right up to it, her fingers gripping the blinds just as Jules grips the front of my pants and releases my belt. Brielle's eyes flame and she looks as though she could tear Jules to shreds, and fuck, I might just let her, but it's me who should be shot dead for this—not Jules. She's nothing but a pawn in a game she doesn't even know she's playing.

My cock springs free and Jules lowers herself to her knees, making a show of spreading her thighs, letting me see just how wet she is through her sheer thong. I smell her arousal and I struggle to keep hard, but that doesn't stop my hand going to the back of her head and curling her hair around it, taking complete control.

Jules grips the base of my cock with one hand and rolls her tongue over her lips just as my stare lifts back to Brielle's, her piercing glare warning me that she's going to destroy me. Jules opens wide and takes me deep in her mouth, putting on a fucking show as her tongue works over my tip, lapping up that small bead of moisture as though it's hers to take. She bobs up and down, wanting to be the best I ever had, but my eyes are glued to Brielle's.

Her stare falls, watching the way Jules works my cock, fire flaring through her blue eyes and making me feel like the worst fucking prick. Her hurt gaze comes back to mine, and with a hard pull, she yanks her blinds closed and her face falls from view, leaving nothing more than a gaping hole in the center of my chest.

"Fucking hell."

"You like that, baby?" Jules asks around my cock.

"No," I spit, pulling against my grip in her hair, forcing her to release my cock, her mouth dropping in horror and embarrassment. "That's enough. You need to go."

"What? No," she rushes out, gripping onto my thighs and pulling back against my hold in her hair. "I can do better. I promise, you'll like it."

Irritation burns through my veins as I release her hair and take a step back, putting space between us. "Jules," I say, tucking myself back into my pants and reaching for her clothes on the end of my bed. I hand them to her, barely able to meet her eyes. "It ain't gonna happen. I'm sorry, I'm just not feeling it."

Devastation washes over her features as she gets to her feet and starts pulling her clothes back on. "It's that new chick, isn't it?" she questions, watching me a little too carefully. "I get it. You like her and want to fuck her out of your system."

"This has got nothing to do with her."

Jules rolls her eyes and starts working on her pants. "You're the most popular guy in school. You're the fucking captain of the football team for fuck's sake. Do you not think that people notice you? They watch you all the time. We know who holds your attention, Tanner, and you have got it bad for her."

She walks toward me, her hand dropping to my shoulder and slowly brushing her fingertips across my skin. "She's nothing, Tanner. Just some poor bitch from Hope Falls. Fuck her, do whatever you have to do to get her out of your system, and when you're ready for someone more your speed, in your own class, you know where to find me."

Just as she goes to step away from me, my bedroom door flies open and Riley barrels in, coming to a screeching halt at seeing Jules in my room. I sigh, knowing what's coming as his gaze flicks between us before sailing across my room to the window.

His stare falls back to me. "Come on, man, really? Low fucking blow."

Guilt tears through me and I give Jules a shove toward the door. "Time to go."

"But—"

"NOW!"

She scurries away without a backward glance, slipping past Riley in the doorway as he just stares at me, disappointment oozing from his narrowed stare. "It's done," I snap, turning away from him and moving across my room, his eye angry and purple from the beating it took earlier. "I don't want to talk about it."

"It doesn't work that way, bro," he says, walking into my room and dropping onto my bed, his arm propped behind his head. "All you've done is hurt her while making yourself feel like shit. She was enough for you to beat the shit out of me, that's not just something that's going to go away."

I drop down into the armchair across my room, letting out a heavy sigh. "It's done, Riley. After that, she won't look at me again, so you and me, we've got nothing to worry about. The season is ours."

"Drop the fucking act for two minutes," he demands. "This girl is in your head and she's there to stay. I was just fucking with you before. You know I'm not going to stand in your way if you want something serious with her. Just say the fucking word."

"There's nothing to say," I tell him, my gaze unintentionally flicking back to the window. "She's a distraction and I took care of it.

End of story."

Riley sits up, his elbows bracing against his knees. "Right, so if she's nothing but a distraction, then you really won't mind if I fuck her. If I go over there right now and rail her so fucking hard you can hear her screaming my name from here, if I feel her tight little cunt squeezing around my cock … That's not going to be a problem for you?"

My hands curl into fists, anger pulsing through my veins once again.

"Yeah, that's what I thought," Riley scoffs. "Just answer me one thing."

I glance up and meet his heavy stare, nerves pounding through my body like they do right before a big game. "What the hell are you so afraid of? You've got this amazing girl, who for some fucked-up reason can't take her eyes off you. She's fucking stunning with a pair of balls bigger than yours. Any one of us would be happy to have her, so why the fuck are you destroying this before it's even started? Why are you trying to push her away?"

I push up from the desk, unable to sit still. "I told you, I don't want to talk about this."

"You used my face as a fucking punching bag. You owe me."

I scoff. "Don't act as though you didn't swing back."

He indicates to his face, and I know exactly what he's going to say. "I played by the rules. No punches to the face, man, and you got me twice. How the fuck am I supposed to explain a black eye and a split lip to my old man?"

Guilt washes through me and I cringe. "Sorry, man. I'll talk to him if you want."

"No, just stop bitching out and answer my fucking question. Why are you pushing her away?"

"FUCK," I groan, stopping to meet his stare. "Because she's in my head. First thing in the morning, I look at her room to make sure she's up and getting ready. The second I get to school, I search for her piece of shit Honda, I memorize her fucking class schedule, know where's she's going to be every single moment of the day, and even that isn't enough. I'm fucking obsessing over this chick, and I don't know how to turn it off."

Riley gapes at me, never in our twelve years of friendship has he ever heard me talk shit like this. "I umm … shit, man."

"Yeah, you think?" I mutter. "I have a fucking championship to win. I have all of your futures riding on my back and scouts to impress. I can't afford to fuck this up because some girl is growing roots inside my head. Not to mention, Addie is in a fucking coma. What kind of asshole does it make me to be out here thinking about how tight Brielle's pussy is over fucking up the bastard who did this to my sister?"

Riley stands and moves toward me, guilt in his eyes for pushing this Brielle thing so far. "You should have told me, man. If I knew …"

"Don't—"

He cuts me off, not interested in hearing me shrug him off. "You keep going like this and you're going to push her right into the arms of somebody else."

"Maybe it's for the best."

Riley pulls his phone from his pocket and tosses it to me. "Really?" he questions, smugness glistening in his eyes. "I never took you for a liar, Tanner. Check my most recent text and tell me how you feel about that."

Rolling my eyes, I swipe my thumb across his screen and enter his passcode, the same fucking one he's had for six years. Finding his texts, I bring up his most recent and my heart stops, finding Brielle's name at the top. I click on it and scan across the message, my fingers tightening around the phone.

Brielle - Gave it some thought and you're right, things between us would be hot. I'm down tonight if you are.

Searing hot panic tears at my chest. Riley is right, me hurting her is doing nothing but sending her into the arms of someone else, and in a perfect world, that's the outcome I should hope for, but the idea of her fucking some other guy terrifies me.

This text was sent twenty minutes ago, probably right after she pulled her blinds closed, and there's no doubt in my mind that she sent this to Riley because she knew I would find out about it. She knew it would hurt me just like I hurt her, and she'd be fucking right. It tears at something deep in my chest, and I deserve every bit of it, but on the other hand, she knows that Riley is a safe bet. There's no way he'd go over there and fuck her, and she knows it. This message was all about playing me, and it worked just how she wanted it to.

Seeing the look on my face, Riley holds his hands out as if to point out that he never responded. "Got that while I was driving home and came straight here instead. Figured a message like that meant you'd done something to hurt her."

The reminder of Jules weighs down on my shoulders, making me feel like a fucking prick, but I don't regret it. She'll pull away from me and it will probably kill me, but I'll get over it, and eventually it won't hurt so bad.

"Let me guess," Riley says, catching his phone as I throw it back at him. "You don't want her, but nobody else can have her either?" I glance away and he shakes his head, a smirk pulling at the corners of his lips. "She's not going to like that."

"No," I agree. "She sure as fuck won't."

Riley stands and his stomach growls. "Shit, I'm raiding your fridge," he says, walking to the door. "You hungry?"

"I could eat."

We make our way downstairs and Riley doesn't waste any time heading for the fridge. He pulls the doors open and his brows furrow, scanning over the contents before him. "Fuck, man. Where's all the good shit?" he groans. "Your mom always has something good in here."

The fuck?

I move in beside him and glance over the fridge before letting out a sigh, a heaviness sinking into my chest. "She must have been at the hospital all day again," I murmur. "She hasn't taken a fucking break in weeks, but she usually heads home during the day to sleep and make sure the house is in order before heading back for the night, but the last few days …"

I don't need to continue, he knows. He always just knows.

"Why don't you head over there, spend the night with Addie, and send your mom home. She could probably use her own bed."

A scoff tears from the back of my throat. "She could, but there's no way in hell she'll actually leave. She's terrified something will happen and she won't be there to hold her hand. We'll both end up crashing there and that's not helping anyone. Besides, every time I suggest staying, she gives me the, *you need your rest for football speech.*"

"Shit, man," Riley says, closing the fridge and pulling out his phone to order in. He drops down in front of the breakfast bar and props his elbows on the counter as he scrolls through his options. "You know," he says. "All you have to do is say the word and you and I will go and deal with Jacobs ourselves. Plus, you know the boys have our backs too."

I shake my head, desperately wishing we could go right fucking now. "Thanks, man," I say, giving him a tight smile, "but no. As much as I hate to admit it, Mom's right. We have to let the law handle this, otherwise all we're doing is throwing away the futures we worked so hard for. Trust me, if there were a way, we'd already have fucked him up."

Riley nods in understanding. "You should talk to Bri about it. She—"

"The fuck?" I demand, cutting him off. "Why the hell would I talk to her about it?"

"She went to Hope Falls," he explains, making something Jules said flash in my head. "She mentioned something today at lunch and it didn't seem as though she had high opinions of the football team. I don't know, this is your business to deal with however you're comfortable. I just think she could probably offer some insight."

"Right," I say, shaking my head. "Like she'll want to sit down and chat with me about the good old days at Hope Falls after what I just did to her."

Riley shrugs his shoulders. "Worth a shot for Addie's sake."

I fucking hate it when he's right.

Not wanting to discuss it any further, I point toward his eyes. "We good?"

He grins and holds out his fist. "Solid," he says as I bump his fist with my own. "But for the record, I fucking smashed you. You're losing your edge."

"Yeah?" I ask, holding my hands out wide. "I'm ready for round two if you want another black eye to match the first. Call it a two for one deal."

Riley laughs and glances up at me, his lips pulling into a wide grin. "Speaking of two for one deals," he says, his brows bouncing, letting me know exactly where this is going. "I swung by Mikenna's place last night and Shantel was there."

"Fucking hell, Riley. Tell me you didn't."

He laughs, looking at me with pride flashing in his eyes. "What the hell was I supposed to do? Say no? Fuck off," he laughs. "Just because Bri has you by the balls doesn't mean I'm not free to swing my cock around, and damn it, bro, I had them on their knees and came on both their faces like a fucking super-soaker 2000."

A grin cracks across my face but he's not nearly done. "Now, if you really want to put Bri behind you, I'm down to swing by Mikenna's again. I'm sure they wouldn't mind adding you to the mix. Just say the word and I'll make it happen." His eyes spring wide with excitement. "Wanna gangbang? I'm sure Jax and Huddy would be down. Trust me, they could handle it, maybe even bring a few of their friends and it can be a party."

"Riley, dude … You're my best friend and I'll always have your back, but I'm not hosting a fucking orgy with you."

He rolls his eyes and shakes his head. "What happened to you, bro?" he sighs dramatically. "The girl showed up and next minute, you're plucking those big-ass balls from between your legs and handing them over. I hope you're happy because now I have to ask Jax, and that fucker always gets way too handsy with me."

CHAPTER 17
Brielle

Erica stumbles out of my car, already wasted before we've even made it to the party. I hastily climb out and lock the car behind me, and I'm left to scurry after her, making sure she doesn't get lost in the crowd and accidentally offer herself up as the lead performer in an orgy porno.

Who knows what could happen tonight. It's the first public party these assholes have thrown since the night that girl was hurt. Nobody really knows what happened or who was involved, just that someone attacked a girl and basically left her for dead. Nobody knows who she was or where she came from, so I can only assume that she was from out of town. Either way, it left every single girl terrified of going out.

You hear stories all the time of what could happen on a night out, and you keep yourself alert, but in the back of your head, you're telling yourself that the chances are so slim, that it'll never happen to you. Then BAM, the very thing you've been warned about happened in the very next room while you were sipping on vodka sunrises and dancing as though you didn't have a care in the world. Just the thought of that night makes me sick.

I spent the rest of my summer being the designated driver, watching over my friends' drinks, and opting for a movie night over going out—not that there were many options after the attack. If there was even a whisper of a gathering, the cops would knock on the door and shut that shit down, but I don't blame them. It was certainly frustrating for some, but I was grateful. I didn't want to see any of my friends get hurt.

School has been back for a week, and while Ilaria, Arizona, and Chanel wanted me to go out with them, when Erica told me the first public party since the attack was going down, I couldn't resist coming to clear my name. I've spent the last five days insisting Colby's bullshit comments and lies haven't bothered me, but now that I'm about to see the people he's been talking to, the idea of clearing my name is just too important. Hell, if I get the chance to sucker punch the asshole in the process, then even better.

Besides, the thought of going out with the girls and running into Tanner doesn't sit well with me. I knew he was an asshole, but I also thought there was something growing between us. How fucked up is that? Seeing him through his window with that girl stung, which is ridiculous. He's not mine and I'm sure as hell not his. I've got nobody to blame but myself. Everyone warned me he was an asshole, and I just had to go push it. I suppose it's better to have found out before I allowed things to get too deep.

Not going to lie, I haven't stopped thinking about it. I can't stand the guy or his bullshit attitude and games. Yet, seeing him with her cut deeper than walking in to see Colby with Ilaria, and he was my damn boyfriend. Tanner is nothing, a nobody, just some dude who lives next door. Yet I can't stop replaying it.

It was a low blow messaging Riley and asking him to come over. A part of me hoped that he saw my message for what it was—a bluff designed to strike back at Tanner, and I think it worked, but that doesn't change the fact that I feel like a stone-cold bitch for doing it. I'm glad Riley never came over, and while our friendship is new, I feel as though I've put an awkward strain on it. He hasn't been his usual flirty self and while that's a relief, I can't help but wonder if I've hurt his feelings by being all too willing to use him as a pawn against Tanner.

All I know is that from here on out, I am officially done with Tanner Morgan. He set out to hurt me, and that's exactly what happened. I'm done playing his games and I'm done retaliating.

Racing to catch Erica, I meet her by the front door of the modest Hope Falls home. I've been here a million times over the past few years with countless parties, but I don't exactly know the guy who owns the place. Don't get me wrong, I know who he is, saw him around school every now and then, but I never paid him much more attention than that.

Familiar faces linger around the house, and out in the garden, some poor girl is already throwing up in the bushes. Rookie error. If you want to drink and have a good night, then you can't hit it hard too fast. You need to know your sweet spot, need to know how much you can have before you start acting like a fucking idiot and embarrassing yourself. For me, it's four shots and five raspberry Cruisers. After that, I end up wearing someone else's bra, stealing watches, and sleeping in Harden Tully's mom's freshly planted garden while snuggling a gnome with his pants down.

Erica's arm loops through mine and together we step through the open door. Bodies fill every available space as the smell of sweat, alcohol, and stale cigarettes linger in the air.

It's dark inside and nearly impossible to see where we're going. If it weren't for the cheap fairy lights strung from the ceilings, we'd be up shit creek without a paddle. The bare minimum effort was put forward for tonight's party, but I didn't expect much else. Around here, all you need are four walls and a bathroom to throw a party.

Erica's excitement is contagious as she drags me through the front part of the house, squeezing past dancing bodies and trying to ignore the couple who have barricaded themselves up against the wall, trying to be discreet about the girl's hand down the front of his pants.

We barely get a few feet into the living room when a loud, piercing sound cracks through the room. "RICCA!"

"Oh, fuck," Erica says, her eyes going wide, trying to find the face through the crowd that belongs to that voice.

There's only one person around here who calls her Ricca and despite Erica's attempts to get her to stop, it just seems to keep happening. She hates it, and I hate it simply on principle, simply because I can't stand the vile creature who decided it was a thing.

Jordy Fucking Livingston.

The bane of my existence pushes her way through the crowd, practically demanding a path to clear for her. She's the kind of girl who believes a crown belongs on her head. Her opinion of herself is outrageous while the rest of the world spends their time dodging her presence in the hopes of just a mere moment of peace.

Jordy is vile and mean and lives off the excitement of exposing others' secrets—the darker the better. When she's coming for you, the only thing you should do is run.

Erica and I have made it our sole obsession to avoid Jordy, and so far, we've been doing an alright job of it, until now. I suppose I couldn't get out of Hope Falls without falling victim to her bullshit one more time. It's almost like a rite of passage. Once someone has suffered at the hands of Jordy Livingston and made it out alive, they may forever more be dubbed with the title of badass, motherfucking survivor bitch.

Jordy barrels toward us, and before we get a chance to fade into the crowd, she's right there, throwing her arms wide and slamming into Erica's chest as though she were her best friend. She gives Erica a tight squeeze. "Ohemgee," she squeals, reminding me far too much of the rich girls from Bradford. "I didn't know you were coming."

My brows furrow as I watch the scene unfold before me. There are a lot of things I can handle, but Jordy Livingston creeping on my best friend ain't one of them. Jordy refuses to release Erica from her clutches, and as Erica meets my stare over Jordy's shoulder, her expression tells me everything I need to know—this feeling definitely isn't mutual, and no matter how much she tries to poach my best friend while I've been away, nothing is going to change.

Erica puts her hands up between them and shoves against Jordy's shoulders, pushing her away. "Ummm … what the hell was that?" she asks, the disgust loud and clear on her face.

Jordy laughs it off as though it's some kind of secret between friends. "Oh, girl. You're too cute," she says, hovering close to Erica before glancing toward me, her expression faltering. "Oh," she sighs. "You're here."

"Well, someone has to be here to keep the vultures away."

Jordy rolls her eyes. "Don't you have a whole new pool of cocks to be sucking? We don't want you here."

A smirk pulls at my lips. If this bitch wants to throw down and start firing insults, then I'm all in. "You're right, but would you believe that after only one week, I've already sucked off every last one of them. You know these bruises on my knees aren't from praying." I pause, watching as she scoffs and rolls her eyes before glancing toward Erica as if she's about to back her up, only to get a scowl in return. "What about you? Found anyone to dust out those cobwebs? You know the way I hear it, Colby is more than available. I know how you like to go after my dirty leftovers."

"The guy deserves a fucking award for putting up with your shit, but the way I hear it, I'm not the only one who wants him." She pauses, glancing toward Erica, and I laugh at the mere suggestion. Nice try, but no. She despises him almost as much as I do.

Seeing that she doesn't get the reaction she was hoping for, she continues. "How much of a bitch does someone have to be to spend months cheating on someone only to talk shit about them behind their back the moment it's over? Fucking hell, Brielle. Have a little self-respect. No wonder he dumped your bitch ass. You look like such a desperate whore. I wouldn't even be surprised if you really had worked your way through Bradford already."

Erica snorts a laugh and steps away from Jordy, moving closer into my side as she looks her up and down, preparing to go in for the kill. "What's the matter, Jordy? Why so sour? Is it because even with his dick swinging around like a revolving door, he still wouldn't touch you, or is it because Blake Darcy shut you down again? You know I heard he's been railing Miss Douglass every Friday after football practice in the teacher's lounge."

"No way," I laugh, glancing at my best friend. "That Miss Douglass is fine. If I were hitting that, I wouldn't want a piece of an overused, bitchy high school skank either."

"Right," Erica agrees before turning back to Jordy. "You don't stand a chance with a guy like Blake Darcy. Though, I'm sure you could get that kid ... what's his name?" she ponders, glancing back at me. "The one who picks his nose when he thinks no one's looking."

"Dale Cummings?"

"Yeah, that's the guy," she beams, turning her violent stare on Jordy. "I'm sure he'll be down to help you clear out those cobwebs. Might need a little training first though."

"Don't worry about me, whore. I've been fucking your brother for the last six months."

Oh fuck.

Erica's fist comes out of nowhere, striking forward and slamming against Jordy's nose like a freight train driving straight through a brick wall. Jordy flies back, nobody stopping to catch her, and as she falls to the ground, Erica moves in, hovering over the bitch and watching as blood spurts from her nose like a fountain. "MY BROTHER IS FIFTEEN, YOU FUCKING PEDOPHILE," she roars, her voice traveling over the whole fucking party, gaining the attention of every last asshole in the room.

Reaching forward, I grip Erica's wrist and pull her back to me, trying to calm her, but there's no stopping this girl when it comes to her little brother. Her parents work so much that she practically raised him herself. "Come on," I tell her, knowing all too well how anger and alcohol aren't a good mix for her. "Let's get out of here. There's a Bradford party we could go to instead."

She shakes her head, her gaze falling back to Jordy as a scowl settles across her lips. "No," she spits. "We came here to do something and we're not leaving until it's done."

"It's okay," I tell her, trying to fight for her stare. "We can do it some other time. We can find another way."

"No, we have to do it now. I'm sick of having people talking shit all the time. It ends now."

"Okay," I tell her, slipping my hand into hers and pulling her deeper into the dancing bodies until we can no longer see Jordy sprawled out on the ground, bleeding all over the floor.

We move toward the big entertaining unit, and she slips my phone out of my hand before lunging for the big-ass TV mounted on the wall behind us. Bringing one foot onto the coffee table, I hoist myself up, the heavy, thumping music dying in the same instant.

The partiers look around in concern, probably thinking the cops are about to raid the place like every other party they've been to in the past few weeks. "GOOD EVENING HOPE FALLS," I sing loudly to the gathered crowd as they turn to look at me, their brows furrowed with confusion. "I won't keep you long. I know you're eager to get batshit wasted and fuck your best friend's girl, so I'm here to clear a few things up."

"SLUT," comes hollered from the crowd.

I laugh and point at the fucktard across the room, clapping my hands together in applause. "Wow, that's an original one," I cheer him on. "Good job. I bet your momma is so proud of you."

"THE FUCK ARE YOU DOING?" I hear Colby screeching through the room, bodies flying out of the way as he barges through the crowd to get to me. He moves in front of me and the anger in his eyes turns to fear as he glances between me and Erica, knowing damn well that I hold his reputation in the palm of my hand.

God, I really haven't missed this asshole over the past week.

"Oh, hey," I say, leaning down and giving him a dazzling smile before bopping his nose and being as condescending as possible, only to realize too late the white powder dusted across the tip of his nose. "If it isn't my asshole ex-boyfriend. How have you been?"

"Brielle," he snaps, fear in his eyes. "What the fuck are you doing? I've been trying to call you all week."

Putting on an automated phone voice, I tell him, "Unfortunately, the number you have dialed has been disconnected. Please check the number and try again."

Rage boils in his eyes and he reaches for me, gripping me by my hair and holding me to him. "Stop being a fucking cunt," he growls, his mouth barely moving. "I'll destroy you for this."

My hand snaps out, my fingers slamming hard against his Adam's apple, sending him sprawling back. He cries out and falls into the thick crowd before flying back at me, rage in his eyes. Panic tears through me, and I'm narrowly saved by his football friends holding him back to keep him from attacking me.

Smugness tears at me, but I'm not going to lie, I'm shaken. This version of him is a complete stranger to me. The guy I dated was patient and kind, but I'm quickly starting to realize that maybe I didn't know him at all.

Smirking at him, I straighten out and shake it off, determined to finish this. "I've come to set the record straight," I tell him. "Don't you think the people of Hope Falls deserve to know the truth? Though to be honest, I'm a little surprised that you've even had a chance to talk shit with all the random pussy you've been slumming through. You should get yourself checked out. Wouldn't want you getting crabs before a big game."

"Bitch," he snaps, his jaw clenching. "Say one more fucking word, I dare you. See what happens. I have a reputation to uphold, and what do you have? Fucking nothing."

I laugh. What the hell is wrong with males these days? Why do they all insist on being assholes? "Your reputation was shit before, so I don't see what you're so worried about." He glares up at me as I let out a heavy sigh, shaking my head, embarrassed by my own stupidity for falling for this guy in the first place. "What the fuck did I ever see in you?"

"Brielle," he warns.

I scoff and glance up at the crowd listening to their gasps and laughter, knowing what they're seeing on the screen behind me. "I give you exhibit A," I announce to them, glancing back and looking at the image I'd taken of Colby fucking Ilaria last week. Though I've blurred her face, she was all too excited to have her tits shown off to the world. She's proud, what can I say? "My boyfriend, Colby Jacobs, cheating on me with a Bradford girl at a party last week. I'm not the slut, you guys. He is."

"Brielle, stop," Colby spits, reaching for me as murmurs sound throughout the room. I evade his advances and watch over my shoulder as Erica changes the image on the TV to a screen recording that I took, scrolling through the slew of texts and missed calls I've received from Colby over the past week, getting worse as the days go on. "Exhibit B," I announce. "Colby Jacobs being a toxic, desperate asshole and begging me to forgive him, insisting that fucking some other girl was purely an accident, and quite frankly, acting like a little bitch. So, there you have it, Hope Falls. I am not the bad guy here, your captain is. Show of hands, ladies. Who here has fucked Colby Jacobs over the past six months?"

Ten fucking hands shoot high into the sky, and I laugh as I shake my head, feeling like the joke of the century. "Thanks for nothing," I tell them, recognizing each of their faces, every last one of them knowing we were together at the time. "Hope you ladies covered the stump before you humped because that is a lot of shared DNA right there. On second thought, I hope you all get chlamydia."

And with that, a chorus of applause sounds through the room right before someone cranks the music back up. Erica disconnects my phone from the big TV, and I jump down as Colby glares at me. "Lose my number, asshole. I'm done with you," I tell him. "And for the record. You never made me come once. I faked it just to get you to hurry the fuck up and get off me. You wouldn't know how to satisfy a woman even with a step-by-step instruction manual. Grow the fuck up, dude. You peaked in high school and from here on out, you'll be nothing but a has been." I give him a dazzling smile. "Always a pleasure."

Not a second later, Erica's arm slides through mine, determined to get the fuck out of here and enjoy the rest of our night.

CHAPTER 18
Brielle

"What the hell are you talking about?" I say, my eyes searching from left to right along the darkened road, not being able to see a damn thing. "I don't see it."

"Just keep going," Ilaria says, yelling over the insane noise behind her. "There's a shitload of bushland and then the dirt road just sneaks up on you. Don't go too fast or you'll fly straight past it. You can't miss it."

Oh God. I can only imagine where this bitch is trying to lead me. I just dropped Erica off at one of the girls' houses, knowing she'll be more than taken care of after insisting I was done for the night, and before even turning my car back on, Ilaria was on the phone demanding my presence, not taking no for an answer. "Where the hell are you leading me?"

"Uh, uh, uh," she says, laughter in her tone. "I'm not ruining this surprise … Well, maybe surprise is the wrong word for it, but it's damn hot and you're going to be sorry if you pass up on it. So, hurry up and get your sweet ass here before you miss it."

"Miss it? Miss what?" I question, unable to even work out a hint of where she's taking me. "If I get to this place and find out that you've led me into a serial killer's lair, I'm going to kill you myself."

Ilaria laughs. "I swear, girl. It's safe—well, actually, knowing you, you'll probably think this is some kind of serial killer lair, but I swear, you're going to have the best time."

"Oh," I cut her off, hitting the brake as I find the small opening in the bushland and roll toward a narrow dirt road that looks like the one place I don't want to be. "I think I found it, but are you sure about this? Where the hell does this lead?"

"Oh my God," she laughs. "Quit being a whiny baby and get your ass down that dirt road. Trust me, you won't regret it."

Turning the wheel, my tires hit the dirt road, and I let out a shaky breath. If it weren't so late and the sun was actually shining down on this road, it probably wouldn't seem so fucked up, but when I'm driving alone and have no idea where I'm going, my mind can't help but lead me straight to the worst possible scenario. I'm driving toward my death, that's the only way I see things right now, but I power on, determined not to bitch out. "I'm already regretting it."

I can practically hear her rolling her eyes. "Keep going for a few miles and then you'll hit this hill, and once you've cleared that, you'll be able to see."

"See what?"

"I'll start walking up now and meet you by the other cars and then we can go down together?"

"Go down where, Ilaria?" I rush out. "Holy shit, is this some fucked-up rich people initiation bullshit? Are you going to strip me naked, steal my shoes, and make me find my way home with a blindfold on and my hands tied behind my back?"

"Fucking hell," Ilaria laughs. "Who hurt you?"

Her words don't do much to ease the ridiculous images flying through my mind, but I do my best to keep calm. I haven't known her long, but I think I know her well enough to be certain she wouldn't lead me astray. She asks me about the party, and I give her the full rundown of exposing Colby's toxic behavior, and by the time I'm finished, my car is hitting the top of the hill and peering over into the vast property below.

"What in the ever-loving fuck is this?" I gasp, pausing at the top of the hill to take in the massive racetrack below. It's fucking huge with big flood lights shining down on the track. Expensive cars fly around the curves with ease, looking as though they've done it a million times before, spitting dust up from beneath their tires.

Crowds of people hover by the sides, screaming and backing their favorite driver, and I can't wait to get down there. I've never seen anything like it. I mean, sure, there was the occasional illegal street racing in Hope Falls, but nothing like this. "This is insane."

"What did I tell you?" Ilaria laughs, the big floodlights of the parking lot highlighting her soft brunette waves as she makes her way toward me.

I ease my car down the hill and into the parking lot, hating the thought of her walking around here by herself. I've heard way too many stories about young girls walking around dodgy areas by themselves and it never ends well.

With so many people already here, it takes a minute to find a parking space, and by the time I'm cutting the engine, Ilaria is right there, tearing my door open and practically yanking me out of my car. "Come on," she says, the excitement in her tone intoxicating. "I don't want you to miss it."

Trusting her word, I let her pull me along while pressing the small button on my key fob to lock my car. We take off through the rows of cars, and with each step, the excitement drums rapidly through my veins. "Who would have known that rich kids knew how to have fun?" I say, discreetly checking the rows of cars to make sure there's no sleek black motorcycles hidden within them.

"Oh, you've got no idea," she tells me.

The roar of the loud engines is deafening, and I have to yell over them, but I love it. I can almost feel the loud rumbles vibrating through my chest.

A black Camaro whips around the final corner of the track, spitting dirt all over the crowd as they wait anxiously for the winner. They all scream louder, and I find myself pulling Ilaria along faster, my eyes wide with anticipation. I never thought I'd be into something like this, but my eyes are glued to the car racing around the track, the danger and adrenaline spiking high within me. There's no way in hell I'd ever race, but fuck, I'd more than happily stand by the sidelines and soak in the adrenaline.

A white car races after the Camaro, but the Camaro has this in the bag, and not a second later, it flies over the finish line and the crowd goes insane. An unbelievable amount of money changes hands and I gape, horrified by the kind of cash these kids are getting around with. Hell, maybe they just bring more when they're coming to things like this.

"Ilaria. Bri. Over here," I hear hollered through the crowd. My head whips to the left to find Arizona's hand shooting up into the air, waving us down, and we immediately make our way toward her. Chanel stands at her side, her attention locked on the track, all but glaring toward the finish line. I follow her gaze to the track and watch as none other than Logan Morgan steps out of the black Camaro.

Well, damn.

I was expecting a lot of things when I realized this was a racetrack, but seeing Logan come out of that Camaro was definitely not one of them. Nervousness rattles me. If Logan is here, there's a good chance Tanner is too.

"You came," Arizona cheers, throwing her arms around me in a quick hug. "I thought you were going to some stupid Hope Falls party."

"I did," I tell her, my gaze discreetly scanning over the cheering crowd. "And it sucked ass, but this is a million times better. What the hell is this place?"

"Jax and Logan's," Arizona says, her eyes flashing back to the track, watching as a throng of people surround Logan and his Camaro, jumping around him and cheering for his win. "Their dad owns a crap-ton of properties around here. He's a bigshot movie producer and is never here, so he hasn't even noticed that the twins turned this place into a racetrack."

My eyes bug out of my head, secretly impressed. "Are you serious? Jax and Logan did all of this?"

"Yup," she says, popping the *p*. "Don't get me wrong, they didn't set out to create some kind of illegal racing ring, it just kind of happened like this. I guess the guys started by just using the property to fuck around and one thing led to another and now this is the place to be every Friday night."

"I'm not going to lie, it's kinda cool," I tell them. "Though, I can't say I expected this from them. I mean, Logan—yes. He seems like the type to thrive on this bullshit, but Jax? I don't know. I haven't spoken to him much, but he doesn't strike me as the racing type."

"He's not," Chanel calls back, her eyes still locked on the Camaro, disdain spilling from her sharp glare. "He's the brains behind the whole thing. He's the one who turned this from a few friends fucking around into a profitable under-the-table business, but don't let that fool you. The dork can still drive like a fucking maniac."

Ilaria scoffs. "That's putting it nicely," she laughs. "All of them are fucking psychos on the track. They're savages."

"Who do you mean by *all*?" I ask, hating how my heart picks up and thunders erratically, just hoping that she'll mention Tanner's name, which is absolutely ridiculous. I shouldn't want to see him, shouldn't crave that spike of adrenaline at hearing his name and seeing him outside of school and home. After all, sitting up on that roof, I was the one who said that the moment he climbed back down, we'd go back to hating each other. How was I supposed to know that after that, he'd set out with the intention to make me ache? I should be running for the hills. "Who else races?"

"Everybody with a car," Ilaria scoffs. "As long as you've got the guts to do it and the ability to shrug it off when you total your car, then you're good to race. Jax and Logan make it pretty damn clear that they're not liable for your fuck ups."

I laugh and shake my head. "Guess that puts me off the roster. If I total my car, I'll be fucked."

"Girl, same," Chanel says. "If I even thought about racing, my dad would ground my ass for the rest of my life."

"Oh, look," Ilaria says, pushing up onto her tippy toes to get a better look. "This is the final race of the night, the one we've been waiting for."

I look down to the track but don't see what the hell she's looking at or how she even knows there's about to be another race when Logan's Camaro is still parked at the finish line with the crowd swarming around him. "I don't see anything."

"Come on," Ilaria says, gripping my hand and tugging me through the crowd of onlookers. "Trust me when I say, you don't want to miss this."

We bump past shoulders until we find a space at the very front, and just as I'm about to ask who or what I'm supposed to be looking at, a roaring engine cuts through the night. My gaze snaps across the track to a gunmetal gray Mustang that makes its way onto the track, its thick, black racing stripe down the center of the hood making it look like sex on wheels.

I don't know shit about cars, but I know a Mustang when I see one because my brother was obsessed. It's his dream car and I had to hear about it every morning over breakfast. Fuck, I miss him. He's only been gone a few months, which doesn't sound like much, but to me, it feels like a lifetime. I'd do anything to hear his mindless chatter about cars again.

The Camaro rolls forward until all four wheels are off the track, and I watch as the beastly Mustang gets into position. "Whose car is—" The door swings open and I watch with wide eyes as Tanner Morgan steps out of the driver's seat. "No fucking way."

"Hell to the motherfucking yes," Ilaria says, a sparkle hitting her eye as my stomach all but drops out of my ass. I don't want to be here anymore. "The guy is an asshole, but he knows what he's doing, and I promise you, by the time he's crossing the finish line, you'll be soaking wet."

I groan, rolling my eyes. The last thing I need is to stand here and watch him being the hero of the night. I'm already a mess over this guy. Watching him dominate this track is only going to have me hurting more. "I ... I don't know about this," I say, my face twisting with unease.

Ilaria goes on as if I didn't say a damn thing. "He's at the top of the leaderboard," she tells me as I watch the crowd around me making bets between themselves, some determined to knock the crown off his head, while others can't wait to see him dominate once again. "No one has ever beaten him. Not even Logan."

I scoff and mutter under my breath. "Does it make me a bitch for wanting him to lose?"

Ilaria laughs as headlights appear up on the hill, and a sleek cherry red Ferrari heads toward the track. "Shit, a Ferrari," I murmur, unsure why I suddenly feel nervous for him. "There's no way his Mustang can beat the Ferrari."

Ilaria smirks at me, excitement brimming in her eyes. "Don't doubt him," she tells me. "He races cars like this every week. It's not the car that wins the race, it's the driver, and Tanner Morgan knows what the fuck he's doing."

A thrill shoots through me and I hate myself for it. We watch as Tanner talks to Jax and Hudson by the starting line, and I can't help but keep my eyes on him. As if sensing my lingering stare, his head snaps right toward me, those dark, penetrative eyes boring into mine from across the track.

Shit. I was hoping I'd be able to get through this undetected.

A smugness settles over his face, and as much as I want to smack it off him, I can't help but keep staring. He knows he's captured my full attention. He's had it from the moment I ran into him at last week's party, and I don't doubt the asshole is assuming that I'm here simply to watch him race. If I knew my night was going to end like this, I would have stayed home, but I can't help but succumb to the excitement of the crowd.

He drops back down into his Mustang, the engine revving so loud that it vibrates right through my chest. The Ferrari hits the track and slowly drives around, putting on a show as he goes. I don't know who's driving, and honestly, I don't give a shit.

The Ferrari settles into place, and I watch as the head cheerleader of Bradford Private struts across the track in nothing but a skimpy bikini top and a pair of shorts that lets her ass hang out the bottom. She holds a scrap of material above her head and meets both the drivers' stares through the tinted windshields. It's too loud to hear anything that's going on down there, but that doesn't make this moment any less intense. My hands are balled into fists at my side as nerves pound through my body. Nerves that have no right to be there.

Ilaria said he was good, and I trust her. No one gets to the top of the leaderboard doing something like this without a hint of talent, but I won't truly understand until I can watch him for myself. Logan was amazing and if Tanner is sitting higher than him, I can only imagine just how good he really is. I'm not going to lie, I want to resent the fact that he's so good at everything he does, yet there's a hint of pride that eats at me. I want him to be the best, but just for a moment, I want him to know how it feels to be knocked back, if only a little. I want him to hurt.

Without wasting another second, the cheerleader drops the material, and the two cars take off like lightning, dirt spitting up beneath their tires and leaving a thick cloud of dust behind them.

My eyes are glued to the track, and I find myself inching forward, needing to be even closer. "They have to do three laps," Ilaria tells me, gripping my hand and squeezing as her eyes remain locked on the two cars across the track, the sound of their engines booming in my ears.

The Ferrari is on the inside and as they hit the first corner, he takes the chance to push out in front of Tanner and my back straightens. Maybe Tanner might just get beat after all, but something tells me that he hasn't even gotten started. He's just playing with the guy.

The Mustang sits right on the Ferrari's ass, not allowing him even a chance to get ahead, despite holding the lead. They hit the next few corners and nothing changes, not even an inch between them. "Don't worry," Ilaria says, squeezing my hand and making me realize that I was cutting off the circulation to her fingers, squeezing so hard with the anticipation of the race. "Tanner's just playing with the guy. He attacks once and once only, but he'll make it count."

I bounce on my feet, unable to stand still as I watch the cloud of dust following behind them. They reach the far corner of the track, quickly drifting around it and bringing them back up the other side, effortlessly gliding as though they've done it a million times over.

Fuck it. I don't want him to lose. I want him to dominate this bastard and I want him to make it count, even if it makes me look like a desperate, needy loser who can't let go of something that was never mine in the first place. I can worry about the hurt later, right now, I want to be in the moment, I want to enjoy this for him.

The cars finally reach the top of the track, the corner closest to me, and while they've only been racing for less than thirty seconds, it feels as though a lifetime has passed. The two cars fly past us and my hair swooshes back over my shoulders, the force of them flying by like nothing I've ever felt before. "HOLY SHIT," I boom, my eyes squinting as the dust cloud follows, covering me head to toe, hating that once again, Tanner Morgan is making me feel something. "That was awesome."

There's no doubt about it now. I'm more than wet. If Tanner asked me, I'd climb him like a fucking tree, sit on his shoulders and suffocate him as he ate my pussy like a fucking animal. I'll deal with the fall out after, no matter the cost to my heart.

What the hell is wrong with me?

Tanner remains on the Ferrari's tail as they complete their first lap, and the second is exactly the same, but as they start the third, I sense the Ferrari driver growing nervous. His movements across the track are sharper, jagged, trying to keep an eye on Tanner, waiting for him to make his move, while also trying to push ahead, going faster and faster, but Tanner sticks to his ass like a bad rash.

They whoosh past us for the third time and my nerves spike like never before. They're running out of corners and Tanner still hasn't made his move, but in the very next moment, they hit the last corner, and rather than slowing like the Ferrari does, Tanner speeds up and cuts inside, both cars drifting around the corner at the exact same time, then like lightning, Tanner hits the gas and flies like a fucking bat out of hell.

The Ferrari driver never even saw it coming, but by the time he completes the corner, Tanner is already long gone, proving again that his crown will never be knocked off his head.

Tanner's performance makes me laugh, and I stand here watching, feeling like the Ferrari. I never saw Tanner coming, and by the time I realized what was happening, he was already gone, his crown still firmly intact.

Tanner flies across the finish line, and just like before, the crowd erupts into ear-shattering applause, and I can't wipe the smile off my face. Hell, I might even cheer for the fucker too. I can't tear my eyes off him, watching as he slows and brings the Mustang to a stop, the Ferrari pulling in behind him.

The crowd surges onto the track and Ilaria and I are pushed with them. "Time to party," she shouts just as loud music blasts through the speakers erected around the property. I laugh, my eyes widening in disbelief. I was wrong, rich kids don't just know how to have fun, they know how to shit all over everything I ever knew and blow my fucking mind.

Chanel and Arizona find us, and before I know it, an hour has passed and we're standing on the outskirts of the property, watching over the massive party, our feet aching from dancing and our throats raw from laughter.

It's been an incredible night, made even better by my ability to avoid Tanner and his band of assholes, but it's not hard. All I have to do is search for the crowd and they're right there in the middle of it.

This party is so much better than the lame Hope Falls party I was just at. No wonder we never saw Bradford kids crashing. Why would they come and hang with us when they were partying it up like this? All I know is that I've been missing out.

We talk shit as the girls point out people in the crowd, telling me everything there is to know about my new classmates. I'm filled in on all the town gossip, whose mom is having an affair with whose dad, which family is committing tax fraud, whose parents are dirt poor ... you know, apart from my mom, and most importantly, they share with me the long line of Tanner's conquests. Not that it should matter to me. In fact, I do my best to zone it out, already scarred with the image of Tanner getting his dick sucked through his bedroom window.

Chanel ends up in a drunk fight with Logan, only it seems more like a contest over who can swing their dick around the most. Insults are flying and with Chanel on the verge of tears and Logan looking as though he's only warming up, Arizona rushes in to save her, leaving Ilaria to drag me back onto the track to dance.

It takes all of two minutes for some guy to move up into Ilaria and she grinds back against him, grinning as his hands fall to her waist.

Ilaria's eyes meet mine, and I don't need another word to know that she'll be going home with this guy tonight. My gaze sweeps over Mr. Handsy. He looks nice enough, and since Ilaria hasn't been drinking, I trust her judgment. Plus, she said only people from Bradford come here, so I'm sure she has known him a lot longer than she's known me.

Grinning back at her, I decide that she's more than okay to handle herself, and I leave her to get her skank on. She didn't give me the save me eyes, and if I'm not fast enough, I'll probably end up witnessing the whole deed right here in the middle of the track.

CHAPTER 19
Brielle

Making my way back to our deserted corner on the outskirts of the track, I feel a familiar set of eyes lingering on my body, and I let out a frustrated groan. Nerves spike in my chest, and I'm immediately on guard, every part of me desperately trying to shut out the feelings I've been trying to smother for the past two days.

"Stop being such a fucking creep, Tanner. I know you're there," I say, turning to face the thick bushland and searching through it until my gaze finally settles on him. He's leaning up against a large tree with his hands deep in his pockets, staring intently and making something die inside of me.

"Why are you here?" he questions, that deep, husky tone rocking right through me as the rest of the people enjoy the party, completely oblivious to the pain pressing against my chest.

Determined not to back down or scurry away in fear, I hold my head high, not allowing him to crush me like he did two nights ago. "Trust me, if I knew you were going to be here, I wouldn't have come."

He doesn't respond, just keeps staring at me through those dark, hard eyes. Frustration claims me and I scoff, shaking my head. "You're wasting my time. Is there something you need? Because if you're just going to stand there and stare at me like a fucking moron, then you can kindly fuck off."

No response.

Turning my back to watch the party around me, I grab my bottle of water and take a hasty sip, determined to ignore him, but when a shiver sails down my spine and goosebumps spread over my skin, I know he's moved closer—*a lot closer*.

I feel his breath on my neck just moments before his big hands circle my waist. One of them sweeps low around my body as the other trails up my ribs and over the curve of my breast until it settles loosely around the base of my throat. His lips move to the side of my neck, and I hear him breathe me in, his body moving in tight against mine.

"Whatever you think you're going to get from me, you can think again, asshole. I'm not hanging around for you to fuck with."

"Mmhmm," he murmurs just as his lips press down against my skin.

Every tiny brain cell inside me demands to push him away, to tell him to fuck off, or in the very least, send a fist hurtling toward his balls.

Who does he think he is coming at me like this? Touching me? Putting his lips on me? No, absolutely not. I won't be some pathetic toy he gets to kick around.

My hand falls to his on my waist, and I yank it off before spinning and shoving him hard, sending him back a step. "What the fuck do you think you're doing?" I demand, rage boiling in my narrowed stare. "You want an easy fuck, then go and pick one of those girls who've been throwing themselves at you for the last hour. I'm done with your games. They were fun while they lasted but dealing with the whiplash that comes from a guy who can't figure out what the fuck he wants is exhausting."

Tanner's eyes darken and the desire pooling in them makes me catch my breath. He moves back into me, his hand curling around the base of my throat, his thumb gently roaming over my skin. He stares down at me, his eyes holding me captive. "That's where you're wrong," he growls. "I know exactly what I want."

I swallow hard, my heart screaming in fear. "Don't do this," I warn him, terrified of the way he so effortlessly draws me in when both of us know that this isn't going anywhere. He's going to hurt me, and the longer this goes on, the harder I'm going to fall.

He drags me back into the darkness of the thick trees and I go willingly, blindly following the devil as a shiver rushes down my spine. My fingers tingle and my core clenches with the anticipation of being lost in the dark with him, all alone.

Tanner moves me until my back is flat against a tree and he inches closer, his arm propped up on the tree above my head, caging me in as his wicked, lethal stare locks onto mine. My hand slips up the front of his shirt and braces against his chest, the feel of his bare skin against mine doing things to me that I'm not nearly ready for. I feel the rapid beat of his heart against my palm, and I spread my fingers, my chest heaving with quick, gasping pants. "You need to walk away."

Tanner leans in even closer, his hand at my waist trailing down my body, passing my hip, and sailing right down my thigh, sending goosebumps over every inch of skin he claims. His dark, intense eyes bore into mine, holding me captive. "You and I both know that's not what you want."

Oh, holy fuck.

Breathe, Brielle. Breathe, damn it.

His voice is deep and full of barely-concealed restraint. It's as though he's barely holding himself back, barely keeping in control, and that thought alone makes my heart thunder erratically in my chest, so heavy that if he moves just an inch closer and presses his wide chest up against mine, he's bound to feel it.

I swallow hard, unable to look away. He holds me captive, my body, my heart, my mind. At this moment, everything I am belongs to him. Whatever he wants from me, it's his to take. "You've gone out of your way to make me hate you. You want me to despise you, and it worked, I despise everything you are. This is only going to confuse things."

"Maybe I want to confuse things."

"When is this going to end? Haven't you fucked with me enough?"

"Not even close."

"What more do you want from me?" I whisper, his intoxicating scent breaking me down. "You've already hurt me. Consider me thoroughly played, or does this not end until you've gotten something out of it too? You want me on my knees? You want me to bend over? You want me to give myself over to you completely, fall madly in love with you until you're the center of my world? When will it be enough for you?"

His eyes linger on mine, and I see the truth shining through them. He has no fucking idea. He doesn't know what he wants from me, doesn't know just how much will be enough.

His body moves in even closer, and I crave him more, his lips barely a breath away. "You don't want this, otherwise you wouldn't have pushed me away."

"Don't I?" he rumbles, his tone dropping even lower, desire thick in his voice. "You said so yourself, every time I walk into a room, you're right there, searching for me just as I am you."

I shake my head. "That was before."

He goes on as though I didn't even speak. "When I'm close, your breath catches, and when I touch you …" he says, pausing as his fingers slowly begin moving back up my thigh, making me clench.

He sees my reaction to his touch and a smugness flashes in his eyes, knowing just how right he is. "Don't lie to me, Killjoy. You want this, maybe even more than I do. You might hate me, you might even despise me, and I deserve that, but it doesn't change the fact that you still want me."

I shake my head, unable to think clearly as his fingers continue moving further up. "You've got me all wrong," I tell him. "I'm not the one searching you out in the middle of the night. I see you, Tanner, watching me through my window, your eyes blazing with desperation every time I walk by. You just can't admit it to yourself. You're a man obsessed, and it kills you that you haven't had a taste."

A low growl rumbles through his chest, desire pouring out of him as his lips brush past mine. "What do you want from me?" I repeat.

"You really want to know what I want?" he questions, his hand slipping between my thighs and cupping my pussy, firmly squeezing and sending a wave of desperation crashing through me. "I want to feel you come on my fingers. I want to feel your tight little cunt squeezing me, and I want to watch your face as it happens, hear my name on your lips as the high rocks through you. But what I want most is for you to know that no matter what, no matter who you're with or what you're doing, nobody will ever make you feel as good as I can."

Breathe. Fucking breathe.

My chin raises, my lips moving over his once more. "Is that really what you want?" I question, pausing as I watch him slowly nodding his head. I lower my voice to a breathy whisper, hating just how right he is about me. No matter how much he hurts me, how much my heart crumbles and the pain paralyzes me, I'll still want him. "Then take it."

Tanner's lips crush against mine and I sink into his touch, his tongue sweeping into my mouth and claiming me like no one has ever done before. My heart races, synching with his, and though he's barely even touched me, this is already more than I could have imagined.

I grind against his hand, and he growls deep in his chest before moving up to the waistband of my pants. His hand slips inside my pants, trailing down until his fingers are brushing over my sensitive clit, making me gasp with need. His lips pause on mine, and he smiles against me before pressing down, his fingers rolling over my clit, the pressure just right.

"Holy fuck," I moan into his mouth. My hand beneath his shirt moves up over his shoulder, and I hold onto him for dear life. Just when I think it can't get any better, he pushes two thick fingers inside me, stretching me wide.

"You haven't been back in my room," I say, not sure why I'm choosing this exact moment to bring this up, but it's bugged me for the past two days. I might even go as far as saying that not seeing his messy handwriting across my mirror had disappointed me.

His eyes sparkle, his lips pulling into a wicked grin as he adjusts the angle of his fingers, making me gasp. "Haven't I?"

Well, shit.

I grin back at him, but before I can respond or even think about what I could have missed in my room, his lips are back on mine. My nails dig into his shoulder as he kisses me fiercely, hungry, and powerful, giving me everything I didn't know I needed. Tanner's fingers curl just right and as he pushes them into me, I gasp and clench around him, completely losing myself to him.

His thumb works my clit as his fingers destroy me, making me feel things I've never felt, and shit, I'm going to come, and it's going to be hard and fast. "Tanner," I breathe, my chest rising and falling with sharp, wild pants, wanting so much more.

"I know," he tells me, closing that final gap between us, his body pressed right up against mine. "Give it to me, baby. Let me see you."

My head tips back and I feel his eyes heavy on my face, watching me as I come undone beneath his touch. He applies more pressure to my clit, his thumb rolling over in small, determined circles as his fingers massage deep inside me.

He doesn't dare give up, pushing me closer and closer to the edge until finally, I explode around him. My orgasm rocks through me, and I cry out his name as I squeeze down around his skilled fingers, coming hard. My pussy contracts as my high pulses through my body, my fingers digging into the warm skin of his shoulders while hard, sharp gasps tear from my throat.

"Fuck, Tanner," I breathe, but he doesn't stop, letting me ride out my high on his fingers, pure elation pulsing through my veins.

"Fucking beautiful," he tells me, his voice raspy and filled with desire.

I come down from my high and as he pulls his fingers free, I immediately feel as though a piece of me is missing, but when he brings those same fingers to my lips and pushes them inside, my heart races all over again. I open wide and his eyes flame like molten lava. "Suck."

My lips close around his fingers, and I roll my tongue over them, watching as desire sweeps through his gaze. He slowly draws them out, and before I get a chance to even swallow, his lips are back on mine, tasting me on my tongue.

He groans into my mouth as I melt into him again, not having nearly enough of him. All too soon, he pulls back, his hand falling to my waist and squeezing as he meets my satisfied stare. "Watch yourself, Killjoy," he murmurs, his tone so low it rumbles against my chest. "You were right, now that I've had a taste, I won't stop until I've destroyed you."

And with that, he turns his back and walks away, leaving me staring after him. I sink to the dirty ground, shame filling me as tears well in my eyes. Well played, Tanner Morgan. Well fucking played.

CHAPTER 20
TANNER

"The fuck?"

The photo of Brielle and Colby Fucking Jacobs stares back at me, and anger tears through my body like a fucking freight train traveling a million miles per hour. The weight bar drops down over Jax's chest and he gasps as Riley grunts and pushes me out of the way, grabbing the heavy bar off Jax before it crushes him.

"You're lying," I spit, grabbing Riley by the scruff of his shirt and pulling him in, rage pouring out of me in waves. "Tell me you're fucking lying."

"Sorry, bro," Riley says as Jax sits up on the bench press table, gasping for air, his elbows braced against his knees. "Brielle is Colby's girl. They've been together for six months or some bullshit like that. She told me she went to Hope Falls and last night at the track, Chanel was drunk and telling Logan how Bri was pissed because her friend didn't tell her that Colby was arrested and then mentioned something about the guy cheating on her. It doesn't take a genius to put all the pieces together."

Jax grunts, grabbing his water bottle and spurting it into his mouth. "The fuck is wrong with you, man?" he says, pissed about the crushing weight on his chest. "She's just some fucking chick. Move on. She's not worth it. You've already fucked up any chances you have with her, so forget her. You need to get your head in the game. We're not losing this season just because you're too busy thinking about getting your dick wet."

Riley pulls away from me and starts re-racking the bar, adjusting the weights for Jax's next round. "Six months?" I ask him. "Are you fucking sure? Because that would mean that she was with him when—"

A heavy clink of weights dropping across the room cuts me off, and I glance over at Hudson to find anger pulsing in his eyes. He catches my stare and all too soon, it falls away, focusing on what he's doing.

"I'm sure, Tanner," Riley says, his voice lowering, filled with pain whenever the topic of Addie comes up, just like all the guys do. The image of Addie naked and alone, bruised and abused on that bed has haunted us all. These guys have grown up with me, and that means they've grown up right along with Addison. She's as much their sister as she is mine. "Have I ever been wrong about this shit?" he asks.

"That photo was taken last night."

Last night.

Fucking hell. If she's with that motherfucker, then last night in the trees …

No, I can't think like that. She's his girl, so what the fuck does that make me? *A joke, that's what.* Is she in on this? Does she know what he did to Addie? Know how he left her for dead, know how he made her scream? Fuck. No. I refuse to believe that. It has to be a coincidence.

I shake my head. "Nah, it's not possible. Brielle was at the track last night. *I* was with her last night."

Jax lays back and Riley gets into position, spotting him as he lifts the heavy weight off the rack. "I don't know what to tell you, man. She didn't get to the track till late, you know that. You fucking saw her drive in. Besides, how well do you really know this girl? She's hot as fuck and she's feisty with a smart mouth that gets me fucking hard, but apart from that, you don't know shit about her. What if she's just trying to get close to you for him?"

"You're wrong," I tell him, holding up the phone and showing him the photo of Bri standing on a coffee table during some cheap party with Colby Jacobs standing right in front of her. His hand is reaching out to her and she's bending down to him, a dazzling smile on her face as she looks at the dude like she's never been so fucking in love. There's no way. This chick … no. I don't believe it, I can't. If she's his girl, then she was with him during the time he attacked Addie six weeks ago, and I can't fucking live with that.

"Suit yourself, man," Riley says. "You asked me to find out

everything there is to know about the fucker, and I did that. I'm just sharing the facts, but don't say I didn't warn you."

"FUCK!"

Anger boils through my veins as I pace through the twins' home gym. I can't stay here. I need to get to the bottom of this. I was with her last night. I fucking kissed her, tasted her, and now my best friend wants to tell me that she belongs to some other man—the same fucking man who hurt my sister. Get fucked. This isn't happening.

Unable to control the vile thoughts infecting my mind, I fly out the door, and before I'm able to even focus on what I'm doing, I'm already tearing down the road, the wind slamming against my chest as I push my motorcycle to its fucking limits.

After pulling into my driveway, I tear my helmet off my head and hang it from the handlebar before cutting across the front lawn onto Channing's property. I don't bother jumping the fence and slipping in through the kitchen window that's always left open, instead, I go straight for the front door.

Brielle's car is out front, and I don't give two shits about anyone else who might be inside the house. Hell, I don't care if they demand I fuck right off. They can say whatever they want, but nothing is stopping me from going upstairs and getting answers out of that little cock tease who somehow has me by the fucking balls.

The door is unlocked, and I push it open, not bothering to close the fucker behind me. Conversation comes from deeper in the house, and I can only assume that's Bri's gold-digging mother, but seeing as though she's distracted with whatever the fuck she's doing, I don't bother making my presence known. Instead, I turn for the stairs and skip up them two at a time.

Her bedroom door is locked, and it's only slowing me down. I back track a few steps to the linen closet down the hall and close the door behind me, reaching up to the crawl space in the ceiling and pushing gently against the door until it slides away. Gripping the edge, I pull myself up into the ceiling, feeling like a fucking creeper, just like every other time I've done this. Crouching as I move through the dark attic space, I take the two steps toward the familiar opening and move the piece of ceiling out of the way before dropping straight down into the middle of Brielle's closet.

I hear the shower running through the adjoining wall and I push my way out through the closet, not hesitating before throwing the bathroom door open and forcing my way inside.

Brielle shrieks and I'm not going to lie, my gaze drops to her naked body, taking in her subtle curves, her perfect full tits and toned waist. "THE FUCK DO YOU THINK YOU'RE DOING?" she yells, throwing her hands up to cover her body, her eyes wide with shock.

Clenching my jaw, I launch her towel through the shower door, and she scrambles to wrap it around her body. "You think because you made me come on your fingers that you can just storm your way in here like some kind of barbarian? Like you're suddenly entitled to my body? What the actual fuck, Tanner? Get the hell out of here."

I slam my phone up against the glass of the shower, showing her the image from the party last night, rage burning through my stare. I don't even care to spare a second glance at her dripping body. "Are you

Colby's girlfriend?"

Her eyes snap to the image and her brows furrow before turning her furious stare back on mine. "What the fuck is wrong with you?" she demands, pushing her way out of the shower and adjusting the towel around herself, boiling with fury. "You come storming in here, bust into my bathroom with absolutely no regard for my privacy just to ask me if I have a boyfriend? Are you that fucking insecure?"

What a fucking joke. Insecure? Me? She clearly hasn't been paying attention, and if I weren't so pissed off, maybe I'd let her know, but not now. I step into her, the rage taking control as my gaze darkens, knowing just how intimidating I can be. Hell, the shit I've put her through is nothing compared to what I'll do if I find out she's been playing me. "Is Colby Jacobs your fucking boyfriend, Brielle. Yes or no?"

"No," she grunts, slamming her hand against my shoulder and forcing me back a step. "What the hell is wrong with you?"

"Was he ever your boyfriend?"

"What does it matter?" she demands, storming out of the bathroom and into the closet, grabbing a dressing gown and pulling it on over her towel and tying it firmly at her waist. "Better yet," she continues as I follow her into the closet and watch her rip the towel out from beneath the robe. "How is it any of your goddamn business? After you just left me in the woods last night with some bullshit comment about destroying me, you now think you can come in here and ask me bullshit like this? I know you're used to swinging your dick around and getting whatever you want, but it's not about to happen here. I'm done with your shit."

"I swear to God, Brielle, just answer the fucking question."

Bri storms out of the closet, completely missing the fact that the attic above her head is wide open, giving away all of my secrets. "Look," she says. "Whatever you think was between us, it's over. The messages on the mirror were cute, but you're crossing so many lines coming in here like this. This is not okay, so fuck off before I find someone to remove you."

"You think I want to be here right now?" I spit. "I will happily fuck off, but unfortunately for you, I'm not going anywhere until you answer my fucking question."

Brielle groans and spins around, shooting me with a lethal stare that could rival one of my own. "You're such a fucking prick," she says, moving to her door and hastily unlocking it. "Get the fuck out, now."

I storm across her room, slamming the door shut and throwing her up against it. "Answer the fucking question. How long were you with him?"

Fear rattles her and for the first time, my dick doesn't get hard seeing her eyes widen. "We got together late February and were hot and heavy for a few months. I wanted to break up with him before the summer, but next thing I know, school was starting and he's still hanging off me like a bad smell. I broke up with him last weekend when I caught him fucking someone else at a party."

"You were with him right up until last weekend?"

"What the fuck is this about, Tanner?" she demands, shoving me off her and moving to the furthest corner of the room, keeping away from me as she crosses her arms and glares daggers at me. "You don't strike me as the jealous type, and don't even think about telling me that you wanted to be the only asshole to ever touch me. I'm not about to apologize for having a past. God knows you've probably already slept your way through every girl at school. Not that it should matter because you'll never fucking touch me again after this bullshit."

"Fucking hell, Brielle. This has nothing to do with you and me and everything to do with him."

"What the fuck is that supposed to mean?" she demands. "You're going to have to give me a little more context than that."

I reach my boiling point and storm toward her again, gripping her arm as I press her back up against the wall, hating how just being so close to her calms me while also sending my emotions into a fucking tailspin. "Your boyfriend is the reason my sister is in the fucking hospital, breathing through a goddamn tube. Tell me you didn't fucking know."

Her hands fly up to mine, gripping my fingers and prying them from her skin. "What the hell are you talking about? I don't even know who your sister is."

I know I shouldn't tell her, shouldn't share what isn't mine to tell, but the words pour out of me before I get a chance to stop them. "He drugged my sister and raped her, left her for fucking dead at a party six weeks ago, all while you were shacked up with the fucking bastard."

Bri's jaw drops, staring at me as though I've lost my fucking mind, but I see the moment she connects the dots. Everybody has heard the stories. They know someone was attacked, they just don't know who.

One thing is for sure, she hasn't denied that he was at the party like he told the cops, confirming what I already know—it was him.

"You're joking, right?" she says, throwing my hand back at me. "That's fucking sick coming in here and accusing him of that. I know him. He wouldn't do that. He's an asshole, but he wouldn't ... he wouldn't do *that*. Six fucking months, Tanner. Not once did he try to force himself on me or try to give me anything. You've got it wrong. I know him, and as much as I hate him, he didn't do this, so find some other sorry asshole to pin this on, and when you do, figure out a way not to accuse me of being some kind of accomplice."

"Holy fucking shit," I say, gaping at her in horror. "You're defending him. He was arrested last week, and you want to stand here and tell me that I don't know what the fuck I'm talking about. Don't be so daft, Brielle. Your boyfriend is a fucking rapist, and you just stood at his side like an idiot, completely blind to what was going on right in front of your face. Where were you that night, huh? Were you at the party? Why the fuck weren't you spreading your legs for him? Why'd he have to steal it from my sister instead?"

Her hand lashes out, burning across my face with a ferocity I wasn't ready for, and I take a step back, knowing damn well that I deserved it. Hell, I feel sick at the fucking vile words spewing out of my mouth, but I can't stop them from coming. This isn't who I am, but when it comes to my sister, there's not a damn thing I wouldn't do to protect her.

"I get it," she spits at me, unshed tears brimming in her eyes that make me feel like shit. "You're angry and frustrated that your sister is hurting, and you want to fuck up whoever did that to her, but nothing gives you the right to come in here and talk to me like that. I'm nobody's whore, and I sure as fuck don't spread my legs just because some asshole demands it."

She moves back to her door and opens it wide, her icy stare slicing straight through me. "I'm not going to say it again. Get the fuck out and don't ever come at me again."

Clenching my jaw, I struggle to control the rage that demands to fly from my mouth, but I hold it down as I make my way toward her. I move into the open doorway before pausing and fixing her with a hard stare as she seethes right back at me. "I know he fucking did this, and you ... you stood by while it was happening, too fucking blind, and because of that, my sister is breathing through a ventilator, and we have no idea if she'll ever wake up again."

Without another word, I storm out of her room, not daring to look back.

CHAPTER 21
Brielle

Painful heaves tear from the back of my throat as I double over, clutching my stomach.

No, no. I refuse to believe it. Tanner's wrong. He has to be wrong because the alternative … No. There's a mix up, there has to be because even though Colby is the bane of my existence, there's no way he would do that, no way he would drug and rape a girl at a party, a party where I was happily dancing in the next room.

He would tell me he loved me every day, how he couldn't wait to see me. Sure, he had his asshole moments, which I can see clearly now that I'm through with him, but rape?

No … I can't believe it, I don't but—

"FUCK!"

My head spins with everything Tanner just said, trying to replay that night over and over while pushing aside the burning rage pulsing through my veins. How dare he storm in here like that. It's one thing to accuse Colby of such a heinous crime, but to come barging into my room and suggest that his sister was attacked because I wasn't spreading my legs enough is an entirely different kind of fucked up.

I've never felt anger like this, and Tanner is going to get his ass handed to him for this bullshit, but if it's true, if Colby did this, then it's so much bigger than what I'm feeling for Tanner right now. I get it, he was angry and clearly just found out that Colby and I were an item. He's somehow feeling betrayed by that piece of information, but I at least owe it to his sister to try and remember the details, to piece together the information I haven't had to think about since that horrendous night.

I was wasted. I drank just about anything I could get my hands on, and that's partly Colby's fault. When I drink, I'm horny. There's nothing more to it, and he figured this out early in our relationship, so any chance he could get, he'd all but pour the liquor down my throat. Erica thought it was hilarious and would encourage it at every turn, and before I knew it, most of my night was already forgotten. It wasn't until that party where I reeled it in and realized just how dangerous my behavior had been. It could have been any of the girls there that night, and I absolutely hate that Tanner's younger sister was the one.

Tears well in my eyes. I knew from overhearing his phone call with his mom that his sister wasn't at a performing arts school.

Something terrible had happened, but never in a million years did I think she was the girl from the party.

And to think Tanner has been dealing with all of that for the past six weeks. No wonder he's such an asshole all the time. I know had that been me, Damien would have been on the first bus home, doing whatever he could to find the asshole who dared touch me. He wouldn't stop until justice was served, and I know without a doubt that Tanner will do the same.

I just hope he's wrong.

It couldn't be Colby. I couldn't have been that blind.

"Yo," comes a voice from just outside my doorway.

My head snaps up to find Jensen hovering awkwardly, looking as though he'd rather be anywhere but here. I wipe my face, not realizing the tears had fallen. "What?" I question, somehow managing to keep the venom out of my tone.

"I, ummm … heard you yell. Are you good?"

Taking a deep breath, I wipe my face a few more times before straightening out and trying to find some semblance of control. I give him a tight smile, pleased to find that for the first time, I'm not getting any creepy, perverted vibes from him, and I instantly feel like shit for judging him so harshly. "I'm fine," I tell him, taking deep breaths. "I didn't realize I'd yelled. Sorry, I didn't mean to disturb you. I'll be sure to keep any future meltdowns to myself."

He gives a curt nod and vanishes down the hallway, and I have to wonder what the hell he would have done had I said I wasn't okay. He may not have been creepy today, but that doesn't make him any less strange.

Using my foot, I kick the door shut before moving across my room, feeling like a ghost without a soul, just going through the motions as I scoop my phone off my desk and find Erica's name. I hit call and press the phone to my ear as I drop down on my bed, listening as the call rings out.

"Come on," I groan, pressing call again. "Answer."

She picks up on the fourth ring and just a sliver of relief fires through me. "What's wrong?" she questions, knowing I never call twice unless it's an emergency.

"Tell me what you remember from the night that girl was attacked."

"I, ummm ... what?" she questions as I hear the loud rumble of Tanner's bike outside, taking off at a million miles an hour and making something break within me. "What's going on? Why are you all worked up?"

"Erica, please. Just tell me what you remember. Where were we? What were we doing? Who was there? I ... I can't remember all the details."

"Bri, you're freaking me out. What the hell is going on?"

"Tanner," I rush out, a panic taking over me and making my words come out as a rambling mess. "The guy from next door. He just came storming in here and told me that Colby was the one who drugged and raped her. She's his sister, Erica. Addison Morgan. She's barely holding on. She was supposed to be a junior this year, so she's probably only sixteen or seventeen and I ... I ... You have to tell me that this isn't true because I can't live with myself if this happened right under my nose and I missed it. Erica, please. Tell me he's wrong. He was so angry, and the look in his eyes, he believes it with every piece of his soul, and he was looking at me as though I had something to do with it."

"Woah, woah," Erica says. "Breathe, Bri. Breathe. You know Colby. That's insane. He wouldn't have done that."

"You saw him last night," I remind her. "The way he grabbed my hair. He's never been violent with me like that before. He was on something, and what if he was on something that night as well. What if he really hurt this girl?"

"Babe," she says slowly. "No. Listen to yourself. You were with him for six months. I know it was shit at the end and you guys barely even hung out anymore, but those months before were good, right? You know him better than anyone, and I know you better than anyone. If you thought for even a second that he would be capable of doing something like that, you would have broken up with him straight away."

I scoff and drop the phone onto my bed, pressing the speaker button and burrowing my face into my hands as the devastation overwhelms me. "I don't think I knew him at all," I tell her. "I didn't know he was doing drugs. How long has he been doing that?"

Erica sighs and I prepare myself for bad news. "Girl, he was doing the hard shit all summer," she finally tells me, regret heavy in her tone. "It started when you began distancing yourself from him, well at least, that's when I first noticed. Whenever there was a party that you skipped out on, he'd hit it hard and get completely fucked up."

"What?" I breathe. "Why wouldn't you tell me that?"

"Why would I? Everyone was doing it. He was just letting off steam like the rest of us and enjoying the summer. We were all dabbling, but why are you getting so worked up over this? It's not like you're an angel or anything like that. You tried it."

"I smoked one joint, Erica. That is not the same thing as getting fucked up every weekend at stupid house parties, so don't try and tell me any different."

"Jesus, Bri. What's gotten into you? Are our shitty house parties too good for you now? Do you only party in mansions with your fancy caterers and bar staff fetching you drinks?"

"What the fuck are you talking about? All I want to know is if you think Colby was the guy who did it. Why are you being so defensive and avoiding my questions? Is there something you're not telling me?"

She groans and I roll my eyes, knowing that she's about to play the victim card like always. "Are you kidding, Brielle?" she spits, using my full name, which she only does when she's pissed. "A girl was attacked and raped, and you think I'm over here keeping secrets? Are you trying to accuse me of something? Holy fuck, girl. That place really is changing you. I don't even recognize you right now."

And with that, she ends the call, leaving me with even more questions than answers.

Frustration burns through me, and before I know it, I'm off my bed and pacing my room, but it's not enough. I need to move, need to get out of this room, need to think.

Following the sound of Mom's voice coming from the oversized living room, I walk in to find her seated on the ground in front of the coffee table with papers sprawled out before her while Orlando and Jensen slouch on the couches watching the game, ignoring whatever my mother is rambling about.

Mom mentions something about having dinner while overlooking the Eiffel Tower and my chest sinks, moving in closer to spy the papers around her. There are brochures in French for hotels and tours, and I shake my head. I should have seen this coming.

"What's going on?" I question, narrowing my gaze.

"Oh, honey," Mom rushes out, whipping around and giving me a dazzling smile as though the tension between us doesn't exist. "Isn't it fabulous news? Orlando is taking me to Paris next weekend. I'm finally going to get to visit the city of love and have dinner overlooking the Eiffel Tower, visit the Louvre, and walk along the Champs-Élysées only to finish beneath the Arc de Triomphe. It will be a weekend filled with romance, just as I've always dreamed."

"Paris?" I ask, hurt blooming through my chest. She's always wanted to go, but she's always said that she wouldn't dream of going without me. We had a pact. When that time came, after saving every last penny, we would go together. We always talked of it being that one special thing we would do together after I graduated. "I thought … I thought we were going to go together."

Her face pales, her eyes widening in horror. "Oh," she says, her gaze shifting toward Orlando's before settling back on mine. "Oh, honey. I'm so sorry. I didn't mean to exclude you. That certainly wasn't my intention. Would you like to come? I'm sure we can arrange another room, or perhaps a suite." She glances at Jensen, her face beaming. "Perhaps it can be a family trip. Jensen? Would you care for a trip to Paris? The four of us away as a family for the first time. It would be a dream."

My gaze flicks across the room toward Jensen and the look of horror on his face probably mirrors the one on mine. I couldn't think of anything worse. "No offense," Jensen says. "But been there and done that with the last two girlfriends who wanted a family trip."

"You know what, Mom?" I say, before she gets the chance to think about that too much. "Why don't you and Orlando enjoy this trip together? Jensen and I wouldn't want to cramp your style. Besides, you guys are in the honeymoon stage, and I'm sure you're going to want time to yourselves."

"Are you sure?" she asks, the look in her eyes suggesting that this is what she wanted anyway. "It's no hassle."

"No, I'm fine," I say a little firmer. "But this isn't why I came down here. I …" I pause, glancing at Orlando and Jensen, hating the way they're listening in on our conversation, but it's not like I can get her alone lately. "I wanted to ask you about Colby."

"Colby?" she questions. "What of him?"

"Colby Jacobs?" Orlando questions, sitting up straighter on the couch, his head whipping toward me.

"Umm, yes," I say, confused. "Do you know him?"

"I think the better question is, how do you know him?" he demands, standing.

Mom stands at his side and places a hand on his wrist as though silently asking him to back off. "Everybody from Hope Falls knows Colby Jacobs. He's the captain of their football team, a bit of a town celebrity. However, Brielle was dating him over the summer and the few months before. Such a cute couple," she adds, glancing toward me. "It's a shame you had to breakup."

I gape at her. "He was cheating on me and was on drugs. Is that really what you want for me?"

"Oh, don't be silly. He's on the football team, he can't afford to be doing drugs, otherwise he'd lose his position. He has a scholarship to think about."

I scoff and the look on Orlando's face suggests that he knows all about Colby's drug use. "You were really dating the boy?" he questions, looking at me through a narrowed, calculating stare.

I nod, feeling uneasy. "Yes."

"And were you there the night the girl was attacked and raped?"

I hesitate, unsure where this is going, but Mom has no qualms. "Yes, she was," she says, gripping onto Orlando's side. "It was such a terrible night. The whole town heard of it. I was terrified for my little girl. Can you believe such a horrid crime was taking place in the very next room while she was dancing with her friend? It could have so easily been her. I think of that every night and am just so blessed to know that my little girl is safe and sound."

Orlando doesn't take his eyes off me, and with every word Mom says, I see his eyes sparkling more, whatever bullshit circling his mind falling right into place.

"Why are you asking?"

"Are you aware that Colby has been falsely accused of hurting that poor girl?" Mom gasps, her hand covering her mouth as I nod, refusing to take my eyes off him, not liking where this is going. "I'm sure it would not come as a surprise to you to learn that the Jacobs family has hired me to represent their son."

"Of course they have," Mom says, moving closer to his side and looking up at him as though he holds all the answers to the world's greatest problems. "This is such a trying time. I am sure they're relieved to have the best in the business."

"Why are you telling me this?" I question, not here for Mom's blatant desperation or the way she tries to blow smoke up the man's ass.

"Do you still care for the boy?"

"Absolutely not."

"Okay," he says thoughtfully. "Well, what are your views on keeping an innocent man out of prison?"

"If the person in question was actually innocent, then I would do my part to help where necessary."

"Excellent," he says. "How would you feel about writing a statement that said Colby was with you the whole night, specifically during the time the attack was taking place and vouch for his character."

Mom rushes in. "Of course she would," she says, glancing at

me. "Wouldn't you? Anything to help."

I shake my head, my brows furrowed. "But I wasn't with him all night. When the girl was hurt, I was dancing with Erica. I have no idea what *or who* Colby was doing, plus I had been drinking heavily, and anyone at that party would be able to vouch for that. I'm not about to falsify an alibi for the guy just so you can win a case. Besides, I know I haven't been to law school or anything like that, but I know enough to know that's illegal."

He shakes his head, shrugging it off. "Technicalities," he says, realizing I'm not about to play ball.

I watch him a little closer, understanding dawning and making me feel sick. "Why would he need me to submit an alibi?" I ask. "Why can't he just get the person he was with to supply one? If he's innocent, he shouldn't have any issues with proving he had an alibi. There were heaps of people there that night, someone would have seen him. Unless … he doesn't have an alibi. Did he …" I suck in a gasp, my eyes going wide. "He did it, didn't he? It was Colby, and you want me to lie and let him walk free just so you can claim another winning case."

"Brielle," Mom snaps, her eyes wide with horror and embarrassment. "Apologize right this instant. How dare you accuse Orlando of such practices. I am appalled by your behavior lately. I don't understand why you keep acting out like this."

I scoff, ignoring her as I step closer to Orlando. "If Colby Jacobs walks because you do something to falsify information, I will make sure the whole world knows about it."

With that, I turn on my heel and storm out of the room, my stomach clenching with the realization that for the past six months, I was dating a man who could potentially be a rapist. I've slept in his bed, defended him, and tried my best to love him. I partied with him, let him use my body, all while blissfully unaware of the real man hidden behind the mask.

Breaking through my bedroom door, I rush through to my bathroom, getting there just in time to drop to my knees in front of the toilet and hurl into the bowl.

My head hangs as I violently throw up, not knowing what to do.

What if it's true? What if I got so drunk that I don't remember Colby slipping away that night? What if I've been blind to it just as Tanner had suggested, and because of my inability to know what's going on around me, his sister was attacked, drugged, raped, and left for dead?

Fuck.

CHAPTER 22
Brielle

Tanner slinks into third period English looking as though he hasn't slept all weekend. I'm not surprised, I haven't slept either. It's been a shit weekend. What started out amazing quickly turned to a steaming pile of horse shit.

I'm so conflicted, so torn over what to believe.

When Tanner stormed into my room, I was so busy raging at him for having no regard for my privacy or the way he'd hurt me that I barely took a chance to truly think over what he was talking about. In that moment, his accusation was insane. I couldn't comprehend what he'd said because it was so alien to me, but I've spent the last two days going over that night six weeks ago.

Most of it is foggy. I remember arriving at the party and having a few drinks. Erica and I danced, and I even draped myself all over Colby like a bad smell. Despite wanting to break up with him, I was still throwing myself at him. What can I say? I'm a horny drunk. Colby had a guaranteed screw at the end of the night, and he knew that, so it doesn't make sense for him to have attacked Tanner's sister.

On the other hand, Tanner was so sure. The conviction in his tone scared me and the desperation in his eyes haunts me, but nothing hurts more than the way he walked out of there. I don't understand this pull between us. I don't know what it is or how it even happened, but the thought of him walking away like that, truly despising … fuck, that aches.

Even now, watching as he walks into the room and looks anywhere but at me … it hurts. I just want to throw myself at him and wrap my arms around him, feel his body against mine and tell him that everything is going to be okay. At some point, we're going to have to talk.

I showed up early this morning, tried to catch him before going in, but he wouldn't talk to me, wouldn't even look at me. He thinks I'm defending Colby, when in reality, I think I might believe him. I think he did it, and I'm terrified of what that means for me. If it's true, if he attacked Tanner's sister, then part of that blame rests on my shoulders. I should have been more aware, should have kept track of him. Should have given him what he needed in order to keep him away from others.

Fuck, how pathetic do I sound?

The fire in Tanner's eyes tells me that he'll do whatever it takes to destroy him. Colby has worked so hard to be the best player that

Hope Falls has ever seen, and something as serious as a rape charge would destroy everything he's worked for. Even if he is proven innocent—which could very well happen considering he has a lawyer like Orlando—the gossip would spread, and he'd never recover. Any chance he has of getting a football scholarship would be gone and he'd be stuck in Hope Falls for the rest of his life.

Tanner walks by me, and I watch his fingers flinch before he curls his hands into tight fists, making me wonder what's going through his head. He's so emotionally destroyed. I want to help him, but he just won't let me.

"Everybody, take your seats," Miss Harper says from behind her desk, her signature scowl resting across her face, only today it seems worse than normal.

I get my notepad out and prepare for the lesson, all too aware of Tanner's eyes lingering on the side of my face. The class scuffles about, taking all too long to get into their seats and settle down, but the moment Miss Harper stands and calls me out, she has their full attention. "Miss Ashford, stand and make your way to the front of the class."

My back stiffens and I meet her horrendous stare before flicking my gaze to Arizona across the room. She shrugs, so I hesitantly get to my feet, making my way down the aisle and putting myself front and center. Tanner's stare is even more intense.

Miss Harper moves from behind her oversized desk, gripping a small stack of familiar papers. She thrusts them into my hand and I hastily glance down at my essay with a big, circled F in the top right corner.

My chest sinks, but before I can start going through the papers, Miss Harper takes her opportunity to scold me. "You're new here so I understand that some things will take some time to become accustomed to, however this is unacceptable. If you are not going to take your studies seriously, then you will not be welcome to take my class."

"I'm sorry?" I ask, shaking my head and wanting to skim over my papers again, desperate to figure out where I went wrong but not wanting to look away from her feral stare. "I don't understand. You asked me to write an essay on a topic of my choice to better understand what concepts I have a firm grasp on, and I believe I delivered exactly what you asked for."

Her eyes widen and she looks at me as though she just caught me kicking a newborn puppy. "Suit yourself, Miss Ashford. If you feel your essay is appropriate for my class, then go ahead and recite it to the class. We shall see what they think of it."

Nervousness trickles through me. There's nothing worse than having to deliver a speech in front of a group of students you don't really know, but to do it without rehearsing it in front of the mirror a million times is simply unheard of. I'm not the type to just wing it when it comes to my schoolwork. I take it seriously because, without good grades, a girl like me has absolutely no hope of getting into college. I don't have a sport to fall back on or a stack of money to bribe the admissions office. I have to get in on my merit alone and hope to whoever exists above that they offer me a scholarship.

My gaze falls to my papers, and I do what I can to ignore the intense stare coming from the back corner of the room. This essay was personal, and I don't exactly feel comfortable sharing it with the class, but I'll do it if it means passing.

Clearing my throat, I prepare myself to read.

Senior year was supposed to be simple. Everything I'd worked toward was finally within reach, and all I had to do was take it, but in a matter of seconds, my world turned on its head. Life threw me a curveball, and instead of hitting it out of the park, I succumbed to its power. Now I'm scrambling, trying to find my feet in this crazy new world.

In the space of twelve hours, I went from being the girlfriend of the most popular guy in school to being the new girl in a world that judges me based on how much money I have in my bank account, which for the record, is none. I live with people who terrify me, and my mom, well, she's nothing but a stranger to me now.

All I have in this world is my brother, who would move heaven and hell to protect me if he were still here. I never planned to have to say goodbye to him, and it broke my heart when he left. Now I live in fear every day that he won't come back, which is ridiculous. He's at boot camp, not at war! He hasn't even been gone that long but I'm already terrified. I suppose I'm just scared of what his future might hold. He's so determined to be nothing like my father, that he left us just the same, and though I know it's different this time, it doesn't seem to hurt less.

This new crazy world isn't all bad. It surprised me in ways that I never expected. There's an asshole next door, sexy as sin, and I want to fuck—

My eyes bug out of my head, my gaze snapping up to Tanner's

across the room as the class erupts into laughter, but he just stares, not even a flicker of emotion on his face.

Embarrassment floods me, and I feel my cheeks heating as I whip around to Miss Harper. "This isn't the essay I wrote," I rush out, only now figuring out what Tanner had been doing in my room. He told me at the track that he had been in my room again, and I searched every corner of it trying to figure out what surprise he'd left for me. I suppose I know now.

Asshole.

Miss Harper leans against the corner of her desk, her arms crossed over her chest and that stoic scowl filled with venom. "Is that your name at the bottom?"

I flip over to the last page and find my name at the bottom, right where I'd originally put it. "Yes, that's my name, but—"

"Did you submit those papers?"

"Yes, but—"

"Then it's your essay," she says, cutting me off.

"I swear," I tell her. "I wrote about the trials and hardships of entering a world that I was unfamiliar with, not some asshole who lives next door. Please, you have to believe me. I didn't write this shit. I wouldn't. My grade—"

Anger blooms through her stare. "Get out of my classroom, Miss Ashford," she snaps, pushing off the edge of her desk. "I do not tolerate that type of language. If you wish to discuss your essay and your grade, then you may do so in your own time. Right now, I have a class to teach."

Well, fuck.

Tanner Morgan is going to die.

Making my way back to my desk, I collect my things, my glare slicing across the room and landing on Tanner's. His elbows are propped against his desk as he braces his chin in his palm, using his fingers to cover his stupid smirk. Rage boils through me, and I know without a doubt that his bitch ass is going to get the full wrath of Brielle Ashford, but it's going to have to wait until I can get him alone.

Fuck, I don't know if I want to rage at him or have a deep conversation about what I've learned of Colby.

"Dead to me," I tell him, my voice low and full of venom, letting him know just how serious I am about this.

His fingers roam over the soft stubble lining his sharp jaw, and his eyes sparkle with the challenge. "Do your worst, Killjoy," he spits, ready to tear me to shreds, "but remember, I bite back."

CHAPTER 23
TANNER

Hudson loops the heavy chain around the tow ball of Logan's new Dodge RAM as the fucker hangs out the driver's window, his hand belting down on the side of his truck and a stupid fucking grin across his face. "Ain't no way you can beat me," he yells to Jax as Hudson grabs the opposite end of the chain and loops it around the tow ball of Jax's new Chevrolet Silverado. "You're a little bitch. You can't handle that."

"That's some big talk for such a little guy."

I roll my eyes. Neither of them are little. Not even close. "We're twins, dickhead," Logan fires back, the smirk on his lips worrying me. "If I'm little, then you're little."

"Have you not seen these gains?" Jax roars, his voice traveling right down the street. "I'm a fucking beast."

"This isn't going to end well," Riley murmurs at my side, his gaze settled on Hudson as he checks the chain firmly secured between the two tow balls, and that nobody is going to end up in the hospital, again. The twins tried a stunt like this before, only last time it was with Logan's Camaro and Addison's brand-new, cherry red Maserati convertible. The only issue was that neither of the cars had a tow ball and the boys had to be creative. It's a shame they're both fucking idiots and their version of being creative meant that everyone around them was suddenly in the fire zone. Which is exactly what happened when the whole bumper of Addie's Maserati flew off and took Riley out. He spent three nights in the hospital and his mom busted our asses.

Fuck, Addie was pissed when she found out what we'd done. She had to drive my Mustang around until hers got out of the shop, and she wasn't impressed.

Jax and Logan turn eighteen in a few weeks, and with their father out of town again, he couldn't resist earning their affection with another bullshit gift that means absolutely nothing to them. But hell, they'll have fun with the trucks until they inevitably destroy them. Looking at them now, that won't take long.

"Your bitch ass ready?" Jax hollers out his window.

"Who you calling a fucking bitch?"

Fucking hell. "Just get on with it," I call back, needing this shit over and done with before my mom comes speeding down the street and puts an end to it and we never get a chance to put this to rest. The twins have been at each other's throats all day, comparing their trucks and insisting that theirs is more powerful than the other. I honestly should have seen this coming, but I've been distracted by the little fireball who's made her way around school all day with a stick stuck right up her ass.

Bri is fucking pissed, and rightfully so after the way I stormed into her room and told her that she was partly at fault for Addison's attack because she didn't spread her legs enough. I've felt sick about that comment for the last three days. I couldn't even face her today. I need to apologize. I was angry and behavior like that doesn't fly with me. I'm a fucking ass, but yet every time I find the nerve to fall to my knees and beg for forgiveness, I remember how she defended that motherfucker. She thinks I'm blindly accusing her ex of raping my sister, as though I'm just some jealous, insecure asshole trying to alienate her from the people around her. I can't wrap my head around it.

"Call it, Bellamy," Logan roars, settling back into his seat, more than ready to smash his twin brother.

"Alright," Hudson calls out. "You assholes ready?"

Both their supercharged engines rumble in response and I shake my head. The trucks are so evenly matched in power that it's going to come down to who's the better driver, and in this case, Logan's got it in the bag. There's no matching him behind the wheel unless I'm the one driving. The asshole has been sour about it for two long years. I don't remember when he finally gave up, but he eventually did. There's just no beating me on the track. I go in for the kill every single time, no matter what odds are against me.

"In three," Hudson roars. "Two. One."

The twins hit the gas, their feet slamming down flat to the ground as their engines roar, snapping the chain tight between them in an epic game of tug-of-war. The trucks jump and groan, rubber burning against the road as smoke billows beneath them.

Jax gives it his all, trying to get the upper hand but Logan is playing with him. He has a gift of reading his opponent, and with the close bond between them, he reads Jax as easily as if he were speaking the words directly into his mind.

"WHAT THE FUCK ARE YOU IDIOTS DOING?" a high-pitched screech comes from behind us.

My head whips around to find Killjoy gaping at us, her essay locked tightly between her fingers. I immediately look back at the trucks, not because I don't want to spend every waking minute gaping at how fucking gorgeous she is, but because every time I look at her, I remember what I said to her and I feel sick.

"Hey, babe," Riley says, practically drooling as he moves closer, draping a heavy arm over her shoulder and pulling her into his side. Not going to lie, I thought his hard-on would have eased by now, especially after learning what we know about her relationship with Colby, but it only seems to be getting worse, and damn it, it grates on my every last nerve. "Come chill with us," he says, dragging her forward and putting her right next to me. "Jax is about to get his ass handed to him."

Bri pushes his arm off her shoulder and watches the scene before her with disinterest. "I'm sure if your asshole friend wasn't such a fucking asshole, I would probably take a second to watch the show," she tells him. "I might even pretend to enjoy watching you idiots swing your dicks around when they're so clearly overcompensating for something else, but right now, all I want to do is tear shreds off the piece of shit standing next to me."

I bite the inside of my cheek, forcing myself not to grin. Can't lie, that fiery attitude gets me worked up in more ways than one, but right now, I really don't know if she's referring to the essay or the intrusion into her room over the weekend.

Riley laughs. "Have at him, babe. There's something special about watching you tear that fucker apart."

I resist glaring at Riley as he steps away, moving toward Hudson to watch the show up close and personal, and just like that, the rest of the world fades away and it's just me, Brielle, and the heaviness resting between us.

She turns to face me, crossing her arms, the essay awkwardly poking out from beneath her elbow. "We need to talk."

"The fuck we do."

The longer I keep my stare on the trucks, the more rage that seems to shoot out of her, and so be it. She finally sighs and drops her arms before stepping out onto the road to turn to face me directly, only a wave of fear rocks through me and I lunge forward, gripping her arm and yanking her back onto the safety of the pavement. "The fuck are you doing? Are you trying to get yourself killed? One slip and these trucks could spiral out of control."

"Bit like how you've been doing?" she throws back at me before huffing and settling back in beside me. She knows I'm right, but that doesn't stop her from arguing about it. "If one of those cars is going to spiral out of control, do you honestly think one step further onto the pavement is really going to save me? Jesus, Tanner. You're not too bright, are you?"

I lower my stare, meeting the rage reflected in her own. "Is there something you need, Killjoy?"

"Yeah," she scoffs, holding the essay up and practically shaking it in my face. "You can stop messing with my life. Do you have any idea how humiliating that was?"

I shrug my shoulders, more than ready to make matters worse. "Don't know what you're talking about."

She gapes at me, and I can see the fury pulsing through her veins, boiling deep in her stomach. "You … You asshole," she screeches. "It's one thing to mess with me, to sneak into my room and write shit on my wall and call me a fucking whore for my ex, but this is too far, Tanner. This is my future. Unlike you, I don't have a long list of colleges begging me to sign on the little dotted line, and I sure as hell don't have parents who'll fork out stacks of cash to secure a spot either. My grades are all I have. They're my only shot at getting into a college and actually making something of myself. Screw with me however you want, call me whatever you want, and use me to rage about your fucking problems—that doesn't matter to me, but don't ruin the one good thing I've got going for my future."

Fucking hell. Why does that make me feel like such a low life cunt?

A loud snap echoes through the street and my eyes bulge out of my head. Before I can even think, I reach for Brielle and slam her down to the ground, my body coming down on top of hers just moments before the heavy chain snaps off the tow balls and flings through the air like a rotating blade, destroying everything in its path.

The trucks launch forward as the chain sails right over our heads, whooshing past us and smashing through the front window of Channing's formal dining room, probably destroying everything inside it.

Brielle stares up at me wide-eyed, her chest heaving with the realization that a split second longer and she could have lost her fucking head. "You saved my life," she breathes.

I stare down at her, the feel of her body beneath mine doing something to me that scares the shit out of me. "I don't suppose this makes us even for the essay?"

"Over my dead body," she tells me as I listen to the sounds of both Jax and Logan trying to regain control of their trucks, both of them probably shitting themselves. I push to my feet, reaching down for her hand and pulling her up and right into me, my gaze roaming over her body, making sure she's not hurt.

Brielle shoves against my chest, forcing space between us that I can't stand, and damn it, I hate that I see hesitation in her eyes, but it's only there because I forced it between us. She's feeling this just as much as I am and I hate how much I've been hurting her, but I'm no good for her, and I think she's finally starting to see that.

She takes another step away, unable to tear her gaze off mine until Riley slams into her, his hands gripping her shoulders and spinning her around, his stare wide and panicked. "Are you okay?" he rushes out, looking over her from head to toe. "Are you hurt?"

"I'm fine," she tells him, discreetly pulling out of his grip as Jax gets out of his truck and checks the back, a booming laugh tearing out of him as Logan just gapes, realizing just how bad that shit could have been.

"HOLY FUCK," Jax laughs. "Did you see that shit?"

"See that shit?" Logan fires back, his eyes wide. "We nearly killed the new chick."

"But we didn't," Jax says, always trying to find the silver-lining with every fucked-up situation we put ourselves into. "Either way, I was killing it. Did you see that? I was smoking your ass."

"In what world were you smoking me?" Logan demands, walking back down the street to meet his brother in the middle. "I had you the whole time. I was just waiting for you to figure it out on your own. The Silverado's got nothing on my RAM."

And so it starts.

They go at each other, and within seconds, fists are flying, leaving Bellamy to dive in after them, taking an elbow to the jaw, which naturally sends Riley into the middle of it too.

"I, ummm …" Brielle says, watching the fight, not impressed in the least. Her gaze flicks back to me before bending and scooping the essay off the ground. "I'm not sticking around for this testosterone fueled shit, but for the record, you need to fix this."

She shoves the essay into my chest, and I watch as she takes off back toward the house, more than likely with the intention to ignore the smashed window in the formal dining room. "And if I don't?" I call after her, knowing damn well that I will. When I changed her essay, we were in a better place. That was before I hurt her, before I crushed her, and before everything I said over the weekend. I owe this to her. Shit, I owe her a lot more than that.

"Then I'll tear shreds off your ass," she tells me.

The door closes between us, and with it, she takes my will to resist. I need to make this right. I've hurt her over and over again and still she's right there.

"Oh, how the mighty have fallen," Hudson says, and without hesitation, all four of my friends drop a knee, their right hand resting over their hearts as they bow their heads in commiseration. "Let us all take a moment to remember our fallen soldier. He was one of the best, a fighter, racer, and proud man with balls the size of Texas, yet so easily broken by none other than a lone, stray pussy. What hope do the rest of us have?"

Shaking my head, I turn on my heel and stalk back toward my house. "For that, you fuckers are on dinner, and it better be good, otherwise, you're running sprints for an hour following practice tomorrow."

"Fuck," Jax mutters behind me.

Making my way back inside, I take off upstairs and slip into my bedroom and come to a standstill, my eyes widening in surprise. Every available space on my walls is taken up with a single word written a million times over, scrawled in a deep plum lipstick, sending a wicked grin stretching across my face and making something settle in my chest.

ASSHOLE!

Well, well, if she's still down to play, then play we shall.

Unable to help myself, my gaze flicks toward her bedroom window to find her staring back at me, a smug grin resting on her face and her middle finger flying proud for every girl who's ever been screwed over by me. Then without even a flicker of regret, she pulls the blinds, leaving me to deal with the mess she's left behind.

CHAPTER 24
Brielle

"Holy shit, she's alive," Ilaria cheers as I walk into homeroom on Tuesday morning, her eyes sparkling with laughter.

Rolling my eyes, I stride toward her and drop down into my seat. "What the hell are you talking about?" I ask, wondering if she's referring to me being a no show before school.

"Rumor has it that the douchebag duo tried to decapitate you yesterday and that the asshole with a god complex saved your pretty little face."

I groan and lean forward onto my desk, not nearly getting enough sleep after being terrified of Tanner's revenge. He's not going to let me off the hook for what I did to his room yesterday. He's going to come for me, the only question is, when? All I know is that whatever it is, it's going to knock me off my feet. It's going to be epic, and it's going to remind me that while things are seriously messed up between us, we still share this strange connection that neither of us truly understand.

"Ugh, how did—"

"Miss Ashford," a stern voice says from the front of the room, cutting off my explanation of yesterday's insane adventures. My head snaps up to find my homeroom teacher staring back at me. "Please make your way to Principal Dormer's office. Your presence has been requested."

"Oh?" I say, my brows furrowed, unsure what the hell he could want with me, mentally going over everything that's happened since being here and struggling to figure it out. "Do you know what this is about?"

"No idea," he says. "I'm just the messenger. Now scram. You're already late."

Shit.

Letting out a heavy breath, I get to my feet and trudge out of the room, wishing I could just catch a break. It feels as though I've been running since the moment I woke up, which as usual, was late, but no matter how late I was, it didn't stop me from spending a few minutes scouring every inch of my room, making sure that Tanner hadn't made himself welcome during the night.

The student office is swarming with bodies, and as I stand in line to check in with the lady at the desk, someone calls my name from down the hall. "Brielle," I hear a feminine tone and turn to find Miss

Harper half hanging out of a doorway, presumably Principal Dormer's office. Dread fills me. This is about the essay. "We're ready for you."

Shit. *We're?* They're going to tag team me, work me from both sides until I crack. Just great. Who doesn't love a little double penetration on a Tuesday morning?

Nerves eat at me as I make my way down the hall and step through to Dormer's office. It's huge, but modest—a little fancy but not over the top as I was expecting. He's an older man with a bit of a silver fox vibe going on, and if he didn't look so serious, I'm sure girls all over the school would be calling him daddy.

"Welcome, Miss Ashford," Dormer says, indicating to the chair opposite his desk as Miss Harper stands off to the side, a copy of my essay clutched in her hand. "Please take a seat. We only need a moment of your time."

"I, ummm …" I start, hesitantly making my way across the room and nervously glancing toward Miss Harper. I drop down on the very edge of the seat, a fight or flight tactic for a speedy getaway. "If this is about the essay, I can explain—"

"This is about your essay," she confirms, cutting me off before I can get lost in a lengthy, ranting explanation about how I was wronged in the most humiliating way. "However, you are not in trouble. We've brought you here to let you know that Tanner Morgan put in a call last night. I don't know how he found my personal cell, but that is beside the point. He explained everything and took full responsibility."

My eyes bug out of my head. "What?"

She nods, stepping forward to hand me the papers. My gaze drops and quickly scans over the words, finding the essay I'd written with a big A+ drawn in the top right-hand corner. "Tanner emailed me your original essay. It was inspiring, Brielle. I am thoroughly pleased with your work. You demonstrated a sound understanding of the concepts discussed and it's clear to me that you take your work very seriously."

My head snaps up, meeting her impressed stare, still reeling with the fact that he called her to make it right. "I do, I take my workload very seriously," I tell her. "I don't have the luxury of paying my way through college as many of the other students do. My grades are the only thing I can count on to get me noticed for a scholarship."

"I assure you," Dormer cuts in. "From the feedback I've heard from your teachers, you should have no issue securing a scholarship."

I give him a tight smile, still feeling weird about this meeting. "Thank you," I tell him before looking between the two of them. "If I may be so bold, I don't understand why this meeting needed to be held under the guidance of the principal. I mean no disrespect, but it seems like this is something that could have been quickly discussed during class time."

Principal Dormer smiles. "It was my decision to bring you here this morning. When Miss Harper shared with me the events of her evening and discussed the grades for your essay, I wanted to meet with you face to face. I believe you are a very bright student and with the right guidance, there is no reason you shouldn't be able to get into the top college of your choice with a scholarship. However," he continues, his expression darkening, "I don't think it would come as a surprise to you to know that young men like Tanner Morgan, while incredibly talented and one of the top performing athletes of this school, spend many hours in my office. You are new here and I am sure you are still learning the ropes and figuring it out as you go. I think it would be a wise decision for you to distance yourself from the likes of Tanner Morgan and his friends. They are bad news, and while I understand you are in a peculiar situation living next door, it seems that Tanner has set his sights on you. I have seen it many times over the past few years, bright students being torn down by his tactics, and it would be a shame to see the same happen to you."

Uhhhhh ... is this guy really trying to warn me away from Tanner? Is that even allowed? More so, how am I supposed to respond to that?

Miss Harper gives me a firm nod, making it clear she agrees with Principal Dormer's judgment, and I quickly nod as well. "Thank you, I'll take that under advisement," I say, sounding way too formal and making me cringe.

"See that you do," Dormer says as the bell sounds through the school. "You may go, Brielle. It was a pleasure chatting with you and I look forward to watching you excel during your time here. Now, hurry along to class, and in the meantime, it would be wise to arrange a visit with our guidance counselor who can look over your college applications and ensure that you've done everything possible to secure your college of choice."

I nod, excitement drumming through my veins. "I will. Thank you," I say before standing and giving Miss Harper a smile. Maybe she isn't such a grinch after all.

Scurrying out of the office, I find my way back into the long hallway and start heading toward my first class of the day, squeezing my way through all the students heading in the opposite direction. My shoulders bump against the masses as I stare ahead in horror. Why is everyone in the whole freaking school going the same way at the same damn time? Who scheduled this? It's as though Billie Eilish just appeared and the masses are rushing to get to her.

I get halfway down the hall when a large body steps directly in front of me, blocking my way and my gaze snaps up to find the very asshole the faculty were just trying to warn me away from. "Do you need something?" I question, a thrill rushing through my veins, quickly becoming addicted to the intense way he stares at me while also trying to block out the way he's hurt me and the nasty things he'll never be able to take back.

"Why are you coming from this way?" he questions, nodding up ahead from the crowded hall I just squeezed through. "Your home room is the opposite way and then you have biology which is across campus."

I arch a brow, my fingers flinching at my side, itching to reach out and slip my hand up his shirt to feel the warmth of his skin beneath my palm. "You keeping tabs on me, Morgan?"

"Wouldn't dream of it."

A smile pulls at my lips, and I hate how obvious I'm being about this ridiculous crush I have on him. He probably thinks I'm so pathetic, acting like every other girl who's ever thrown themselves at him, despite his efforts to scare me off. "You called Miss Harper and gave her my real essay."

He shakes his head. "Don't know what you're talking about," he says, smirking right back at me. "Must have been someone else."

"Really now?" I laugh, leaning my shoulder against the wall as he moves closer into me, that heavenly scent overwhelming my senses and making me weak. "She called you out by name, and also, she's a bit concerned about how you got her personal cell number. I mean, if you're into the whole teacher student thing, just say the word and I'll take my hat out of the ring."

"Really? You're admitting that your hat's in the ring?"

My eyes bug out, realizing what I just said. "It's not," I rush out. "It's so far out of the ring that I don't even have a hat. It disintegrated the second I spilled beer down your shirt and you opened your big mouth."

"Uh-huh," he says, getting even closer, my chin unintentionally tipping back in the hopes that maybe, just maybe he might kiss me and make all the pain go away.

"I'm torn," I murmur. "I don't know if I should thank you for fixing things with Miss Harper, or if I should knee you in the balls for screwing with my essay in the first place … actually, knee you twice in the balls for all the other bullshit as well."

He takes a subtle step back, knowing that after dropping Riley last week, I won't hesitate to do the same to him, and to be fair, he deserves it a shitload more. "I mean, there's always one thing you could do to make it up to me."

Rolling my eyes, I shuffle back a step, needing to put a little space between us so I can think clearly. "I ummm … I think I owe you a conversation," I tell him, skipping right to the chase, done with this strange tension between us.

"About what?"

"Your sister," I tell him, watching as his eyes harden and become full of anger. "What you said the other day ... I was angry that you'd busted into my room without invitation—not that you've ever waited for an invitation before—and I was hurt about the way you'd just walked away at the track." I pause, meeting his cautious stare. "We've both calmed down and I've been thinking about that night at the party and everything that went down. I think maybe I can offer you something more now that I'm not so busy wanting to pull your balls out through your throat."

His eyes flicker around us, making sure we're not overheard, and not a moment later, his warm fingers curl around my wrist and pull me toward him before he drops his hand to my lower back and leads me up the hallway. He reaches around me, opening an empty classroom and ushers me inside before closing the door behind him and shutting out the world around us.

I lean back against one of the desks, watching as Tanner moves deeper into the room. He steps into me, takes my first period books out of my hands and places them on the desk beside me. "I just need to know one thing," he starts, a nervous hesitation in his voice. "Do you believe me? Do you think Colby did it?"

I swallow hard, knowing that admitting it out loud is going to kill me. "I think he did it," I say, meeting his strained stare, watching as relief washes over him. "You need to understand that when I was with him, right at the beginning, he was charming and kind. He never pushed me to do anything I didn't want to do, and I never once saw him indulge in drugs or any of that shit. What you were saying didn't make sense to me. It was shocking and you were painting a picture of someone I didn't know while also being a complete ass and saying things that—"

"Listen—"

"No," I say, cutting him off. "I've been trying to get this out for three days, so just let me talk." I meet his stare and he nods, letting me go on. "I was kind of a mess after I kicked you out and I started thinking about that night, replaying everything and trying to clear the fog. I was drinking a lot at the party and by that stage of our relationship, he'd started turning into an asshole, so no, I wasn't putting out, but I shouldn't be held accountable for that."

"I know," he rushes out. "That was a dick thing for me to say and you need to know that I don't honestly think that. I was angry and words just started spewing out of my mouth. I didn't mean any of it."

I nod, swallowing hard. Maybe we'll circle back to that, but for now, I just need to get it all out. "I called Erica and was asking her about it, and she told me that over the summer, Colby started to get harder into drugs, which was news to me because I didn't even know that he was doing it before that. His attitude started to change, and I hated being around him. I'd been planning to break up with him all summer but was afraid of how he'd react."

"What do you mean afraid of how he'd react?" he questions, his hands falling to my thighs.

Letting out a sigh, I pull my phone from my pocket and bring up the texts from Colby, not having even bothered to read the thirty or so new messages which have all come through since Friday night. Handing it over, I watch as he scrolls through them, his brows arching higher by the second. "The fuck is this dude's problem? Is this how he always talks to you?"

"By the end, yes," I say. "He wasn't the same person I knew, and I resented going anywhere with him."

"Fucking hell," he says. "Why didn't you tell me you were getting threats from him?"

"Why would I?" I question. "You and I … we're not … I don't even know what this is, but it's not your responsibility to fight my fights, and besides, I've known you all of two seconds, and the majority of that time, we've been at each other's throats. Plus, you made sure I had front row tickets to the blowjob of the century and that kinda killed the vibe."

He cringes, guilt flashing in his dark eyes and a part of me loves that he hates himself for doing that to me. "I don't care, Killjoy. If someone is threatening to fuck with you, I want to know about it."

"Let me get this right," I say, a smile pulling at my lips. "You can fuck with me, but no one else can?"

"Damn straight," he says, pressing my phone back into my hand.

A moment of silence passes between us before I find the nerve to continue. "Look, the guy I thought I knew, the one I got to know, he would never have hurt your sister," I tell him. "But this guy, this stranger who's messaging me with all this anger and ugliness, the guy who tried to hurt me at the party on Friday night, I believe that guy did exactly what you're accusing him of doing."

Tanner steps into me, his hand curling around the back of my neck and using his thumb to press under my chin to raise my gaze to him. "You're with me?"

My mind swirls with images from that night, little snippets I've been trying to remember while also taking me back to the conversation I had with Orlando, needing me to create a bullshit alibi. "I'm with you," I whisper. "I'll stand with you right to the grave. I want justice for your sister, and if the cops aren't going to do it, then it's up to us. I just … I wish I could remember everything clearer, but it's all so foggy. I feel like I'm letting you down … letting Addison down."

His thumb rubs back and forth across my jaw and he shakes his head. "That's not possible," he murmurs, his voice thick with emotion.

"How did you know it was him?" I ask. "Did someone come forward?"

Tanner nods and his hands tighten on my thighs. "His name was put forward to the police. They haven't given us any details about the case. All they've said is that he claimed he wasn't there that night, which we both know is bullshit, but I don't need their evidence, I just know it was him."

My brows furrow and I meet his stare. "What are you talking about?"

He shakes his head. "This is ugly, Bri. I don't want to have to tell you this."

"I can handle it."

He swallows and takes a hesitant step back and my heart pounds, fearing what's about to come out of his mouth. "A few years ago, there was a party at that piece of shit lake house in Hope Falls." I nod, knowing the one. "Riley and I went, and I met this girl and—"

"You fucked her?"

Tanner nods, hesitation in his eyes. "Yeah, it was Colby's older sister."

My eyes bug out of my head, my back stiffening as pieces start to fall into place. "Rachael?" I gasp. "Everybody knows the story from that night. She was caught cheating on her boyfriend with some Bradford rich kid and ended up being labeled the school slut. She eventually dropped out of school and apparently went to live with some uncle out of state. I heard she didn't even bother completing her school year and never graduated."

Tanner presses his lips into a hard line before indicating toward himself. "Bradford rich kid."

"Holy fuck. That was you," I say, having heard this all from Colby at the beginning of our relationship, knowing just how much he despised Tanner for what happened. He never told me his name but would always say how he would destroy him if he ever got the chance. "He's always blamed you for what happened to his sister, but you weren't the one cheating on her boyf—wait. You would have only been a sophomore."

"I know," he murmurs, the corner of his lips pulling into a cocky smirk. "But Colby doesn't see it that way, and now my sister is breathing through tubes because I fucked some random girl at a party two years ago."

Reaching out, I take his hands and pull him back into me, my eyes expressing everything I don't know how to say. "He really did it, didn't he?" Tanner nods and curls his hand around the back of my neck before dropping his forehead to mine. "This isn't your fault, Tanner. This is all on Colby, and now that I know, there's nothing stopping me from helping you destroy him. Whatever you need, *I'm all yours.*"

"Don't say that," he warns me. "I might just take it literally."

A thrill shoots through me and I quickly squash it down, knowing we're not nearly done with this conversation. "You need to know that Colby hired Orlando to represent him."

Tanner nods, his gaze darkening, telling me this single piece of information has already made plenty of rounds through his head. "I know."

"He asked me to falsify an alibi, stating that Colby was with me during the time of your sister's attack," I explain. "I refused to do it, but you need to know that with Orlando working his case, he's going to do whatever it takes to make sure Colby's name is scrubbed free of this, and we can't let that happen."

Tanner shakes his head, anger blazing in his dark eyes. "I'd sooner lay my life down than allow Colby Jacobs to walk free. He will pay for hurting Addie," he vows, "even if I have to take the law into my own hands."

My hand slips up the front of his shirt and curves around his waist before pulling him in closer. As he hovers over me, I tip my head forward to his chest. "I feel like such an idiot for not seeing it," I tell him. "Colby was different around his football friends, but I figured it was the usual, trying to look like a man's man in front of his friends, trying to be cool, and now I wonder if that was the real him all along and he was just playing me in the hope of me spreading my legs."

Tanner cringes at that last comment. "I owe you a proper apology," he says. "I never should have suggested that you were at fault for my sister getting hurt because you weren't giving it up to him. That was a low blow for me."

"It was," I agree, "but you were angry, and while that's no excuse for your behavior, I understand it."

"Let me take you out this weekend."

A laugh bubbles up my throat and he grins back at me, amused by my reaction. I push him back a step, giving me space to push away from the desk. "You and I both know that's the worst idea you've ever had."

"Couldn't be any worse than any of my other ideas."

"Your last idea nearly killed me with a flying chain," I remind him. "And for the record, Orlando was pissed, but don't worry, I threw you right under the bus."

"I wouldn't expect anything else."

Stepping around him, I walk to the door before he can convince me to do something he and I are really not ready for. Pausing, I glance back. "For what it's worth, your contribution to my essay sucked. You need to work on your adjectives. You called yourself sexy fifteen times. *Fifteen, Tanner.* I don't know if you've heard of it before, but there's this crazy thing called a thesaurus. You should look into that."

"Oh yeah?" he says, a smirk pulling at his lips, light pulsing back into his eyes and sending just the slightest ray of hope coursing through me. "What word would you use?"

A soft laugh rumbles through my chest as I reach for the door and pull it open, truly thinking about my response before glancing back one more time, holding his complete attention. "Intoxicating and irresistibly delicious in every possible way."

CHAPTER 25
Brielle

I've always hated football. I don't know if it's because I simply don't understand the game or because it's just a bunch of men running after a stupid ball and taking it from one end to the other. But one thing is for sure, sitting up in the grandstand and watching as Tanner dominates the field is the most exhilarating thing I've ever seen.

He's a beast, and it finally makes sense to me why the whole school turns up to watch these games. He's incredible and with Riley, Hudson, and the twins working along with him, the five of them are unstoppable.

It's the hottest thing I've ever seen.

There are only five minutes left on the clock, and I've watched every second of it with wide eyes, cheering at all the right times despite not even knowing what I'm cheering for half the time. Hell, anyone who looks my way right now wouldn't have a damn clue that I don't know what's happening down on that field. I look like a seasoned pro.

The team huddles around their coach, more than ready to smash out these last five minutes against their disheveled and exhausted opponents. Bradford is up against the Broken Hill High team and they're good, really good, but they're no competition for Bradford.

I sit between Ilaria and Arizona, cheering for Chanel down on the field with her blue poms-poms. The cheerleaders have been giving their all for the first game of the season, and I've listened intently as Ilaria has told me about the Ryder brothers who go to Broken Hill—Nate and Jesse. She's apparently been crushing on them for years. Nate sounds like the untouchable type while Ilaria describes Jesse as the *any hole's a goal* type, a complete flirt, and honestly, he sounds like my kinda guy. You know, apart from the brooding asshole down on the field who has looked up here every chance he gets.

The players make their way back to the field and I sit straighter, far too excited for these last five minutes. They get into position and the whistle blows, and just like that, everyone is moving again. Bradford is up by four, but the Broken Hill players have been putting in a good fight, doing everything they can not to let their opponents get away from them. But they're tired. Bradford is pushing too hard and they're quickly falling behind.

My gaze locks on Tanner, watching how he plays, and it's clear he takes this seriously. The whole way through the game, he's been checking in on his teammates, pushing them to their limits, and making sure everyone is playing a good, safe game. No wonder he's team captain.

There's a scuffle on the field between players, and the ref blows his whistle again, only adding to the intensity of the last few minutes. The crowd gets to their feet with wide eyes, and even Ilaria shuts up about the Ryder brothers, too captivated by the game playing out before her.

Two minutes on the clock and the opposition gets the ball, storming through the exhausted players, until Hudson and Riley intercept. Jax gets an elbow to the face and blood spurts everywhere, but Hudson is right there, saving their play. The elbow dude is benched and Jax hovers by the sideline, not giving two shits about his nose as the game picks back up.

Hudson takes off like lightning and gets the ball to Tanner, and I grip onto Ilaria and Arizona, watching intently as the impressive quarterback launches the ball down the field, Logan racing for it with a storm of Broken Hill players right on his ass.

Riley forges forward having Logan's back, throwing himself at another player and clearing the way for Logan to shoot through. He launches himself up into the air and collects the ball with ease, the crowd roaring for their team.

We watch with wide eyes as one after another, Bradford players take the opposition out of the game, dropping them to their asses and clearing a path for Logan to get through to the center of the end goal and slam the ball down into the grass.

The crowd roars, chanting the Bradford war cry as Logan launches the ball high into the sky, letting it crash down in the middle of the overcrowded grandstand. A wide grin stretches across my face as the buzzer sounds, and I can't help but notice the way Logan seeks out Chanel, making sure she just witnessed his show-stopping moment. The poor guy. He's got it bad.

The entire team races toward Logan, throwing themselves around him as the crowd begins spilling out onto the field, more than ready to celebrate with their winning team. I watch in awe. It was never like this at Hope Falls, never filled with this kind of all-round school spirit. Arizona tried to warn me, but I shrugged it off, not believing it for one minute, but now, after witnessing this, I know that from here until the end of the season, I won't miss a single home game.

"Come on," Ilaria says, gripping my hand and dragging me along with Arizona sticking to my back. "You get it now? Our game nights are epic, but not as good as the party that will follow."

I roll my eyes and laugh as we try to navigate the stands and avoid being trampled by the masses. "Don't even think about it," I tell her. "I'm not going to the party. Me around Tanner Morgan is not a smart move, and besides, I was hoping to catch my mom before Orlando flies her to Paris for the weekend. We still haven't spoken since our fight last week, and I'm starting to wonder if she actually remembers I live with her."

"Ughhhhh," Ilaria groans. "That's shit about your mom, but YOU'RE SO FREAKING BORING! You can't tell me that you'd rather stay home with Jensen over coming to the track with us. Come on, stop being such an old lady. We'll hitch a ride and then we can all drink and have a good night."

"Nope," I say, hitting the stairs. "Absolutely not."

They don't push me on it. They see the connection between me and Tanner, it's obvious to anyone who knows to look for it, and while I haven't told them what happened up against that tree last Friday night, or the million things that followed, they know something happened. Something has shifted.

They haven't demanded answers, and I have offered them the same privacy, but sooner or later, their curiosity is going to get the best of them.

Arizona laughs. "Yep, she's going to be an old lady," she tells Ilaria. "She'll have matching knitted sweaters made for us within the week."

"Don't knock the knitted sweaters," I laugh as we finally reach the bottom of the grandstand and make our way onto the field, only to get bulldozed by Chanel.

"Holy shit," she says, her pom-poms flying around mine and Arizona's faces. "Did you see that game? They were amazing."

"Hell yeah, they were," Ilaria says.

"So, what's the plan?" Chanel asks, her gaze shifting toward the crowd, searching but not finding whatever or whoever it is she's looking for. "I didn't bring any clothes with me, so I was going to head home and get dressed before heading to the track. Did you guys wanna come with me, or should I just find my own way there?"

"We'll come," Arizona says, "But Marjorie over here is ditching us for a night in with her new stepbro."

Chanel gapes at me in horror and I rush to fill in the blanks. "I am not. I'm just not down for the track tonight. I need to keep my distance before I do something I regret."

Chanel grins at me. "By doing something you'll regret, what *or who* do you mean exactly?"

I grin right back at her. "Who knows? But I'm more curious about what *or who* you'll end up regretting," I say. "Who do you keep looking for in this crowd?"

She holds my stare, and in that exact moment, Logan rushes past, her cheeks flaming, unable to deny what's now so clearly obvious. "One can only hope."

Well, damn.

She bursts into a booming laugh, and I can't help but love her. I've been here for two weeks now, and these three assholes have somehow found their way into my heart and are clutching onto it with sharp talons, refusing to let go, and I wouldn't have it any other way. They've made being the new girl so easy, and every day I learn something more that makes me love them.

If I'm completely honest, the connection I've built with them rivals the friendship I've had with Erica for the past million years, and a part of me feels guilty for letting them in so much. If Erica knew how high I held these new friendships, she'd be hurt, but on the other hand, Erica has been distant.

Chanel takes off to do whatever it is she needs to do with the rest of the cheerleaders, and without skipping a beat, Ilaria, Arizona, and I make our way back toward the student parking lot, cutting through the center of the field.

The crowd lingers, celebrating with the team, and as we cut

through the thickest part of it, a soft brush against my hand has my head whipping back over my shoulder. I see the big number 14 on the front of his jersey first and flick my stare up to meet Tanner's hungry gaze. He's walking the opposite way but is turned backward with a cocky grin resting on his lips. He doesn't say a word, but he doesn't have to.

His message is loud and clear—you're mine.

A shiver sails down my spine as butterflies erupt in my stomach. Things really have shifted since our talk in the empty classroom and while it terrifies me, and the ghost of all that hurt still lingers, I can't help but notice how that hesitation seems to have disappeared from Tanner's gaze. It's as though he no longer fears what this could be and instead, he embraces it. Either way, I'm nervous as all shit. One moment alone with him could change it all.

He knows I watched him the whole game, and he knows just how hot and heavy he made me, and the way he's watching me now, he plans to ease that animalistic hunger that's burning deep inside of me. But there will be no easing of anything, not if I get my way.

This stupid crush on the most dangerous guy in school needs to be smothered for the sake of my sanity.

"Keep dreaming, 14," I tell him, smirking right back at him, all too aware that he's going to take my words as nothing but a challenge. "It's never going to happen."

And with that, I turn back and keep walking, terrified of just how deep I'm getting.

CHAPTER 26
TANNER

There's nothing better than a Friday night game but winning it while Brielle's eyes were on me was even better. Fuck, I could barely concentrate, but I promised my boys that my head was in the game, and I made sure of it. There's no way we're ending our season without that championship trophy. Not after the work we've put in. Broken Hill was good, but they were no match for us.

She watched me like a hawk, every step, every throw, every tackle, her eyes were only for me, and it pushed me harder. I wanted to perform for her, I wanted her to understand exactly why I'm the king of this fucking school. It was only the first game of the season and I'm already addicted.

The boys party around me as the girls are already going wild, grinding against anything they can get their hands on. The whole team showed up tonight, and because of how many people are already here, we're only accepting a few races. Too many races means too many opportunities for people to get hurt, and we're not about that, especially now that the majority of the people here are already wasted.

A beer rests in my hand, the condensation dripping down the side as I walk around the track. I've been looking out for Killjoy all fucking night but haven't found her, and I know that after that game and the look she gave me, there's no way she would have skipped out.

"Come on, bro," I hear Jax holler from behind me as he watches me bat away another chick who tries to cling to me. I spent twenty minutes just trying to get Jules off me. Letting her suck my dick was a mistake, and now she thinks there's something between us. She couldn't be more wrong, but Riley took her off my hands, not wanting a willing participant to go to waste. "Just pick one. They're all throwing themselves at you. Forget about Brielle."

"Worry about your own dick, man."

A booming laugh tears through him, and I shake my head, already knowing what's coming out of his mouth before he even bothers to say it. "Don't need to. Karleigh already has it under control."

A feminine laugh sounds, and I don't even bother looking back. I know what I'll find, and it's not exactly something I wanna watch my cousin doing. After all, I've already been there with Karleigh, and so has the rest of the team. At least she's a fast worker. She'll get him off in no time and he'll be back to celebrating with the boys.

A familiar mop of golden blonde hair cuts past me and I reach out, gripping Chanel's arm and pulling her up short. She goes to bitch at me before seeing it's me, and the irritation in her eyes is quickly replaced with anger. She still hasn't forgiven me for the bullshit that went down last year, and I don't blame her.

Chanel yanks her arm out of my grip and stares at me with a raised brow, not impressed to be standing in my presence. "What do you want?"

"Where's Brielle?"

Her brows furrow and I watch as that irritation comes storming back full force. Her arms cross over her slender body, unintentionally boosting her tits up higher. "How is that any of your business?"

She's right. It's not, but that doesn't mean I won't do anything it takes to get the answer out of her.

I step closer, my eyes narrowing on her, and I watch as she sucks in a breath, remembering just how lethal I can be. Hell, our little fuck-fest didn't end last year only because I was bored with her, it ended because I put her brother in the hospital, and I know she thinks of that every time she looks at me. He was a senior last year and on the team. We all knew he liked his girls young, but when I caught the fucker with a thirteen-year-old girl in his bedroom, making her feel like shit for telling him no, I couldn't help myself. It nearly lost me my spot on the team but once the girl came forward and my name was cleared, I was welcomed back as a hero. "Where is she, Chanel?" I repeat, my tone lowering as goosebumps sail over her skin.

"She's not here," she finally says.

I pull back, confusion lacing my tone. "What do you mean she's not here?"

"Holy shit, Tanner. Are you seriously that self-absorbed that the idea of a girl not wanting to be near you is that horrifying? She didn't want to see you because she knows that sooner or later, you're going to screw her over just like you do everyone, and honestly, can you blame her?" She backs up a step. "Just … leave her alone. She doesn't know what she's doing getting involved with you. I care about her, and I don't want to see her get hurt."

"Same could be said about you."

"What's that supposed to mean?"

"You're playing with Logan and have been for twelve fucking months," I tell her, voicing the thing we've all been tiptoeing around. "Either do something about it or let him go but stop stringing him along. He's better than that and you know it. You're just too fucking scared, and sure, that could be my fault, but he's a good guy, and if you let him in, he's not going to screw you over like I did."

I don't wait for her response because honestly, it really doesn't matter to me. All that I care about is the fact that Brielle isn't here. I have an hour until I'm due to race, and when I do, she'll be right there with those bright blue eyes on me.

Taking off through the throng of drunken seniors, I shove my untouched beer into the hands of one of my teammates before breaking out through the parking lot. My bike is parked right up front, and I waste no time throwing my leg over it and storming off like a bat out of hell.

Wind whips past me, my shirt sticking to my body as I fly back up the road. It takes ten minutes before I'm pulling into my driveway and even less time for me to break into the house next door. Her door is unlocked, and despite our conversation about welcoming myself into her room uninvited, I still push it open and slip inside, grinning as I hear the sound of her shower running.

How is it that every time I come in here, she's in the shower?

Soft moans come from inside the bathroom, and I groan, barely keeping control. She's so fucking gorgeous when she comes. I should go in there and help her, but I'm not about to ruin tonight before it's even really started.

So instead, I take it upon myself to have a little fun. I make my way across her room and search through her wide array of lipstick colors before picking out a deep red, one that hasn't already been destroyed by our ridiculous messages, and I get busy scrawling a new message across the mirror.

Making a mental note to order her new lipsticks, I step back and admire my handiwork before settling down on her bed and helping myself to the small box of skittles on her bedside table. The smell of her perfume lingers in the air, and I listen to the sweet sounds of her coming, my name whispered on her lips, almost making me feel bad for the message left on her mirror. But fuck, now I know I should have gone in there and joined her.

Another minute passes before she finishes in the shower, and I listen as she wraps a towel around her tight little body and grips the door handle. Anticipation pulses through my veins, every passing second making me hold my breath until the door finally opens and she steps out.

Her soft gasp fills the room as she sees the deep red words on the mirror staring back at her.

DO YOU THINK ABOUT ME WHEN YOU CUM?

"That fucking ass—"

"Watch it, Killjoy. You wouldn't want to say anything that'll get you in trouble now, would you?"

She spins around, her eyes wide as she clutches her towel tighter. "What the hell are you doing in here?" she demands, her cheeks flushing with the most stunning blush. "I thought we covered the whole *coming into my room uninvited* thing."

Getting up from her bed, I cross her room and put myself right in front of her, reaching up and fingering a loose strand of blonde hair that curls from the water of her shower. "I came to get you," I tell her. "There's a party, but it seems that you're having more fun here by yourself."

"What's the matter, Tanner? Jealous?"

I lean into her, my hand gripping her waist and pulling her in rough against my chest. Her stare meets mine and I hold her captive, loving the way she gasps and pants for breath, just as affected by me as I am by her. "Immensely."

Her cheeks flush again and she pulls back from me. "Seriously though, what are you doing here?"

"I'm taking you to the track," I tell her, moving across to her closet and pushing through the door before tearing open her underwear drawer and pulling out the smallest thong I can possibly find. I toss it toward her, and she fumbles to catch it without dropping her towel. "I'm racing and I want you there. And then as soon as I've defended my title, I'm spending the rest of the night showing you just how fucking good it gets."

Bri scoffs and moves into the closet before shoving me out of the way and dropping the thong back in. "I'm not going to the party. I'm glad you won your game, and I'm sure you'll win your race too, but you and me in the same room together is dangerous."

Finding a black lace bra, I pull it out and shove it toward her before searching through the rest of her drawers and finding an old band tee and a pair of ripped jeans that I know curves around her ass in all the right places.

"Get dressed, Brielle," I say, turning toward her and meeting her stare. "You're coming with me whether you like it or not, so you can either dress yourself and come willingly—"

"Or?" she cuts me off.

"Or I will more than happily tear that towel off your sexy as fuck body and dress you myself. Don't think for one second I won't throw you over my shoulder and drag you there kicking and screaming. I'm not leaving here without you, and I'm not missing my race either, so take your pick."

Brielle glares at me, and I see the exact moment she gives in. "Fine," she mutters before jamming her hand against my chest and pushing me out of her closet.

High on the adrenaline of getting my way, I lumber toward her bed and drop down again, knowing it won't be a long wait. I've seen her getting ready for school in the mornings and it takes her all of three seconds to race through her morning routine, though as a general rule, she's always running late.

She emerges from the closet a few minutes later, dressed in the outfit I'd chosen for her, looking good enough to eat … fuck, maybe that's exactly what I'll do.

She crosses the room to the full-length mirror, studiously ignoring the words blocking her view as she grabs a tube of mascara and brushes it along her thick lashes. She's fucking captivating. I can't look away.

She doesn't apply any more makeup and I'm glad. She doesn't need it. She's so fucking stunning that it knocks the oxygen right out of my lungs every time I see her.

Before I know it, we're out the door and she's making her way toward her piece of shit Civic. "Nah," I laugh, pulling the keys out of her hand and shoving them deep into my pocket.

She just stands there, watching me straddle my bike as though she's never seen one before. "There's no way in hell I'm about to get on that with you."

A grin pulls at the corners of my lips as I hold my helmet out to her. "I wasn't kidding, Killjoy. Either get your ass on my bike, or I'll put you there myself, and trust me, throwing you around is only going to make me want you more."

Her eyes flash with hunger and she catches her breath, making me painfully hard inside my jeans. Deciding to play the game, she strides toward me and shoves the helmet over her head before placing her delicate hand on my shoulder. She throws her leg over my bike and settles in behind me, her thighs pressed right up against mine.

I turn the key and the engine roars to life, making Bri yelp and throw her hands around me, clutching on for dear life. "You good?"

"If you kill me, I'm going to tell the whole fucking school that you suffer from premature ejaculation."

A laugh rumbles through my chest, and without another word, I take off into the night, Bri's hold getting tighter by the second.

I take the ride back to the track slower, wanting to savor this moment as long as possible, but despite riding slower than the speed limit, we arrive at the track way sooner than I'd hoped. There's still half an hour before my race, and as I pull into the parking lot, I see the students of Bradford Private gaping toward us. I'm sure Bri probably assumes it's because we've shown up together, whereas I know it's because I've broken my one cardinal rule—no chick will ever ride with me, no matter what. But Brielle ... fuck, she has me breaking all kinds of rules.

I don't bother filling her in on the secret as I drive right through the property, passing through the parking lot and down into the crowd. They create a path for me just as I knew they would, and I don't stop until I've crossed the track and pull onto the side where the boys and I usually chill.

Everyone is here and I know it's going to be a night to remember.

Before I've even cut the engine, Riley is stepping in beside my bike and offering Bri his hand. "You couldn't resist me after all," he says. "I knew you'd come running."

I knock his hand out of the way and send a scathing glare toward him. "Want another black eye?" I ask him. "You had your week, bro. She's not interested."

The dick grins back at me. "Afraid of a little competition?"

Bri scoffs and grips my shoulder as she climbs off my bike. "There is no competition," she says, my chest filling with pride until she goes and shuts it down. "I'm not fucking either of you."

And not a moment later, Arizona, Chanel, and Ilaria come bursting through the crowd and slam right into her, scooping her into their arms. "Is that you, Marjorie?" Arizona teases. "I didn't recognize you without your sweater."

They burst into laughter as the boys and I just stare. "Who the fuck is Marjorie?" Riley murmurs.

"I've got no idea."

The girls start talking shit and press a drink into Bri's hand, insisting she catch up, and within the space of three seconds, they're rummaging through the back of Logan's RAM, searching out the good shit. As they start doing shots of Fireball, I realize that maybe she was safer locked up in her ivory tower after all.

Jax shows up from who the hell knows where, a cocky, satisfied grin playing on his lips as he barrels into his brother, dropping his arm over his shoulder. "I'm racing tonight."

"The hell you are," Logan grunts. "You're drunk."

"Nah, I've only had like … five or nine."

Logan rolls his eyes, his gaze falling toward Chanel as she laughs with the girls. "Exactly my point, man. Mom's off fucking some billionaire Italian and Dad's on a shoot, so I'm not being the one responsible for wiping your ass after you lose control of your car and need a full-time caretaker."

"Don't be such a little bitch," Jax says, his grin widening. "We'll obviously hire a fresh out of college caretaker with big tits who'll sit on my dick every night. It'll be romantic. A modern-day love story."

Logan pushes his brother off him with a frustrated grunt before shaking his head and letting out a heavy breath. He's more frustrated than usual, and his stare hasn't left Chanel for even a second, and when he starts bouncing his shoulders, my brows fly up.

Riley gapes, seeing what I'm seeing. "Is he—"

"Doing his pregame mental pep talk bullshit he does before facing down our biggest rivals? He sure fucking is."

"You don't think he'll—" Without a moment of hesitation, Logan takes off toward the group of girls, looking as though he's about to shit himself. "Yup. He's going in for the kill," Riley says, the four of us watching with wide eyes.

Logan's been working up to this very moment for twelve long months. He's been with her plenty of times, not that any of her friends know. He's got absolutely no issues when it comes to sex. They end up screwing at every party, but he's never had the guts to tell her that he's madly in love with her. They're constantly at each other's throats, and while it's entertaining as hell, it kills him that he can't have her in the way he wants.

Jax laughs, bumping into me. "Nah, there's no fucking way. He's too sober for this shit. He's going to shit the bed."

Logan reaches the girls, and just as he goes to reach out to Chanel, he pauses, his whole body stiffening with fear. "Come on, man," I murmur, wanting this for him despite knowing there's probably some other girl who's better suited for him. "Just do it."

As he glances back at us, his steps falter nervously, and instead of approaching the group of girls, he takes off at high speed into the thick crowd, bitching out like a fucking pussy. We burst into booming laughter as Jax snatches up Logan's discarded beer. "Called it."

Our laughter has the girls whipping around, and Brielle's gaze falls to mine. "What's so funny?" she asks as Chanel glances around our group, her brows furrowed.

"What happened to Logan? I could have sworn he was just here."

Jax laughs, lifting his beer to his lips. "Motherfucker shit his pants, that's what."

Bri holds my stare and I lift my chin, silently asking her to come to me, and she doesn't hesitate, the few shots making her brave. She steps into me, her hand resting against my chest, right where it belongs. "What's up?"

"Come with me," I tell her, indicating toward my bike. "There's something I need to do."

CHAPTER 27
Brielle

The engine of the sleek, black bike roars to life between my legs as my arms fly around Tanner's waist. "Where are we going?" I ask as he propels us through the crowd, a sharp yelp tearing from my throat.

He doesn't respond, but I feel the rumble of laughter vibrating through his chest.

"Tanner?" I warn.

Nothing.

"Asshole."

All I can do is watch as the bike cuts through the crowd along the same path we drove thirty minutes ago. The ground is rocky and uneven, and I'm forced to hold onto him tighter to keep from slipping off the stupid bike, but I'm not going to lie, holding onto him like this … shit. I should have just let Riley have me, then none of this would be happening. Tanner would have backed away after I slept with his friend, and Riley would have been through with me after getting what he wanted, but now … I'm caught up and I don't know what to do.

Tanner gets to the track, and instead of cutting through it like he had on our way down, he turns the handlebars, putting us directly on the track's path and my body flinches. "What are you doing?" I call over the loud thumping music and the roar of the engine. "Where are you taking me?"

Silence.

God, he's infuriating.

He keeps going, creeping through the throng of people who seem to be clearing away from the track, and when the music falls silent and a second engine rumbles near the parking lot, my stomach sinks.

"Tanner," I say louder as he brings his bike to a stop right at the starting line. The track is completely clear while familiar faces hover around the boundary line, their curious eyes lingering on me as they place bets. This fucker plans on racing with me on the back of his bike.

"Oh, fuck no!"

I start pulling away, but Tanner's hand comes down over mine to hold me still. "You didn't think you'd get away with covering my whole fucking room with the word *asshole*, did you? That shit took me nearly three hours to scrub clean."

"It was worth it, but this? No, absolutely not."

Tanner laughs as he eyes the other bike slowly making his way toward the starting line. "You're not scared, are you?" he questions, a smirk playing on his lips, knowing damn well that he's throwing down a challenge I won't be able to resist. "Funny, I didn't take you as the type to bitch out at the very last moment."

My fingers bunch into the material of his shirt, nerves pounding through me like hot lava destroying everything in its path. "Fucking fuckity fuck," I grunt, scooching in as close as physically possible and plastering my chest to his muscled back. "I really hate you right now."

"Sure you do," he murmurs, the other rider settling in beside us.

I don't recognize the guy but honestly, even if I did, I don't think I'd be able to place him. I'm too nervous and worked up to even think straight. He nods at Tanner before scanning a curious gaze over me and smirking, probably assuming that he's got this in the bag seeing as though Tanner's carrying extra luggage.

"Isn't there some kind of rule about this?"

Tanner scoffs. "You telling me you've never broken the rules before, Killjoy?" he questions as the head cheerleader from Bradford struts out onto the track in nothing but a red strappy bikini, hooker heels, and a scrap of material hanging from her taloned fingers.

"Fuck, fuck, fuck."

She moves to the center, and I watch her with wide eyes, needing something ... *anything* to focus on that isn't my imminent death. "Hold tight, Killjoy," Tanner says as the cheerleader raises her hand high in the sky, pausing to make a show out of her two seconds of fame. "Don't fucking let go. You need to stay so fucking tight to my back that I feel the heat of your tight little cunt rubbing against me."

"Fucking kill me now."

"Clear, Killjoy?" he questions, his eyes glued to the cheerleader. "I lean, you lean."

"Uh-huh."

"Repeat it to me."

"I lean, you lean."

His hand squeezes mine for only a moment before returning to the handlebar, and despite how terrified I am of turning into roadkill, I know I can trust him. Hell, despite my desperation to pull away, he's one of the only people in my life who I trust.

How messed up is that? Tanner Morgan has weaseled his way into my soul and resides there as if he's entitled to it. Shit, he's such an asshole.

I lean, you lean.

Why the hell does that speak to me on such a deep level?

As the cheerleader drops the scrap of material, the bikes take off, spitting dust from beneath their tires. My eyes bug out of my head, my heart lurching in my chest and racing faster than the bikes ever could. My stomach all but sinks out my ass, and I'm pretty sure my whole fucking soul just left my body.

I tighten my grip around Tanner's strong waist, my nails digging in. "HOOOOOOOOLLLYYYY FUUCCKKKKKKKIIINNNGGGG SSHHHHIIIITTTTTTT," I scream, my throat immediately going raw.

Terror plagues me as the world whips by at a million miles an hour. I feel Tanner's heartbeat beneath my hand, and he's cool, calm, and collected. He's confident and sailing around the track as though he's done this a million times before, and I suppose he has.

My head ducks down, curling behind his back and blocking the wind from whipping me in the face. He goes so fast that the people around the track blur, the only other solid figure is our opponent's bike, directly beside us, its rider determined to get ahead.

Before I know it, we're approaching the first corner. "TANNER, I SWEAR TO—"

"I LEAN, YOU LEAN," he calls over the roar of the engines.

And not a second later, we hit the corner.

Clenching my eyes, I let out a breath and let my body glide to the side, following Tanner as he leans into the corner, the track seeming to come closer and closer to my face, and before I know it, the bike is hitting the straight and I'm upright once again.

Fucking hell. The second this is done, I'm jamming his helmet right up his ass.

As we complete the first lap, my body starts to relax, and rather than clenching my arms around his body, I simply hold him, getting used to the feel of it and starting to finally enjoy myself. I raise my head from behind him, letting the wind cut past me, sending my golden waves flowing out behind me.

Shit, if I hadn't taken those few shots before he decided this was a good idea, it could have gone very differently. Though one thing is for sure, the vibration of the seat beneath me and the way I'm pressed right up against him has the inside seam of my jeans rubbing against my clit, and if I'm not careful, I'm going to come undone in front of all these people.

Feeling me relaxing behind him, he turns his head as if to glance over his shoulder but keeps his sharp gaze locked on the track ahead, always watching his opponent and calculating every moment. "There she is," he tells me. "I was worried you couldn't cut it for a moment."

A laugh booms from my chest as we ride side by side with this guy. My gaze lingers on him, watching as he pushes his bike to its limits, desperate to keep up with us as Tanner expertly maneuvers around each of the corners.

A grin pulls at my lips and my hand slips up under his shirt, right where it belongs, loving the feel of his toned abs beneath. We cross over the starting line again, one lap to go. "Hey Tanner," I call, pressing my chest firmer against his, rocking my hips forward and gasping at the intense pleasure pressing against my core.

He turns his head again and my other hand moves up to his shoulder, getting far too comfortable on the back of this thing. "What?"

"Are you done playing with him yet?"

He laughs, a cocky grin pulling at the corner of his lips. "Why?"

"I don't want you to just win," I tell him. "I want you to smoke him."

I feel his appreciative groan vibrating through his chest, and not a moment later, Tanner hits the fucking gas, launching the bike forward. A sharp yelp tears from my throat, making me wonder if he'd been holding back just to keep me from freaking out. The other bike is left in our dust, the crowd cheering for their defending champion as we fly around the track.

The adrenaline pulses through me, and I feel more alive than ever, gripping onto him as my hand shoots up into the sky, feeling the intense pressure of the wind slamming against my arm. We hit the final corner and I jolt off balance as he begins to lean into it, and I have no choice but to grip his waist again, his hand shooting back to my thigh, silently checking I'm not currently becoming roadkill.

He straightens out and I glance across the track, our opponent embarrassingly far behind. We barrel toward the finish line and a wide, exhilarated grin stretches across my face, anticipation brimming within me.

We fly across the line and a loud buzzer sounds, the crowd's roaring cheers blasting through the twins' property. Holy shit, I'm so turned on by all of this. The power, the speed, the win. It's like nothing I've ever felt before.

"That was incredible," I call, waiting for him to slow down to meet the crowd of adoring fans, more than ready to spend the rest of the night partying until I can't remember that my world is burning to ashes around me.

Tanner squeezes my thigh as he continues around the track, and a thrill shoots through me as I curiously watch him pull off the side through an opening in the crowd. He slows as we move away from the massive flood lights erected around the track, but we're still close enough to see everything that's going down. He drives into the trees surrounding the property, and the loud cheering of the party begins to fade away, covering us in a tension filled silence.

My heart thrums through my ears as he brings the bike to a stop, a sense of nervousness washing over me. Darkness surrounds us, and if it weren't for the glow coming from the track, we wouldn't be able to see a damn thing.

Gripping his shoulder, I balance myself as I slip off the edge of his bike, my ass numb from the ride. The whole race couldn't have taken more than three minutes, but the intensity of the vibrations through the seat and the tires flying over the track was enough to turn my legs into jelly.

He remains straddled on the bike but doesn't let me get far before his hand falls to my waist, pulling me back into his side. He takes my chin and meets my stare, his eyes narrowing in curiosity. "Why do you look so nervous?"

I grin up at him, a flush settling onto my cheeks. "Because the big bad wolf has brought me out into the woods all alone, and I'm still trying to decide if I want to play his game or not."

My hand falls to his strong thigh and a rush pulses through me, sailing right down to my core. "You should be running from me."

A smile spreads across my lips, the nervousness growing into anticipation as I make my decision to stay. My voice lowers, need slamming through my chest as my hand slowly trails up his thigh, leaning into him, his lips only a breath away. "Maybe you're the one who should be running from me."

His hand curls around the back of my neck and pulls me in, closing the distance and making me melt into him, every second between us working up to this one defining moment. Neither of us can back away now, whatever this is, it's here and now, the connection and pull between us too strong for either of us to deny.

He deepens the kiss, his tongue fighting for dominance as his hands roam over my body. I groan into his mouth, needing so much more from him, and damn it, he reads me like a fucking book.

He pulls my old band tee over my head and drops it to the dirty ground before reaching around and unclasping my bra. The soft material slips down my arms, and I let it fall away, my pussy clenching with anticipation.

Tanner explores my body, committing every curve to memory as my hand trails higher up his thigh. I've always been shy with making my move when it comes to sex, but with Tanner, there's no judgment. He wants to feel my body just as desperately as I want his.

His cock strains through his pants and he groans as my hand brushes over his thick length, sending a shiver down my spine. I knew he was big, but hell, this is going to be so much better than I could have ever anticipated.

His thumb skims over my nipple and it pebbles beneath his touch, making a smirk pull at his lips. I guess Tanner Morgan appreciates a responsive woman. "Do it again," I whisper, pulling back from his lips and tipping my head back as pleasure rocks through my body.

He doesn't hesitate, gently rolling my nipple between his thumb and forefinger, and with my head tipped back, he draws me back in and brings his lips down on the sensitive skin of my neck. I open up for him, wanting to feel it all, and I grip the hem of his shirt, lifting it over his head.

His body is perfect, so tall, sculpted, and strong. He's every woman's version of a wet dream, and I need to have him.

My hands fall to his belt, and he wastes no time stripping me of my jeans. I slip my shoes off and before I know it, Tanner is lifting me on top of him. He seats me down on his thighs, the position pushing my legs wide and exposing my most intimate parts.

His arm bands around my waist, holding me up and feeling my nervous energy beginning to creep back in, he kisses me again. And like butter, I melt.

I pull his cock free from the confines of his pants and my fist barely fits around him, but I'm up for the challenge. My fist moves up and down his thick cock, my thumb roaming over his tip and feeling the smooth bead of moisture. Hunger surges through me, and without thinking, I meet his heated stare and lift my thumb to my mouth.

Opening wide, I suck my thumb clean and his eyes blaze like molten lava. "Fucking hell," he murmurs. "And here I was wondering just how innocent you were."

Tanner's fingers brush against my clit, and I gasp, his touch sending a shot of electricity coursing through my veins. "There's not an innocent thing about me." And as if to drive my point home, he lowers his hand, his thumb remaining on my clit as he applies just a hint of pressure and pushes two thick fingers inside me, curling them at just the right time.

He draws them back and my grip tightens on his cock, needing him inside of me. I've been craving this moment since the second I met him, and as his fingers move in and out, teasing me with undeniable bliss and pleasure, that intensity only grows.

My chest rises and falls with rapid pants, my body so wound up, desperate for everything that he is.

I feel myself flooding, growing wetter with every second. "Tanner," I breathe, my arm curling around his neck and holding him closer. "I need you inside me. I can't wait any longer."

He groans, desire pooling in his eyes, and within seconds, his hand is slipping into the pocket of his jeans and pulling out a small foil packet. He tears it open with his teeth, keeping his other hand on me, and as his grip tightens around my waist and he lifts me up, a thrill fires through me.

Tanner lines his cock up with my entrance and I feel the tip right there as I take his shoulder. He lowers me down, so fucking slowly that I could die from anticipation. With each new inch I take of him, he stretches me wider, and I drop my head to his shoulder, groaning with his full intrusion until he's finally seated fully inside me.

Tanner's grip tightens on my waist, and he groans as my pussy clenches around him, adjusting to his sheer size. I raise my head and meet his stare, his soft breath brushing over my lips as his hand finds the back of my neck. "You good?" I nod and a desperate grunt sounds in the back of his throat. "Good, because I'm going to need you to start moving. You're so fucking tight around me, so warm, and perfect, like you were made just for me."

His words send butterflies swarming through my stomach, and without hesitation, I rock my hips, getting used to the feel of his rock-hard cock moving inside of me. The slight movement sends waves of pleasure washing through me.

"Oh, fuck," I pant, doing it again only to bite my bottom lip between my teeth and grip onto him tighter. I do it again, this time taking him deeper, and he groans before pulling me back in, his lips slamming down on mine. I move faster, taking exactly what I need from him, never feeling so alive. Is this what it's like to be high? To be so one with your body while also feeling as though it's not even your own?

This isn't the easiest position to move in, but I give it my all, rocking, swaying, bouncing. Anything he needs, I give him, reading his body as easily as though it were my own.

That familiar pull begins to grow, intensifying with every passing second. "Shit, Tanner," I gasp, panting for breath, my arm tightening around his neck as our bodies grow sweaty. "I'm going to come."

"Not without me, you're not," he rumbles, his voice thick with desire as his thumb presses harder against my clit, drawing tight little circles and sending my eyes rolling into the back of my head.

"Oh, fuck, fuck, fuck. Yes. Tanner, more."

He's only so happy to oblige, and give me exactly what I want, and I feel myself growing closer and closer to the edge, barely holding on. "Tanner," I warn, knowing there's no way I'm going to be able to hold on much longer, my body far too wound up.

"I know, baby. I fucking know," he tells me, his fingers digging into my skin. "I'm right there with you. Give it to me, Killer. I wanna feel your tight little cunt squeezing me."

His words are my undoing, and I explode around him, my orgasm blasting through me, pulsing through every last nerve in my body and sending me into an intense bliss. My pussy spasms, convulsing around his thick cock as he continues working my clit. I don't dare stop, my hips rocking and grinding, feeling him so deep inside me as I ride out my high, watching his face as he comes with me.

Coming down from my high, my head drops to his shoulder and he holds me up, his fingers drawing soft circles against my skin as he remains seated inside me. A moment passes when I finally catch my breath and raise my head to meet his stare, his dark eyes already on mine. A million things rush through my mind, but when I open my mouth to say something, not a damn word comes out.

The cocky bastard winks. "Speechless, huh?"

A laugh tears out of me and I shove at his chest. "Is this the part where I tell you I think we should just be friends?"

Tanner smirks back at me, his eyes dancing as though he's never been so happy. "Wow, your pussy is still clenched around my cock and you're already trying to shoot me down."

I lean in and brush my lips over his, clenching a little tighter just to make a point and almost die of desire at the sound of his hungry groans. "Figured an ego like yours could handle being knocked back."

He captures my lips in his and kisses me with greed before gently pulling back, his eyes sparkling. "If only you meant it," he tells me, his arm scooping under my leg and lifting me off him. His cock pulls free, and a hollowness shatters me just as my back slams against the rough bark of a tree.

Tanner's body presses against me and I gasp, desire pooling between my legs, needing him all over again. He adjusts his hold on me and I groan as he pushes back inside me, this new position taking him so much deeper. "You ready, Killer?" he asks, his tongue rolling over his lips and warning me that this is about to get rough in all the best ways. "What we did on my bike was nothing but a warmup."

Well, shit.

I can't say that this is what I expected of my night, but now that he's right here, staring me in the face … Well, he's more than just staring me in the face, he's already so deep inside of me that if I'm not careful, I'll be feeling him in my throat soon. Either way, I'm not about to say no. If Tanner Morgan wants to spend his night making me come over and over again, then who the hell am I to deny him?

CHAPTER 28
Brielle

Four times. Four fucking times. I haven't even come that much when I'm on my own.

My knees shake as Tanner helps me back onto his bike, my arms curling around his waist. I have no idea where we stand, but what I do know is that when it comes to sex, we are more than compatible. It was everything and more.

I'm not going to lie, despite how much he's pushed me away and how much I've tried to hate him, I always knew it would come down to this. I knew we were going to end up having this moment together, I just didn't expect that it would be out in the middle of some half-abandoned property with the rest of my classmates on the other side of the trees. In my head, I'd imagined it happening in either one of our rooms, and I have to be honest, I may have had one or two sex dreams that involved fucking on the roof outside my bedroom window, but never in a million years did I expect to have fucked Tanner Morgan on his bike and up against a tree. We ended up on the ground at some point, and my brain is too full of post sex-fog to even remember at what point he ate my pussy like a starving man at an all you can eat buffet. All I remember is that it was the most erotic thing I'd ever seen.

Tanner Morgan—ten out of ten, highly recommended.

The bike rumbles beneath me and my head rests against Tanner's back, too exhausted to even think about having to spend the next few hours socializing and partying with my new friends, but I don't doubt the moment the vibe of the track party settles into my soul, I'll somehow find the energy to party all night. What can I say? Tanner made me come four times, and to me, I can't find a better excuse to celebrate. Besides, the thought of going home and ending this night hurts something deep in my chest.

My fingers dance across the ink decorating his strong arms as we ride toward the glowing lights surrounding the track. It has to be well past midnight by now, but there's even more people here than before.

The crowd is rowdy, and I don't miss the way curious glances linger on the bike as we re-emerge into the world. I was so much happier out there, covered by the darkness of the trees, but I just know the moment I get off his bike and the girls swallow me into their arms, they're going to demand an explanation, and honestly, how can I explain something I don't completely understand?

Tanner cuts back through the crowd, and I see the catty stares coming from the group of cheerleaders hovering directly in the center of the crowd. The words slut and whore are thrown at me, and my fingers flinch on Tanner's arm. "Just say the word and I'll end them," he murmurs, having the power to do just that.

I shake my head. The girls of Bradford Private have been mostly welcoming, despite seeing this connection between me and Tanner, and up until now, they haven't said a damn thing, but I see it in their eyes. They think I'm stealing something that belongs to them, something they're entitled to, but I doubt Tanner sees it that way. "Nah," I tell him, more than able to handle myself. "I'm not looking to start a war with a bunch of cheerleaders. They'll quickly learn that I won't fall victim to their bullshit and get bored."

We ride right across the track and back up to where we'd been hanging out before, and I'm surprised to find Ilaria and Arizona still chilling with the guys.

Tanner cuts the engine, his gaze lifting to the back of Logan's RAM to where Logan and Chanel stand locked in some kind of argument, looking as though they're about to start tearing shreds off each other. "They've been going at it for twenty minutes," Hudson says, noticing Tanner's stare. "But looks like they're not the only ones who've been working out their issues."

My cheeks flush as Ilaria laughs, holding that same scrap of material the cheerleader started the race with and spinning it around like some kind of lasso. "Damn straight, girl," she cheers, a drink in her other hand. "Hope you gave it to him good."

Jax and Arizona laugh as I brace my hand against Tanner's

shoulder for balance as I slide off the bike, my pussy clenching with the movements. "The next one of you to say anything gets a fist straight up your ass," I warn them, eyeing Riley and Jax, knowing they're the most-likely culprits.

Riley grins back at me and makes a show of zipping his lips, but it only lasts a second. "For the record," he says, unable to help himself. "I would have at least taken you to dinner before fucking you in the woods."

"For the record," I throw back at him. "You would have fumbled around with my bra strap and come in your pants before I'd even touched you."

He narrows his eyes and I grin wide. "You know damn well that I can handle my shit."

I shrug my shoulders. "I'm yet to see it," I tease, watching Tanner from the corner of my eye as he moves off his bike and saunters toward the back of Logan's RAM, probably finding himself a beer.

Riley scoffs. "You want to see me in action?" he questions, up for the challenge. "Pick one girl, any single one of them, and I bet I could have her bent over within ten minutes."

"Bullshit."

Riley laughs and steps toward me, his brows bouncing with excitement. "Oh, baby girl. You're about to witness a god at work." He slings an arm over my shoulders and, in the same instant, turns us to face the crowd at our back. "Who's it gonna be?"

My gaze scans the dancing bodies, being careful with my selection until finally landing on a girl from my biology class. She's popular, and I'm sure all of the guys have already slept with her at some point. "Her," I tell him, pointing her out. "Maddison Matthews."

Riley grins as Tanner appears at my side, and just as I thought, there's a drink in his hand, but when he presses some girly shit into mine, a wave of butterflies swarm through my stomach. Tanner follows my gaze and scoffs. "Ain't no way, man. Maddi won't go for a round two with you after you fucked her sister."

Riley's eyes dance with the challenge as he glances back at Tanner. "I suppose we'll see," and with that, he struts toward the dancing crowd, moving in toward her and glancing back over his shoulder, his brows bouncing as if to tease just how easy this is going to be.

He starts dancing with the crowd around her, looking at her friends and eye fucking every last one of them but her, and I watch as she notices. "Holy shit, he's really going to do it," I murmur, watching as Maddi moves closer toward him, now desperate for his attention.

"Damn right, he will," Tanner smirks, shaking his head at his best friend's performance. "Consider yourself lucky that he forgot to set the terms of the bet before going for it. That asshole would have had you in skimpy lingerie, hand feeding him grapes for a week."

I grin up at him, loving the way his eyes are only for me. "Don't assume that had he set terms, I wouldn't have made it interesting too. I don't lose bets, Tanner."

Fire burns through his stare as his hand falls to my waist, pulling me in closer, both of us locked in each other's stare.

"No, absolutely not," Ilaria says, barging between us and yanking me away. "You've been holed up with him for like … forever, and there's no way you're about to stand there and suck face with the guy while we're trying to party. Not happening on my watch, baby."

Arizona cheers to Ilaria's demands and throws herself to her feet only to have Jax's arm snake out around her waist and yank her back onto his lap. "And where the fuck do you think you're going?"

Arizona laughs and my brows shoot up, gaping between the two of them and just how comfortable they are with one another. "What the hell is this?"

She grins up at me, her eyes darkening with a wicked heat. "Oh, Jax and I go way back," she explains, her legs dangling over the side of his. She loops her arm around his neck and he pulls her in closer. "Lost the big V to this guy," she says. "Not gonna lie, it wasn't great for either of us, but the guy is a fast learner and that thing he does with his tongue … ooffft."

Pride surges through Jax's features and the cockiest grin I've ever seen stretches across his face. His hand drops to her thigh, sailing high. "And don't you forget it."

"Has this been staring me in the face the whole time and I just haven't seen it? Are you two like … a thing?"

"Oh, God no," Arizona booms. "Jax is the biggest manwhore you'll ever meet, worse than Riley, Tanner, and Hudson put together. "

"Not Logan as well?"

She scoffs and our eyes wander toward Logan and Chanel half hidden behind his RAM, the two of them still deep in an argument. "No, not Logan," she laughs. "At least, not anymore. At this point, the dude's dick is going to fall off from lack of use."

Jax laughs. "Trust me, his dick is getting plenty of action, just not the kind of action he wants."

My brows furrow and Hudson is quick to clear up any confusion. "He jerks off like it's going out of style. He's hitting it so often that I wouldn't be surprised if it does fall off. But hey, that's what sexual frustration gets ya."

"You guys are so gross," Ilaria laughs, getting up to grab a new drink, and as time flies, the alcohol has more than worked its way through my blood system.

Tanner sits with his friends talking shit and laughing as the girls and I work out the size of our classmates' dicks based on the size of their egos, and unfortunately, some of them aren't doing so well. "Oh shit," I rush out, my head whipping around and scanning through the bodies down on the track. The boys' conversation falls short as all eyes come to me. "We forgot about Riley. Where did he go? Was anybody timing him?"

Hudson laughs. "Seeing as though he's not here acting a fool, we can safely assume he's buried deep inside cheerleader pussy. He'll be back soon, but don't worry, he'll be sure to share every last detail."

I scrunch my face in disgust and the boys laugh before falling back into their easy conversation, discussing the game and how Logan killed it. "Come on," Ilaria says, gripping my hand and dragging me back to the RAM. "We're doing shots and then I'm going to teach you how to dance like a ho."

"Deal."

We get messy and I'm not going to lie, there's maybe a few too many shots making their way through my system. While Ilaria dances up on some guy, Jax steals Arizona away, and I can't resist glancing back toward the guys, my eyes lingering on Tanner.

I dance for him as Riley returns, and judging by the looks on the guys' faces, he's more than sharing all the details. His hands flail around, doing all the actions and giving a detailed run down of how he screwed Maddi, and from the looks of it, he just got the best blowjob of his life.

I turn back to the girls as Chanel joins us again, her eyes brimming with secrets that have me desperate for information, and the way she dances … Well, damn. Someone just got dicked down, and her grin can only suggest just how good it was. I suppose Logan won't be rubbing one out tonight. Chanel's already handled that for him … literally.

A hard body presses into my back as a warm hand circles my waist, sending a smile tearing across my face, but as Chanel pauses and looks to the person behind me, confusion flickers in her eyes. "Who the fuck are you?"

I whip around, my eyes wide coming face to face with Colby. I shove him hard, pushing him away from me. "What the hell do you think you're doing?" I demand, glancing over his shoulder to see Tanner in the distance, getting to his feet.

Colby's back is to him and, seeing as though he's not already storming down here, he hasn't figured out who this is. But there's no doubt about it, if he's dumb enough to show up here, then he's asking for a thorough beating, and he'll damn well get it.

Colby reaches for me but I dodge his advance. "You and I need to talk," he spits, anger blooming in his stare as he tries for me again. "You think I was just going to let you walk away after the shit you pulled last week. You've been blocking my calls and not responding to my messages, so you leave me no fucking choice."

Done with my evasion, he lunges forward and grips my arm, yanking me into his chest, his fingers easily bruising my skin. "Ain't no girl of mine going to whore herself around like this. You're coming with me, and you won't be fucking leaving until I'm done with you."

He drags me back through the crowd as panic surges through me. I yank on my arm, forcing him to turn back and without hesitation, my knee slams up into his junk. Colby doubles over while refusing to release my arm, but it's enough to gain the attention of the people around us, and I have no doubt that Tanner and the boys are already on their way. "If you think I'm going anywhere with you, you're sorely mistaken," I tell him, leaning in and lowering my voice to a threatening whisper. "I know what you did to Addison Morgan, and you're going to go down for it. Mark my fucking words, Colby. Tanner is going to bury you."

He groans, his fingers digging into my skin as he pulls me back into him. "Shut the fuck up about it. You don't know what you're talking about, and if you aren't careful, I'll make sure you're next."

As if on cue, Tanner barges through the crowd, rage burning through his wild eyes as the boys fail to hold him back. He's too fast. Not even Logan can get him, and there's no denying it now, he knows this is Colby, the same piece of shit who left his sister for dead, the same son of a bitch who held her down and raped her.

He grips Colby around the back of the throat and tears him away from me, launching him across the track and shoving him to the ground. Without skipping a beat, his heavy fist rears back, and with every ounce of anger bursting through his body, he smashes his fist right into Colby's jaw.

I hear the sickening crunch, and all I can do is stand back and watch, hoping like hell Tanner hits him harder. Fuck, I don't even care if Tanner breaks every bone in his hand and up his arm. I will nurse him back to health if that's what I have to do. He'll recover, and while none of this changes what happened to Addison or the fact she's still fighting for her life in the hospital, it will lift a weight off Tanner's shoulders. For the first time in six long weeks, he'll finally feel as though he's doing something to help his sister.

He beats the shit out of him as people around us pull out their phones, capturing every last brutal second of it, and then all too soon, the boys are there, tearing him off Colby.

Sirens blast in the distance and all hell breaks loose. Someone grabs my wrist and I stumble along after them, my gaze snapping back to Colby's unconscious body, beaten and broken in the middle of the track. People scramble and scream, bodies flying left and right. The flood lights shut off, plunging the track into darkness, and the music drops away, leaving nothing but the sound of anxious high school students desperate to flee.

"Is he dead?" I yell, glancing back again, Colby still not moving.

No one answers, but someone shoves me into the back of the RAM, and before I even right myself in the seat, we're peeling out of the property. There's a separate exit in the back, far from the one the rest of our classmates are using.

The property is aglow with red and blue lights, and as the cops chase the stragglers through the main exit, we disappear into the cover of trees. Logan knows the track like the back of his hand, and within moments, we're breaking out onto the main road, tires screeching against the pavement and sending us soaring back toward Bradford.

CHAPTER 29
Brielle

Logan pulls to a stop outside mine and Tanner's homes and a nervousness tears through me. No one has said a word the whole way here, and I don't know what to do. Tanner sits in the front, his chest heaving with rage as his knuckles bleed. I don't know what he needs or how to calm him. This is all too new, and I'm sure he doesn't want me telling him that it's all going to be okay.

Colby could be dead. He just laid there, not moving, not even a flinch.

If Tanner killed him … fuck. I can't even begin to think how bad this is going to get. This is only the beginning. I should have tried to pull him away, should have tried to stop him. He has a whole future to think about, a career with the NFL that hangs in the balance, and

I stupidly just stood back and let it happen, hoping he would hit him harder.

Fuck, what kind of asshole does that make me?

Logan gets out and moves to my door, opening it for me and helping me down. "You should go home," he tells me. "We'll handle this."

I nod, not sure what *this* really is. "Okay," I murmur, my gaze trailing back to Tanner, watching as he barges his way out of the RAM, Jax and Riley right beside him, holding onto him to make sure he doesn't take off to finish the job. "What's ... what's going to happen?"

Logan shakes his head. "Your guess is as good as mine," he tells me. "Hudson stayed at the track to keep an eye on things. He'll let us know how bad it is once he gets some information. In the meantime, can you message the girls, make sure they got out okay?"

"Of course," I say, stepping toward the Channing residence, my gaze lifting to Tanner once again. God, I would do anything to barrel into his arms right now, to hold him and make his pain go away, but I don't think that's what he needs. I don't know how to help him and it's crushing me.

The boys make their way up Tanner's driveway, and I stop to watch them, meeting Tanner's dark gaze as he glances back at me. Pain lingers in his eyes, and with every step the boys take, I feel as though something is being torn away from me.

"Logan," I call as Jax and Riley take Tanner inside. Logan turns back, his eyes lifting to mine. "All the people," I say. "They were recording him. If that gets out, he's going to lose football. No colleges will sign him."

"I know," he says, nodding, his face grim and filled with concern for his cousin and everything this could mean. "Don't worry about it. I've got it handled. Tanner isn't going down for this."

And with that, he disappears inside the house, leaving me an absolute mess.

I make my way toward the door, getting only a few steps inside before my phone begins blasting in my pocket. Fishing it out, I find Ilaria's name scrawled across the screen, and I hastily answer it as I fly up the stairs two at a time. "Ilaria?" I rush out. "Are you guys okay? Did you get out?"

"We're fine. We looked for you, but Chanel thought she saw you getting man-handled into Logan's RAM."

"Yeah," I tell her, listening to the heavy sigh that quickly follows. "We all got out. I'm home now and the boys are all dealing with Tanner, but that was insane."

"Damn right it was," she says. "Did Tanner beat the crap out of him because of you?"

"No, it has nothing to do with me," I rush out, not wanting to be the one to have to explain what this was really about, but also not wanting a false story to begin spreading. "It's … it's personal between them. They have issues that go far beyond me, and unfortunately, I just happen to be right in the middle of it."

I barge through to my room and drop down on the edge of the bed, unable to get the haunting pain in his eyes out of my head. "He's going to be okay," Ilaria murmurs, her tone softening, being able to sense just how much he really means to me. "It will all get cleared up. This isn't the first fight Tanner's been involved in and probably won't be the last. Your ex most likely has a broken jaw and a mad concussion. He was probably just knocked out cold. He'll be fine."

"I hope so," I murmur, letting out a heavy sigh, and while I know I'm lying, wanting Colby to suffer in the worst possible ways, I also need him to be fine because if he's not, Tanner is fucked.

"Okay, girl," she says. "If you want to talk …"

She leaves her words hanging in the air and a smile pulls at the corners of my lips, but I don't feel it. "Thanks. I'll let you know if I hear anything."

"Same goes," she says before ending the call.

I drop my phone onto my bed and make my way into my bathroom before settling into a hot shower, letting the water wash over me. I'm filthy from spending a good portion of my night screwing around with Tanner on the dirty ground, and I know for a fact that there are at least three spilled drinks from drunk high schoolers that have left me feeling all kinds of sticky.

Taking my time, I wash my hair and scrub my body while still being able to feel Tanner between my legs. It was dirty work, but someone had to do it. Being with him was so much more than I imagined. Sex is one thing, but to have that connection as well, it meant something. Our messed-up little relationship has shifted, and just the thought of meaning something to him or what we have being something real brings butterflies to my stomach.

Finished with my shower, I turn off the lights and settle into my bed, pulling the sheets right up to my chin and snuggling into the blanket. I hear loud noises from the guys next door and try to zone them out, knowing they're fixing this with alcohol, which will only end in disaster.

Sleep doesn't come, and I lay in bed staring at the ceiling.

An hour passes, and then another before a noise has my heart leaping out of my chest. A loud thud sounds in my closet and my head whips around, wide-eyed as I reach for the lamp on my side table and fill my room with its dull light.

I find Tanner stepping out of my closet and his eyes come to mine. He's so clearly wasted and looks like shit. His hand hasn't been bandaged properly and I'm pretty sure he's only moments from breaking down.

Pushing my blankets back, I move out of my bed and walk into his open arms. "You're going to be fine," I tell him, letting him wrap me in his warmth and closing my eyes as my face presses against his wide chest. "Remember," I murmur. "*You lean, I lean.*"

We stand in silence for just a moment before I take his hand and lead him into my bathroom. I strip him of his stained and bloodied clothes, dumping them in my hamper and peeling off the bandage the boys must have stuck on him, checking the damage below.

His knuckles are split and bruised, and by morning, there will be plenty of swelling, but I'm sure it's nothing he hasn't dealt with before. I reach into my shower and as the water warms, I peel off my pajamas and lead him into the warm spray of water.

We stand in silence as I slowly massage his hand, washing away the dried blood before moving onto the rest of his body and hoping the shower can somehow help settle the alcohol sitting in the bottom of his stomach.

I lead him out of the shower and find the small first aid kit hidden in the cupboard beneath the sink. I get him fixed up, neither of us saying a word, and once I'm finally done, I lead him to my bed.

The moment my head hits my pillow, Tanner pulls me into his arms, my head resting against his chest, and once again feeling something shift between us. What we have, while still very new, is so much more than just some bullshit high school relationship. This is real, so damn real.

"*You lean, I lean*," he tells me, pressing his lips to the top of my head, and not a moment later, he closes his eyes and falls asleep, settling something deep inside my chest.

Sun streams in through my room and I groan, knowing damn well I drank far too much last night, but it was fun until it all went to shit. The memories from the night come streaming back to me, and I let out a heavy sigh. It was so good until Colby showed up. Why did he have to ruin everything?

Tanner and I …

I don't know. I think we're something. He was a broken man last night, fearing for his future. He knew he fucked up by putting his hands on Colby, but I didn't see a hint of regret in his eyes, only fear for the repercussions, fear of letting his mom and sister down, fear for throwing away everything he's worked for.

He came to me vulnerable. He was broken and silently screaming for help, and I did what I could to make it better, but I don't know if it was enough … I hope I'm enough.

Rolling over, my hand spreads out over the bed, searching for him only to find it empty. Devastation rocks through me. I should have seen this coming. Judging by the position of the sun streaming through my window, it's well after midday and after everything that happened last night, I can't expect him to wait around to talk it out with me. He has shit to deal with and another whole human being to ensure isn't dead. To assume he'd be thinking about me today is selfish.

Peering through my bedroom, my eyes stop on red lipstick scrawled across my mirror.

I'M SORRY.
HE'S ALIVE.
DON'T BE SCARED OF ME.

My heart shatters, feeling so much depth in those words, so much to unpack, and so much to be thankful for. How could I ever be scared of him, and why would he assume that I am? After everything he's told me, his actions were justified, but what's important is that Colby Jacobs is alive. At least, for now.

Throwing my blanket back, I trudge out of my room and make my way downstairs as my stomach grumbles. I had dinner after the game last night, but since then, I've been riding high on nothing but adrenaline, and now I'm starving.

With breakfast well and truly missed, I put together lunch when I hear someone on the stairs. "Mom?" I call out, my eyes widening as my heart pounds just a little bit faster. I still haven't had a chance to speak with her after all the bullshit of the past two weeks, and I hate the thought of her taking off to Paris for the weekend without talking it through first.

"Try again," Jensen calls out, making his way through the foyer and into the kitchen. He glances my way before his brows arch at the sight of food on the table. "You making lunch?"

Rolling my eyes, I let out a sigh and resist telling him to fuck off. "I'm assuming you're hungry?"

"Starving," he says, moving around my side of the island counter to help. He grabs a chopping board and gets busy slicing tomatoes. "Your mom isn't here," he says, almost as an afterthought. "They took a late flight last night to make the most of the weekend."

Hurt tears at my chest. "What do you mean a late flight? They're already gone?"

"Mmhmm," he murmurs, doing a decent job of the tomatoes and keeping his eyes down. "Dad's driver swung by at nine to pick them up."

I shake my head, his timeline not matching up. "No, that couldn't be right. I was home then. I didn't go out till after. Mom wouldn't have left without saying goodbye."

Jensen shrugs his shoulders. "I don't know what to tell you, Bri.

You can check the security footage if you want. All I know is that I was trying to get out of here when they left, and your mom held me up for twenty minutes talking about shit that I had absolutely no interest in."

I gape at him, unable to believe that she'd really leave without saying goodbye. "Did she know I was home? I texted her that I was coming home after the game to chat."

"She was playing on her phone all night organizing last minute details for their trip, so I'm assuming she definitely knew you were coming home. That woman doesn't miss anything," he says, "and for the record, yes. When we were talking out front, she mentioned that you were home and suggested that I take you out so you weren't stuck at home alone."

"She knew I was home," I repeat, really trying not to let the hurt tear me apart, but how can I not? She left without saying goodbye.

"Look," he says with a sigh, stopping his chopping. "I've seen it all before. My mom was exactly the same. Once the money starts coming in and they climb the social ladder, your wants and needs become less of a priority. It's when she joins the country club that you really need to worry."

Well, shit.

I go about getting lunch prepared, my heart heavy, and soon enough, we're sitting at the breakfast bar in silence, both of us happy to eat as fast as possible and get the fuck away from each other.

I scarf my food down in record time, and as I walk around the kitchen island to place my plate in the dishwasher and clean up, I pause and glance at Jensen. "Why aren't you being creepy?" I ask, always suspicious. "What happened to all the fucked-up leering, winking, and calling me little sis?"

A smirk plays on his lips. "Why? Do you miss it?"

"No," I rush out.

"Then what's the problem?"

"I … I don't know. I don't trust people who so effortlessly change who they are."

Jensen holds my stare before finally letting out a heavy sigh. "You aren't the first step sister I was required to play nice with, Bri. I've honestly lost count. It's easier to push people away with leers and innuendos than to demand my personal space. When I realized you bought into those bullshit rapist rumors at school, I couldn't do it anymore. It's one thing to have people whispering behind my back but having someone I live with being afraid to be in the same room with me was a kick in the gut."

"I'm not scared of you."

His brow arches as his lips press into a hard line. "Uh-huh."

I study him, watching as he gets back to eating his lunch. "You really didn't do it?"

"Hurt that girl?" he clarifies, glancing my way. I nod and he shakes his head. "Wouldn't dream of it. Believe what you want to believe, but I'm not a bad guy. She'd been sending me nudes for weeks and asking to fuck, so when she approached me at school and dragged me into the bathroom, I was all too eager. When some guy walked in on us, she got embarrassed and ran off. By the end of the day, the whole school knew we'd been hooking up. I don't know who got her parents involved, but

I guess they were angry. She said I'd forced myself on her, and that split-second decision fucked with my whole future."

"How so?"

"I had three Ivy league colleges lined up, and her parents saw to it that my acceptance letters were rescinded. Even after the girl came clean and her parents made a statement to the colleges, the damage was done. The world thinks I'm a fucking rapist, and no matter how many courts rule in my favor and clear my name, I'll always be seen that way. Even the asshole who walked in on us testified that everything seemed consensual from his point of view, and that's a lot coming from him. Brady and I didn't exactly get along in high school. I was a bit of an outcast, so it was only too easy for the masses to believe the lie."

I lean against the counter, that same heaviness from earlier coming back twofold. I can't imagine how hard an accusation like that must be, and for the slightest moment, I wonder if that's what I've been doing to Colby, but my gut tells me he's guilty. As for Jensen, looking at him now, I see just how genuine he is. Don't get me wrong, he's still definitely weird, but a rapist? Far from it. "I'm sorry," I tell him, "I judged you too soon, and I feel like shit about that."

He shrugs his shoulders. "It's fine. I'm used to it."

"Nobody should ever be used to something like that," I tell him. "Though there's just one thing I don't understand."

"What's that?"

"What was with all the step-sibling relationship shit? I mean, I know that shit is hot in porn and books, but that's fucked up."

Jensen laughs, embarrassment flooding his features. "Fuck," he mutters under his breath before raising his gaze, his lips pressed into a hard line. "You want the complete truth?"

"Always."

"I was trying to scare you and your mom off," he says. "You guys are the third mother-daughter duo my father has moved in here over the past two years, and honestly, I'm fucking bored of the routine. I don't mean to offend you, I kind of like the way you stand up to my father. It's entertaining, but I'm sick of having to pretend like each new woman is something special when they're not. In the sincerest way possible, you and your mom will be out on your ass in three months tops."

I nod, getting it. "I kinda figured as much."

"Yep," he says. "That day at brunch when I was staring at you, I wanted you to fear me. I did the same thing to your mom, but she was too caught up doting on my father while he paid her absolutely no attention. No offense, but the woman is kinda daft. That's beside the point, though. I wanted you both to feel uneasy about moving in here, but it clearly didn't work. Your mom was all too eager to throw you to the wolves, even after I followed you into the bathroom."

"That was fucked up by the way."

He laughs. "I consider it some of my best work," he says, his eyes sparkling with laughter. "You were freaked out and wary about being here, and at first, I think your mom was too, but anything my father says is religion to her."

Letting out a sigh, I meet his stare. "Okay, here's the deal," I tell him. "You and I don't have to be friends, we don't even have to acknowledge each other when we're here, but I'll chill on the bitchy attitude if you promise to keep being normal."

"Sounds good, sis."

My hands slam down on the counter only to find the asshole smirking back at me. "I swear to God, Jensen Channing, call me *sis* one more time and I'll shove a ten-inch dildo up your ass and pull it out through your throat."

He gets up from the table and drops his plate in the sink. "I'd like to see you try," and with that, he's gone, leaving his plate staring back at me. I scowl at it. Did the asshole not see me cleaning the kitchen and filling the dishwasher? Am I invisible or is he just an entitled, rich kid who assumes everyone else is going to clean up after him?

Out of principle, I leave the plate in the sink and make my way back up to my room, determined not to allow the day to go to waste. I get myself dressed, and as I'm pulling on a shirt, something on the ceiling captures my attention.

My gaze lifts to find a small piece of the ceiling slightly sitting out of place and realize it's access into the roof, like some kind of crawl space.

That asshole.

I saw Tanner come in through my closet last night but hadn't taken a moment to understand how he was making it happen. It's bugged me for the past two weeks, especially after making a point of locking both the windows and the door. I never would have guessed that he was coming in through the ceiling. I mean, how did he even work that out?

I finish getting dressed when I hear the familiar beep of my phone, and I hurry across my room to scoop it off my bedside table. There's a slew of unread texts, most of them from the girls, checking in and making sure everything is okay.

Quickly scanning through them and responding to what I can, I come to my latest message—a text from Erica.

I open it and scan over it before my stomach turns to lead. I force myself to read it again, pain paralyzing me.

Erica - What the fuck, Brielle? You had your new boyfriend beat the shit out of Colby? What a low fucking blow. I told you he didn't do it and now look at what you've done. Those rich assholes are changing you. Where's your fucking loyalty? He was just going there to talk to you because you keep skipping out on his texts. It's one thing to humiliate him for cheating on you, but this? Really, Brielle? You're not who I thought you were.

What. The. Ever. Loving. Fuck?

CHAPTER 30

TANNER

One message sent around the student body is all it took to ensure every last video of me beating the shit out of Colby Jacobs was deleted. Don't get me wrong, I know there's bound to be someone who's going to hold on to it for safekeeping, but it'll never see the light of day.

Leaving Brielle's bed this morning was the hardest thing I've ever done. I wanted nothing more than to lay with her all day, feeling her head resting against my chest as she slept, feeling her tight little body pressed up against mine, but there was shit to do.

I've had cops on my doorstep, questioning me about Colby and demanding answers, but with so little information, they walked away. Colby apparently woke in the early hours of the morning and refused to speak, but he'd be wise not to open his damn mouth because that's only going to draw attention to the reason why I felt so obliged to break his fucking jaw.

Not going to lie, a part of me had hoped the fucker would have suffered more. Perhaps a coma and ventilator would have sedated the need for vengeance living inside me, but nothing, not even my fists can change what happened that night. Nothing will ever take away Addie's suffering, the torment and memories she'll wake to remember. If she wakes up at all.

The moment the cops left, the boys were here, going over everything and making sure that I wasn't about to spiral out of control. Hudson explained how he'd camped out on the property overnight, watching as the ambulance showed up and delivered first aid. Colby was out cold, but he was alive, and despite needing that to have been the outcome, it didn't offer me any relief.

Riley, Logan, and Jax left late last night, assuming I'd passed out, but I laid in my bed, unable to sleep and glancing through Bri's window, finding her just as lost as I felt. I couldn't resist heading over there.

It's been a long fucking day, and the killer hangover isn't helping. I tried to work it out down in my home gym, but my mind kept going back to last night, kept telling me that I should have stayed just a moment longer, should have delivered just one more punch. No amount of broken bones will ever make up for what he did to Addie.

It's well past dinner time when I finally head up to my room, desperate to sleep it off, only my first grin all day cracks across my face.

SCARED? OF A BITCH LIKE YOU? DON'T BE RIDICULOUS! I'VE SEEN MY GRANDMOTHER THROW HARDER PUNCHES THAN THAT!

How the fuck does she do it? Even on my worst day, she has me grinning like a fucking idiot. I can't help but make my way across my room and open my window, finding Bri alone in her room, books spread out over her bed as she annihilates her homework.

Her window is cracked just a sliver and I call out. "Hey, Killer."

Bri's head snaps up, her eyes coming to mine. "Ugh, it's you," she says, keeping a straight face, only her hungry eyes give away the thrill shooting through her body. "It's only been a day and you're already desperate for my attention. I didn't pin you as the stage-five-clinger type."

"Shut the fuck up and get your ass over here. I'm ordering in."

A brilliant smile spreads across her face and she all but launches herself off her bed and crosses to her window. "I want it stated for the record that I'm coming over for food, not because I want to see you."

I grin back at her, hating how fucking obvious I'm being. "Noted."

Bri closes her window, and after one last glance toward me, she dashes out of her bedroom, slamming the door behind her. I make my way downstairs, and by the time I'm at the door, Bri is already dashing across the front lawn. When she glances up and sees me here waiting, she slows her pace, trying not to appear so excited about spending the night with me.

I lean against the open doorframe, watching as she moves toward me, her eyes locked on mine. She steps into me, and as I go to reach for her, she catches my hand instead, holding it up to look over my cracked knuckles. They should probably be bandaged, but when I'm working out a red-hot rage in the gym, the bandages only slow me down.

A frown mars her pretty face as she raises her bright blue eyes to mine. "Does it hurt?" she murmurs, her thumb slowly roaming over the top of my knuckles in a gentle massage.

I shake my head. "It's fine. I've got so much going on that I haven't even stopped to think about it."

Bri gives me a blank stare. "You're such a liar," she says, rolling her eyes. "Your hand is swollen, bruised, and cracked. I bet it's going to make football practice on Monday hell. So, don't try and tell me that it's fine when it's not. There's no way in hell it doesn't hurt."

I let out a heavy sigh and steal my hand back. "Fine," I tell her. "It stings like a fucking bitch, but I can handle it."

Her lips press into a tight line, and judging by the way her eyes shimmer, she's biting her tongue, so fucking smug that she was right. "Did you at least put ice on it?"

I stare back at her, matching her blank expression. "Do you think I put ice on it?"

Bri rolls her eyes and groans before barging past me. "You're such a typical male," she mutters, storming through the kitchen as I follow behind, watching the way her ass moves in those pants.

"Am I just?" I ask, amusement brimming in my chest. "And what makes me such a typical male? Please share for the class."

Bri reaches the fridge and rifles around until she finds what she's looking for. "Because," she starts, grabbing an ice pack and going for the paper towel across the kitchen. "Without a shadow of doubt in my mind, the whole time I was storming through here, your eyes were on my ass. Prove me wrong."

A grin cuts across my face as I make my way around the island counter, moving right into her, only to have the ice pack shoved into my hands. "Don't even dream about lying to me again."

Leaning down into her, my lips brush over hers and I watch the way she melts into me, leaning closer and pressing her hand to my chest, unable to help herself. "You're right, I was staring at your ass, but what did you expect? It's the finest ass I've ever seen." I place the ice pack down on the counter beside us and take her waist, pulling her in even closer. "You see, every time I see that ass, I can't stop thinking about all the filthy things I want to do to it."

"Really?" she questions, her tone lowering and her eyes becoming hooded, reminding me of every fucking second with her in those woods. "What kind of filthy things?"

"Things that would make even Riley and Jax blush."

She swallows hard and I laugh at the way her eyes fill with lust, but she squashes it down quickly, knowing all too well that there's a shitload of things that we should talk through before I can even dream about touching her again. "I hope you didn't ask me here just to get your dick wet because I'm not that girl. I'm not some ditzy booty call who's going to come running every time you call her name, so if that's what you're wanting from me, then you need to rethink all of this."

"That's not why I asked you here," I tell her, my hand taking hers on my chest. "Come on. Let me order something so you don't starve and get grouchy, and then we can talk."

"Talk?" she questions nervously as I lead her into the oversized den that Jax spent most of his day scrubbing clean after deciding we were all getting wasted last night. "I don't think our version of talking has ever ended well."

I drop onto the couch as she sits across the room as if needing that space between us. She crosses her legs and scans the big room, and after quickly ordering something to eat, I sit patiently, waiting for her gaze to make its way back to mine.

I sit forward, leaning my elbows against my knees as my chest tightens, unsure how to do this whole apologizing thing, and as if seeing the hesitation in my eyes, she gets up and walks across the room, gently pushing me back against the couch and climbing onto my lap.

She straddles me while also leaving enough distance between us to talk. "You don't need to do this, Tanner," she tells me, reading me better than I read myself. "Last night was … complicated. We were having a great time, and don't for one second think that I regret what happened between us. It was … well, you know exactly how it was," she murmurs, a slight flush spreading over her cheeks. "The race, and you and me … I've never felt so exhilarated in my life. Being with you was like an adrenaline rush I never wanted to come down from. It wasn't until Colby showed up that everything went to shit. I don't blame you for what you did, but more importantly, I'm not scared of you."

"Killer," I warn, hating how accepting she is of this. "Don't excuse what I did. I almost fucking killed him. He was out cold and I couldn't stop, and a part of me can't even tell if it was for what he did to Addie or for the way he was grabbing you. I saw fucking red, and while I don't regret what I did, it's not something I'm proud of."

"I'm not scared of you," she repeats as if knowing just how much I fear she is.

I let out a sigh and prepare for this to crash and burn. "He's not the first asshole I've almost killed in a blind rage, Bri," I tell her. "It's a fucking pattern, and if you were smart, you'd get out now before you get too attached. I'm not a good guy."

Her face falls as her brows furrow, watching me with caution. "What are you talking about?"

Lead sinks into my gut as I glance away, unable to handle the intensity in her eyes. Shame fills my veins, spreading through my body like wildfire. "Last year when Chanel and I were hooking up, we were messing around at her place when I heard her brother—"

"Brother?" she asks. "Chanel doesn't have a brother."

"She does," I confirm. "But I don't blame her for not mentioning him. The fucker has issues."

"Okay," she says slowly. "What happened?"

Anger drums at the memory of that night, and I have to focus on the feel of her skin beneath my palm to keep myself centered. "I could hear him down the hall in his bedroom, he was trying to kick some girl out because she wasn't ready to fuck him. He was calling her all this nasty shit and she was sobbing. Something about her tone made me get up and check it out. She was thirteen. *Thirteen*. She was barely even in high school, a fucking child. I can't even remember what happened next. I know there was yelling and Chanel was trying to drag me back to her room. One thing led to another, and I was holding him down, beating the fucking shit out of him. He was hospitalized for two weeks and needed reconstructive surgery to his face. I was arrested for assault, but after Chanel and the girl made their statements, I was free, and the asshole got nothing but a slap on the wrist. I'm pretty sure their family disowned him and sent him away, but I honestly haven't spared a thought for him or bothered to look into where he is now."

"Fuck."

"Yeah."

She presses her lips into a hard line, her eyes lingering on mine. "I think you're a good guy, Tanner. I think you try really hard not to let that show, but deep down, you care about what's right, and you advocate for those who can't do it for themselves. That's nothing to be ashamed of and certainly not something I should fear. Should you take some anger management classes? Probably, but you and I both know that you'll never hurt me. You were completely justified in lashing out at both Colby and Chanel's brother."

"You think?"

"Uh-huh," she says, her eyes darkening. "Besides, the whole time you were beating the crap out of Colby, I was hoping you'd hit him harder."

My brow arches, always so surprised by the shit that comes flying out of her mouth. My hands fall to her thighs and slowly move to her hips. "Yeah?"

"Uh-huh," she says, a smirk pulling at her lips. "As bad as it sounds, I didn't even care if you broke every bone in your hand and could never play football again. I was prepared to nurse you back to health."

A soft laugh builds deep in my chest. "Okay, we're going to come back to your blatant lack of respect for my football career," I tell her. "But I'm more interested in this whole nursing me back to health thing. What exactly does that entail? Sponge baths? Outfits? Twenty-four-seven, around the clock care? Because there's this pain right here, high on my inner thigh …"

Bri laughs and shakes her head. "It'll be gloves, lube, and probing if you're not careful, and trust me, it's not me who'll be getting probed."

"Okay, okay," I say, putting my hands up. "I know when to back down."

"Do you now?" she questions. "Breaking into my bedroom to leave creepy messages on my mirror and making sure I witness some bitch going down on you would suggest otherwise."

A smirk tears across my face as she holds my stare, and when the moment passes, a seriousness comes over me. "How can I make it up to you?"

She shakes her head, moving in just a little bit closer. "There's nothing to make up for, I mean, apart from the whole Jules blowjob thing. You knocked out the guy who left your sister for dead. The cops aren't doing enough, and his lawyer is going to make sure he walks free, so you took it into your own hands, which is exactly what I expected you to do. You don't need to make up for doing what's right for your sister."

"I ruined our night, got plastered, and then broke into your room."

"You did," she tells me, "And I'm not going to lie, I liked having you there, and I liked it even more when I got to see the real you. I was more pissed about the fact you slipped out without saying goodbye. Now, that was a low blow."

"I knew that was going to bite me on the ass," I mutter.

"Mmmm," she murmurs, her voice lowering to a deep rasp as her eyes fill with desire, making me uncomfortably hard. "I'd like to bite you on the ass."

Well, fuck. This girl never fails to surprise me.

"Stay on track, babe. I'm trying to apologize for beating the shit out of your ex."

She shrugs her shoulders. "Colby deserved it, and honestly, watching you like that, all wild and out of control, it was hot as fuck. I've never been so wet," she says. "But, if you really insist on making it up to me, there is one thing you can do."

Her eyes light up and my cock twitches in my pants, having a good idea what she's about to ask for, and damn it, I'm not one to say no. "Oh yeah?" I ask, watching as her eyes become hooded and she rocks forward on my lap. "And what's that?"

She grins, biting her bottom lip. "Nah, you know what? I don't think you can handle it."

I scoff, my arm curling around her back and pulling her in closer. "There's nothing I can't handle when it comes to you."

"You really want to know?" she questions. "The one thing I want most in this world?"

"Mmhmm."

"I want *Jason Momoa* in character of *Khal Drogo* giving me a strip tease while whispering in my ear in *Dothraki*. But here's the kicker," she says. "He's gotta be hard, like rock fucking hard, and if you could get him to throw me around a bit … goddamn."

Okay, so that's not where I thought this was going.

I stare at her, not understanding a damn word she said, but the thought of some guy throwing her around makes me want to punch something. "What the hell is a *Khal Drogo* and why do you want to fuck it?"

She laughs, and after a moment, her face begins to fall when she realizes that I'm being serious. "Wait. You really don't know?"

I shake my head and she stares at me in horror.

"Holy shit. I knew you must have taken a few hits over the years, but I didn't realize it could get this bad. No wonder you struggle with the basics." She lets out a heavy sigh. "You're lucky to have someone like me willing to bring you up to speed."

I narrow my stare, slowly working it out. "Whatever it is, I'm not watching it."

"Oh yeah?" she laughs. "How else are you going to make it up to me?"

I laugh. She makes it too fucking easy.

My grip tightens around her waist, and I throw her down on the couch, listening to the shrieking yelp that tears from between her lips. My hips settle firmly between her legs as I hover over her, staring down into her wide blue eyes. "Like this."

My lips press down over hers and she sighs into my mouth as her body relaxes, and just like that, the rest of the world fades away. Colby Jacobs no longer exists, my sister is no longer dying, and the cops weren't just on my doorstep. Everything revolves around only her.

Bri's arms wrap around my neck as her leg hitches high over my hip and I grind down against her. She kisses me back and her grip tightens around me, silently begging me not to stop, and while I've made a game out of continuously disappointing her, now is not going to be one of those times. No, I need to hear her scream, need to feel her body jolting under my touch, need her on my tongue.

The anticipation is too much, and I start moving down her body, my lips brushing over her neck. She turns her head, allowing me more space, and the sweetest moan sails from between her lips. It's like a whisper straight from the lips of an angel.

She's going to be the fucking death of me. I'm so addicted to this girl. Every touch, every breath, every taste. I need it all. Last night with her was incredible, but we were covered in darkness, fucking on my bike. Here, there's no hiding. I see every inch of her body, every rise of her chest, every damn time her eyes flash with desperation, needing so much more.

Working my way down her body, my hands slip between the fabric of her cropped shirt, pushing it up and over her head, her perfect, full tits staring back at me. She's not wearing a bra, and just the thought of her bare nipples rubbing against the fabric of her shirt has my cock straining to get inside her.

My mouth closes over her pebbled nipple and her back arches off the couch, pressing up into me. "Oh, God, Tanner."

I can't wait another fucking second.

My hand trails down her body and slips inside her pants, listening to that sweet gasp of anticipation. She squirms beneath me, and I can't help the smile that pulls at my lips. She's so fucking gorgeous, so damn responsive. I'll never get enough of this.

She's ready for me, and as my fingers brush over her clit, she groans, pushing her hips up for more. I give her exactly what she wants, what she's been craving since the moment she crossed the room and climbed onto my lap.

My thumb presses down over her clit, rubbing lazy circles as I push two fingers into her waiting pussy. She groans again and the pure satisfaction running through my veins is like nothing I've ever felt before. I want to make her feel alive, to make her come like no man has ever done before. When someone asks her what's the best sex she's ever had, I want her to think of me, no hesitation.

I continue moving down her body, my lips brushing over the curve of her breast and down past her ribs. She sucks in a breath as I skim over her waist, and as I pull my hand free from within her and hook my thumbs into the waistband of her pants, she's all too eager to get the show on the road.

Her pants are gone in a matter of seconds, and I meet her eyes as I settle between her legs, loving the wild desperation staring back at me. My lips skim along the soft skin of her inner thigh, moving down toward her core as I watch her head tip back and her hands drop to her body.

She sucks in a breath and just as my mouth closes over her clit, her back arches up off the couch. "Tanner," she moans, her hand moving up her body and brushing over her full tits.

I get to fucking work.

I suck and nip at her clit as I push my fingers deep inside, watching as she bucks and squirms under my touch. She's fucking delicious, but I knew she would be. I got a taste of her last night, but nothing is better than this moment right here.

I don't dare stop, curving my fingers just right and massaging deep inside her as my tongue flicks over her clit. "Oh, fuck," she groans, her hand roaming down her body and bunching into my hair. She squeezes tight, knotting her fingers and holding me right where she wants me. "Yes, Tanner."

I'm relentless. Giving her what she needs and more, fucking her with my tongue and watching the way she becomes dependent on my touch. If I were a patient man, I'd drag this moment out, lay here for hours teasing her sweet cunt, but I need her to come almost as much as she does. I need to feel her come undone, need to feel the way her orgasm sends her into a quivering mess, convulsing around my fingers and know that it was me who made that happen.

Her fingers knot tighter and I push her further. Flicking, nipping, sucking, squeezing.

She cries out, her head thrown back against the cushions as her other hand clutches her tit. Her legs tighten around me, almost holding me down, and fuck, she could suffocate me right here and I'd die a happy man. I'll fucking drown in her if that's what I have to do.

Sucking her clit and flicking my tongue, she gasps, and just like that, she comes hard. Her body spasms and she calls my name, making a grin pull at my lips. I can't help but watch her, taking in the way her fingers squeeze her tit, watching how she gasps for breath and clenches her stunning eyes. Her grip tightens in my hair, and I almost come in my fucking pants feeling how her cunt convulses around my fingers.

She's fucking angelic.

There's no one else like her.

I don't stop working her body as she rides out her high and only when her body relaxes, do I ease up on her. She pants, gasping for breath as she comes down and I pull back, unable to take my eyes off her as her taste lingers in my mouth.

Bri meets my stare and shakes her head, disbelief flashing in her eyes. "Holy shit, Tanner Morgan," she says, pushing up from the couch cushion. "That was incredible."

There's a distant knocking coming from the door and a nagging thought in the back of my head tells me it's the UberEats driver, but we both ignore it, too captivated by one another to even risk glancing away. "Oh yeah?" I smirk, watching as her eyes darken with desire. "You should see what else I can do."

I adjust myself on the couch and have barely settled against the cushion before she's straddled over my lap, her tits right there for the taking. She reaches down between us, freeing my cock from the restriction of my pants, her eyes shimmering with the same hunger I know she sees in mine. "Oh yeah?" she questions, a flush appearing on her cheeks. "You'll have to show me some time, but right now, it's your turn to see what else I can do."

And with that, she reaches into my pocket and pulls out a condom, tearing it open with her teeth. She sheaths my cock, and not a moment later, drops down on top of me, her tight little cunt squeezing me like never before, all while the UberEats driver continues to knock at the door.

CHAPTER 31
Brielle

The Sunday afternoon sun shines through the front windshield of my Honda, blinding me despite the visor being down, but what's new? I learned pretty quickly there's not a lot I can do about it, apart from holding my hand up and trying to not kill anyone in the process. Short girl problems.

I turn down my street, still not used to the winding roads of Bradford. They all look the same, and if it weren't for the house with the naked woman sculpture at the very corner, I'd never remember which street to turn down.

I see the yellow Beetle almost immediately and my stomach sinks. Erica.

I haven't been able to stop thinking about her bullshit text since it first came through yesterday morning. What the hell was she thinking defending Colby like that? Did she not hear me when I told her he was responsible for attacking Addison?

Her words have sat in the back of my mind, playing on a loop, reminding me that since the moment I left Hope Falls, things haven't been the same between us. Is something bothering her? Is she pissed that my life has been uprooted and I moved away, or are we already growing apart?

My car pulls to a stop on the curb, and I get out to find Erica hovering awkwardly by the door, her arms crossed over her chest, nibbling on her bottom lip. Giving the door a push, it closes with a hard thud and I stare up toward her, unease resting in my chest. "What are you doing here?"

"We've never fought like this," she says. "I just wanted to clear the air. I don't like this."

I scoff and stride up to the big house, passing her to jam the key in the lock. "Maybe you should have considered that before sending me that bullshit text," I mutter, unlocking the door and pushing it wide. I stride in and Erica follows behind, keeping an awkward distance.

Erica mutters something behind me that I can't make out, and knowing her well enough to know it wasn't anything kind, it sends venom pulsing through my veins. I storm right through the house, refusing to go upstairs and make this some kind of comfortable chill session. Instead, I move through the kitchen and out to the backyard while pulling out my phone.

I spin on her, sending a scathing glare her way as I bring up the text I've read over a million times since yesterday. Clearing my throat, I recite it for her, just so we're both clear on what the fuck is going down right now. "What the fuck, Brielle? You had your new boyfriend beat the shit out of Colby? What a low fucking blow. I told you he didn't do it and now look at what you've done," I start, meeting her stare to see nothing but guilt and anger shining back at me. "Those rich assholes are changing you. Where's your fucking loyalty? He was just going there to talk to you because you keep skipping out on his texts. It's one thing to humiliate him for cheating on you, but this? Really, Brielle? You're not who I thought you were."

"Bri—"

"No," I cut her off, ignoring the sound of Tanner's bike as he screeches down the road. I can't get distracted now, this is too important. "You had absolutely no right to say any of that to me. I told you what he did, Erica. I told you how he hurt Tanner's sister, how he drugged her, how he held her down and fucking raped her, and you have the fucking audacity to take his side on this."

"This isn't about what he did to that girl, it's about what you allowed to happen to him at the stupid Bradford party with all your stupid new friends."

"Are you hearing yourself?" I yell at her. "You weren't even there. You have no idea how it went down, which could only mean that you've been talking to Colby, and he's been feeding you bullshit lies."

"He hasn't."

"Really?" I scoff. "Did he tell you how he grabbed me, how he dug his fingers in and when I tried to pull away, he told me if I wasn't careful, he'd fucking rape me next? No, I bet he skipped over those little details, didn't he? Look at me, Erica. Look at my arms," I demand, pointing out the scratches and bruises that mar my skin. "All of this is from Colby. I didn't do this to myself. That's the asshole you're defending right now, and honestly, I really can't believe that you are. You've seen the messages he's been sending me."

"I know, I just ... you shouldn't have let your boyfriend hurt him. That was uncalled for."

I gape at her, unable to believe what I'm hearing. "Colby came onto our turf. He came to a Bradford party looking to hurt me. He assaulted me in front of the whole senior class, so whether Tanner was there or not, whether he hurt Addison or not, he was going to get his ass handed to him, and rightfully so."

She looks away from me, guilt heavy in her eyes.

"Are you serious right now?" I question. "You said in your message that I'm not who you thought I was, but honestly, Erica, you're the stranger right now. You're defending Colby. What if that had been me who he raped and left in a coma? Would you be defending him then? What if it was your little brother who'd been hurt? What if—" I let my sentence trail off, hating that she won't even look at me. "Am I missing something? Is there something you're keeping from me? This doesn't make sense. You shouldn't be defending him like this."

"I'm not defending him, I'm just ... you're turning your back on everything. Colby is our star player and you let your boyfriend beat him senseless. Where's your loyalty—"

"COLBY RAPED HIS FUCKING SISTER, ERICA," I yell, the

wild rage burning up inside of me. "He should be rotting in a fucking prison. How can you not see that? The beating Tanner gave him wasn't even a portion of what he deserves. The asshole drugged her, held her down, and stripped her bare while she screamed through the phone for Tanner to save her. Colby fucking laughed while he raped her and then left her for fucking dead. Can't you—"

"THAT'S NOT HOW IT HAPPENED," she fires back at me. "THAT BITCH TOOK THOSE DRUGS HERSELF. SHE KNEW WHAT SHE WAS DOING."

My eyes bug out of my head, my jaw dropping as I watch Erica realize what the fuck she just said. She shakes her head, her eyes widening and beginning to flick around, desperate to start backtracking. "No, no," she rushes out, her hands flying up as if to express her innocence. "That's not what I meant. She just—"

"You were there," I say, bile rising in my throat. "You and Colby. You were both in on this."

"No," she rushes out. "I swear, I didn't know he was going to hurt her. We just wanted to take a few pills and she was down so Colby gave her some. I … I didn't know he—"

I shake my head, not even recognizing the girl standing across from me. "Tell me you're lying. Tell me you had nothing to do with this."

"I … I …"

"I swear to fucking God, Erica, stop trying to come up with some bullshit story and be honest for once in your fucking life. WHAT THE FUCK HAPPENED THAT NIGHT?"

Heaving sobs tear from the back of Erica's throat and she drops to her knees, her face falling into her hands. "I didn't know," she cries. "I didn't know he was going to hurt her."

"Erica," I snap, silently demanding the whole story.

"We've been fucking, okay," she rushes out. "All summer long. You weren't giving him what he needed and so he came to me the night of your eighteenth, and you know how I've always liked him. Ever since sophomore year and—"

"You were fucking my boyfriend? On my birthday? What the fuck, Erica?"

She swallows hard and nods, her eyes filling with tears. "I … I didn't mean to. It just—"

I look away, unable to meet her stare as the betrayal shoots through my body, tears falling down my face. "Let me guess, you fell and your loose fucking vagina landed on his three-inch cock and all the moving trying to get back up just happened to make you both come?" I question, shaking my head. "Just stop with your bullshit excuses and tell me what happened to Addison."

Erica sobs and crumbles a little bit more. "Colby and I … we were taking pills and getting fucked up out back when she asked if she could have some. I'd seen her earlier dancing on all the guys, and she was looking at Colby like she wanted to fuck him, and I didn't like it. I told her to fuck off, but Colby was down, so he gave her a bunch of pills. He was all over her and I was jealous, so we got in a fight and he shoved me away. That's when I went back to you. The next thing I know," she continues, her relentless sobbing making it hard to follow,

"I had a call from Colby and he was panicking. I went to find him and he was in the bedroom with her. She was naked and they'd clearly just fucked, and I didn't even notice her torn clothing or how she was bleeding because she was seizing on the ground."

Erica stops as if that's a good ending for her story, but I step toward her, not nearly finished with her. "What did you do?"

Her eyes widen. "What do you mean? We fucking ran. She was a rich kid from Bradford. The cops were coming and we … we just grabbed you and took off. What else were we supposed to do?"

My hand whips out, smacking hard across her face. "Addison has been in a fucking coma for six weeks," I roar. "SIX FUCKING WEEKS AND THAT'S ALL ON YOU."

Erica throws herself to her feet, shoving me hard in the chest. "Don't you dare put this on my shoulders," she spits. "I didn't shove those pills down her fucking throat, and I sure as fuck wasn't the one to put my hands on her. This has nothing to do with me."

"You fucking ran while a girl was lying there seizing, just moments after being brutally attacked while on a cocktail of drugs. Who the fuck are you, Erica?" I spit. "You may not have given her those drugs or physically raped her, but you are just as guilty as he is, and I swear to you, Erica, if you don't go and hand yourself in to the cops right fucking now, I will do it for you."

Her face pales and she stares at me in horror, betrayal slicing through her stare. "What did you just say?"

"You heard me."

"But I'm your best friend."

I shake my head. "You stopped being my best friend the moment you decided to fuck my boyfriend. Right now, all you are is the girl who helped Colby Jacobs assault a minor. You're nothing to me, Erica. Don't ever come here again."

Tears stream down her face and she turns to make a break for it only we both gasp at finding Tanner standing just inside, staring straight back at us. The door is wide open and there's no doubt in my mind that he heard every last word.

He doesn't say a damn thing, just stands there and stares, the rage pouring out of his stare telling me exactly what's going through his mind. Erica squeaks, fear rattling her and, in an instant, she storms past him. "Erica," I call to her fleeing back.

She stops and looks back at me, her eyes desperate. "If she dies," I tell her, my tone thick with venom. "I'm coming for you."

Erica whimpers a horrid yelping sound before spinning on her heel and flying straight out the front door, more than determined to get the fuck out of here before Tanner decides to tear her to shreds.

I fall to the ground, my knees hitting the pavement as my face falls into my hands, heaving sobs catching in my throat. The devastation and betrayal claim me. "I'm so sorry," I cry, glancing up at him and seeing pure murder in his eyes. "I didn't know."

Tanner just stares a moment longer, his hands balling into fists, and as the moment passes between us, his fury only grows.

Fear begins pounding in my chest. I shake my head, throwing myself to my feet, but it's too late, Tanner is already halfway to the door. "TANNER, NO," I call after him, racing to catch his long strides.

He bursts through the front door and I race after him, but by the time I catch him, his leg is already flying over his bike. I hurry around the front of his bike, blocking his way while having no idea what he plans to do. All I know is that it's not going to be good. "Tanner, please. Don't do this. It's going to be okay. We're going to make sure they pay for what they did."

"Move," he roars.

"No. Don't do this."

"I'm not asking again. Move."

I hold my ground, my heated stare locking onto his and like a flash of lightning, his arm strikes out and curls around my waist. He lifts me off the ground and pulls me up onto the seat, my body plastered to his, chest to chest.

Tanner reaches around me, gripping the handlebars and takes off at a million miles an hour, screeching out of his driveway as my arms fly around him, holding on for dear life.

My lips brush against Tanner's warm skin, and I bury my face into his neck, the harsh wind slapping against my back. He's furious, reckless even, but I know he'll never let anything happen to me.

I hold on with everything I have, my legs wrapped around his waist and my fingers clutching onto his back. Our chests press up against each other and I feel the rapid heavy thumping of his heart. He's out of control, but I don't blame him. I would be too after hearing that.

How else is he supposed to react? He just learned that the girl I called my best friend for thirteen years had something to do with his sister's attack, that after being raped and falling into a seizure, they just left her there, naked and dying on the cold ground. It's a miracle he didn't kill her right then and there in the middle of Orlando's living room.

We fly through the streets of Bradford, twisting and winding our way through the turns that are all too familiar for Tanner. "It's going to be okay," I murmur against his skin, closing my eyes as he hits the highway and doubles in speed. "Addie is going to get through this. If she's anything like you, she's going to survive, and when she does, she'll come back with a vengeance."

Horns blast as we fly past and we get more than a few curious glances, but it's not every day that you see some dude flying down the road with a girl straddling his lap.

Ten minutes turn to twenty, and soon enough, the roads become all too familiar. We pass my old high school, sail through the streets where I learned to drive, and pass the old bakery where I had my first kiss. I hold onto him tighter, the desperation pounding through my veins. "You're better than this, Tanner. Don't let them win."

My lips linger on his neck, my face still buried against his warm skin as my hair whips around us. I feel the heavy beating of his pulse against my lips, and I can't resist him a moment longer. I kiss him right there, my hand moving up into his hair and clutching onto him with everything I have. "Please. Whatever you need, I'm right here, but don't do this. Don't throw away your future for them."

My body is plastered to his like never before, and as my lips work over his skin, I feel the bike begin to slow. His body relaxes against mine, the tension seeping out of his tight muscles, and as Tanner eases onto the brake at a red light, he pulls up onto the curb and comes to a complete stop on the sidewalk.

I don't dare let go of him, but when my lips stop moving, he releases the handlebars to wrap his arms around me, and I know I've got him back.

I let out a heavy sigh, my heart slowly beginning to calm. "Whatever you need from me, Tanner, I'm all yours."

A moment passes before he finally raises his head off my shoulder and his eyes come to mine, wild, raw, and terrified. "I—"

"Don't," I tell him, seeing the apology clear in his dark eyes. "You don't owe me anything. I'm here with you, where you go, I go. *You lean, I lean.* You don't need to apologize for feeling, especially after hearing what they did."

His hand slides up and clutches the back of my neck, holding me so close that I feel his breath brushing over my cheek. "I don't even know what I was going to do. I saw red and couldn't stop."

"I know, but you did stop."

"No," he says, shaking his head. "You stopped me. If it weren't for you …"

He leaves his comment hanging in the air and a weight drops down over my shoulders, imagining how this could have ended. "You stopped, Tanner," I tell him. "You eased up on the brake, you pulled off to the curb. You did that, not me. You're stronger than you give yourself credit for."

A soft smile pulls at the corner of his lips, and it takes me a moment to realize he pities himself, or maybe me for thinking so highly of him. "Nobody has ever kept me grounded in the way you do. Not the boys, not my mom or Addie, only you."

I swallow hard, feeling the whole weight of his heart in the palm of my hands. I've never seen him so open like this, so broken yet so strong. Leaning in, I brush my lips over his and he captures them in a gentle, lingering kiss. "Tanner?" I question when he finally releases me. His eyes come to mine and I move my hand around his big shoulder and down to his chest. "Take me home."

And just like that, he swings me around on his bike and takes off. My arms coil tightly around his waist as the bike rumbles beneath me, moving us onto the road and whipping around to send us back toward Bradford.

CHAPTER 32
Brielle

"Tanner's so hot and cold that it's impossible to tell where we stand. I wish I could just enter his brain and figure it out," I tell Ilaria as I walk out of her place on Wednesday afternoon, desperate to get home after I realized Tanner would be finishing up with football practice soon.

Shit, that makes me sound desperate, but this connection between us … I can't explain it. It's unlike anything I've ever felt before. Every spare moment is spent with him, and if I'm not with him, I'm thinking about just how good it is when I am.

Ilaria laughs, gripping on to the handle and hovering in the doorway. "You know, over the past few years that I've been going to school with the guy, I've never once seen him so taken by a girl before, so obviously your little *we secretly hate each other* act is paying off."

Rolling my eyes, I take off down the path toward my car on the curb. "We do hate each other," I tell her, both of us knowing damn well I'm lying. There may have been a time where Tanner Morgan was the bane of my existence, but over the past week or so ... things have shifted.

"Uh-huh."

"When he admits this is something more, I will," I laugh. "Until then, he's nothing but my asshole neighbor who I secretly fantasize about barging in on me in the shower."

Ilaria shakes her head, grinning back at me. "You're playing a dangerous game, Bri. Tanner is famous for being a prick. The only way you're getting something out of him is if you hire an exorcist."

I laugh as I reach my Honda, my hand hovering over the handle. "Trust me, it's not that hard to get something to come spurting out of him."

A booming laugh tears from the back of her throat. "Girl, I need a guy like Tanner who's going to make me scream at him one minute and rail me the next," she says. "What are those things you blow to make a wish?"

A smirk stretches across my face as I open my car door. "You mean a sugar daddy?"

"That is so wrong," she calls after me. "So fucking wrong."

I hold my hand up to wave bye before hitting the gas and taking off down the street. Ilaria doesn't live too far from Orlando's place, maybe only a few minutes. Her parents are filthy rich and they come from old money, so they have that classic *too good for everyone* vibe, and honestly, I don't think they like me very much. They probably assume I'm here to screw them out of their wealth, just as everyone else does.

Turning onto my street, I sail down the road and am just starting to vibe with *Halestorm's 'I Get Off'* when a familiar black Charger comes screaming down the road. My eyes widen and I get a flash of his face, so full of determination and anger, but it's too late.

Colby's Charger T-bones me, smashing into the side of my Civic, and I scream as I'm thrashed around inside my car. Colby doesn't ease up, and the Charger forces me across the street as I frantically hold onto the steering wheel, desperately trying to brace myself.

My car slams into an old oak tree across the road, shattering the windows as my head bounces from left to right. My vision blurs and everything goes quiet. Shadows dance behind my eyes, and when a hand curls around my arm, I scream.

Colby drags me from my car, and my body falls to the ground with a heavy thump before I'm pulled toward the bushes. Twigs and branches tear at my skin, and I heave a gasp as a heavy weight drops over my chest.

Something tightens around my throat, cutting off my airway, and my eyes spring open, finding Colby on top of me with his hands locked tightly around my throat. I try to scream but nothing comes out, and I grip on to his hand, frantically digging at his skin.

His eyes are wild and angry, fury rippling through his nasty gaze. "Say a damn word to the cops and I'll fucking end you," he spits, his face full of the evidence of Tanner's beating. "I ain't going down for this. Erica doesn't know what the fuck she's talking about, and if I'm going down, then you two bitches are too."

He squeezes harder and my lungs scream for relief. "You hear me?" he growls, getting down into my face. "Say a damn word, and I'll fucking slit your throat faster than I fucked that bitch."

Anger blooms through my chest, but my oxygen is quickly dwindling, and needing to get him off me, I reach up and dig my nails into his face, clawing at his eyes, more than ready to gouge them out if I have to.

Colby growls and tears away from me. I suck in a desperate breath, gasping for sweet oxygen, but I don't dare look away from him. Fresh blood trails down his face and his anger only gets worse. My fear skyrockets, knowing he's not even close to being through with me. He goes to make his move when something has his back stiffening.

His head whips around, listening intently. "Fuck," he spits, looking back at me.

A moment passes as if trying to decide what he's going to do, panic beginning to overwhelm him. He glances to his car and then back at me, his lips pressing into a hard line. "Fuck," he roars again, and the next thing I know, his heavy boot slams into my ribs.

I hear a distinct crack and scream out, clutching at my side as the familiar sound of Tanner's bike brings a new hope surging through my veins. Colby dashes back to his Charger and drops down into it as I try to claw my way out of the bushes, crying out at the pain that rocks through my body.

The sound of Tanner's bike becomes more distinct as he grows closer and heavy sobs tear from the back of my throat. Colby doesn't hang around another moment, knowing damn well what will happen to him if he's caught here right now. The Charger disappears, screeching down the street, and I continue pulling myself from the bushes, unable to get up.

I hear the very moment Tanner turns the corner and finds my car, his speed doubling as he races to get to me. The roar of his bike is deafening, but it's welcomed, knowing that soon enough, I'll be out of this pain and back in his arms.

He skids to a stop and I hear his helmet hit the concrete. "BRIELLE?"

"Tanner," I call, tears streaming down my face. "Tanner. Help."

He races around my wrecked car, his eyes frantic as he searches me out beneath the bushes. "Fuck, Bri," he rushes out, storming toward me as he spots me amongst the thick bushes. His gaze sails up and down my body, taking in every last scratch, bruise, and cut before focusing on the way I clutch my ribs. "Are you okay? What happened?"

I reach for him and groan as the pain doubles with my movements. "Colby T-boned me," I grunt, trying to speak over the pain while slowly drowning in it. "I think he knows that Erica told me. He dragged me out of the car and held me down with his hands around my throat. He said something about not going down for what he did to your sister. This was supposed to be some kind of warning, and I think he wanted to hurt me more, but he heard your bike and got scared."

Tanner's head whips back to my car, giving it a second look, and I watch as the anger pours out of him. "I'm going to fucking kill him."

He pulls his phone out and presses a few buttons before jamming it between his shoulder and ear. He talks to the 911 operator while reaching for me and doing his best to pull me from the bushes and into a safe place without causing me any more hell.

"You're going to be okay," he promises me. "We'll get you better, and then we'll fucking destroy him."

I meet his panicked eyes and reach for his face. "Damn fucking straight we will."

CHAPTER 33
TANNER

The image of Bri's Honda wrapped around that tree has haunted me all afternoon. I've only ever felt fear like that once before, and that was the night Addison called me screaming for help.

It's well past eight when I finally get Bri into the back of Jax's Silverado, and to say I'm pissed is an understatement. I called the boys the moment she was settled in the emergency room, and after three hours of searching the streets of both Hope Falls and Bradford, the fucker can't be found. But mark my words, I will find Colby Jacobs, and when I do, he'll have hell to pay.

Bri was seen immediately, and her injuries were cared for while we waited for the results of her x-ray, only to confirm that Colby had indeed broken her rib. It's only a small fracture, but enough to leave Bri in tremendous pain.

She called her mom to let her know, and it didn't take long to realize Orlando and her mom still hadn't returned from Paris, which only aggravated me more. Bri deserves better than that. Once she ended the call, Bri explained that her mom was getting on the first flight home, and as much as she needs her mom right now, a part of me wanted her to keep away so I could have Bri all to myself.

The trip to the hospital allowed me a moment to check in on Mom and Addison, but with Bri in pain, I didn't get to stay long. But it was enough to get the latest update and make sure Addison was doing alright. But fuck, I'm not going to lie, seeing her in that hospital bed and not being able to wake her up kills me. She'll get through this. I'm sure of it.

By the time Jax is pulling into my driveway, there's a whole fucking party on my front lawn.

Logan has Bri's wrecked car on a trailer and Hudson is helping him back it in while Jenson watches from the front porch. Riley strides out of my garage with my bike parked safely behind him, and all the girls are huddled in a corner watching the show, only the moment they see Jax's Silverado pull in and make out Bri through the window, they start running.

"What do you want?" I ask Bri, my thumb brushing over the back of her hand. "I can tell them all to fuck off and take you up to your bed."

She shakes her head. "I don't want to be alone," she says, her voice hoarse from being strangled. "Can we all just … chill out?"

"Yeah, Killer," I tell her. "Whatever you want."

Pushing the door open, we are immediately flooded by screeching girls trying to check on their friend, and I have to barge my way past them just to be able to get out of Jax's truck. They all but climb in my vacated spot as I make my way around to Bri, and if she didn't want them here, I would have sent them away the second I opened my door.

Bri's voice sails out through her open door, and I listen as she consoles her friends. Chanel quietly sobs while Arizona pouts, hating seeing her friend like this, but Ilaria is the one who gets my vote. Her face is bunched up and full of rage as she explains in explicit detail exactly what she plans on doing to Colby Jacobs, and I soak it in, loving every minute of it.

"Come on," I tell her, reaching up for her.

She loops her arm around my neck and tries not to cringe as I lift her off the seat. She's on some strong painkillers but they're not enough to make her forget the pain of a broken rib. The guys fall around us, checking over her injuries as Chanel races ahead to get my front door open.

Within the space of two minutes, our whole crew is down in my home gym. I sit on the couch with Brielle in my arms and an ice pack pressed to the side of her head. The girls sit opposite her, listening to her rehash all the details of her afternoon while the boys get started on their weight training, telling me every last detail they were able to find on Colby Jacobs—his friends, his family, where he likes to hang out, and every now and then, Bri will add snippets of what she's learned about him over the past six months.

Once she's done answering all the girls' questions, she sighs and glances toward the boys. "How bad is my car?" she asks, her hand unintentionally moving away from her face, taking the ice pack off the lump on her head.

Jax scoffs as I push her hand back against her head. "It's pretty fucking bad, babe," Jax says as Arizona gets up to stack more weight onto his bar. "But it's no big loss. That car was a piece of shit anyway. We'll get you something real nice."

Bri sends him a scathing glare that has him shrinking back. "I'll have you know I worked my ass off to be able to afford that piece of shit."

Guilt tears across Jax's face and he glances to me as though I'm about to help him out of the hole he just dug himself. "You're on your own, asshole."

Jax gapes at me before turning back to Bri. "I'm sorry," he says. "I don't know what I was thinking. It's been a long day and I was worried about you, and the words just slipped out. Forgive me?"

"Wow, Jax. I'm impressed," she says, her hand on her heart as a wicked smirk crosses her face. "For a moment, I thought you Morgans were incapable of admitting when you're wrong."

Chanel chokes on a laugh as both Logan and I roll our eyes, but damn it, if it makes her smile right now, then I'll fucking cop it on the chin. "Nope," Chanel says, her gaze flicking toward Logan. "You were right, these Morgans really don't know how to admit when they're wrong. In fact, they don't know how to admit to anything at all."

Logan stands and looks at Chanel, his eyes narrowed. "Really?" he demands as the girls look between them like this is some kind of TV drama special. "You want to do this now?"

"What's the point?" Chanel throws back at him. "The moment one of us says something a little too deep, you're only going to run away like a little bitch."

"Oh, fuck," Jax laughs, finishing his set and dragging Arizona into his lap. "Shots fired."

Logan storms toward Chanel, the two of them locked in an intense trance and I can't help but wonder if this is what it looks like when Bri and I are at each other's throats. "A little bitch?" he demands, reaching for her wrist and yanking her up off the couch. "I ain't no fucking bitch."

Logan grabs Chanel, hoisting her over his shoulder and storming out of my home gym, all while she belts her fists against his back, demanding he put her down. They've barely even moved into the den and closed the door before they start screaming at each other.

Ilaria laughs. "Those two just need to put their weapons down and realize that they're good together."

Hudson laughs and swivels his gaze toward me and Bri. "They're not the only ones."

"Huh?" Bri questions, having zoned out, her hand dropping away from her head again.

I push it back, making sure the ice is firmly in place before glaring at Hudson. "Nothing. He's talking shit."

"What's the deal between you guys anyway?" Arizona pushes,

making Bri's eyes bug out of her head, neither of us knowing how the fuck to answer that question. "Are you together, fuck buddies, still hating each other but secretly pining for one another's attention?"

Bri looks anywhere but at me and my heart starts to race. "I, ummm … we … we're—"

Riley's booming laugh cuts me off and my gaze falls to Bri's, never seeing anyone look so relieved in my life. "They clearly haven't had that conversation yet," Riley says, taking amusement out of our awkward pain. "Why don't we hash it out right now? Let's get to the bottom of this so we're all on the same page, because Bri, babe, if you're really not feeling it, you know I'm down."

Reaching over the side of the couch, I grab a water bottle and launch it at Riley's head. "Fuck you, man," I say, knowing that at some point, Bri and I are going to have to define this thing between us, but I'm sure as fuck not ready for that, and I know damn well that she's not either.

The bottle smacks the asshole right in the center of his forehead and he whines, rubbing his head. "Ahhhh, fuck," he groans, snatching it up and hurtling it straight back at me, but unlike Riley, my reflexes are on point.

My movement jostles Bri and she sucks in a breath, immediately making me feel like an ass. "See what you made me do," I spit at Riley, knowing damn well that's on me, but hell, if I get the opportunity to blame Riley for something, I'll take it with both hands.

"You guys are idiots," Bri tells us as the sound of Chanel being slammed up against the wall echoes through the gym, quickly followed by a low groan. Bri's eyes widen. "No, please, no," she says in horror as the rest of us laugh.

They quickly get into it and it takes only a moment for Jax to start commentating the whole deed. "The clothes are gone, and the stud is let out of the gate. He's racing hard, determination in his veins, but she wants it more," he says, Arizona chuckling in his lap. "We're in for a treat, folks, it's the race of a lifetime. The socialite princess up against the football superstar, who will take the prize? The stud has the stamina and is the favorite to win, but the princess packs a nasty bite and could squeeze any man into submission. It's anyone's game."

There's a loud oomph followed by a throaty moan as Chanel fights back and pushes off the wall, giving Jax all he needs to keep going. "They're a pedigree pair, each putting up a fight as they get into position. The race is dragging on, the stud ready to drive this home. There are plenty of other players on the field, but where these two are concerned, there is no competition."

Bri laughs, her hand shifting away from her head again, and I promptly push it back, unable to block out Jax's commentary, as we hear the obvious sounds of Logan and Chanel mid-fuck. "The opening is narrow, but the stud is going for it, pushing harder and harder, not relenting in his determination. But—oh no. OH NO! He's going too hard. The stud is at risk of finishing this race early, but it seems the princess won't accept second place. She's forging ahead, holding the stud in line. For those watching at home, it seems this is going to be a quick game. Blink and you'll miss it. This pair have fought it out for so long, it was bound to come to an explosive end and—" Jax pauses, his eyes wide as a stupid grin cuts across all of our faces, hearing Chanel scream Logan's name. "YES! YES! The princess pushes ahead, taking control of this race and flying across the finish, making the stud her bitch as he comes in a close second, equally as proud."

Everybody cackles as they come down from their high, and I'm not surprised when they remain in the den, the soft murmurs of their conversation coming through the wall.

Light conversation fills the room and all too soon, Bri disappears inside her own head. "What's wrong?" I murmur, stealing her attention.

She shakes her head. "Nothing, I just …"

"This isn't about what Jax said earlier, is it? About where you and I stand with each other?"

"No," she rushes out, her eyes widening at the thought. "Don't get me wrong, I'm just as curious as everybody else, but if I'm honest, I don't think you and I can get through a conversation like that without ending up in bed or screaming at each other. I don't know what's in your head, Tanner, and I have a slight suspicion that you don't either."

A grin pulls at the corners of my lips. I hate how clearly she reads me. It makes it far too hard to get away with shit. "So what's bothering you then?"

She glances away, her gaze dropping to her hand in her lap. "Every time I breathe in, I feel the way he was weighing down on me, and every time I swallow, I remember his hands and how scared I was not being able to breathe. I thought I was going to die."

"I would have never let that happen."

"But what if you weren't there? What if your coach had asked you to do one more drill or if you'd decided to stop for gas on the way home?"

"Then you would have fought back and annihilated him," I tell her, damn sure of it too. "I've seen how easily you drop a guy, Killer. You're brutal. You're not the kind to sit back and take it. If someone swings at you, you swing back with twice as much force."

"Are you sure about that?"

"Damn sure."

Bri nods and settles back in beside me before allowing herself to get lost in the girls' conversation, but her usual spark isn't there. I don't blame her though, getting in a car wreck and having your asshole ex-boyfriend pin you down and strangle you isn't exactly the highlight of anyone's day.

I hate seeing her like this. Hate that out of all the people to bring her down, it's him. Hate that the same fucker that messed with my sister is now messing with Brielle.

This asshole is going to die, and it's going to be by my hand. Fuck the consequences. Fuck the future I've worked for. Nothing else matters to me now. He won't get away with this. Not if I have anything to do with it.

Knowing damn well that there's nothing I can do about Colby Jacobs tonight, I focus my attention on Bri because I'm damn sure I can do something about that frown marring her gorgeous face, even if it means making a complete ass of myself. There's nothing I won't do to see her smile, especially after the shit she's been through.

Pulling out my phone, I start searching for my best work to date, and once I'm satisfied with my selection, I pull up a new message and briefly hesitate. This is the stupidest fucking shit I've ever done, and despite knowing that, I hit send.

With Bri putting her phone on silent at the hospital, I give her a soft nudge and wait as her bright blue eyes meet mine. "What's up?"

"Check your phone."

Her brows furrow as she drops the ice pack on my thigh and digs into her pocket for her phone before swiping her thumb across the screen. All the movements jostle her around and she tries to muffle her groans. With her phone unlocked, she stares down at the screen and shakes her head. "What am I supposed to be looking at?"

"I sent you a message."

"There's no message from y—"

"WHAT THE FUCK," Logan roars, storming back into my home gym with his phone in his hand and his stare locked on mine.

My gaze drops to my phone, and I hastily check the message I just sent, dread sinking heavily into my gut. "Oh no," I groan, cringing as I glance back at Bri and hand her my phone. "I was trying to send you my award-winning dick pic, and sent it to Logan instead."

Bri howls with laughter and practically launches herself at my phone, her broken rib all but forgotten. She clicks on the image and laughs even more as it fills the entire screen, the girls racing in to look over her shoulder.

Jax laughs and glances toward his brother. "I gotta see this."

Without hesitation, Logan tosses his phone across the room and by the time Jax is pulling up the message, Riley and Hudson are already there, looking in.

Ilaria snorts a laugh. "Ten out of ten for lighting," she says, preparing to critique. "Nice angle too, manscaped just right, and you can even see the angry veins."

"Fucking hell. This isn't happening."

"Bonus points for the firm grip. Sometimes guys just don't have enough meat to get a grip shot, you know what I mean? Their fist usually hides the main attraction, but that clearly isn't an issue for you," she says as both Riley and Jax nod along as if they know exactly what she's talking about, "and you also seem to get the ball proportion just right."

"Ball proportion?" I ask, regretting the words the moment they leave my mouth.

"Yeah," Ilaria continues as if this has turned into dick pics for beginners. "Some guys get too much balls in the shot and it's distracting. You know there's nothing worse than opening up your phone to get blasted by a wrinkly ball sack. It's like the underboob, you have to get it just right."

Chanel and Arizona nod in agreement as I catch Bri zooming in as though she hasn't already had an up-close look at the thing. "You know what," she murmurs to herself, going about opening a new message to herself. "I might just save this for later."

She hits send and we all hear the soft vibration of her incoming message before she glances up at me. "Got any more I can add to my Tanner folder?" she asks, her bright blue eyes making it almost impossible to say no.

I grin back at her. "Just say the word, and I'll send you anything you want."

"Good," she murmurs, raising her chin and lowering her voice. "But for the record, dick pics are out. If you really want to make me squirm, send me a live cumshot with the volume turned up. I wanna hear you come, and you better be groaning my name."

Well, fuck.

Who the hell am I to say no?

CHAPTER 34
TANNER

Bri curls into my side as I help her up the stairs toward her bedroom, hating the pained curses she tries to hide. It's creeping up on midnight and she's well overdue for some more painkillers.

The moment everyone left, I had Bri out the door. Every part of me wanted to take her up to my room and keep her here for as long as I could, but the rational part of my brain told me that her mom was going to return home some time during the night, and when she does, she's probably going to want to check on her daughter. I can't imagine that her mom is going to be very forgiving if she walked in to find her daughter not in her bed, especially after just being told that she'd been in a car wreck.

I lead her down the hallway to her room, and as I take the handle and push her door open, she smirks up at me, looking far too proud of herself. "It must be nice not having to squeeze through the crawl space to get in here."

"Don't know what you're talking about."

"Right," she scoffs, moving across her room to perch on the side of her bed.

She watches me as I start to unload all her painkillers and fresh bandages onto her bedside table. "Do you need anything?" I ask, making sure everything is there before spilling a few pills into the center of my hand and passing them to her. "Pajamas? Water?"

"Both," she says, her face scrunching as she goes to get up again. "But don't worry. You've already done so much. I can figure it out from here."

I scoff and push her back to bed before making my way into her walk-in and scanning through all the drawers. I have no idea where she keeps her pajamas but, judging from what I've seen over the few weeks she's been living next door, an old comfortable shirt and underwear usually does the trick.

Making my way out of her closet, I toss her clothes onto the edge of her bed before going through to her private bathroom and filling a glass of water. I come back out just in time to see her place the painkillers into her mouth, and I hand her the glass to wash them down.

She makes quick work of it, cringing as the pills make their way down her sore throat, and I step into her before reaching for the top button of her school blouse. "You don't have to do this," she tells me, her eyes locked on me while I focus on her buttons. "It will suck, but I can manage."

I shake my head, reaching the final button and popping it open before pushing her school blouse off her shoulders and letting the soft material fall to the bed behind her. "It's no problem," I tell her, feeling more than responsible for what happened to her today. "I don't like to see you hurting."

"Really?" she says, a soft chuckle in her tone. "And here I was thinking you loved seeing me in pain."

I roll my eyes. "I like getting under your skin, making you squirm and rage at me for inconveniencing you. That's a shitload different than hurting you or seeing you in real, physical pain." My gaze drops to her bandaged ribs and scans over the bruises peeking out from beneath it. "I don't like this."

Grabbing her pajama shirt off the edge of the bed, I carefully pull it over her head and help her get her arms through the holes, hating how she tries to be strong, despite knowing all too well how much a broken rib sucks. I pull the blankets back and help her into bed before taking her phone and plugging it into the charger. "You, umm …" she says, scrunching her face as if unsure if she should continue. "Do you want to stay here tonight?"

I pause and look at her, my heart beating just a fraction faster. "You want me to stay?"

Bri bites her bottom lip and nods. "I don't want to be alone."

Decisions. Decisions. Spend the rest of my night with her in my arms or go back to my room and spend countless hours staring up at my ceiling and wishing I could be here. It's a no-brainer. "Okay," I tell her, moving around the other side of her bed and kicking off my shoes as I dump all my things on the bedside table. "Your mom isn't going to have a problem with this?"

"I don't think my mom has spared a single thought for what I do since we first got here."

I fucking hate that she's right. "You deserve better, Bri," I tell her, slipping into her bed and reaching out for her. "Come here."

She crawls into my arms and rests her head on my chest, right where she belongs and I find peace settling over me. This just feels right. Me and Brielle ... maybe I should be looking deeper into this. She's so much more than some chick I wanted to fuck out of my system, but the idea of this being something real terrifies me. It makes me vulnerable and hands her the power to destroy me, and at some point, I'm going to fuck it up. I'm going to end up hurting her and she deserves so much better than that ... better than me.

The exhaustion of the day quickly catches up to her and she falls into a restless sleep. I can only imagine what kind of bullshit nightmares are terrorizing her sleep. I bet Colby's face is flashing in her mind, the fear of seeing his car hurtling toward hers and not being able to stop it, or the way he crushed her and tightened his grip around her neck. That moment will stay with her for the rest of her life, and I hate that there's not a goddamn thing I can do to take it away.

I turn into her, my chin resting on top of her head as her fruity shampoo lingers in the air. I close my eyes and am just drifting to sleep when my phone buzzes on the bedside table. I cringe and reach for it, hoping the call doesn't wake Bri.

I'm just about to silence it when I see it's an incoming call from Mom and my eyes widen, my heart leaping in my chest. Dread fills my veins as I pull out of bed, trying not to jostle Bri while also hurrying not to miss the call. There's only one reason my mother would call me in the middle of the night and I … fuck. Addison better be okay. I need her to be okay.

"Mom?" I question, answering her call as I move away from Bri. "What's going on?"

Harsh sobbing cuts through the line. "Oh, Tanner," she wails, her tone full of grief. "I only went to get a coffee and when I returned—"

"What happened?" I demand, unable to catch my breath. "Fuck, tell me she's still alive."

"I … I …"

"MOM," I rush out, grabbing my shoes and flying out the door, halfway down the stairs before she can get out another sob. "What happened? Is Addison alright?"

"Barely," she cries. "Someone came in here and tried to hurt her."

"What?" I spit, racing through the bottom story of Channing's home and breaking out into the cold night. I dash across to my house, the front door still unlocked. "What do you mean someone tried to hurt her? What happened?"

I break through the internal door to my garage and slam my hand down over the automatic door opener before racing toward my bike, searching over it for the key but finding it nowhere. "I don't know," Mom sobs. "No one is telling me anything, they just keep racing around. Two seconds, Tanner. I was gone for two seconds."

Anger boils through my veins as I give up the search for my keys, certain Riley must have forgotten to leave them after he returned my bike, and I go for my Mustang instead, the keys already in the ignition. "WHAT HAPPENED?"

The tires screech as I hit the gas and like lightning, the Mustang lurches forward, shooting me out of the garage and down the street. "All I know," she says as I struggle to hear her over the roar of my engine, "is that when I returned, all the doctors and nurses were racing in. The wires to her monitors and medication had all been cut and the ventilator ... it looked as though someone had yanked it out of her throat. I just ... I don't understand who would do such a thing."

I have a good fucking idea.

"Just stay with her," I tell Mom. "Hold her hand. I'm coming."

Mom ends the call and I push my Mustang faster, flying around corners until I finally hit the highway and put my foot to the floor. What's usually a ten-minute drive is done in three and I park right out front before storming through the front doors.

Bradford Hospital is huge, but over the past six weeks, I've become all too familiar with this place. Being the dead of the night, it's almost silent inside, and I grow frustrated having to wait for the elevator to arrive. I almost bail and take the stairs when it finally dings and I barrel into it, slamming my hand down over the button for the ICU.

I arrive on Addison's level, and the moment the elevator door dings its arrival and opens wide, I'm already flying down the long hall. I hear Mom's cries before I've even reached Addie's room, and it pushes me faster. My feet pound against the linoleum and I grip the edge of the doorframe, using it to swing around and propel myself into Addison's room.

I come to a screeching halt, needing a moment to take in everything that's happening. There are two doctors and four nurses, each of them hovering over my sister, but none of them seem rushed, telling me that the brunt of the emergency has passed, but nothing—nothing—is sweeter than the soft rhythmic beep of her heart monitor.

I double over, catching my breath while keeping my eyes locked on Addison, scanning over her beautiful face and taking in the ventilator that's keeping her alive.

Holy fuck. We almost lost her, and I was too fucking busy playing boyfriend to a girl I vowed meant nothing to me. I should have been here, should have been watching out for her, at least that way no one would have been able to come in while Mom was out. She would have been protected and I let her down.

What the fuck is wrong with me?

I let Bri talk me out of beating his ass the other day. I was right there in Hope Falls, and I let her stop me. I let her take my pain and convince me to turn around. I've been so busy trying to play boyfriend that I've let it cloud what's really important, and now, Addison has been hurt again. If I had just intervened, this could have been avoided.

"Oh, Tanner," Mom sobs, finally seeing me at the entry of the private room. She throws herself into my arms and I catch her before she crumbles. "Who would do such a thing? Who would try to hurt my baby?"

Mom cries into my chest as I keep my eyes on Addison, watching as the doctors do everything they can to help her, and after twenty minutes, they move away and I'm faced with one of her regular doctors.

"Mrs. Morgan," he says, placing a calming hand on her arm and giving me a tight smile.

Mom pulls away from me and hastily wipes her face on the back of her arms, trying to find some composure to speak with the doctor. "Is my baby going to be alright?"

"Yes," he tells her. "We need to take her for routine testing just to be sure, however we believe this setback has not affected her chances in any way. The most damage would have been from the tubes being pulled from her throat. We can assume some bruising will occur, which we will look out for."

"How did this happen?" I demand.

"That is the question we have all been wondering, Mr. Morgan," the doctor says. "The police have been notified and are on their way, and as you can see," he adds, indicating to the top corner of the room, "there are security cameras in each of our ICU rooms, the hallways, and reception areas. So, I am sure whoever did this will be caught and brought to justice. You have my word on that. The hospital will push for a result."

"Thank you," Mom says, her gaze falling back to Addison.

The doctor excuses himself and I walk over to my sister, scooping her hand into mine. I feel her pulse at her wrist and it calms the fear in my chest, but does nothing to ease the burning hot fury. She's so beautiful, and I hate that I've never told her that. We have the typical sibling relationship. She comes into my space and I tell her to fuck off, and when I do the same, she whines to Mom and makes sure I'm punished, but I love her all the same, no matter how much she gets on my nerves.

She looks just like Mom. They're the spitting image of each other, and with Mom's need to shoot herself up with botox and have her hair and nails done, they could almost pass as sisters.

Addison's hair is swept to the side, looking almost freshly brushed, clear evidence of Mom continuously running her fingers through her hair. Seeing her like this destroys me, but with her lying here so calm, I can almost imagine she was just sleeping, tucked in her bed at home without a care in the world.

If it weren't for Colby Fucking Jacobs.

The asshole will die, and he'll fucking die tonight.

Releasing her hand, I lay it back by her side, being as gentle as possible before taking a step back. Mom glances toward me, and I swear she can either feel the tension rolling off me or hear my thoughts screaming through my mind. "Tanner, don't," she warns. "Don't do this. I can't lose both of you."

But it's too late, I'm already storming out the door.

In the space of two minutes, I'm already back in my Mustang and flying toward Hope Falls, determination rippling through my body. Riley got me the fucker's address the same night we learned who he was, and I'm not too proud to say that I've done countless drive-bys, casing the area, just hoping for a chance to get my hands on him.

Tonight, it ends.

I pull up in front of Colby's place, a run-down piece of shit in Hope Falls. It's falling apart and not worth a damn thing, making it even easier to shove my boot through the front door and watch as it goes flying off its hinges.

I storm into the small three-bedroom home, my nose turned up at the state of things. There are dirty dishes left all over the place and it looks as though it hasn't been cared for in years. A pungent smell lingers in the air, but I put it to the back of my head as I storm through the house, heading for the bedrooms at the end of the narrow hall.

Gripping the handle of the first room, I turn it and shove my shoulder into it, letting the door fly open and smash into the wall behind it. Peering into the room, I find what looks to be a teenage girl's room that hasn't been touched in years, and I realize this must belong to Colby's sister, the single worst mistake of my life.

I hear movement in the room furthest down the hall and quickly make my way to door number two, my anger spurring me on. The door is locked and I waste no time shoving my foot against it and splintering the wood. The door breaks off its hinges and I race in as it falls to the floor, roaring with frustration as I find the room just as empty as the last.

"Leave now and we won't call the police," I hear, coming from an older man in the hallway behind me. I move out of Colby's room and stare at the man standing protectively in front of his wife. He looks just like Colby, only thirty years older and wasting his life away on booze and McDonalds.

I slam my hand against Colby's bedroom door. "Where is he?"

"What do you want with Colby?"

"I'm going to ask you one more fucking time," I say, letting the rage pour out in my tone, not giving a shit if I'm scaring him or his wife. They fucking deserve it for raising such a piece of shit. "WHERE THE FUCK IS HE?"

"I don't know," Colby's father rushes out, throwing his hands up and making me realize I've begun stalking toward them. "He hasn't been home in two weeks."

"FUCK."

Colby's mom grabs her husband's arm and moves it out of her way before stepping toward me, raising her chin and showing a type of bravery that I wasn't expecting. "What did my son do to you?"

I stare her down, letting her receive the full intensity of my rage. "Six weeks ago, he fed my little sister a cocktail of drugs during a party and then attacked and raped her while she screamed for him to stop. She had a seizure, and instead of getting help, he left her naked and broken on the ground. She's been a in a coma ever since."

Her gaze shifts from my eyes, her stare hardening as if already knowing every damn word I just spoke is true. "No, there must be a mistake," she murmurs, looking guilty as shit, absolutely no conviction in her tone.

"No. Ramming Brielle's car into a tree, strangling her, and breaking her rib was his mistake," I tell her, my harsh tone forcing her stare back to mine. "But showing up in my sister's hospital room tonight and tearing her breathing tube out of her throat to ensure her silence, was nothing but a death wish. Mark my words, your son is not going to prison, he's going to the fucking grave."

Her husband pulls her back behind him, his hard stare locked on mine. "That's enough," he spits as she crumbles to the ground, knowing every word I speak is the truth. "Leave my house and never come back. We don't have what you need here."

I hold his stare for a moment longer, the fury overwhelming me, and as Colby's mom sobs on the ground, I back away from them before tearing off into the night, my Mustang screeching against the road.

CHAPTER 35
Brielle

My phone blares on my bedside table and I groan as I reach across to silence it, my ribs screaming at me to stay still. It must only be two or three in the morning and the painkillers are making my head foggy.

Gripping my phone, I quickly press the button on the side to get it to shut up, not wanting to wake Tanner. I take an extra second, squinting into the bright light of the phone to see that Riley was calling me and make a mental note to kick his ass whenever I see him next.

He was at Tanner's place last night and knows damn well that something is growing between us. If he's looking for a booty call, then he's calling the wrong girl, and I'm sure Tanner will have something to say when he finds out.

Yawning, I roll back over and reach across the bed, searching for Tanner. "Sorry," I murmur, my eyes already closed, only when I don't feel him across the bed, they fly open again.

Where the fuck is he?

My phone rings again and this time, I sit up and accept the call. "Bri," Riley yells into the phone, not allowing me the chance to even wake up properly. "You gotta get down here, girl. Tanner's out of control and we can't help him. We thought maybe you could work whatever pussy magic you've got going on and see if you can calm him down."

"What the hell are you talking about? Where is he?"

"At the track, babe. Just get down here."

Riley ends the call before I can ask any more questions and frustration overwhelms me. "FUCK," I yell, throwing my blankets back and reaching for the lamp on my bedside table.

Dim light fills my room and I pull myself out of bed while gripping my side, my ribs aching with every slight movement. I can barely get myself around. How the hell does Riley expect me to drive out to the track in the middle of the night? Besides, it's not as though I have a car anymore. Colby made sure of that.

Despite it being early fall, I grab a coat and shove my arms into it before finding a pair of sweatpants and hating every minute as I try to yank them up my legs. I shove my phone into my pocket before jamming another few painkillers down my throat and rushing out of my room.

My fists pound against Jensen's door. "GET UP."

I knock again and then knock some more, only stopping when I finally hear movement from within his room. The door opens and Jensen hovers in front of me, a pissed-off scowl stretching across his face. "What the fuck do you want? It's 3:30 in the morning."

"You need to drive me to the track, and you need to do it right fucking now. Consider it a peace offering for being such a jerk over the last few weeks."

"What?" he grunts, his face scrunching with frustration. "Absolutely not."

"Stop being an ass for just two seconds and grab your keys. Either you drive me there or I'm taking your car. Take your pick."

"FUCCCCK," he groans, pushing away from his bedroom door and diving into his room to find a shirt, shoes, and his keys. He returns a moment later and barges past me, clearly not a morning person.

I hurry to keep up with him and he takes pity on me on the stairs, even stopping to offer me a hand. We hurry to the bottom and rush out the door, his stupid little sports car roaring to life.

By the time I get in and close the door, Jensen is already taking off. The bumps and turns of the road bring flashes of Colby's black Charger to mind as it races toward me, but I swallow it down, terrified of what I'm about to find at the track.

Neither of us say a word until Jensen is pulling onto the dirt road leading toward the track. "What is this all about?" he asks. "If I'm driving you any further, I better not get in there to find some fucking sacrificial witch ceremony."

I groan, the anticipation of what we're about to find scarring my chest. "All I know is that Tanner's in some kind of trouble and needs my help."

"What's so special about this fucking idiot anyway? You know he's been sneaking into your room in the middle of the night, right? The guy is a fucking creep."

"You knew he was sneaking into my room and didn't say a damn thing? Holy fuck, Jensen. That's messed up, but for the record, I've known he was sneaking into my room since the very first time he did it. The first time was fucked up, I'll give you that, but it's fine now."

Jensen shakes his head. "No matter what kind of spin you put on it, it's still messed up."

I roll my eyes as Jensen pulls into the parking lot at the end of the dirt road, and we find Tanner's Mustang shooting around the track, the boys standing by, doing absolutely nothing. "What the fuck?" Jensen says, driving down past the parking lot and toward the track. "He must be going at least 200 miles an hour, 220 maybe. That's way too fast for this track. He's either going to kill himself or the assholes standing around watching."

Panic tears at me, and I bounce in my seat as he moves painfully slow toward the track, not wanting to damage his precious car. I can't take my eyes off the sleek Mustang, watching as he whips around the track, taking risks that no driver should take. Jensen is right, he's going to get himself killed, and I can't stand by and let it happen.

Riley stands with the twins, all three of them staring at Tanner with grim expressions, just waiting for this to go south. With each new lap Tanner takes, the dread sinks heavier onto my shoulders. "What the fuck happened?" I call out the second Jensen stops his car and I get my door open.

Riley looks back before jogging to meet me, his eyes dark as night. "I don't fucking know. The most we could get out of him is that there was some kind of attack on Addie."

My eyes bug out of my head. "What?"

"Yeah, Hudson took off to the hospital to check it out," he explains, unease flooding my stomach, having a good fucking idea who's behind all of this, "but as for Tanner, he's out of control. He's been going like this for almost forty-five minutes. He tripped the security sensors on his way in and has been going ever since. We've all fucking tried, but he won't stop and soon enough—"

"He's going to get in a wreck," I finish for him.

Riley nods as we catch up to the others, watching as Tanner shoots by us, pushing his car even faster at the sight of me standing with his friends.

"Fuck," Logan mutters, shaking his head. "We shouldn't have called her. It's going to fuck with him more."

"Nah, if anyone can talk him down, it's Bri," Riley says, his confidence in me definitely misplaced.

I shake my head, way out of my league. "I don't know what you guys expect me to do," I say. "How the hell am I supposed to help this?"

"I don't know," Jax says, not taking his eyes off Tanner as he reaches the top of the track, just seconds from turning the corner to bring him back down toward us. "But you better figure it out quickly.

There's only two reasons why Tanner is so messed up right now, and you're one of them."

Fuck.

What the hell am I supposed to do?

"Does he have his phone?"

Riley shakes his head, watching as he barrels this way, dust spitting up from beneath his tires. "Threw it out the window fifteen minutes ago."

"Shit."

Tanner gets closer and closer and if I don't do something soon, he'll be heading for another lap.

Time slows and pressure weighs down on me, squeezing my chest like never before, and without even a moment of thought, I throw myself onto the track, racing out, right in Tanner's line of sight. "BRIELLE," Riley hollers as I slip out and evade his grasp. "NOOO!"

My heart races as I stare down the Mustang speeding toward me, and I raise my chin in challenge, knowing he sees me perfectly well, but he doesn't dare hit the brake. He thinks I'm going to move but I sure as hell didn't get dragged out of bed at 3:30 in the morning with a broken rib just to fuck around here for hours, waiting for him to run out of gas.

If we're doing this, then we're doing it now.

Each passing second has my heart racing faster. My palms begin to sweat as my knees shake. I don't take my eyes off the Mustang, knowing with each passing second I wait, the harder it's going to be to spring out of the way, but I hold my ground. I am not backing down.

It's a game of cat and mouse, the only question is, who is the cat and who is the mouse?

Tanner hits the final corner, drifting around it with ease and just like that, he's coming right for me, his eyes piercing through the windshield and right through to my soul. He's angry, tired, broken, and confused, and I'm not about to let him give up like this.

He's getting close, too fucking close.

My heart thunders, my eyes widening with fear.

Even if I run, I won't make it out of the way. I have to trust him. I have no choice.

He's going to hit me, and I have to accept my fate.

A scream tears from the back of my throat and at the last possible second, Tanner slams his foot down on the brake, sending a wave of dirt flying up behind him. The tires screech and skid against the dirt as his car hurtles toward me and turns to the side. He struggles to stop, but I don't fucking move, determination clouding my judgment.

I gasp for air, sucking it between my clenched jaw, and just as I expect the Mustang to take me out, it comes to a jarring stop, barely an inch between us.

"WHAT THE FUCK WERE YOU THINKING?" Tanner roars, bailing out of the Mustang and storming toward me. "I COULD HAVE FUCKING KILLED YOU."

Fury burns in his eyes, and I try to reach for him, but he pulls away from my touch. "I had no choice," I tell him. "You're racing around the track like a fucking idiot. You're the one who's going to get himself killed, Tanner. What the hell is wrong with you?"

"Me?" he spits as the boys race in, trying to grab him before he completely loses his mind. "You shouldn't even be here. Why the fuck do you keep shoving your nose where it doesn't belong?"

"Riley called me. They were worr—"

"Riley?" he scoffs, spinning around, his fist already in motion. He clocks his best friend in the face and I gasp, watching as Riley falls to the ground, taking it like a fucking pro. Logan and Jax grab his arms, holding him back as he focuses all his anger on his friend. "You had no fucking right to call her. She's not my fucking girl. We're not together. She's just some bitch I fucked a few times. She means nothing to me."

Pain blasts through my chest and I hold back tears, knowing he's only saying this to hurt me. He's out of control, emotional, and scared for his sister while probably imagining all the different ways he could slaughter Colby.

He didn't mean it. If I meant nothing to him, he wouldn't have come to me the night he beat Colby, and he sure as hell wouldn't have cared for me the way he did last night. No, he wants to hurt me because he is terrified of letting me in, allowing me to see the monster hidden within him, and being vulnerable to what he feels for me. I can't let his anger win.

I scoff, demanding his attention and doing whatever I have to do to keep him from lunging out with his fists and hurting his friends. "If that's how you really feel, then at least have the balls to say it to my face."

His eyes are wild, regret shining brightly, but he's too far gone to pull himself up. He's going to push and push until he loses everything, and if that's what he needs to do to pull himself out of this reckless tornado, then that's what I'm going to let him do, my heart be damned. If he has to shatter me just to feel something again, then I hope he makes it count and hits me right where it hurts.

"You don't think I will?" Tanner demands, tugging against his cousins and grabbing hold of my challenge with both hands, rising to the bait. "You were a fucking bet, nothing more than a bitch with nice tits who needed the attitude fucked out of her, and look at you now, chasing after me in the middle of the night as if you mean anything to me. You're pathetic."

His words sting and tear at my chest, killing something within me, but I hold my head high, not afraid of him or his ugly words. "I'm pathetic?" I laugh, more than prepared to throw it right back in his face. After all, if I'm going down, then I'm not going without a fight. "Look at you, Tanner. You're falling apart because you're too fucking scared to allow yourself to feel something. Colby hurt your sister again and instead of doing something about it, you're going to waste away on a fucking track and get yourself killed. Congratulations, you're going to leave your mom without any of her kids while Colby's still out there, free as a fucking bird to hurt the next girl who comes along. You're a real hero."

"You don't fucking know me at all," Tanner tells me, that fire in him only burning brighter. "You think I just found out what he did and came here? No," he scoffs, needing to lash out more than he needs his next breath. "I went to his fucking house, kicked in the door, and if it wasn't for the fact that little bitch has been hiding out, he'd already be dead. I'm here, racing fucking laps to keep from going home to you because you're the fucking reason I wasn't there for her in the first place."

My heart shatters but I don't dare break, don't let him see how much he's hurting me, despite the horrid truths spurting from between his lips. "Wow, that's two out of four," I tell him, welcoming his insults just so he can get it all out. "Riley's down and you pushed me away. How quickly can you make Logan and Jax hate you too? You excel at everything, right Mr. Captain Of The Football Team? Gotta be the best. Let me guess, you're lining up a cheap shot at Chanel for Logan and preparing a stab at Jax's ego just to hit him where it hurts. It's like a fucked-up little game. I know how you like those. We'll call it *how much can Tanner Morgan lose in one night?*"

Tanner breaks free from the twins' tight grasp and steps into me, his hand striking up and gripping my throat, much like Colby had done to me when he held me down in the bushes. "That's just the thing," he tells me, drawing me in until I feel his breath against my cheek, making it hard to believe that only a few short hours ago we were this close, only his arms were wrapped around me and his lips brushing against my temple in the sweetest kiss. "They're my cousins and Riley is my best friend, no matter what happens, they'll have my back, but you … you're nothing, just the kid of the gold-digging whore from next door. You'll be gone in no time. Channing will send you on your way and he'll be fucking the next bitch before you've even walked out the door. You'll be left with nothing, and you'll be so far below me that I won't even remember who you are. You'll be cleaning up after assholes like me the rest of your life unless you play your cards right. Jensen might take you in as a pity fuck, but if he's not interested in used goods, there's a brothel just out of town. I'm sure they'll take you. Your tits are nice enough, and I'm sure a girl like you would be happy to shake her ass for a dollar."

My hand cracks across his face. "You know what, Tanner?" I say, shoving him hard in the chest and hating how he doesn't even rock back a step, but at least he releases my throat. "I'm done with you. Maybe I will fuck Jensen. Hell, maybe I'll fuck Riley too and you guys can form a special little club for assholes who've screwed me over and trade notes on just how well I suck dick. Do what you want, kill Colby for all I care. Throw your future away and be this pathetic version of yourself who doesn't know how to control his emotions and lashes out at the people who only want to help you. You'll get nowhere in life like this, but what does it matter? You'll either be locked up or dead and when your sister eventually wakes, she'll have no one to lean on. Push me away all you like, Tanner, it doesn't matter to me, but don't let yourself spiral out of control because soon enough, Addison is going to need you, and you won't be there. Don't let her down like you did me."

With that, I turn my back and walk away, hating the traitorous tears that roll down my cheeks.

Jensen gives me a pitying stare and I avoid his eyes as I climb back into his car. "I don't want to hear it."

He glances away, watching the boys try to tackle Tanner into submission. "I wasn't going to say anything."

"Good."

Jensen gets in and closes the door, his car rumbling to life, and as he hits the gas and turns around, I can't help but glance up at the boys on the track, Riley only just getting to his feet as Logan and Jax pull Tanner back toward Logan's Dodge RAM. He fights them with every step, and as Jensen rolls away, Tanner looks back toward me, pain in his eyes and his heart broken on his sleeve, knowing damn well he just lost the best thing that ever happened to him.

CHAPTER 36
Brielle

The early morning sun shines through my bedroom window as I stare up at the ceiling. Hell, I haven't stopped staring at the ceiling since the moment I got back into bed.

Last night was shit. I said some things, Tanner said some things, and while I know deep in my heart that he didn't mean any of it, it doesn't keep the sting from tearing me apart. He needed to scream, needed to push everybody away to be able to feel something, and I volunteered myself as tribute.

How fucking stupid was that? All I know is the things he said, I don't think we'll be able to come back from. I was his personal punching bag. Nothing was off-limits and he went in for the kill, shattering every single one of my insecurities. I told him I was done, and honestly, I think I really meant it.

Today is going to be interesting.

If I were smart, I'd stay right here. I'd whine and complain about how badly my injuries are hurting from the wreck yesterday and Mom will happily turn a blind eye to my absence from school, but as much as I don't want to be there, the thought of not having a perfect attendance record kills something inside me. Call me a nerd or a loser, but there's nothing I won't face to ensure I appear to be a perfect student for every last college in the country.

Peeling myself out of bed, I trudge into the bathroom and go about my morning. The sun has barely appeared in the sky, so I have plenty of time to waste away in a hot shower. I try to wash my hair but end up only getting halfway through after realizing just how hard it is. Any movement which involves raising my arm above my head can be strictly cut from my routine today.

Adjusting myself under the spray, I rinse off what I can and shut off the shower before pulling my towel firmly around me. I spend a good ten minutes rubbing cream into my injuries and cringing at the way the bruise has developed over my ribs. It's bad, so fucking bad, but it still pales in comparison to the emotional wounds I carry from last night.

Pain rocks through me as I do my best to tape my ribs, but I force myself through it quickly, all too aware that the sooner I get it done, the sooner I can breathe again. Feeling too messed up to bother with makeup, I pull on a clean uniform and make my way downstairs.

Mom's over-the-top laugh flows up from the kitchen and something constricts around my heart, holding it captive. I haven't seen her since she left for Paris on Friday night without so much as a goodbye. She didn't call or text the whole time she was gone, and when I called her yesterday from the hospital, she acted as though my call was nothing more than an inconvenience ... that is until I explained Colby had T-boned me into a tree, strangled me then broke a rib. She was all too happy to play the doting mother then, though anyone would think a doting mother would have come to check on her daughter the moment she arrived back. Not mine though.

Forcing myself down the rest of the stairs, I make my way through to the kitchen, needing something in my stomach with all of these painkillers. "Oh honey," Mom gasps from behind the kitchen island, placing the knife down on the chopping board and racing toward me. She throws her arms around me and squeezes tight.

Pain blasts through my body and for a moment, I think I could pass out. Tears immediately spring to my eyes and I shove her away with a ferocity I wasn't aware I was capable of. "MOM. STOP," I scream, gripping my ribs and trying not to pass out.

Mom stares at me in horror, her eyes wide. "Oh, Brielle. I'm so sorry. I wasn't thinking. I was just so excited to see you. I've never been away from you for so long before."

I shove past her, needing the counter to hold me up and grip onto it with everything I have before sliding my ass onto the bar stool. Sucking in deep breaths, I try to breathe through the pain, unable to trust myself to speak until it finally begins to ease.

Mom steps in beside me, her hand gently rubbing up and down my back. "How can I help? Do you need an ice pack or some painkillers?"

I shake my head. "I just need a minute," I say, the hostility clear in my tone.

"Perhaps you should be taking the day off," she suggests. "No one expects you to go to school. I can call your principal and explain what happened. I'm sure he'll understand. Besides," she adds. "I haven't seen you in so long. We have so much to catch up on and I want to share everything about my trip. Paris was wonderful. It's a shame we had to cut it short though."

I scoff. "Cut it short? You were supposed to be home days ago."

She shakes her head. "What do you mean, darling? We extended it to a week-long trip. Did Jensen not tell you? Orlando said he was going to call and let you both know."

"Wow, so nice of you to have called me yourself," I mutter darkly, my stare locked on the fruit bowl in front of me. "And no, Jensen had no idea that you had extended your trip."

"That's peculiar," she mutters to herself.

I shake my head, more than done with her this morning. I'm sure had she not decided to squeeze me so soon after breaking a rib, I probably would have had more patience for her. Grabbing a banana from the fruit bowl, I prepare myself to stand again. "I need to get to school."

Mom's hand falls away but a shimmer catches in the light and my head whips down to her hand. As if seeing where my attention has gone she hastily covers the massive rock resting on her ring finger. "What the fuck is that?" I demand, flying to my feet, my banana dropping to the ground as I grab her hand instead. "You're engaged?"

Mom cringes and tries to pull her hand free. "I … no, it's not quite what you're thinking."

My eyes are wide, confusion tearing at my chest. "Then what?" I demand. "You don't have the money to buy something like that for yourself, and if a man gives you a ring, it only means one thing."

"We …" she cringes again, and it makes me want to shake her. "We got married, darling."

A different kind of pain rocks through me, and I fall back a step, staring at her in horror. "You got married to this guy? Without even talking to me or Damien about it? You just went ahead and uprooted our lives to become some kind of Stepford wife?"

"No, Brielle, it's not like that at all. Why are you making such a big deal about this? You're eighteen now and soon enough you'll be away at college. Damien is already away, and I'm sure the moment he gets back from bootcamp, he'll be right out the door again, then what am I supposed to do? I'll be all alone. Orlando loves me and wants to show me the world and shower me in diamonds, so why shouldn't I allow myself to be happy?"

"It's not that I don't want you to be happy, Mom. I do. Of course I want that for you, but didn't you think for one second that this is something you should at least have the decency to tell me first so I'm not blindsided by it? Or was I so far down on your agenda that you didn't even consider how Damien or I might have felt? Hell, you took off to Paris without even a goodbye, so I suppose that answers my question."

Without another word, I storm past her, but she grabs my wrist and yanks me back. "Don't you speak to me like that," she spits as I cry out, the pain tearing through me. "I am your mother and you will show respect for me."

"Respect?" I demand, trying not to cry. "Maybe I'll respect you when you start to show that you have respect for yourself. Look at you Mom. Everything we did together, the life we grew, you threw it all away for the chance at being some rich guy's bitch. Do you even love him, Mom? Have you ever looked deeper than the surface to get to know him? Because I sure as hell know that he's not the kind of guy I'd want to spend the rest of my life with."

"Brielle," she snaps.

"Don't," I spit back at her, yanking my wrist free of her flimsy grasp. "I'm late."

I spin around and storm for the door, scooping up Mom's keys on the entryway table as I go. Screw her and screw this bullshit life she's trying to fake. This isn't us. How could she want a life with that man? Orlando Channing is as bad as they come. He has deep pockets and a charming smile, but that's as far as it goes, everything else below the surface is nothing but evil. The man cares about nothing except for his ability to win court cases, he doesn't even care if his client deserves to be in prison or not. He has the ability to manipulate the people around him, and that's exactly what he's done to my mom, and she's stupid enough to go and marry him.

Great. Just fucking great.

Anger pounds through my veins as I get into Mom's car and take off at the speed of light, only by the time I'm reaching the front gates of Bradford Private, the anger has turned into nothing but hurt.

She moved us into Orlando's home without a thought for what I needed.

She enrolled me into a school without even talking to me.

She quit her jobs to become his office fuck toy.

She took off to another country without a goodbye.

And now ...

She got married without even thinking about me.

If she truly loved this man and he was everything she ever dreamed about, I would have stood by her side, I would have walked down the aisle as her maid-of-honor, and I would have cried the happiest tears watching her say her vows, but this?

This isn't the woman who raised me. She is so blinded by the money and lifestyle that she can't even see how Orlando has simply taken control of every aspect of her life. She's no longer an independent woman. Everything she has relies solely on him.

By the time I'm pulling into a parking space and cutting the engine, I realize tears have been streaming down my face and I hastily wipe them away before glancing at my reflection in the rearview mirror.

I do my best to look presentable. I'm sure word has gotten out about the accident yesterday and I'm going to be the topic of conversation. Glancing up at the big school, I lock Mom's car and get only a few steps before Chanel is at my side, slipping her arm through mine and helping me up to the school. "You shouldn't be here," she tells me, as though I don't already know that.

I shrug my shoulders, not really sure what to say that's going to make my being here sound like a good idea. We reach the main part of the school and there are bodies everywhere, making me fear for the walk to my locker. One shoulder charge is all I need to drop me to the ground, and as if sensing that, Chanel switches sides with me to put herself between me and the crowd.

By the time I reach my locker, the bell for homeroom is already ringing and Chanel scurries off, leaving Ilaria to be my guide.

The morning is slow and I don't see Tanner until I'm sitting in third period English. He walks through the door, late as usual, and the moment he raises his head and finds me, he stops. His dark eyes lingering on mine and causing my heart to race.

The words he said to me fill every space in my mind, so loud it's like they're screaming at me, trying to hurt me all over again. He left me broken last night, broken and fucking destroyed just as he always said he would.

Regret shines heavy in his eyes and the intensity is too strong, I'm forced to look away.

"Find your seat, Mr. Morgan," Miss Harper says. "You're holding up my lesson."

Tanner drops his gaze, and a wave of relief washes over my body, only it doesn't last as he starts to walk toward his seat at the back of the room. Every step he takes in my direction kills me, and I find myself holding my breath, desperate for him to pass, only he doesn't.

Tanner pauses by my desk, and it takes every bit of willpower not to look up into those eyes that have claimed every part of my soul. "You shouldn't be here," he murmurs, his tone low but so full of authority. "You need to be home resting."

"And now you care?" I question, refusing to meet his eyes.

"Bri," he says, leaving my name lingering in the air between us.

"Miss Harper is waiting," I remind him. "You're wasting her time."

I see his hands ball into fists at his side, not liking this one bit. He drops down beside me, his gaze lingering on the side of my face. "Come on, Killjoy. Just talk to me. You know I didn't mean any of it. Let me make this right."

I shake my head before slowly turning to take him in. "Careful," I say, hating how his eyes penetrate deeply into mine, capturing everything that I am. "You wouldn't want to be caught slumming it with the good for nothing whore from Hope Falls. You know I'm going to be a prostitute one day?"

Hurt flashes in his eyes, but before he can say a damn word, Miss Harper calls out. "Tanner. Get in your seat now or you'll spend your Friday afternoon in detention with me."

Knowing damn well Miss Harper will follow through on her threat, Tanner stands, not willing to risk missing Friday night's game. "This isn't over," he tells me.

I scoff. "I told you last night. I'm done."

He clenches his jaw before taking a step, only to pause again and steal Arizona's attention. "As soon as class is done, make sure she goes home." With that, he walks away and drops down into his seat, my heart shattering all over again. I know he was hurting last night, his sister was attacked for a second time and could have lost her life. If

I hadn't stopped him on that track, he could have easily ended up in the ICU right beside her, and if I hadn't allowed him to use me as his verbal punching bag, he would have hurt his friends and gotten straight back in his Mustang. It was a necessary evil that's left us both broken.

A heaviness settles into my chest as Arizona reaches across to my desk, taking my hand. "He's right. You should go home," she says, a hint of confusion lacing her tone. The last time I saw her, I was held tightly in Tanner's arms, and now, there's nothing but disdain between us. "You've had your attendance marked off. There's nothing stopping you from taking off."

I shake my head, the idea of going home to face my mother only making things worse. "I can't go home."

"What do you—"

A knock at the door cuts off Arizona's question, and we all glance up to find Principal Dormer accompanying two police officers.

My blood instantly turns cold.

They step through the doorway and Miss Harper murmurs to herself. "Great, another hold up," she says before giving Principal Dormer a welcoming smile. "How can I help you?"

My gaze snaps back to Tanner's, all the bullshit between us suddenly not so important. He broke into Colby's home last night, destroyed their property, and scared the shit out of his parents. There's only one reason why the cops would be here, either that or they have news about his sister, but I doubt it. His mom would have called him first.

Tanner stares back at me, the same fear reflected in his own eyes.

"I'll be fine," he tells me, his voice so low that I barely hear it, even despite the words we can't take back, he's still looking out for me, not wanting me to fear for what he's about to go through. "Don't worry about me."

Don't worry about him? That's not possible.

Principal Dormer glances over the class before his heavy gaze lands on me. "Miss Ashford. Please stand."

"Me?" I question, my brows furrowed.

"Please do not resist," Dormer says. "These officers would like to have a chat with you."

I glance back at Tanner to see confusion brimming in his stare as I reluctantly stand, keeping myself half braced behind my desk. "What's this about?"

"Miss Ashford, please mak—"

The cop closest to the aisle decides he's had enough of Dormer's slow and steady approach and storms down the aisle toward me, gripping his cuffs at his hip. "Brielle Ashford," he states, reaching me in two seconds and gripping me by my wrist. He whips me around and I scream out as he slams my chest down on my desk, tackling my arms behind my back. "You're under arrest for the brutal attack, rape, and attempted murder of Miss Addison Morgan."

Unbelievable pain tears through me and I scream as the edge of my desk presses against my ribs, the cop holding me down as shocked gasps fill the room. This is the first the school is hearing about Addison's attack, and now they're all going to think it was me.

"I DIDN'T DO IT," I cry out, grunting against the pain as

students whip out their phones to record the show. "You've got the wrong person. It was Colby Jacobs. He admitted it. I swear, it has noth—"

"LET HER GO," Tanner roars and not a second later, the weight of the cop is torn off me. I spin around as the other cop barrels past Dormer and lunges for me, gripping me by the arm and yanking me away. I'm shoved toward Dormer and he holds onto me as I crumble to the ground, the pain too much to handle.

Agony fills my veins as I watch in horror as Tanner evades the first cop and comes for me.

The second cop reaches for his gun and my eyes widen, fear like I've never known pounding through my veins. "STOP, TANNER," I scream as the man whips his gun from its holster and points it right at his chest. "Please stop."

Tanner pauses as the other students scream and duck for cover, Miss Harper throwing herself in front of the closest student. "Back away, son," the gun-wielding cop says as the other gets to his feet behind Tanner, caging him in.

Tanner holds his ground, remaining still with his hands held up, his eyes flicking between me and the cop. "She didn't do it," he spits as the cop behind him grips his arms and forces them behind his back, cuffing him too. "My name is Tanner Morgan, Addison is my sister," he says, pleading with him to listen as the cop behind him shoves him down to his knees. "You've got the wrong person. Brielle didn't do this."

"We have an arrest warrant with Brielle Ashford's name on it," the cop says, slowly holstering his gun again. "We have eyewitnesses, sworn statements, and all the evidence we need. As far as we're aware, Brielle Ashford will be spending the rest of her life behind bars."

And with that, the cop drags me out of Miss Harper's classroom as Tanner is shoved down to the ground, sobs tearing from the back of my throat.

THANKS FOR READING

If you enjoyed reading this book as much as I enjoyed writing it, please consider leaving an Amazon review to let me know.

https://www.amazon.com/dp/B09Y3H2JH8

STALK ME

Facebook Page
www.facebook.com/SheridanAnneAuthor
Facebook Reader Group
www.facebook.com/SheridansBookishBabes
Instagram
www.instagram.com/Sheridan.Anne.Author

OTHER SERIES
www.amazon.com/Sheridan-Anne/e/B079TLXN6K

YOUNG ADULT / NEW ADULT DARK ROMANCE
The Broken Hill High Series | Haven Falls | Broken Hill Boys | Aston Creek High | Rejects Paradise | Boys of Winter | Depraved Sinners | Bradford Bastard | Empire

NEW ADULT SPORTS ROMANCE
Kings of Denver | Denver Royalty | Rebels Advocate

CONTEMPORARY ROMANCE (standalones)
Play With Fire | Until Autumn (Happily Eva Alpha World)

URBAN FANTASY - PEN NAME: CASSIDY SUMMERS
Slayer Academy

Printed in Great Britain
by Amazon